# Turnabout's Fair Play

# Turnabout's Fair Play

## MATCHMAKERS

# KAYE DACUS

BARBOUR
PUBLISHING

For more information about Kaye Dacus, please access the author's website at the following Internet address: www.kayedacus.com

Cover design: Lookout Design, Inc.

Published by Barbour Publishing, Inc., P.O. Box 719, Uhrichsville, OH 44683, www.barbourbooks.com

*Our mission is to publish and distribute inspirational products offering exceptional value and biblical encouragement to the masses.*

ecpa Member of the
Evangelical Christian
Publishers Association

Printed in the United States of America.

# Dedication

This book is possible only because of the real
Cookie and Big Daddy—married for more than forty-five years
and more supportive and loving than I deserve.

# Prologue

*I*'m not a child, you know."

Maureen O'Connor turned at the deep, masculine voice. It was not often that someone walking in to the senior adult Sunday school class at Acklen Avenue Fellowship Church was accused of being anything less than old.

Her breath hitched a little when she saw the source of the deep, gravelly voice. An oak tree. That's what he reminded her of: tall, sturdy, and craggy. But even the weathered wear on his face and the thinning silver hair did not keep him from being quite a looker.

"Zarah has about made herself sick over this whole thing. Thank goodness the wedding is next weekend, because I don't know how much more of this she could handle." Katrina Breitinger looked around as if to make sure everybody in the general vicinity could hear her and knew her granddaughter was getting married this coming Saturday. Trina turned to another friend of theirs, Sassy Evans. "Have Caylor and Dylan set a date yet?"

Less than a year ago, Maureen and her four closest friends—Trina, Lindy, Sassy, and Perty—had made a pact with each other to try to see at least one of their grandchildren married. So far, it had worked out that their grandchildren had fallen in love with each other—Trina's granddaughter with Lindy's grandson, and Sassy's granddaughter with

7

Perty's grandson—though all of them had multiple grandchildren to work with. Maureen, on the other hand, had only one grandson, and though he dated frequently, he seemed to have no interest in settling down. Only Sassy had a granddaughter of the right age for Jamie, but no matter how much Maureen loved her college friend, she wouldn't wish the flighty young woman on anyone's grandson.

As her four friends talked about the impending wedding, Maureen let her attention travel around the room. And in short order, it arrived back at the handsome stranger.

"I am not so old and feeble that I can't figure out how to visit a Sunday school class on my own." The older gentleman towered over a beautiful, blond young woman, as if trying to intimidate her. The young woman looked familiar, but Maureen could not immediately place her.

"It's been thirty years since you've even visited another church. Please just let me introduce you around a little bit."

The young woman looked like her grandson's type: tall, slender, and beautiful. Her thick blond hair fell in a cascade of loose curls and waves to the middle of her back, and the tailored suit she wore showed off her curves and long legs to perfection. Yet even in high heels, the top of the young woman's head barely reached the older gentleman's nose. He rolled his eyes and then gave her an indulgent smile.

The young woman groaned, took him by the hand, and led him straight over to Maureen and her group of friends.

"Flannery!" Sassy reached out and pulled the tall young woman into a hug. Of course. Flannery McNeill, Sassy's older granddaughter's best friend. Maureen had met her last fall at a cookout when all four families got together. A cookout at which Maureen's grandson, Jamie, had been present. The two had spent very little time together there, but Maureen would have sworn she saw a few sparks of interest fly between them.

"Sassy, this is my grandfather Kirby McNeill." Flannery went around and introduced the other four friends as well. Maureen was impressed; perhaps Flannery had met Trina, Lindy, and Perty before, but Maureen knew she had only met the young woman once. And if Sassy had not said her name, Maureen never would have remembered it.

When it came Maureen's turn to shake hands with Kirby McNeill, she found herself no longer an eighty-four-year-old woman widowed for forty-seven years, but an eighteen-year-old debutante at her first cotillion. The large hand that enveloped hers was soft. . .but with rough places. She imagined it was a good representation of the man himself.

Once the introductions were complete, Flannery led her grandfather away to introduce him to a group of men standing on the other side of the room. Because Flannery was one of the maids of honor in Zarah's wedding, talk naturally turned back to that subject. Maureen's attention, however, stayed on the oak tree of a man she'd just met.

Was he married? If not, how long had he been single? And why, at her age, was she even entertaining thoughts like this? She needed to be concentrating on finding a wife for Jamie. Her gaze fell on Flannery McNeill.

If she could get Jamie and Flannery together, she might get to see more of Kirby McNeill. Hopefully a lot more.

# Chapter 1

*I* hate weddings."

Flannery McNeill sank down on the top step of the broad stage as the rest of the wedding party gathered around the wedding planner. She didn't need to hear all of the dickering and whys and wherefores. She just wanted the bottom line: where to stand and how to get there.

"You don't mean that." A gorgeous man with sandy brown hair, vivid blue eyes, and dimples to die for plopped down on the step beside her.

Flannery looked at her boss and friend, Jack Colby. "Yes, I do. A wedding is a flashing neon sign warning everyone that they're never going to have the same relationship with these people ever again."

Jack's broad forehead creased. "What do you mean?"

Flannery braced her hands on the stage floor behind her and locked her elbows. "Take my sisters, for example. They were fine before they got engaged. But then they couldn't carry on an intelligent conversation. They morphed into this unrecognizable *we-us* entity and couldn't see anything in terms of *me-I* or make their own decisions."

Jack laughed. "People just get caught up in the excitement of planning a wedding. They've both been married a long time—it can't still be that bad."

"Ha!" Flannery's cheeks burned a little when several people

turned at her echoing derision. "Emily was one of the youngest junior executives in the bank where she worked before she had kids—now she can't even balance her own checkbook; her husband does it."

"Maybe she just got tired of—"

"And Sylvia, who is a sound engineering programmer in the recording industry, has to get her husband to program the clock on the DVD player every time the electricity goes out. 'He *has* to do it; I just *can't* figure it out.'" Flannery imitated the high-pitched, baby-talk voice Sylvia sometimes used when talking to or about her husband. It made Flannery's skin crawl, especially hearing it come from someone now thirty-six years old.

When Jack said nothing, she glanced at him and then looked away in disgust at the smile of amused pity on his otherwise handsome face. "You just don't get it. You don't have sisters."

"Is this about your sisters. . .or about the fact that your two best friends recently got hitched up and you feel somewhat left out?"

"I—" Flannery clamped her lips down on the denial about to pop out of her mouth. Zarah and Caylor were nowhere near as bad as Emily and Sylvia had gotten as soon as those diamond rings went on their fingers—well, Caylor didn't have a ring yet, even though she'd been officially engaged for five weeks now. After all, when Flannery, Zarah, and Caylor got together for their regular Sunday afternoon coffee-and-chat sessions, they still talked about many of the same things they discussed before Bobby and Dylan entered the picture— their jobs, their families, their hopes and fears. Of course that last part, of late, included more discussion of Bobby and Dylan. . .and Zarah and Bobby's Memorial Day weekend wedding. She leaned forward and wrapped her arms around her knees.

"Who's the hottie?"

Flannery followed Jack's gaze to the back of the room. She groaned. "Oh, you've got to be kidding me."

Jack leaned back on his elbows, his expensive silk tie flopping to the side. "What's the matter?"

Flannery shook her head, pushing her hair behind her ears.

"Nothing. Just someone I'd hoped never to see again."

Jack's gaze remained for a moment longer on the guy introducing himself to the few others at the back of the sanctuary, and then he sighed. "I'm just saying that you need to start taking note of men like that. I'm not going to be around to be your platonic date forever, you know."

Flannery turned her head so she could indulge in rolling her eyes without his seeing it. "Whatever."

The rest of the wedding party moved toward the back of the room. Caylor turned, caught Flannery's attention, and motioned her to follow.

Jack stood and offered her a hand up. But he didn't let go immediately once she got to her feet. "Flannery, you're a good friend, and I hate to see you so miserable. Have you talked to Caylor and Zarah about this?"

She shook her head and looked everywhere but into his piercing blue eyes.

He dropped her hand. "Fine. Just remember that I reserve the right to do the I-told-you-so dance of victory later on down the road when you lose it because you've decided to keep everything bottled up and aren't woman enough to talk to your best friends about your innermost thoughts and fears." He turned and did a soft-shoe dance down the steps, waving an imaginary top hat and cane. "Now, I'm off to go ush. . .or whatever an usher is supposed to do." He flashed her a megawatt smile, turned on the balls of his feet, and sashayed up the aisle.

Flannery's face hurt from trying to hold in her amusement at Jack's blatant attempts to jolly her into a better frame of mind. By the time she joined the rest of the wedding party out in the foyer, a smile had forced its way through.

Zarah and Caylor were not as far gone as her sisters—and they'd made a concerted effort to ensure the three of them continued spending time together without Bobby and Dylan present.

"Well, that solves it." The wedding planner grabbed Flannery by the elbow and placed her in front of Caylor, right beside Chase Denney, a friend of Bobby's from work.

Flannery looked over her shoulder—and realized what needed to be solved. Since Zarah had asked both Caylor and Flannery to be her maids of honor, she'd stressed over which would be the one to stand beside her during the ceremony. At six feet tall—and the shoes Zarah's mother-in-law picked out for them to wear would add to that—Caylor would be taller than any of the men in the wedding party other than Bobby's best man, Patrick MacDonald, who dwarfed everyone present at six foot six.

Just three inches shorter than Caylor, Flannery had worried about towering over her escort wearing the inch-and-a-half high heels. But with the boost of the slightly higher heels of the tasseled, kiltie-style, burgundy pumps she'd worn to work today, she was still a little shorter than Chase.

They practiced processing in and out a couple more times.

"Maid of Honor Number Two—quit talking to your escort on the way down the aisle," the wedding planner called from the foyer behind them when Flannery and Chase reached the front of the sanctuary the third time.

"Busted," Flannery whispered as she and Chase parted at the bottom step. His laugh boomed through the large sanctuary. Flannery pretended to lift the long A-line skirt of the black gown she'd be wearing Saturday evening.

"Stop!"

She froze, foot hovering over the next step.

"Wait at the bottom until the bride arrives—you have to help arrange her train."

"Oh yeah. I forgot." Flannery turned, almost lost her balance, righted herself, and stepped back down onto the floor. Ugh. The *train*.

Poor Zarah. Since Zarah's mother had died when Zarah was very young, Bobby's mom had taken over the wedding planning—even taking Zarah, Caylor, and Flannery to New York City to go dress shopping. And while Zarah wanted something simple, Beth wanted drama. Thank goodness Caylor had found a compromise. From the front, Zarah's dress was an elegant A-line that suited her figure and personality perfectly. The back, however, was all about Beth and her desire for sensation. . .bustles and silk roses and a long train that Beth thought of as "presence" and Flannery viewed as powdered sugar on top of whipped cream on top of meringue.

Though she'd promised to turn it off, her phone started vibrating in her pocket. The muscles in the back of her neck and down her left arm twitched with the need to see if it was the call she'd waited for all day—the final decision on a major book deal she'd been working on for months.

But she couldn't insult Zarah and Bobby—or anyone else—by pulling out the phone and looking at the caller ID. . .or worse yet, answering it. Which she would be tempted to do if she looked.

Her hand sneaked toward her pocket, but she pulled it back and gripped the invisible stems of the invisible flowers she was pretending to hold. "Wait—if we're holding flowers, how are we supposed to arrange the train?"

Caylor reached the end of the aisle, her expression clearly telling Flannery that if they weren't in public, Caylor would gladly pummel her.

"We each use our free hand and work together," Caylor hissed between clenched teeth as she took her place beside Flannery.

"Oh, right. I remember that now."

"What is with you tonight?"

Flannery couldn't tell her the truth—about how much turmoil this wedding. . .no, rewind. . .how much turmoil her best friends' falling in love and getting engaged caused her. "Um. . .it's been a stressful week?"

"Whatever it is, try to keep it to a dull roar—and try to pay attention. Zarah's stressed out enough about this wedding. She doesn't need your flaking out to add to it."

All of Flannery's former annoyance turned into guilt. She shouldn't be thinking about herself. One of her best friends in the whole wide world was getting married day after tomorrow. Flannery should be doing whatever she could to make it the happiest day in Zarah's life.

The blushing bride—whose face had been bright red all evening from the attention lavished on her—arrived on her grandfather's arm, and after the pastor talked about giving the opening prayer here, Pops handed her over to Bobby, who would assist her up the steps. Once she reached the top, Flannery and Caylor mimed arranging the long train and then climbed the steps and took their places on the stage.

As she stood listening to the pastor talk to Zarah and Bobby about the vows they would be making to each other day after tomorrow, Flannery repeated the vow she'd made to herself at both of her sisters' weddings: She would never let falling in love change who she was, what she did, what she thought, and how she acted. She would always remain true to herself.

Not only did the phone in her pocket—which had buzzed a second time, indicating a voice mail message—torment her during the remainder of the rehearsal, but the presence of the good-looking, dark-haired guy talking and laughing with Jack and the other ushers at the back of the sanctuary also proved a continuing distraction.

The third time Jack caught her looking and responded with that knowing grin of his, Flannery returned her attention to the goings-on onstage, promising herself she would ignore Jack for the rest of the night.

After two practice recessionals—Flannery was making Chase walk too fast, apparently—the wedding planner released them. Flannery grabbed her purse off the front pew and bolted toward the doors, pulling her phone out of her pocket.

"Not so fast there, Speedy Gonzales." Jack caught her arm, forcing her to stop. He was her boss, after all. "I wanted to introduce you to Jamie O'Connor."

Flannery glared at Jack for all she was worth, then turned her most professional and sunny demeanor toward the dark-haired guy. Cataloging the fact that he was a little bit shorter than she (though she *was* wearing heels), she extended her right hand. "Mr. O'Connor and I have already met."

Talk about someone with a red face. Jamie looked as if he'd stuck

15

his head in an oven for six hours on EXTREME BAKE. Or whatever the highest temperature setting was on an oven.

Jamie shook her hand, giving her an equally detached, professional smile. "Yes. Fanny, right?"

She jerked her hand out of his, and his eyes crinkled up a little more. Maybe he thought he'd come up with a unique way of teasing her, but she'd heard that little play on her name one too many times growing up. She could think of a few choice things to call him, but her grandfather would wash her mouth out with soap if he heard her say anything unkind to anyone. And she was in church.

"It's *Fllllann-er-y*." She wasn't about to bring up the fact that she'd been named after the author who shared his last name. She'd heard that far too many times in her life, too. *"Oh, Flannery—just like Flannery O'Connor, the author!"*

"I was just saying that parking is limited over by the restaurant, so maybe a few of us could carpool." Jack winked at her.

She was about to argue when Jamie spoke.

"Much as I'd love to, I can't. I told Bobby that I wasn't going to be able to make it to the dinner—other plans." Jamie looked comfortable, at ease, standing here surrounded by *her* people. . .well, hers and Caylor's and Zarah's. The three ushers other than Jamie were Zarah's boss, Dennis Forrester; Caylor's fiancé, Dylan Bradley; and Jack.

Last fall Zarah had invited Flannery to a cookout at Bobby's grandparents'. Jamie had been there with his grandmother, and even though Flannery tried to avoid him most of the night, she'd had the distinct feeling he was homing in on her friends and their families. She had the same feeling tonight. Smarmy advertising salesman in an expensive suit that. . .showed off his broad shoulders and trim waist. Truthfully, the fact that he was even better looking than Jack made it easier for her to dislike Jamie. No guy that good looking had ever brought her anything but trouble.

She'd always known she'd fall for a nerdy, glasses-wearing, bookwormy type. Or at least that's what she told herself every time she broke up with one of the good-looking, alpha-male, jock types who seemed to be the only ones who'd ask her out. And she was the one to do the breaking up—not giving any of them a chance to break her heart.

"Hot date?" Jack asked, and though his voice had a lilt of humor in it, he glanced at Flannery with what could only be categorized as concern.

Jamie shrugged and gave an enigmatic, somewhat suggestive smile. "Something like that."

*Jerk.*

When Zarah mentioned that Bobby asked Jamie to be an usher in the wedding, Flannery had hoped and prayed the self-absorbed, annoying, arrogant salesman would turn down the opportunity. But he wouldn't be at dinner tonight, and as an usher and not a true member of the wedding party, he would be easy to ignore on Saturday. She could put up with anybody for a few hours, especially from across the room—she had to do it often enough for her job. But she hoped after this weekend, she would never have the displeasure of Jamie O'Connor's company again.

∞

Though he didn't usually, Jamie O'Connor ordered his latte with a double shot of espresso on Friday morning. He pulled forward to the pickup window and gave his favorite barista a flirtatious smile and a few kind words, though his head buzzed with the need for caffeine.

After sleeping through the alarm for half an hour, he'd rushed out of the house this morning. But he hadn't accounted for the lighter traffic—and shorter line in the Starbucks drive-through—due to this being the day before the Memorial Day weekend. What usually took him thirty-five to forty minutes took fifteen, and he pulled into the parking garage twenty minutes early.

Great. Just that much more time to stew. He finished off the last two sips of the coffee and climbed out of the car.

"Hey, Jamie *dawg!*" Darrell Keesey jogged down the parking-garage ramp.

"'Sup, man?" Jamie turned and held out his fist, which his coworker bumped his own against. He despised being called a dog. But it was an epithet that had caught on at the office in recent months—even though he was pretty sure no one said it in the real world anymore.

"Dude, you look rough." Darrell threw open the door to the stairwell and started down. "Big date last night keep you out late?"

Jamie shrugged noncommittally. Using a hint of big plans, he'd begged off going out drinking with most of the others from the office after yesterday's golf invitational for clients. He had to spend eight to twelve hours a day with these people; he didn't have to share the intimate details of his life with them, too—like attending a new friend's wedding rehearsal and then. . .what he'd done afterward. Besides, a reputation as a playboy—just another *dawg*—went far in an office like this.

"I'll get tightened up as soon as we get in there." He ran his knuckles along his jaw, wishing he'd checked the traffic report so he'd have known he had time to shave before leaving the house.

Unfortunately, the Gregg Agency's definition of casual Friday didn't include going unshaven.

From the parking garage across the street to the second-tallest building in Nashville and all the way up to the eighteenth floor, Darrell regaled him with tales about who'd gotten drunk, which account executive had made a pass at which client—and vice versa—and where the staff had ended up after the open bar at their boss's country club closed.

They turned into the hallway leading to the Sports Marketing Department, and Darrell paused beside the closed door of the first—and largest—office. "Hey—the meeting. Today's the big day and the announcement Armando's been promising." Darrell jerked his chin toward Jamie. "Odds are four to one in favor of you moving into this office after this morning's meeting."

In an office where betting on everything from sports to political elections was a way of life, they'd started a pool on who would be promoted to Sports Marketing director. He just *loved* being bet on like a racehorse.

"Smart money's on you, dude. Mitch may have more years of experience, but you've been at Gregg a lot longer, and Armando rewards loyalty."

Jamie knew the job was his—had to be. Both he and Mitch had been called in, separately, three weeks ago to give presentations on how the agency could make up for the loss of business caused by a couple of expired and non-replaced sponsorship contracts, and the defection of their former director to work directly for one of the professional sports teams in town. It hadn't been a formal interview, but why would a formal interview be needed for the only two senior account executives in the small department?

Several times since then, when Jamie had run into Armando Gregg, the agency's owner and CEO had acted like he wanted to tell Jamie something but then clammed up.

"I hope so, Darrell." Jamie pressed his lips together and drew in a slow breath through his nose. "I hope so."

Approaching footsteps on the tile floor alerted them a few seconds before two more of their team rounded the corner. Both tall and blond, the junior account executive and administrative assistant stopped, not needing a lot of imagination to figure out what Jamie and Darrell had been discussing while standing outside the vacant director's office.

"Today's the day, huh, *Boss*?" Wade asked, flinging his surfer-boy hair out of his eyes with a toss of his head.

"Don't jinx it." But Ainslee didn't look at all worried. "I have the requisitions for your new nameplate, business cards, and letterhead all written up and ready to go to accounting as soon as we get out of the meeting, Jamie."

Wade nudged the former women's college and professional basketball player with his elbow. "And for yourself with *Junior Account Executive* on them? And me with *Senior Account Executive*?"

Ainslee shrugged, her brown eyes twinkling. "Maybe."

"I hope you wrote up a set of requisitions with Mitch's name on them, too, just in case." Glancing toward the corner that joined the department to the main corridor, Jamie ushered his team—minus

Mitch—toward the common area at the end of the short hall. Ainslee dropped her giant purse on her desk. The two graphic designers, whom she shared the large space with—which also contained the couch and chairs that made up their brainstorming area—hadn't made it in yet, apparently.

"Didn't you guys hear?" Wade glanced over his shoulder.

"No, what?" Ainslee and Darrell turned. Gossip was more virulent than Ebola in this office.

"Apparently Armando and Mitch got into it at the clubhouse yesterday afternoon." Wade picked up a foam basketball from the wire in-basket on Ainslee's desk and tossed it toward the hoop hanging on his office door. It bounced off the rim and rolled under one of the designers' desks.

"How? They weren't even on the same team." Darrell once again jerked his chin in Jamie's direction. "And I was surprised you weren't with Armando's group—but I guess he didn't want to tip his hand about the big announcement."

No lover of golf—proficient, though, from years of hosting clients at Armando's biannual golf invitationals—Jamie was glad he hadn't been on Armando's team. The ad agency's owner took the game far too seriously.

"Dunno." Wade tossed another foam ball at the hoop. "But probably blew his chances."

"Maybe he pressed Mr. Gregg for an answer and didn't like what he heard." Ainslee lobbed a small plastic football toward the hoop, over Wade's head, and it swished through. She raised her arms in triumph. "Nothin' but net."

Growing uncomfortable with the topic—and worried Mitch might arrive and overhear them—Jamie glanced at the large wall clock with the minor-league baseball team's logo in the center. "Eight o'clock. Time to get to work."

Ainslee tossed one more ball toward Wade's door, which also swished through the small hoop and net. "Yes, Boss." She winked at him and then crossed the room to start the coffee as the two graphic designers arrived and started up their computers.

Jamie opened his office door and snapped the light on. "*Boss.*" A chill crawled over his shoulders and down his arms. No one here could ever know what he'd talked about until two this morning with the only person privy to the private life of James Clarence O'Connor III.

He closed the door and pulled out the electric razor he kept in his credenza for days like today. Stepping up to the mirror hanging on the back of the door, he grimaced. Though not nearly as red as yesterday, this sunburn would start peeling in another day or two. At least with the holiday, he wouldn't be seeing clients until Tuesday.

The electric razor intensified the irritation in his skin. He stepped back when Ainslee opened the door to hand him his coffee mug.

"T minus forty-five minutes."

"Thanks." He closed the door behind her and finished shaving before moving on to checking his e-mail and appointment calendar. Only some phone calls to make this morning and then he could concentrate on catching up on his paperwork and month-end reports.

Time ticked by in an eternity as call after call ended with him leaving messages for his clients and prospects, but finally Ainslee knocked on the door.

"Ready, Boss?"

He shrugged into his navy sport coat. "Don't let anyone hear you say that until it's official."

"It's got to be." The administrative assistant—who would indeed be promoted to junior account executive if Jamie got the director position—fell in step beside him. Darrell, Wade, and the two designers rounded the corner into the main hall ahead of them, merging with the flow of dozens of others from all departments of the largest independent advertising agency in Nashville.

"I wish I had your confidence." Jamie held open the door of the theater-style conference room for Ainslee.

She paused halfway through, towering over him. "No, it's *got* to be you. Mitch never showed up this morning," she whispered.

"What?"

A loudly cleared throat alerted them to the traffic jam behind them. Jamie took Ainslee by the elbow and pulled her into the room. "Mitch isn't here?"

She grinned and shook her head. "And the penalty for unsportsmanlike conduct goes to. . ." She waggled her eyebrows.

He followed her to the row where the rest of the team—dare he think of them as *his* team?—sat.

As soon as Armando Gregg walked into the room, all chatter—mostly about plans for the holiday weekend—ended.

The normally well-groomed and laid-back forty-five-year-old looked harried and stressed. Not like someone about to impart good news. But Jamie didn't let that worry him. Good news was good news whether Armando was stressed or not.

Would his promotion to Sports Marketing director really be good news, though?

A middle-aged woman stepped up onto the platform to join Armando. While everyone else in the room wore the casual Friday standard—a variation of chinos and an open-collar, button-down shirt with a blazer—the woman who stood beside Armando wore a severe, dark-gray business suit. And her expression made an even more somber statement than her clothing did.

Armando set the papers he carried in with him on the podium, looked at the woman to his left, licked his lips nervously, and turned to look around the room without actually making eye contact with anyone.

"As some of you may have already figured out, the Gregg Agency was struck pretty hard by the recent recession. I know I pushed all of you harder than I ever did before over the last couple of years, but I did not want you to know just how dire circumstances had become. When it looked like I might have to shutter the agency forever, I was approached by Hampton, Dixon, and Holcomb Marketing Solutions out of Memphis about a partial buyout and partnership. After six months of negotiations and business model development, I'm pleased this morning to announce that as of June 1, our name is officially changing to Hampton, Dixon, Holcomb, and Gregg—HDHG Marketing Solutions."

Armando turned the meeting over to Ms. Gray Business Suit, who gave a little history of the Memphis agency that had just bought out Armando's pride and joy. After boring everyone to tears, she turned the meeting back over to Armando.

"So what does this mean for us?" Again, Armando looked around the room without focusing on anyone. "The most important thing to keep in mind is that this partnership allows us to stay in business. But it also means that between the two locations—here and Memphis— we now have some redundancies. There are certain divisions that we need in both locations, such as graphic design and editorial. However other departments will be affected in both places. Major Accounts, for example. Account executives in both locations handle the same clients. Fortunately we do have some open positions that we can begin the eliminations with. . . ."

Jamie tuned the boss's voice out when a new idea struck him. What if Armando was going to announce that Jamie would be the director not only of Sports Marketing here but also over the department at the Memphis office? The magnitude of that kind of responsibility made him a little queasy.

"Unfortunately, it isn't just open positions that we'll be eliminating. And we're telling you all this at the same time so there will be no misunderstandings—I wish we could have met with each person individually first, but confidentiality needed to be maintained." Armando took a deep breath, his eyes focused on the papers in front of him. "The biggest and hardest cut that we've had to make is eliminating the Nashville Sports Marketing Department and transferring everything over to the larger and better-equipped Sports Marketing Department in Memphis. We're also cutting. . ."

Beside him, Jamie's coworkers reacted in not-so-hushed tones and words of disbelief. But Jamie couldn't breathe. Couldn't comprehend. . .

He'd shaved for this?

# Chapter 2

At the sound of a car in the driveway, Maureen stood and brushed the dirt and grass off the knees of her floral-print, rayon pants. She left the garden and made her way around the corner of the house, tucking her gloves into the short tool apron she wore.

She stopped at the gate, the air suddenly going chill. "Jamie?"

Her grandson looked exactly the same as he had at his thirteenth birthday party when the paramedics declared his father dead.

She flung the gate open and rushed to him. "What is it? What's wrong? Why are you here at ten o'clock in the morning?"

"I. . ." Jamie's slate-gray eyes remained fixed at a distant point.

She grabbed his arms and shook him. "Tell me what's wrong."

"I lost my job." His eyes came into focus, and he finally looked at her, seeming surprised to see her. "Cookie, I got laid off."

"You. . .but what about the promotion? Last night, you were so certain—"

"There never was a promotion. The presentation wasn't an interview. It was so the department in Memphis would be able to do our jobs for us."

Maureen rubbed his hand between hers. "You're not making any sense. Memphis?"

"Our new parent company. Armando sold us out. So much for

rewarding loyalty." Jamie pulled away from her and began pacing the sidewalk between the driveway and front porch. "The whole department—and not just us, but a lot of other people, too. But is anyone in Memphis losing their jobs? No! Of course not!"

Maureen's concern for her grandson grew along with his agitation.

"Let's go inside and talk about this." She led him around the house, through the back door, and to the kitchen.

Jamie sank into one of the dinette chairs and dropped his head to the table so his forehead, nose, and chin were pressed against the polished, dark wood surface. His arms dangled at his sides.

Maureen's heart wrenched.

He muttered something, but it came out garbled.

"What's that?" She wrapped one arm around his waist and caressed the back of his head with her other hand.

He turned so his cheek pressed against the tabletop. "Thirteen years. I worked there thirteen years. And just like that"—he raised his right hand to shoulder height and snapped his fingers—"no more job." Turning, he pressed his face to the table again.

Maureen couldn't stand it. She turned and raised her eyes. *Why him, Lord? What has he ever done that deserves what he's gone through in his life?*

She filled the kettle and put it on the stove to heat and then opened the plastic container holding the cookies she'd made for game night at church. She had plenty of time to make something else, and Jamie's need outweighed the time she'd spent with the new recipe. She put four on a plate and then set the plate and a tall glass of milk on the table.

"Sit up."

"I don't want to."

She almost smiled at his petulant tone. It'd been a long time since she'd heard it. Instead, she placed both hands on his strong shoulders—shoulders that had already borne more than most men twice his age—and pulled.

He gave another mild protest but then sat up. He pulled the

cookies and milk closer, and Maureen returned to the stove to make a cup of tea for herself. After setting the cup and saucer on the table—along with the container holding the rest of the cookies—she sat down beside him. "Tell me what happened."

Never one to recoil from detail, Jamie took his time, starting with waking up late, his double-espresso latte, the encouragement from his coworkers, and his boss's unwelcome announcement. "A couple of Major Accounts reps are losing their jobs, a few designers and editors, and some department directors are being demoted back down to account executives."

"But your department was the only one cut in its entirety?"

Jamie broke off a piece of the cookie he'd been turning over and over in his fingers as he talked. "Yep. Just us. And you know what? That's the worst thing of all. Ainslee just finished her MBA. She's been slaving away as an assistant for years now on the promise that as soon as a junior account exec position came open in our department, it was hers. And Wade was ready to be promoted to senior account exec. And Darrell. . .no one was better suited to do this job than him. What are they going to do now? It's not like there are a whole bunch of sports-marketing jobs available here. Ainslee's master's degree is *in* sports management for crying out loud!"

Maureen rose to fix another cup of tea—so Jamie wouldn't see her smile or the tears pooling in her eyes. To see him so indignant on behalf of others instead of himself made her grandmother heart swell with pride.

He snorted and then shoved an entire cookie into his mouth. "Guess we found out why Mitch and Armando got into it yesterday and why Mitch didn't show up for work today."

"James. . ."

He covered his full mouth with his hand. "Sorry, Cookie." After swallowing and guzzling half the glass of milk, he continued, "They're giving us a week's severance pay for every year we've worked there, plus our accrued vacation time. So I'm the lucky one. I get thirteen weeks and eight vacation days. Darrell gets eight weeks, and Wade and

Ainslee get five. Mitch—unless Armando fired him yesterday—only gets two weeks."

"Do you really think—"

"No. I doubt Armando would have done that to him. He probably told him not to come in today to keep him from saying anything to the rest of us."

"So they let you go home after the meeting?"

Jamie swallowed the half cookie he'd just bitten off. "The HR rep came in and talked to all of us together, then took us aside one by one. Fortunately, I got to go first. Armando couldn't even be bothered to sit in on the meeting. But the gal from HR told us he'd said we didn't have to stay for the rest of the day if we didn't want to."

Maureen reached for one of the cookies and dunked it in her tea. Her grandson's voice had started mellowing under the effects of the chocolate cookies with crushed toffee candy inside. "Your job ends today?"

"Next Friday." He squinched his face in a sardonic expression. "I still have month-end reports to finish and expenses and mileage reimbursements to request and other paperwork to finish before I can be officially released from work. Talk about adding insult to injury. I can't even use getting laid off as an excuse to get out of month-end reports."

He pushed back the plate, still holding two cookies, and once again pressed his face to the table. "I hate my life."

After a few minutes of silence, Maureen decided to broach the topic that had been bouncing around in the back of her mind ever since her quick, accusatory prayer. "Remember what we talked about last night?"

"About how much I hate my life?" he muttered against the table.

"About how much you really wish you'd chosen a different path in life. About how much you feel like working in marketing is sucking the life out of you. About how much you wish you had a job that impacted people in a positive way."

He didn't respond. Maureen wasn't sure if she should take that as positive or negative, so she pressed on. "Maybe this is God's way of giving you the chance to make that change. Maybe He's been trying to tell you in little ways over the years that this wasn't the path He intended for you, but you weren't listening. So maybe this is your wake-up call."

For a long time, Jamie didn't move, didn't speak. Finally, he sat up, rubbing his nose. "Why couldn't God have just sent me a registered letter instead?"

Maureen chuckled. Nothing kept her grandson down long. She leaned over, wrapped her arm around his shoulders, and gave him a squeeze. "Now's your chance, Jamie. Your chance to start all over again and figure out what you really want to do with your life. And you can start by going to Bobby Patterson's bachelor party tonight."

"But I told you I'd come help with game night at church."

So proud of him she couldn't stand it, Maureen pinched his cheeks. "You are so precious. But the senior adults of Acklen Avenue Fellowship can manage on our own. Besides, after calling bingo for two hours at the nursing home last night and then coming home and talking to me until the wee hours, you need a break from hanging out with old folks. Go. Have a boys' night out. Make new friends. And open up your heart for whatever it is God might be trying to tell you."

He leaned over and kissed her cheek. "I'll go. And I'll try to have a good time."

"Every time you start feeling low, just remember the old song about turning your frown upside down."

"You used to sing that to me after Mom left."

She nodded. "I know."

He pressed his forehead to hers. "What did I ever do to deserve a grandmother like you?"

"I don't know, but it must have been something wonderful."

"Sorry I'm late, Big Daddy. I couldn't get away from the office. Not from lack of trying, though."

Kirby McNeill set the menu down and stood to greet his youngest granddaughter with a kiss on the forehead. "I thought you were supposed to be off work today, helping out with last-minute things for your friend's wedding."

Flannery sat in the chair he held out for her, shaking her head. "Got bad news last night. That big contract I've been working on for months, which they were supposed to give me a final answer on yesterday—there were more pieces they wanted to negotiate, so I've been haggling with the contracts manager and my boss all morning. But Bobby's mother and Caylor are with Zarah, helping her with what needs to be done."

After ordering, Flannery went back to talking about her job. Kirby fought the urge to give her advice on how to deal with the coworkers, agents, authors, and production people who seemed to do nothing but add stress to her life. But sixty years as a pastor had taught him that young people didn't want counseling or advice unless they specifically asked for it—and then, most of them didn't take it anyway.

"I got the final changes done and the new contract sent over right before I left to come here. The agent promised me a final answer before end of business today. And since he's in Atlanta, hopefully he means eastern time, which means I might actually get to leave work by five o'clock our time." She dug around in the large pile of salad greens remaining in her bowl for the last piece of fried chicken. "How's your room at Union Station? Did you get checked in okay?"

"It is much nicer than it was when your grandmother and I stayed there the night after we got married." He watched her plunge the breaded nugget into the dressing and eat it.

"Sorry things didn't work out for you to stay with me on the weekends."

With only one parking space in the garage under the high-rise condo building and her determination to give up her own bed and sleep on the not-quite-long-enough sofa in what she called "an open-concept one-bedroom"—meaning that only an angled half wall separated the bedroom from the rest of the apartment—Kirby had put his foot down and told her he would stay in a hotel when he came up on the weekends to visit with her and attend church.

"You need your privacy—especially on your only days off from work." Not that she ever truly took any time off from work. Just sitting here for forty-five minutes without her phone ringing was a rarity—

Flannery looked down at the smartphone clipped onto her purse. Her eyes widened. "Big Daddy, I hate to do this. . . ."

"It's the agent, isn't it?"

"It is." She dug around in the large satchel for her keys. "Are you still planning on going to the game night for the seniors' group at church tonight?"

"Don't worry about me. I know you have responsibilities this weekend. I can entertain myself. There are so many new things to see and do in Nashville, I could spend every day here for six months and still not see it all."

Flannery leaned over and gave him a peck on the cheek. "Thanks for understanding. I'll meet you at the hotel for breakfast tomorrow at nine."

"I'll see you then."

After paying the lunch tab—and wondering for the hundredth time why Flannery insisted on ordering a salad when all she ate off of it was the fried chicken—Kirby left the restaurant and drove from Brentwood back into downtown Nashville.

He missed the farm already, even after only a few hours away. But getting away from the farm—and getting involved in a new church—would be good for him. He'd spent so much of his life as Pastor McNeill and not enough as just plain Kirby—always a part of what was going on, but always apart from the people.

He spent the afternoon at the Country Music Hall of Fame, enjoying the displays on the beginnings of the musical style that made the city famous—and the music he'd listened to for so many years.

After a light supper at the hotel, Kirby dressed in slacks and a button-down shirt and headed over to Acklen Avenue Fellowship. Game night sounded a bit juvenile to him, but he couldn't miss the opportunity to fellowship with others and start getting to know them.

The fellowship hall—community center, this church called it—was in a separate building across a small plaza from the back entrance of the main part of the church. The floor-to-ceiling glass windows of the ultra-modern community center contrasted greatly with the traditional red-brick exterior of the rest of the church complex.

He'd no more than stepped into the cavernous fellowship space than an older lady with red hair—dyed, obviously, but looking quite natural with her porcelain skin and smoky-gray eyes—looked up from the name-tag table. Her red lips split into a wide smile.

"Kirby McNeill, isn't it?" She extended her right hand, the knuckles slightly bent and bulging.

Kirby took the arthritic hand and exerted gentle pressure on it. "Mrs. O'Connor."

Her smile widened. "Yes, but you must call me Maureen. I'm impressed you remember—you must have met so many people Sunday." She handed him a felt-tip pen to make a name tag for himself. "We're so happy you decided to come back and socialize with us."

Being able to put faces and names together after one meeting was a gift—one that apparently had passed on to Flannery alone of all his offspring. "After so many years of being the one in charge of these types of shindigs, it will be nice just to be able to take it all in for once."

Maureen came around the table, a slight hitch in her giddyup. "It's early yet, so not a lot of folks have arrived, but let me introduce you around a little bit." She looked up at him, almost craning her neck to do so. "You said you were accustomed to leading these types of gatherings. May I ask why?"

"I'm a pastor—or, I *was* a pastor. I've recently retired. Again."

"Again?"

He rubbed the back of his neck. "I officially retired two years ago. But I'd been at the church for nearly thirty years. It was the church that supported me through losing my wife and through. . .many other difficult times, so I figured I'd stay on as a member. But when they

31

couldn't find an interim they liked, they asked me to fill in until they found a new pastor."

"And after two years, they'd stopped looking?" Maureen stopped in between two tables displaying a couple dozen games, puzzles, and decks of cards.

"Something like that. I think everyone would have been content for me to stay on until I keeled over in the pulpit." Kirby could hear those words echo through his head in Flannery's mellow alto voice. "So I gave them a date that would be my last day to preach. And that was two weeks ago. Then I took my granddaughter's advice and skedaddled out of town on the weekends."

"Out of town?" Maureen's ample forehead crinkled in a frown. "You're not from Nashville?"

"No—Pulaski. A bit south of Columbia." As soon as he said it, recognition flashed in Maureen's eyes, marking the explanation as unnecessary. "I just need to find a more permanent situation than staying in a hotel every weekend."

"Your granddaughter can't house you?" Maureen started walking again toward where everyone was clustered around the refreshments.

"Her apartment is too small. And with as many hours as she works during the week, I don't want to infringe on her only downtime." Though she rarely took weekends off, either. He'd seen the stacks of paperwork on her desk and suspected the computer tablet thing she carried around everywhere with her had work stuff on it, too.

"What will you find to fill your time? Though I suppose you will want to make sure that you see all of the sights around town, and that will take some time."

"I went to the Country Music Hall of Fame this afternoon. And since my granddaughter is tied up all day tomorrow with her best friend's wedding, I guess I could visit the Frist art museum and the Tennessee State Museum." He turned his gaze to the table laden with all kinds of baked goods and desserts. His blood sugar spiked just looking at all of it.

"You don't sound overly enthusiastic about it, though."

He shrugged, struggling to put words to the restless feeling that had been growing in his chest all day. "It's all well and good to take in the sights and be entertained. But I feel like I should be doing something...useful. Something helpful. Something to make whatever time I have left mean something."

At eighty-six, he had long since passed the years of denying his own mortality. No sense in pretending he had decades remaining on his account. Though he didn't usually like to talk about it.

"I know what you mean. When I retired from nursing twenty years ago, I almost went crazy feeling like my life had ceased to matter. That's when I started volunteering at the hospital and the nursing home our church supports. And I try to find a service project for the group each month. So if you're interested, we'll be going down to the food bank Monday morning to pack boxes and then over to the women's and children's shelter around lunchtime to host a Memorial Day cookout for the residents. We should be finished by three or four o'clock."

"I hadn't planned on staying on through Monday...." He regretted it as soon as he said it. "But I can drive home just as easily after the cookout."

Maureen's eyes sparkled, and her wide smile appeared again. "Do you have access to e-mail while you're here? I can send you all of the information."

He reached for his wallet and pulled out a business card.

"*Doctor* Kirby McNeill? Doctor of theology?"

He shook his head. "Ph.D. in agricultural sciences. I was going to be one of those space-age farmers who improved everything with technology before God got ahold of me and led me to the pulpit. I still keep a vegetable garden, though."

"So do I." She tucked the card into her pocket. "I'll e-mail you all the particulars when I get home tonight."

Apparently deciding she'd kept him to herself long enough, she turned toward the group that had been edging closer and closer down the table toward them and began the introductions.

She'd asked for his e-mail address. Was that the modern-day equivalent of asking for his phone number?

He rather hoped it was. He'd always had a soft spot for redheads.

# Chapter 3

❧

"*If directions to your house include 'Turn off the paved road'. . .*"

The line from Jeff Foxworthy's famous comedy routine about rednecks ran through Jamie's head as he turned off the narrow road—which barely qualified as paved—and onto a gravel drive that disappeared into the woods.

He should have accepted the ride out here that Bobby offered—let Bobby's car get dinged up from the gravel. But Jamie wanted to leave his options open, just in case he felt the need to bolt. Which he was pretty sure he would.

Turning on his headlights, he slowed to a crawl, unable to see beyond the next curve, and with the dense canopy of branches and leaves overhead, little afternoon light broke through to help. Last thing he needed today was to wreck his car. Actually, if he wrecked the car and then got home later to find out his townhouse had burned down, he'd have hit the trifecta.

He hadn't been this far out in the country since Mom sold the house outside Murfreesboro and sent Jamie to live with Cookie in her little cottage in the Crieve Hall area of Nashville. And though the house had been in a rural area, it had been surrounded by small farms, not out in the wilderness like this place—Bobby's parents' hunting cabin.

Seriously? They had their own hunting cabin? Jamie tightened his grip on the steering wheel. Must have been nice to grow up privileged and have everything handed to him. Cookie had worked long and hard hours as a nurse to support him after Mom left—

No. He wasn't going to do this to himself tonight. He'd come to have a good time, to do something to try to get his mind off losing his job. He didn't know what that *something* was, but he imagined out here that it would probably be something physical. And since he hadn't gotten his run in this morning—though he could have gone after he got home from Cookie's house—he needed some way to expend all his pent-up energy.

Light ahead—the end of the forest, or someone coming toward him? Not that it mattered; the encroaching trees left no margin for passing. He continued on slowly—and breathed a relieved sigh when he broke through the trees into a sun-drenched clearing.

The large yard surrounding the log cabin sent up a scent indicating it had been mowed today, and several cars already sat in a row on the gravel pad beside the cabin. He pulled up beside the farthest car, parked, and climbed out.

"Jamie, man, glad you could make it." Bobby Patterson opened the side door at Jamie's knock and then ushered him into the house. "I was kinda surprised when you changed your mind, but it's great you did—now our teams are even."

Jamie tried to tamp down a recurrence of jealousy over the size and grandeur of the "hunting cabin." He'd gone skiing in Colorado once and stayed at a luxury resort that hadn't been this lavishly appointed. Some guys had all the luck. He put his game face on. "My schedule cleared up at the last minute."

Bobby's coworkers from the Tennessee Criminal Investigations Unit greeted Jamie and immediately started grilling him. Had he ever played capture the flag? How was his marksmanship? His stealthiness?

"Wait—we're playing capture the flag? Paintball or laser?"

Chase Denney pointed to the stacks of vests in the corner. "Laser."

"With time-out or kill?" A spark of excitement ignited in Jamie's gut.

Chase and the other two agents grinned at each other. "Time-out.

I think Bobby said he has the sensors set to ten minutes."

Oh, if only Danny could be here. The urge to geek out on these guys rose up in the back of Jamie's throat, but he controlled it. How many Friday nights and Saturdays during high school and college had he and his childhood best friend spent out in the small patch of woods behind Danny's folks' place with their paintball guns? But they hadn't been playing capture the flag with a bunch of military- and police-trained experts.

A few more guys arrived—including the mountain of a man serving as Bobby's best man in the wedding and two who hadn't been at the rehearsal. Jamie's fellow usher, Dylan Bradley, arrived looking distinctly uncertain with what appeared to be a sketchpad tucked under his arm, but he was the only one of the other three ushers to make an appearance. That didn't surprise Jamie. This kind of activity didn't seem suited to Jack Colby or Dennis Forrester—not from what Jamie had observed of them yesterday.

"Okay. Now that we're all here"—Bobby's raised voice immediately quieted everyone else—"let's get started."

They followed him into the kitchen of the log mansion, where two piles of equipment sat on a long, wide, stone-topped island.

"There are two teams of seven. Since we're the two former military guys, Chase and I are team captains and, as such, will be defending the flags. The other six players on the teams will be divided into pairs. Each pair will have a GPS into which is programmed the location of the other team's flag—and a locator signal for each and every team. We're working with forty-six acres here, people, so don't expect this to be easy. Remember—the winning team is the one that not only captures the opposing team's flag but also returns safely to their own base of operations with it.

"We are using laser guns." Bobby lifted one of the lifelike toy weapons. "If your vest registers a hit, you and your partner must get to the infirmary—which is here at the house—as fast as possible to wait out your ten-minute penalty and get your vest reset by our acting medic—Dylan."

Jamie joined in the chorus of groans, smiling as he did so.

"Equipment." Bobby moved to the stack of stuff closest to him. "Vest and gun, obviously. Night-vision goggles. GPS. Canteen. Two-way radios. Oh, and I should mention—cell phone service out here stinks. So *don't* lose the radios."

Clenching his teeth together to keep his jaw from hanging open, Jamie looked around at the other guys, wondering if any of the rest of them found this abnormal. He and Danny had worked an entire summer to be able to afford the low-end paintball starter kits and walkie-talkies they'd used throughout high school and college.

"Gage, Jamie, Patrick, Jim, Mike, and Steve—you're with me." Bobby motioned them to join him on his side of the island.

Thank goodness the teams had been determined ahead of time. There hadn't even been time for the knot of uneasiness to form from worrying about whether or not he'd be picked last because no one here knew him.

Jamie shrugged into the vest—lighter weight than it appeared—hooked the strap of the realistically weighted gun over his head and one shoulder, and took the goggles, canteen, and radio Bobby handed him, all of which he found straps or pockets for on the vest.

"I think this is the wrong vest." Patrick tugged at the front of his, trying to get it closed.

"That's the one that has your name written on the tag."

"Well, it shrank or something."

Bobby laughed. "Or something. . .like the fact that your fiancée loves to bake?"

"Nah. I think this kind of material shrinks up after a few years." Patrick sucked in his slight paunch and got the plastic buckles to snap closed.

Jamie tightened the straps on his vest and adjusted the gun so that it lay at a comfortable angle across his back, leaving his hands free for the moment.

Bobby looked across the kitchen at Chase's team. "If y'all are ready?"

"We've been waiting on you guys." The African American guy gave Bobby a wicked grin.

"Well then"—Bobby lifted his left arm, revealing a large, expensive sportsman's watch, and Chase did the same—"on my mark, we set the timers for twenty minutes to get to our bases of operation. Let the better team prevail."

"Oh, we will, don't worry," Chase teased.

"Three, two, one. . .*mark*."

Instead of trying to beat the other team through the door in the kitchen to get outside, Bobby led them back through the living room, out a sliding glass door, and across the back deck.

"Gage and Jamie, you two are partners. Patrick and Jim, Mike and Steve, same." He set a quick pace into the woods, and Jamie hurried to keep from being left behind.

The guy named Gage dropped back beside Jamie. "Rick Gage. I work with Bobby at the TCIU."

"Jamie O'Connor." He shook Gage's hand. "Do y'all do this kind of thing often?"

"First time for me, at least with this group. Used to do it all the time with my church youth group as a kid—though not with the guns and electronic equipment and all. You?"

"Had a friend growing up I went paintballing with on the weekends." And this whole experience made him miss Danny more forcefully than he had in the five years since he'd failed to respond to Danny's last e-mail. Why had he let that relationship go?

Ahead, Bobby continued streaming instructions and ideas and strategy as he broke through the undergrowth toward where their flag was hidden.

Running half a dozen miles in his neighborhood every day made Jamie feel like he was staying fit. But tromping through the wilderness—uphill—showed him just how out of shape he was.

The fresh air—with a much different quality than the "fresh air" of the suburbs—rugged landscape, and companionship of guys who weren't interested in image or appearance cracked something open inside Jamie. Something he'd packed up and plastered over a long time ago. Something he needed to unpack and explore again.

His life had just changed—drastically. Maybe taking a step back into the past to see if there had been another choice he'd missed could help him pull the pieces apart and put them back together again.

❧

The extra-sweet, extra-tall swirl of cream cheese–flavored buttercream frosting made Flannery slightly nauseated by the time she finished licking it off the white cupcake. But she just couldn't help herself. She needed the second cupcake to restore her energy after running around downtown all evening.

Besides, it wasn't every weekend a girl's best friend got married. And since she didn't drink, she needed some way to drown her sorrows. Gigi's cupcakes to the rescue!

Of course, after fried green tomatoes and fried shrimp for dinner at Chappy's, she would not only have to increase the incline on the treadmill tomorrow, but she'd also have to add at least two or three more miles to her regular ten-mile morning run. But that's why she'd started running back in college—so she didn't have to give up eating the foods she loved.

"He's not juggling, is he?" Caylor moved closer to Zarah's thirty-two-inch flat-panel TV to get a better view of the digital photo. She pressed her fingertips to the corners of her eyes, then rolled them and blinked several times—a clear indication her contacts were bothering her. "And this one doesn't count, even if he is really juggling, because Flannery's already been in three pictures."

Stacy and the other girls on Flannery's team protested. "This guy really could juggle—several of us got video of him on our phones juggling five shot glasses. But flip to the next picture, and you'll see I'm with him. But that was his price for juggling for us—a picture with Flannery and one of her business cards. You know how these guys get when they see someone like her—tall, blond, and built like a supermodel."

Teeth half sunk into the cupcake, Flannery raised her eyes, narrowing them and trying to shoot lightning bolts out of them at the petite brunette.

"And in addition to being a bouncer at Rippy's, he's a musician, so you know Flan will go out with him when he calls."

Flannery swallowed her bite and debated with outrage for a second before joining in the laughter. "Three musicians—and y'all act like that's all I ever date. I'd like to see someone who grew up in Nashville who's never dated a wannabe singer or musician."

Caylor raised her hand.

Flannery shook her head. "Doesn't count—you sing in at least four different groups, not including your church choir, Caylor."

Even Zarah, who'd reverted back to quiet and pensive after exerting her social skills and having fun during the photo scavenger hunt bachelorette party downtown, laughed this time.

After sorting out the scores—with Caylor's and Zarah's teams tying and Flannery's winning by one point—Caylor and Flannery called it a night, though barely nine o'clock. The other women understood and departed with well-wishes and well-intentioned advice from the married gals on how to sleep the night before the wedding.

As soon as the last one left, Flannery turned off the porch light and joined her two best friends on the sofa.

Caylor's phone chirped. She looked at it, smiled, and then dropped it into her purse sitting on the floor beside her feet. "That was Dylan. They're just finishing and should be headed back to Nashville shortly. No injuries, and no one got lost in the woods."

"Good." Though Zarah didn't look as relieved as she sounded. "At least I won't have to worry about Beth losing it tomorrow if one of the guys had to cancel with a sprained ankle or something."

"So. . .has Bobby told you yet where you're going on your honeymoon?" Caylor waggled her eyebrows. Zarah went from pale to full-on blush in under one second. Had to be a new land-speed record. "We're going to New Mexico—Las Cruces first, to revisit all the places we went when we were dating the first time, just for a couple of days. And then we'll be spending a week at a resort in Santa Fe—somewhere we talked about visiting back then."

"Aw, that's too sweet." Caylor's eyes took on a dreamy quality.

Flannery sighed. Here they went—now Caylor would speculate on where she and Dylan might go on *their* honeymoon—

"Flan—are you okay with this?"

The concern in Zarah's voice blasted through Flannery's annoyance. What had she missed? Been volunteered for? "Okay with what?"

"With me getting married. With Caylor's being engaged. With. . .well, with having other people in our lives now. You've been acting kind of. . .different lately. Withdrawn."

"I'd almost call it sulking"—Caylor turned to sit with her back against the plush arm of the sofa, her feet tucked up under her—"except I've seen you sulk many times over the past thirty-odd years, and that usually lasts only a couple of hours, not a few weeks or months."

A cold hand of sorrow linked with a hot hand of embarrassment and wrapped around Flannery's throat and squeezed, making even shallow breaths difficult.

Zarah reached over and took Flannery's hand in both of hers. "You know that you're not going to lose us, right? That we're not going to drop you in favor of the guys the way your sisters did, right?"

Here they were, the night before Zarah's wedding, when Flannery and Caylor should be scraping Zarah off the ceiling, and instead, Zarah and Caylor were trying to comfort Flannery.

She burst into tears and flung her arms around Zarah. "I am so, so sorry. I've been narcissistic, making this whole thing about me, when I should have been focusing on you."

As usual, she'd been unable to clarify her feelings in her own mind until the words tumbled out of her mouth. "I've been a horrible best friend, thinking only of myself and my fears of how your engagements and weddings are going to change everything for me. I've forgotten to be happy for you—and for Bobby. I have to remember that I'm not losing a friend; I'm regaining a high school classmate."

The statement came out just as ridiculous as it'd sounded in her head, and she sat back, releasing Zarah and joining in with Zarah's and Caylor's chuckles. Flannery wiped the tears from her face with the backs of her hands. At least Jack wasn't here to do his I-told-you-so dance.

"I don't know where you've gotten the idea that you're losing either of us, just because we're getting married—wait, yes, I do." Caylor cut Flannery off before she could interrupt. "It's because of your sisters. But come on. Think about what we've been through and done together over the years. Friendship like that doesn't go away."

Flannery shrugged. "I guess."

"You guess?" Caylor scoffed, and even Zarah smiled. "Who else would, in their thirties, take a day off work, have a sleepover, and stay up all night so that they could watch a royal wedding together at five o'clock in the morning?"

"Or what about that trip to Gatlinburg last month?" Zarah raised her brows. "Who else but us would put up with your being on the phone the entire tour of Cade's Cove?"

A snort escaped before Flannery could stop it. "Caylor, you're a romance novelist. You would have stayed up—or gotten up—to watch the royal wedding. You just talked us into doing it with you so that you wouldn't feel like such a nerd. And about the phone thing...I'm trying to get better. You notice I haven't been on it all night, except when we were coordinating our meet-ups downtown with the other girls."

"You know what the solution to your problem is, don't you?" Caylor looked down at her fingernails.

Flannery was pretty sure she knew what her lifelong friend was going to say—and certain she wasn't going to like it. "What's that? Chocolate? Sushi? Chocolate sushi?"

The left side of Caylor's broad mouth quirked up in an expression that was more familiar to Flannery than one of her own from a lifetime of knowing her. "No—let us help you find a guy. You know, Dylan does have three brothers. . . ."

Flannery snorted. "*Younger* brothers. I'm not interested in being a cradle robber like you, thank you very much." Although Dylan's brother

Spencer was *quite* handsome—but there was that pesky eleven-year age difference. Besides, she'd already determined: no good-looking men. Ever.

"Hey, you never know till you try it." Thank goodness Caylor, a year older than Flannery at thirty-five, had gotten over her issue with the seven-year age gap between her and Dylan. Much as Flannery hated to admit it, Caylor and Dylan were perfect for each other.

"It's only fair that you let us try to find you someone—after what you put me through last year trying to set me up with someone." Zarah poked Flannery's knee and then hid a yawn behind her hand.

"If I recall, I only managed to match you up with one or two guys—and nothing ever came of those." But if she read the expressions on her friends' faces correctly, they weren't going to let go of this idea anytime soon. "Oh, all right. I'll do it. But I reserve the right to veto any of them I don't think I'll like."

Caylor and Zarah exchanged an exasperated look.

"One condition to the veto exception." Caylor crossed her arms.

Flannery turned and matched her position. "What's that?"

"That you agree to go out with Dylan's brother Pax. You're always insisting that geeky scientist guys are more your type—and he fits the bill perfectly, in addition to being cute. And I don't want to hear about the age difference. As you once said, using his age as a reason not to go out with him is just an excuse. And you're not getting any younger, you know. So *tick-tock*, honey."

The reference to her age infuriated Flannery. How dare Caylor use Flannery's own words—spoken when trying to get Caylor to admit she had feelings for Dylan a few months ago—against her?

Caylor extended her right hand across Zarah toward Flannery. "Deal?"

Flannery narrowed her eyes, chewing the inside of her cheek. Go out with Dylan's younger brother? Let Zarah and Caylor—who'd managed to snare absolutely fabulous men—set her up on dates?

She sighed and shook Caylor's hand. "Deal."

# Chapter 4

*Jamie* dashed the sweat from his eyes as he ran up the steep part of the road that circled the townhouse community. How could it be possible that only twenty-four hours had passed since his life derailed from the tracks? Twenty-four hours ago, he'd been intoxicated with the idea of promotion, of attaining that next step on the career ladder. A career he'd never planned on, a career that took more than it gave, a career that completely changed him and his outlook on life. A career that had been so unceremoniously yanked out from under him.

He rounded the curve and started across the top of the irregular circle. Two times around was about a mile. He usually ran twelve to fourteen laps, depending on if he'd snoozed the alarm clock or not. This morning he was on twenty and counting. Running. Heart pounding. Matching his breathing to the rhythm of his feet pounding the pavement. Moving. Round and round, getting nowhere fast.

What would he do now? He was a little ahead on his mortgage payment—maybe two months—and only had five or six car payments remaining. And he had been socking away at least a hundred dollars a month for the past few years. But without steady income, his savings would dwindle quickly. And then what? Unemployment checks? How did one even go about getting those?

He supposed the answer to that would be in the thick envelope of paperwork and booklets the HR rep had given him before he left Friday. And maybe she'd even explained it, but he'd been in such a haze of shock, he could barely remember how he'd gotten from the office to Cookie's house.

Another job was a must—because he couldn't just sit around doing nothing every day. He'd flip fast-food burgers—and if it took too long to find a real job and money started to run out, he could sell the townhouse and downsize, move to a less-expensive area of town.

Even back to Murfreesboro.

He stopped at his driveway, pacing the length of it to cool down. Never. He'd worked too hard and too long to get out of the 'Boro. He'd die before going back.

Too many thoughts. Too much silence. He needed to get out, to go somewhere active, crowded. Somewhere the noise would drown out the questions and worries in his head. Somewhere he could think straight.

After a quick shower, he threw on jeans, a Country Music Marathon T-shirt, and athletic shoes. No point in shaving right now—might as well wait until it was time to get ready for the wedding.

He grabbed his netbook on the way out the door and shoved his sunglasses on against the blaze of the early-morning sun.

The Starbucks in Nipper's Corner was, as he'd hoped, crowded. He placed his order and then nabbed one of the armchairs by the window before someone else could.

The buzz of voices combined with the grinding and hissing of the coffee-making equipment soothed Jamie's mind—almost as if the chaos were being transferred from the inside out.

After picking up his venti, triple-shot, nonfat, sugar-free, caramel-flavored latte and breakfast sandwich, he opened the mini-laptop.

E-mail first.

Only a few. Not a single one from church, even though he'd e-mailed his small-group leader about getting laid off and asked to be put on the group's prayer list.

Instead of dealing with the junk e-mails from places he shopped and newsletters and newspaper headline subscriptions still sitting in the virtual in-box, he clicked a button on his quick-link toolbar and was instantly transported to one of his absolute favorite websites. He scanned the front page. No new news items since he'd last logged in.

He thought about browsing the forums, just to see what new discussions he might like to join in on, but something told him to check his profile, to see if he had any private messages first.

No. No messages. But he did have an alert about a new post by one of his favorite contributors. He clicked the link, settled back in the plush chair, grabbed his sandwich, and started reading, happily discovering the piece was a continuation of the writer's previous work.

"Excuse me, are these seats taken?"

Jamie tore his eyes away from the small screen and looked up to find the question had come from a beautiful Asian-looking woman. Not what he'd expected from the soft Southern accent.

Jamie looked around. Last time he'd noticed, the other three over-stuffed armchairs had been occupied. Now he was the only one in this nook of the coffee shop. "No, they're available as far as I know."

She pushed her shiny, long, black hair behind her ear, and the diamond wedding ring set on her left hand sparkled in the sunlight streaming in from outside.

Something about her seemed familiar, but the rings told him not to even go there. Oh well. She was out of his league anyway. Especially given what he'd just been reading. Exchanging a polite smile with the woman, he returned his attention to the computer screen.

"Chae, here's your—"

Jamie snapped his head up at the male voice, almost as familiar to him as his own. "Danny? Danny Seung?" He slapped the netbook closed, hopped to his feet, and pulled the Korean American man into a backslapping hug. "What are you doing here?"

Stepping back, Jamie held his childhood best friend at arm's length. One thing he'd always appreciated about Danny: the fact he was a good two inches shorter.

"We're meeting our real estate agent here in a half hour or so to go house hunting. I'm starting a new job up at Southern Hills Medical Center, so we're looking to move to this area to be close." Danny set his coffee down on the low table between the four chairs. "You remember my wife, Chae Koh Seung."

Jamie turned again toward the gorgeous woman. "I can't believe I didn't recognize you. You should have said something." He took her hands in his and leaned forward to exchange a kiss on the cheek.

"I'm not surprised you didn't remember me." Chae sat down, looking like nothing less than a queen holding court. "We only saw each other a couple of times before you stopped coming around."

Though Chae continued smiling, the waspish tone in her voice stung. As if he needed her censure to feel any worse than he already did.

Having just settled into his chair, Danny went stiff. "Chae, that's not—"

"No, Danny, it's okay." Jamie sat, leaned forward, and braced his elbows on his knees. "Believe it or not, I've been thinking about you a lot the last couple of days. In fact, I'd decided to call you to see if you'd have time soon to get together for dinner or something so we could talk. But now's as good a time as any." Though he hadn't planned on doing this in front of Chae.

Danny sipped his coffee. "We're here. No time like the present."

"The way things ended. . .I mean, not really ended, but. . .I mean, I dropped the ball big time. And you have every right to never want to talk to me again. But now things are different, and I've got to make changes. And the rehearsal and bachelor party reminded me of you and how much I missed you and how I'd screwed up, not responding to that last e-mail."

Danny's eyebrows raised higher and higher during Jamie's verbal vomit. "Is there an apology in there, or are you just throwing words at each other?"

Jamie lost all control of the muscles in his face and couldn't get his mouth to close.

After several long moments, Danny's expression cracked into a smile, then into laughter. "Your face is priceless. I'm still confused at what you were trying to say, but I'm pretty sure there was regret and remorse in there somewhere."

Relieved, Jamie scrubbed his hands over his face. "So, you forgive me for being the biggest jerk of a friend?"

"Forgive. . .yes. But I may hold this over you for a long time to come."

Jamie groaned but couldn't help smiling at the same time. He didn't care if Danny brought this up every day from now until doomsday—so long as they were friends again. "And if anyone can hold a grudge, you can. But I deserve it."

"You said something about a wedding rehearsal and bachelor party. Don't tell me you're finally getting married."

He didn't miss the hurt tone in Danny's voice. "No—see, I don't have a grandmother who insists on hiring a matchmaker the way yours did." He slipped easily into the neutral topic of Bobby Patterson's wedding.

He was trying to figuring out how to work his layoff into the conversation when a very familiar-looking woman entered. Quite petite with long brown hair, she came directly over to them. He and Danny both stood.

"Danny, Chae, I hope I haven't kept you waiting. And Jamie, I didn't expect to see you again before the wedding tonight."

Wedding—right. She was one of the bridesmaids—the one engaged to Bobby's best man, Patrick. He reached over the coffee table to shake her hand. "Good morning, Stacy. I didn't know you were a real estate agent."

Almost before the words were out of his mouth, she whipped out a business card from her trousers pocket. "Yep. Helped Zarah buy her house, and Bobby his condo—which I'll now be helping him sell. Call me if you're ever in the market."

Jamie tucked the card into the outer pocket of his netbook sleeve. Might come in handy if he did end up needing to sell the townhouse. Sometimes agents connected with mutual friends were more willing to negotiate for a lower commission. That way, he could keep more of the money from selling. . .if things got that bad.

Chae walked over to the counter with Stacy. Jamie took advantage of the moment alone with Danny.

"I'd really like to get together with you soon—just us—so we can talk. Are your e-mail and phone number still the same?" Jamie pulled out his phone, just in case he needed to change one or the other in his contact list.

"Still the same. Yeah, we need to get together to talk. I'm working evenings for the next two weeks, but then once I start the new job, I'll be on the day shift. Just let me know what works for you." Danny extended his right hand.

Jamie shook it, resisting the urge to clasp it with both of his. "Will do."

Chae called his name, and Danny picked up his cup to dispose of it. "Oh, and if you're interested, a couple of other guys and I have started a gaming group. You'd be more than welcome to join us, if you're still into that kind of thing." Danny explained the concept behind the fantasy-world war game.

Jamie's heart leaped at the idea, but his professional persona tamped down the enthusiasm. "I'll have to let you know about that." He'd buried that part of his past so deep, he wasn't certain it could—or should—be resurrected. At least not publicly.

Danny, Chae, and Stacy departed, and Jamie sat and picked up the computer again. Before getting back into what he'd been reading, he opened up a new browser window and wrote an e-mail that was five years late. This time, he wasn't going to let his career, his delusions of grandeur, come in between him and the best friend he'd ever had.

After sending the missive—with a few suggested dates to get together—he switched back to the other website. He read a few more sentences. . .and then stopped.

He'd read this kind of stuff privately, in a way no one else would know about it, but he wouldn't join his best friend in gaming because he was afraid of letting other enthusiasts know he was one of them? What a hypocrite.

Frankly, the more he thought about it, the more Jamie didn't like the person he'd become, the person who thought that having a hobby and being enthusiastic about it was something wrong, something bad.

Yes, he needed to make changes in his life. And the first step was rediscovering who Jamie O'Connor really was.

∞

Tight, searing pain blocked Flannery's throat. Tears stung her eyes. Bright white dots danced in her peripheral vision. She needed to sit down.

"Bend your knees just a little, or you're going to pass out." Caylor's whisper almost vanished in the *whoosh* and rustle of more than five hundred people rising as the small string-and-brass ensemble transitioned from Handel's "Water Music Suite" to join the pipe organ in playing "The Prince of Denmark's March" trumpet voluntary.

Flannery unlocked her knees. Immediately the dizziness and dancing lights went away. But the pain in her throat grew worse when the doors at the rear of the sanctuary opened. Carrying a cascading bouquet of white flowers—roses, lily of the valley, white lilacs, and orange blossoms—and on her grandfather's arm, Zarah moved slowly down the central aisle of the fan-shaped sanctuary, her eyes fixed on the front of the church.

Blinking to clear her vision, Flannery glanced at Bobby. His large, square jaw worked back and forth—making the muscles in his cheek appear to be twitching. He blinked, and a tear ran down his face.

Quickly, Flannery looked away, taking shallow breaths so she didn't dissolve into the threatening sobs. She always got choked up at weddings—but this was different. This was her best friend's wedding, one of them, anyway. Yet it wasn't for Zarah that the emotion nearly overwhelmed her—not entirely.

Though Caylor and Dylan hadn't set a date yet, they, too, would be getting married soon. Flannery had other unmarried friends, sure, but no one as close as these two. And in a short time, she would be absolutely and utterly alone.

And she'd discovered her greatest fear last night—while tossing and turning from her emotional encounter with her best friends after the bachelorette party. More than anything else in life, she feared growing old and dying alone. She feared going through life not sharing it with someone else in more than just friendship.

She looked past Zarah to the now-closed doors. Standing beside them, hands clasped fig-leaf style in front of him, was Jamie O'Connor.

Did she fear dying alone enough to put up with someone like him?

A manic laugh bubbled in her chest, and she nearly choked trying to keep it from escaping. She might be afraid, but she wasn't desperate. Not yet, anyway.

Somehow, she remembered all of her responsibilities during the ceremony and—after shocking herself back into the present with the wild thought about Jamie O'Connor—managed to push everything else aside, get over her own selfishness, and truly experience Zarah's happiness. She did allow herself the weakness of a few tears when Bobby's voice trembled and then cracked completely when reciting his portion of the vows. Zarah, on the other hand, hadn't been this calm, cool, and confident since. . .well, ever, in the time Flannery had known her.

Since most of the photos had been taken before the ceremony—except for those with Zarah and Bobby together—it didn't take long before the wedding party and close family of the bride and groom were herded onto a bus for the trek out to the Opryland Hotel.

Flannery tried to join in the chatter amongst the crowd, but it seemed no matter where she turned or with whom she spoke, Jamie O'Connor's voice and laughter drowned out everyone else's.

"I knew you had a thing for him." Jack Colby dropped into the seat beside Flannery.

"What *are* you talking about?" Flannery crossed her arms—and uncrossed them to keep from creasing the front of the black silk gown.

Jack raised his chin, indicating Jamie, who stood in the aisle and leaned over the seats where Stacy and Patrick sat.

"You should have seen this guy." Jamie rested his hand on Patrick's shoulder. Flannery couldn't see Stacy over the high seat back, but she was certain Patrick's fiancée had a slightly punch-drunk expression on her face. Jamie seemed to affect most women that way. "He starts going up the hill after—what was his name? Milligan? Yeah, Milligan—he starts going up the hill after Milligan, who's just grabbed our flag. . . ."

Flannery turned back to her boss. "Whatever. If you think I'd be interested in someone like him just because he's good looking, you don't know me very well."

Jack sighed. "Look, kiddo, I know you think I'm shallow and vain"—he grinned—"which, truthfully, I am. But I know you're not. And you're shortchanging this guy if you think all he has going for him is his looks. I'm just suggesting you take the time to get to know him. I haven't been around him all that much—and haven't really had a chance to talk to him at length—but I've got a feeling. There's something more to this guy than what's on the surface, than this persona he puts out there for everyone to see. And have you ever known me to be wrong about anyone?"

"Well, there was that one editor you hired—"

"Yeah—besides people who falsify their résumés, I mean."

Flannery gaped at Jack. In all the years they'd worked together, he'd never been this interested in her personal life—only in deflecting the occasional speculation around the office about the two of them being linked romantically. "Who died and made you my fairy godmother all of a sudden?"

"Believe me, if I could, I'd do some magic on you to knock whatever created this negativity toward nice guys out of your head." He tapped his forefinger against her temple.

"I've only ever dated 'nice' guys. Maybe *too* nice sometimes."

"Yeah? What's this I hear about you giving your number to a bouncer at Rippy's?"

Couldn't anyone keep a secret these days? "He's a law student, just working there to pay rent and bills."

"Uh-huh. That's what they all say when they see a five-foot-nine blond who looks like a Scandinavian goddess. Sweetie, guys will say anything to get a woman like you to go out with them."

Flannery rolled her eyes. "Yeah, I figured that out a long time ago. And hello—I'm Irish, not Scandinavian. I probably won't go out with him anyway. He totally wasn't my type."

"And who is?" Jack jerked his head toward Jamie a couple of times.

Flannery punched him in the upper arm. "Stop it already. I don't know why I'm telling you this, but last night I agreed to let Zarah and Caylor start setting me up with guys they know, starting with Dylan's brother, the physicist."

"There you go. A nice, smart guy."

"Who's too young for me."

"Age doesn't matter if he's the right one."

Funny, Flannery remembered saying something very much like that to Caylor not long ago.

The bus rolled to a stop under the portico leading into the conference-center portion of the enormous hotel. Jack stood and offered Flannery a hand up. Having spent several hours here this afternoon taking photos in the world-famous atrium, Flannery's mood improved upon discovering the Tennessee Ballroom was just inside these doors instead of half a mile away. Though she loved this pair of strappy, mid-heeled sandals Zarah's new mother-in-law had helped them pick out, she'd learned they definitely weren't made for walking and had spent most of the afternoon going from place to place in the atrium barefoot.

She followed the slow-moving group in the aisle ahead of her and warned Jack about not stepping on her skirt as she picked her way down the bus's steps. She took the outstretched hand offered her when she reached the bottom step—which sat just a little too high for comfort off the pavement below—and started to step down. But when she looked up to thank the helpful guy, she almost took a header into the asphalt.

Jamie O'Connor grinned at her. "Flannery."

"Jamie." She yanked her hand out of his as soon as both feet hit the ground. But she couldn't be rude. "Thank you."

He inclined his head. "My pleasure."

Before she could say anything else to him, he turned to assist an older woman down. Flannery lifted the long skirt of the evening gown and, slipping her hand through the crook of Jack's elbow, headed into the hotel.

Yep, she might be envious of her friends' happiness and coupledom, and she might even be lonely and afraid of being alone for the rest of her life. But she was nowhere near desperate enough to go out with someone like Jamie O'Connor. No matter how polite he'd decided to be tonight or how highly Jack thought of him.

# Chapter 5

*Aside* from the towering white cake and the beautiful woman in the wedding dress, the ballroom reminded Jamie forcefully of a formal dinner at the end of a sales conference. Seats had apparently been very carefully assigned; even though the salad course was just being cleared away, from his position at a table near the front of the cavernous room, he'd already counted eighteen instances of business cards being exchanged.

Why hadn't he thought to print up some cards with his personal contact information to bring with him tonight? Oh yeah—because he'd been under the impression he'd be attending a *wedding*, not a business-networking event.

Instead of joining in the get-to-know-you chatter around his table, Jamie just listened. Only one of the other three ushers sat at the table with him, and out of the three, Dennis Forrester was the one Jamie would have picked last if forced to choose. But as Dylan and Jack sat at the head table with their dates—the two maids of honor—Jamie had to make do.

Usually he'd be in his element in a room full of five hundred people. Tonight, though, the noise of the voices, the silver against china, and even the soft sound of the band on the stage at the other side of the room clawed all the way up his last nerve and jumped all over it.

He stole another glance at the front of the room. He hadn't imagined it during the wedding—Flannery McNeill looked decidedly unhappy. Oh, she tried to hide it, laughing and talking with Jack Colby on her right and Caylor on her left, but an almost-visible aura of melancholy surrounded her.

Not his problem. He returned his attention to the dinner plate in front of him. Filet mignon and salmon. Could this get any more cliché? The small, bacon-wrapped steak did at least come with a blue-cheese butter sauce on top of it, so that added something a little different.

"Jamie, you said you work in sports marketing?" Dennis Forrester, now apparently finished finding out everything about their table companions, turned his focus on Jamie.

Jamie cut a small bite of the steak. Right between rare and medium rare—just the way he liked his beef. "Yes, for the Gregg Agency." As far as Jamie had seen, the news of the merger with the Memphis company hadn't hit the business journals yet.

"Ah." A flash of something—speculation? knowing?—flashed through Dennis's brown eyes. "I've worked with Armando Gregg on a few boards and committees of different charities around town. Good man."

*If you insist.* Jamie nodded.

"How long have you been there?"

"Thirteen years." Actually, when he'd looked at the calendar, his final day would be just two weeks shy of the anniversary of his start date.

"So I guess you know Cole Samuels, then." Dennis cut into his sweet potato puree–stuffed, roasted Portobello mushroom. For a fleeting second, Jamie wished he'd ordered a vegetarian plate, too. He didn't like a lot of veggies, but he could eat yams and mushrooms with every meal.

"I haven't had the chance to meet him, but I've been talking with his agent about a few opportunities." The steak was pretty good, too. Jamie glanced over to the table on the other side of the long head table where Cole Samuels sat. After catching four touchdown passes to help win the Super Bowl—and then being named league MVP for the year—Cole Samuels was recognized by everyone in the room.

But if Jamie wasn't going to be working at the Gregg Agency anymore, what was the point in trying to meet the star football player?

Applause broke out as the last of the dinner plates were removed from Jamie's table. He looked around. Bobby and Zarah had risen and made their way to the side table where the wedding cake dwarfed even six-foot-three Bobby Patterson.

The addition of flashes from digital cameras around the room to the three from the professional photographers turned the scene into a brief paparazzi frenzy of flashing lights and people jostling for the best, least-obstructed angle.

Seriously? Who needed that many photos of someone else's wedding and reception? He scanned the tables he'd had his back to all evening. Several women purposely caught his eye. He knew what they were selling. . .and he wasn't buying. But it put him on his guard against the advances that were certain to come later. After working in the marketing and sales industry for more than a decade, not only had he become someone who could sell a sloppy joe to a bride wearing white gloves, but he'd also learned how to handle come-ons from beautiful, rich, lonely women—even the persistent ones.

Jamie swiveled, twisting the black fabric chair cover with him. Seeing the wait staff emerge from the kitchen carrying silver carafes, he turned his coffee cup right side up. He'd stuck with the watered-down iced tea throughout dinner while many at the table indulged in wine and cocktails from the open bar.

The first couple of years at the advertising agency, he'd gone out on Thursday and Friday nights with the guys—and it hadn't taken him long to realize just how stupid and unlikable alcohol made them. Not everyone was like that, sure, and he'd been around plenty of people who could have a glass or two of wine and seemingly not be affected by it at all. But he preferred to keep his wits about him—and not take any risks when it came to driving himself home from such events.

Coffee, however, was his vice. Black, creamed, straight, sweet, plain, flavored—it didn't matter. He'd take it any way he could get it.

"Regular or decaf, sir?" their waitress asked.

"Regular, please."

Dennis Forrester raised an eyebrow before requesting decaffeinated coffee. "I don't know how you young people can do it, so much caffeine so late at night."

Jamie almost snorted. The head of the historical society where Zarah Mitchell. . .Patterson worked acted like people in their thirties were teenagers. He couldn't be that much older. "What can I say? I'm a night person, so it doesn't bother me." He doctored the brew with one pack of artificial sweetener and a splash of half-and-half.

More servers came around with plates of the wedding cake. "The cake layers are french vanilla, dark chocolate, and red velvet." The main server for the table nodded, and he and each of the other three set dessert plates with a generous-sized slice of the three-layer cake in front of each person at the table. "The frosting on the outside is cream cheese buttercream. The filling between the vanilla and chocolate layers is raspberry, and the filling between the chocolate and red velvet layers is Italian cherry. Enjoy."

Jamie cut into the red velvet layer—at the back of the piece so he got the thick layer of frosting with the first bite. The moist, light cake with its almost-chocolate flavor mingled on his tongue with the creamy sweetness of the frosting and then melted. He started to groan—then remembered where he was.

Perfection.

If coffee was his vice, sugar was his addiction. And with his family's history of heart problems, he didn't give in to that temptation often—especially since he'd been somewhat tubby as a kid. But hey, wedding cakes were a rarity in his life. He'd shed the puppy fat as a teen running around the woods with paintball guns some days after school and almost all day on the weekends. He wasn't about to let his predilection for sweets cause him health problems or stop him from looking his best. Not when people were apt to judge someone negatively if the least bit overweight.

The music started, and the bandleader announced the bride and groom would have their first dance. Then the dance with the mother of the groom and father—no, grandfather of the bride. Jamie had a clear view of the dance floor when the full wedding party took to the floor and the band started playing Patsy Cline's "Today, Tomorrow, and Forever."

Jamie's eyes locked on to the tall blond being two-stepped around by the smoothest dancer on the floor—and he wasn't at all surprised that Jack Colby was a good dancer. In her heels, Flannery was almost as tall as her boss, which made them seem well suited for dancing together. For the first time tonight, she looked like she was truly enjoying herself. Jack apparently said something funny, because she threw her head back and laughed.

The song drew to a close, and Jack dipped her, just like in all the old Astaire-Rogers movies the ladies at the nursing home loved watching so much.

"Come on. They'll want everyone involved in the wedding out there to help encourage folks to dance." Dennis stood and motioned Jamie to follow him.

Wait—had Dennis Forrester just asked him to dance? Jamie rose slowly and followed him. . .at a distance. But Zarah's boss stopped at the table just short of the dance floor and asked an older woman there to dance, apparently someone he knew.

Jamie looked around. Really, there was only one person here he wanted to dance with tonight. He took a deep breath and moved forward with purpose.

Flannery's little toe on her right foot hurt where the sandal's strap rubbed on the knuckle. All she wanted to do was sit down and maybe surreptitiously take the shoes off under the table, since the tablecloth touched the floor in front and on the sides.

She stepped off the dance floor and—found her way blocked by Jamie O'Connor.

"Hey, Flannery."

It didn't matter how handsome he was. The way he looked at her—no, *scrutinized* would be a better word—creeped her out a little.

"Hi, Jamie."

"You look really nice tonight." He rocked from heel to toe—which only emphasized the fact that, with her in these shoes, he was a little bit shorter than she. Which meant they were probably about the same height in actuality.

"Um, thanks. You look nice tonight, too." No lie—he was breath stealing dressed in a tuxedo. She hadn't missed the fact that almost every woman in attendance tonight had, at one time or another, been eyeing him as if he were a plate of caviar in a room full of Spam sandwiches.

"I like your hair up like that, how it shows off your neck. With that dress, it's almost like you're the lead actress in a vampire movie, just waiting for Dracula to come along and bite you."

Flannery's hands flew to her throat—which had just closed in around her windpipe. "Ex*cuse* me?"

Jamie's mouth flopped open and closed a few times. "N–no, I meant. . .what I meant to say—" His face glowed like Chernobyl's meltdown.

Flannery was pretty sure hers was in the same condition. She returned her hands to her sides, gathering up her skirt just in case she needed to run away.

He took a deep breath and a step back. "I didn't m–mean to say that. I wanted to ask you to d–dance."

*Not in this lifetime.* "Yeah. . .um, look. Thanks, but my foot really hurts, so I'm going to go sit down."

Instead of moving closer to get past him between the tables where they stood, she turned and went around the table to her right.

Dracula? Really? That was his idea of a pickup line? At least he'd had the good grace to look embarrassed when he realized he'd totally wigged her out. *Dracula?*

Back at the head table, she pulled the sandals off, flagged down the waiter, and asked for another piece of cake and a refill of her coffee.

Out on the dance floor, Jack was making Zarah, now without the ridiculous tiered bustle and train attached to her elegant A-line wedding gown, look like the woman in the fluffy dresses in the old musicals Caylor liked watching whenever they got together for movie nights, whirling her around the floor to a 1940s tune. Zarah'd made Bobby take dance lessons with her—if she was going to be forced to dance, she didn't want to embarrass herself in front of so many people—and it showed in the ease and comfort with which she moved around the floor.

And Jamie. . .

Flannery sat up a little straighter. Jamie O'Connor danced with Bobby's grandmother. And when that song ended, he danced with Zarah's grandmother. Then he danced with another older lady. All this despite the fact that several cougars prowled the perimeter of the dance floor, obviously waiting for a chance to pounce on one of the best looking—and obviously single—men here.

She sighed, propped her chin on her fist, and scraped the frosting off the cake, saving it for last. Jack, the jerk, had told her after three dances that she'd have to find another partner, because he wasn't going to dance with her again tonight.

A dapper man, probably in his forties, came up to the table. "Would you like to dance?"

"No, thank you." Flannery smiled at him—and when he realized she wasn't going to explain why, he frowned and left. She returned her full attention to the cake. There were plenty of men here she could dance with, and in other circumstances she might—

"May I ask you to dance?" A twentysomething guy—she was pretty sure she'd seen him with a petite brunette during supper—stood across the table from her.

"You may, but I'm not dancing tonight."

After what Jack had said, followed by another unfortunate encounter with Jamie O'Connor, she was officially off men tonight.

It only took declining six other offers for the men in the room to get the clue—she didn't want to dance.

She finished off the cake and coffee and sat watching the few hundred guests who hadn't left right after the cake cutting mill about the room. It reminded her of a dinner at a writers' conference—everyone seemed to have an agenda of whom they wanted to talk to before the evening ended and they missed their chance. She'd figured with the caliber of friends and acquaintances Bobby's folks had—the majority of people here tonight—it would be more of a see-and-be-seen kind of event. But too many business cards had been exchanged in the last thirty minutes to write this off as a simple high-profile society event.

Would anyone notice if she got another piece of cake?

A familiar sound echoed from what seemed to be a great distance. She straightened from her slumped position in the chair and grabbed for her purse under the table. She pulled out the phone. New text message from. . .Jack Colby?

NEED TO SEE YOU ASAP. JC

Flannery looked around—there, on the far side of the dance floor. Jack raised his arm and motioned her over.

The thought of putting her shoes back on made her groan, so she left them under the table with her purse—but carried her phone with her. If something had come up at work, she might need it.

The hem of her skirt dragged on the floor, since it had been altered to just skim it when she had shoes on. She lifted it a little to keep from tripping, not caring if anyone noticed she was barefoot. Bridesmaids *always* took their shoes off during the reception.

Apologizing her way through the clusters of people blocking her path, she finally made it over to the group Jack stood with.

Immediately she dropped the skirt, regretting the decision to leave the shoes on the other end of the room. She swapped the phone to her left hand and extended her right. "Cole Samuels—good to see you again."

The professional football player engulfed her hand with both of his. "Wow, you look fantastic. I couldn't believe it when I saw you coming down the aisle." He turned to the woman by his side. In normal circumstances, she'd be an average-height woman; beside this meat mountain, she looked positively tiny. "Amy Joy, this is Flannery McNeill, my editor." He beamed at Flannery on those last two words.

His wife's smile broadened, and she shook Flannery's hand. "Flannery? Like the author, Flannery O'Connor?"

Flannery kept her cool. Why had her mother named her after someone famous? *Let the standard explanation begin.* "Yes. My mother was a big fan of literature, so she named her daughters after three of her favorite authors."

"Ooh—what are your sister's names?" Amy Joy asked.

"Emily and Sylvia."

"Emily. . .for Emily Dickinson, the poet, right?"

Flannery nodded.

"And Sylvia. . ." Amy Joy's porcelain-doll features crumpled into a frown. "I can't think of who that would be for."

*Whom*, Flannery mentally corrected. "Sylvia Plath. I can't say I share my mom's taste in literature completely."

Not only did Amy Joy resemble a china doll, but she also had a music box–worthy tinkling laugh. "It's so nice to meet you. Cole hasn't stopped talking about his book finally getting published. You're the first publisher who took him seriously and didn't try to talk him out of writing fiction and into writing about his experience winning college and pro championships and being an MVP and all that."

Flannery's smile returned, and she shrugged. "I'm a fiction editor. If Cole wrote nonfiction, I wouldn't be the one working with him, so why would I try to talk him into that? I have to say I'm kind of surprised to see y'all here. I thought you lived in South Carolina during the off-season."

Cole nodded. "Oh, we do. But Tank Patterson is my mentor. He's part of a group of former players who offer to kinda take rookies under their wings and help them out throughout their careers. When I found out Tank Patterson wanted to mentor me, I couldn't have been happier. He's always been one of my role models. I don't know Bobby as well as

I'd like, but I couldn't miss the wedding of Tank's son."

Of course. Zarah had told her about the connection when Flannery first mentioned she was considering acquiring Cole's novels.

Jack touched her elbow. "Cole, Jamie, and I were just chatting— brainstorming, really—about some marketing ideas for Cole's books."

She cricked her neck, turning her head too fast, finally noticing someone else stood on the other side of her boss. Jamie gave her a tight smile and a dorky little wave.

"Jamie is a sports marketing rep at a large agency, so he's got a lot of ideas for how we can possibly use some of Cole's other endorsements to help leverage the marketing and sales of the novels." Jack beamed at her as if he'd planned this turn of events all along.

"Is that so?" Flannery kept her smile plastered on—no need for Cole to know how much she loathed Jamie O'Connor. "Well, I'd be happy to listen to your ideas and take them to the marketing director when it comes time for that."

"Oh, we can do better than that." Jack wrapped his arm around Flannery's waist and pulled her close into his side. "I've asked Jamie to set up a time when you and he can sit down with Cole and discuss some marketing ideas together. It'll have to be this week, as Cole and Amy Joy are headed back to South Carolina on Friday."

Amy Joy pulled a beeping phone out of her purse. "Oh, look at the time. I told the sitter service we'd be back to the room by eleven, and it's ten after. It's going to take us forever to get back through this hotel and find our room again."

Jamie stepped forward and extended his right hand to Cole. "Good to talk to you tonight. I'll give you a call Tuesday morning to set up that meeting time."

"Great, we should know by then what our plans are for the rest of the week." Cole inclined his head to Flannery and Jack. "It was great seeing you guys again. I'm really excited about working with your publishing house on this project." He took his wife's hand, and they left—though not easily, with many people wanting to speak to the sports star.

Flannery tried to pull away from Jack to escape, but he pulled her up against his side again. "Not so fast there, Speed Racer." He turned, forcing her to face Jamie. "Jamie, based on the ideas we've already discussed, will you be able to find out before your meeting with Cole what endorsement deals he has and which ones might be to our advantage?"

"Sure. It'll take some work, but I can do it." Jamie glanced furtively at Flannery, then returned his dark-gray eyes to focus on Jack.

Still embarrassed? He should be. "Jack, why do I need to be at that meeting?" Did she sound like she was whining? She cleared her throat. "Jamie and Cole can meet and talk about his endorsements, and then Jamie can e-mail me—"

"No." Jack squeezed her a little tighter, his expression clearly indicating he knew what she was trying to do. "I want you there in that meeting, too. No matter how much Jamie knows about sports marketing, he's not an expert on publishing and marketing fiction. And before you ask, no, I'm not going to send Shandi or anyone from our marketing department. They don't know anything about the project, and it would take you longer to get them up to speed than it would for you to just go to the meeting yourself."

Flannery hoped her eyes conveyed to Jack just how much she absolutely and totally hated him at this moment. Work with Jamie O'Connor?

She'd rather let Dracula chow down on her neck.

# Chapter 6

*D*racula? Really?"

Jamie glared at Danny, whose eyes almost disappeared behind the high, full apples of his cheeks in his effort to contain his laughter. "It was just like seventh grade and Lisa Jackson all over again."

Danny leaned forward, his elbows on the table, his coffee cup held in both hands. "She didn't slap you, too?"

"No—but I wouldn't have blamed her if she had." Jamie scrubbed his hands over his face. He probably should have shaved for church this morning, but frankly, the only reasons he attended that church were because it was just down Old Hickory Boulevard from his townhouse community, and it was where all the big money in town attended—and he really didn't care about impressing them anymore. "Man, I was such a *dork*."

The word tasted foul in his mouth, so he took a swig of the strong house coffee: black today, just like his mood.

"And you couldn't just laugh it off with a wink and a smile and get her to see the humor in it?"

"No. I totally lost it. Started stammering like an imbecile. A dorky imbecile. I don't know what it is about her that's so different from every other beautiful woman I've been around. I can usually handle myself. Flirt. Laugh. Make them fall in love with me, even if just for five minutes."

"I remember. You got really good at it in college. As I recall, that's the only way you made it through Advanced Macroeconomic Theory—because the professor thought you were cute."

"See—that's what I'm talking about. Even sixty-year-old women, who should know better, fall for me. So why do I completely lose my cool whenever I'm near Flannery McNeill? I'm such an idiot." Jamie pushed his cup back, leaned over, and pressed his forehead, nose, and chin against the table. He hoped it had been cleaned recently. He let his arms dangle from his shoulders.

Danny's bolt of laughter brought Jamie upright again.

"What?"

Wiping his eyes with the backs of his hands, Danny shook his head. "I can't believe you still do that face-plant move. Remember the time—"

"You swore you'd never bring that up." The memory of a face-plant leading to getting his forehead stuck to a table in the middle-school cafeteria only added to his current sense of self-scorn. "I blame it on the job. If I hadn't found out Friday morning that I'm losing my job, I might have had it more together last night and not embarrassed myself like that."

"Whoa—what? You're losing your job? What happened?"

Jamie started the story with rushing to get to work on Friday morning, and the more he talked about it—about the sense of expectation he'd walked into the meeting with only to have it crushed—the better he started feeling, not just about the fact that he'd be unemployed by the end of the week, but about what happened with Flannery last night.

How long had it been since he'd had someone other than Cookie with whom he could talk about things like this? Oh, yeah. . .five years, since the last time he'd communicated with Danny.

Before he realized it, he'd launched into the details of Bobby Patterson's bachelor party, wanting to focus on the one patch of fun he'd had this weekend. He imagined his own eyes held a nostalgic gleam similar to the one that came into Danny's eyes.

"I miss our paintball days." Danny nodded, rubbing his chin in a contemplative manner. "But I have to say, the gaming I'm into now is a lot safer."

"Yeah—I was going to ask you about that."

"Really? Because you looked a little scared when I mentioned it yesterday." Danny grinned at him, and the years fell away. Jamie forgot about getting laid off and embarrassing himself in front of Flannery. All that remained, all that mattered, was the lifetime of shared experiences he had with the man who sat across the table from him.

"I know. But that was the other me—that was the me I don't want to be anymore. That was the marketing-account-exec me. I want to get back to being the real me—the one who wouldn't have stopped answering your e-mails. So tell me about this gaming."

Danny looked at his watch. "I'll have to give you the short version—I've got to be at work in half an hour."

He listened with fascination as Danny described the lengths he and his new group of friends went to entertain themselves—a table containing a three-dimensional topography, several locales, and the miniature characters they created with painstaking detail.

"We don't get together as often as we used to, since we're all married now and a couple of guys have kids, but we set aside one Saturday a month to spend the day playing." Danny stuffed his napkins down into his cup and carried it to the nearby trash can.

Jamie followed him and disposed of his own cup and napkins. "How did you get hooked up with these guys?"

"I went to nursing school with three of them. I met the other two at the hospital when I started working there." Danny fished his keys from his pocket. "Speaking of work, have you thought about what you're going to do now?"

Jamie followed him from the café toward the front doors. The coffee shop in the big-box bookstore in the new shopping center in Murfreesboro had been the best place for them to meet, close to the medical center where Danny worked. "Not really. I want to take a few weeks off—maybe go out to Utah and see my mom—before I start looking for something else. I have three months of severance pay and money in savings, so I'm not desperate to find a job immediately."

Danny pulled his sunglasses down from the top of his head and paused at the main doors. "Are you still volunteering at the senior center with your grandmother?"

"Of course. Why wouldn't I?"

Danny shrugged. "Well, you gave up a lot of other things to become that marketing-account-exec you."

He had a point. "I know. And that's one of the reasons I want to take my time with this next job decision. I want to make sure I'm not doing something because someone else thinks I should." He crossed his arms and leaned against a display table. "When you left the ad agency where you worked after college to go to nursing school, what was it that made you realize that's what you wanted to do?"

"I realized I didn't want to sell people stuff. I wanted to help them. I wanted to make people feel better—literally." Danny pushed the door open. "I know you don't want people trying to influence you, but I saw you working with the elderly at the nursing home back in the day. You're good at it. Maybe it's something you should consider."

Jamie's spine stiffened in rebellion against Danny's words—but he forced himself to relax. It had merely been a suggestion, not a shove in one particular direction. "Thanks, I'll think about it."

"See you later." Danny raised his hand and pushed through the outer door. Moments later, the roar of a motorcycle sounded and retreated.

Jamie turned and scanned the large bookstore. His childhood best friend, who, like Jamie, had majored in marketing in college, interned at a prestigious Nashville advertising agency, and then been offered a job there upon graduation, was now a nurse. A nurse who rode a motorcycle. And who played fantasy-based war games with other male nurses.

One of the last things Dad had said to him before he died was that he wanted Jamie to grow up to be a real man. Dad had been so frustrated with him. He flinched when Dad threw a football at him.

The only class he ever failed was PE. The peewee-football coach kicked him off the team because he avoided physical contact with others—and he was supposed to be a tackler. Dad, a former Marine turned cop, had wanted Jamie to be an athlete, a man's man, someone confident in his own abilities. What he'd gotten was a doughy stammerer who'd been more interested in computer games and fantasy novels.

For his thirteenth birthday, Jamie had gotten a full set of free weights and dumbbells from his father. He'd hated them. He'd asked for a medieval figurine- and castle-model kit. But half an hour later, standing over his father's body waiting for the paramedics, Jamie had vowed he'd become the kind of man his father would be proud of.

And that was not the kind of man who became a nurse. When Danny told him twelve years ago he'd quit his job and enrolled in MTSU's School of Nursing, Jamie experienced a moment's jealousy. Danny's parents supported him in his decision to enter a somewhat-nontraditional field for a man. But Danny didn't have the specter of his father looking over his shoulder, constantly reminding him to buck up and be a man. A real man. A man who did manly things, who shouldered manly responsibilities. And who had a manly job. A man who could talk to a beautiful woman without completely embarrassing himself.

∞

"I'm thinking about applying for an editor position up in New York City. Can you imagine me living and working in the Big Apple?" Flannery shaded her eyes and looked off in the distance over her grandfather's shoulder toward. . .nothing in particular. She just didn't want to see his reaction.

"New York? Why? Are you unhappy with your job here? I thought you enjoyed working for Lindsley House." His voice sounded neutral enough—not shocked or horrified—but with perhaps a slight tone of disappointment.

Disappointment in her or in the idea of her moving so far away? "I'm happy at Lindsley. I love my job and everyone I work with."

A warm breeze gusted, and the edges of the umbrella shading the table on the deck outside of the Rosepepper Cantina in East Nashville fluttered, shadows dancing across the remnants of their early dinner.

"But?" Big Daddy prompted.

She sighed and returned her attention to him and away from the other patrons there for an early Sunday-evening dinner. "But I figure since I'm losing everything here anyway, why not take the opportunity to see if I could get a job working at one of the big New York publishers."

Big Daddy pushed his plate aside and leaned forward, hands clasped together atop the table. "What do you mean you're losing everything?"

She groaned. "I shouldn't have put it like that. I just mean that with Zarah and Caylor getting married, it's not going to be long before I'm pretty much on my own—once they start living their own lives with their husbands and spending time with all their new, married friends. Maybe it's time for me to start over somewhere else where I won't have to watch it happen."

"Ah." He leaned back in his chair again, nodding. "I see. So you'd rather call it quits, assume your friends are going to behave like your sisters, and run away rather than stick it out and make sure that doesn't happen."

"No, it's not—" But it was just like that. She crossed her arms, furious with him for calling her on her own cowardice. "I don't want to be left behind again, left out. Made to feel like there's something wrong with me because they're married and I'm not."

"Flan, can I let you in on a little secret?"

Now she leaned forward on the table, arms still crossed. "What's that?"

"I always knew you'd be older when you got married. Even when you were a little girl, I knew you'd most likely be in your thirties before you married."

She frowned, not sure she liked what his secret implied. "You mean you knew that no man would want me?"

"No. I mean that I knew you had things to do with your life. You didn't dream about being a princess and having your Prince Charming come rescue you the way your sisters did. You didn't want to constantly play house or with baby dolls. You climbed trees. You made up magical worlds full of fantastical creatures for you to battle—not for a prince to rescue you from. You were the warrior, the one slaying the dragons."

But once she'd hit her teens and that playacting had gone the way of her sisters' dolls, she'd turned the fantasy inward—where there had always been handsome heroes fighting beside the strong females she imagined, wooing and winning them in the end.

"And I knew you would grow into a woman who wanted to stand on her own, who wanted to make her own way before marrying. And that it would take a special man to be able to see you not as a princess who needed rescuing and coddling, but as a strong woman who wanted someone to come alongside her and slay dragons with her."

Flannery wasn't sure how to respond. "So. . .you're saying I'm too strong and that I intimidate men?"

"I'm saying it's harder for a woman like you to find that special someone because men like that are unique and rare." He grinned at her. "Like me."

She had to laugh at that. "Yes, Big Daddy, you are unique and rare. Zarah and Caylor are going to have a hard time finding someone who can compare to you."

"What do you mean?"

Her expression warped into that of a pouting child. "They strong-armed me into agreeing to let them set me up on dates."

"And you don't want to let them do that?"

She shrugged. "I don't know. I don't really want to think about it."

"If we're going to make it to the concert, we'd better be going, don't you think?"

Flannery picked up her phone and checked the time. Almost six o'clock already. "Yep, we'd better go." It would take about fifteen minutes to get to the Scarritt-Bennett Center, but she was less worried about being late and more worried about parking.

She needn't have worried, though, as she found one last space on Nineteenth Street just in front of the Gothic reproduction Wightman Chapel.

While she loved her church and the contemporary, modern feel to the sanctuary that had been built shortly after she finished college, there was something worshipful about the simple act of entering the ninety-year-old chapel built in the style of the European chapels of the Middle Ages. The stonework, the woodwork, the arched openings and windows, and especially the large pipe organ dominating the nave—all worked together to help her understand what the writers of the Bible meant when they wrote about the *fear* of God. It wasn't a terror or a horror, but a sense of awe, of God's ultimate power and greatness and her own smallness.

In Acklen Avenue Fellowship's modern worship center, she felt close to God, as if He was a personal friend with whom she could share anything. She liked to come here—or occasionally attend special services and concerts at the Episcopal cathedral downtown—just to feel the sense of awe that came from experiencing the greatness, the glory, the untouchableness of God through the majestic quality of the architecture and the reverence with which services were undertaken.

Of course, the fact that they were here for a music service that combined experimental jazz with liturgical worship music created an entirely new sense of experiencing God.

Throughout the forty-five-minute musical worship service, Flannery's thoughts kept going back to Caylor and Zarah's offer to set her up. She'd been the one to press Zarah into agreeing to be set up less than a year ago. So why was she so resistant to the idea of Zarah and Caylor doing it for her?

Maybe it was less about the idea of being set up with guys she'd never met and more about the idea that her friends weren't going to be happy until they saw her paired off, too—that they saw her as incomplete on her own.

No, they wouldn't think that. Would they?

She turned her gaze to the rays of the sunset angling in through the arched, mullioned windows. No. Caylor and Zarah were much more grounded than Flannery's sisters had been. Both had found fulfillment in God's calling on their lives first. Then they'd found the loves of their lives.

Still, she worried that falling in love and getting married would change them. She shook her head and returned her attention to the music. She wouldn't worry about that now. She'd worry about it later. Maybe tomorrow. Or the day after.

When she dropped Big Daddy off at Union Station after the service, he was still talking about the sense of wonder evoked by the way the small jazz ensemble interpreted the music and about attending again.

She headed home with a smile, happy she'd been able to share that experience with her grandfather, who—she was pretty sure—wasn't thrilled with the contemporary bent to the worship style at Acklen Ave. But he did plan to participate in the senior adults' service project tomorrow and then go to lunch with them before heading back home to Pulaski. So maybe he didn't mind it too much.

After parking in her designated spot in the underground garage, she rode the elevator up to the eighth floor of the condominium building in downtown Nashville. She entered the quiet condo—though it didn't stay quiet for long. As soon as she set her keys and purse down on the end of the high breakfast bar on the back of the kitchen island, the begging started.

A furry creature wrapped itself around and around her ankles, crying as if it had been abandoned for weeks, not mere hours.

She bent over and picked up the cat, tucking him under her arm as she went to the refrigerator to get a snack for herself. Almost pure white, save for his gray face, ears, and tail, the animal flopped over her arm like the ragdoll his breed was named for. She didn't see anything in the fridge that interested her—mostly boxes of leftovers from restaurants or takeout. She grabbed a can of caffeine-free diet soda and closed the fridge.

"You're too heavy to carry around like this, you know, Liam." She dropped him on the floor, which he protested with a *meow* and a head-butt to her shin—before he started rubbing against her legs and weaving in and out of them.

"I know, I know, I'm almost an hour late feeding you dinner. Mercy, you'd think I hadn't fed you this morning, either." She crossed to the pantry and pulled out a granola bar for herself and a can of salmon-and shrimp-flavored food. She'd never had a cat before two years ago, when a neighbor's cat had a litter and Flannery fell in love with this one's cute face and blue eyes. She'd quickly learned that if she didn't want him waking her up at 4:00 a.m., she needed to feed him dry food in the morning and save the canned stuff for night. That way, he was always eager to greet her when she came home in the evenings... begging for his dinner.

He sat at her feet, fluffy tail twitching, meowing his heart out as she dumped the foul-smelling and worse-looking concoction into his bowl. She held him back with one foot when she leaned over and put the bowl back down on the mat at the end of the island. After emptying, rinsing, and refilling his water dish, she washed her hands and went through her bathroom from the guest entrance and into the closet that connected the bathroom to her bedroom to change clothes.

She hung the skirt and blouse—she'd wear them again tomorrow to the singles' group cookout—and changed into long knit pajama pants and a cotton tank. Grabbing her laptop computer off the stand attached to her treadmill, she carried it to the bed. It was too early to sleep. It was a holiday weekend, and she'd promised herself she wouldn't work at all; but she didn't have any new books just begging to be read at the moment.

So that left her with only one thing to do.

Settling several pillows around her, she grabbed the wooden lap desk and got comfortable while the computer started up. She crunched on the granola bar and sipped her soda while she checked her personal e-mail, smiling when she saw Zarah had sent her and Caylor a message letting them know they'd arrived safely in Las Cruces and were on their way out for dinner at a restaurant called La Posta.

Out of habit, she started to pull up her work e-mail—but stopped before she opened the in-box (which showed more than twenty new messages just since yesterday when, okay, she had gone through and read the forty-odd messages that she'd gotten since Friday).

No, instead…she pulled up an e-mail account she didn't check very often, because the only messages that came into it were notifications, not anything she could respond to directly.

She had one new message. She opened it:

> *I've never written to anyone through one of these sites before,*
> *but I just wanted to let you know I like what I've seen so far.*

Aw. That was sweet. Not overtly creepy like a lot of the other notes she'd gotten through this site. She wasn't going to respond to it. She hadn't been a member of this site very long, and she still wasn't sure about communicating with anyone directly through the e-mail feature, especially if it meant risking that someone might figure out a way to learn her true identity. Because she didn't want anyone knowing she'd ever even visited a site like this, much less joined. If anyone found out…

No, that was unthinkable. No one could *ever* know.

# Chapter 7

❧

$\mathcal{E}$ven as he checked out of the hotel Monday morning, Kirby prayed for his youngest granddaughter. Though she'd tried to laugh it off and change the subject, he hadn't missed the pain in her eyes and voice when talking about her friends and her fear of being forgotten by them.

He took a couple of wrong turns on his way to the food bank, but he managed to pull up just as some others from the senior adult group arrived. He and a few others who'd never been before were taken on a short tour of the facility and then back to the warehouse, where they would be making up weekly meal boxes.

He spotted a flash of red hair and smiled to himself. Looked like there was an open spot right next to her.

Maureen O'Connor looked up and smiled her broad, beaming smile at him. He could almost pretend he was a young buck seeing the girl he was sweet on with the little leap in his chest. Either that or his defibrillator had just given his heart a kick.

"I thought I saw you with the tour group. You didn't have any trouble finding the place?"

"No, no trouble." Just a few one-way streets leading him in circles. "So what are we doing?"

Maureen showed him what went in the boxes. He took her lead and set five boxes in front of him to do multiples of each product at a time.

"You seem pensive this morning." Maureen stacked cans of green beans in her box.

"I suppose I am." Kirby reached up to a high shelf and brought down a flat of canned soup to share with her.

"Anything I can help you with?"

She probably had daughters and granddaughters with similar experiences to Flannery's. "My youngest granddaughter has me a little concerned. Her two best friends recently got engaged, and she's worried that they're going to forget all about her and leave her behind. I understand her worry—her sisters did that to her when she was younger. But she's talking about applying for jobs in New York City just because her friends are getting married. She thinks she's losing everything."

He finished adding his products and pushed the first of his boxes down the rollered belt for the next volunteer to continue filling. "Have you ever gone through this with your girls?"

Maureen's expression turned pensive. "I never had girls. One son, one grandson. I would have thought that as a pastor for so many years, you would have helped church members through problems like this before."

"Oh, I know. I should be adept at giving counsel in these kinds of situations."

"But when it's your own child—or grandchild—that makes a big difference." Maureen nodded, experience echoing in her voice. "If I may speak from my own experiences...?"

"Yes, please." Kirby took her completed box and sent it on down the line with two more of his.

"It's very hard on a young woman to see everyone around her getting paired off, engaged, and married. Especially when she doesn't have a boyfriend herself. I do understand her fear of losing her friends or feeling left out. When my husband was still living, we had a very active social life—dinners and parties with friends from work and church, dancing on the weekends, concerts. . . . Everything I asked to do, we did it. But then after James died, I couldn't go and do all the things we'd done as a couple—the dancing, the concerts. And couples we'd been friends with for decades slowly stopped inviting me around—not only was there the issue of my widowhood reminding them of the fragility of life and making them unsure of what to say to me, but there was also the fact that I made for an odd number at dinner parties. So it was easier for them not to invite me. But it was especially hard on me because I was so young. I didn't fit in anywhere."

Kirby paused, his hands resting on the flap of the box in front of him. "How young?"

"Thirty-seven. There was no 'singles' group' back then. There were the young people—in their twenties, just out of college. Career girls, we called the women. But their highest priority was in finding husbands. I definitely didn't fit in there. All the other widows in the church were old"—she smirked—"around my age now. So I didn't fit in there, either. And I had a fifteen-year-old son who was angry and resentful that God would take his father away like that. So we stopped going to church. If it hadn't been for four dear friends from college who rallied around me—around us—we never would have made it."

Kirby seized on that. "You were friends with those women before you married?"

Maureen nodded, not a hair of her brilliant red hair moving out of place. "Yes. We shared a suite together in the sorority at college. After James died, I was ready to cut myself off from everyone simply because of those who had cut me off. But Trina, Lindy, Sassy, and Perty wouldn't let me do that. Instead of leaving me out of invitations, they made a special effort to make me—and Jimmy—feel included in everything. And they wouldn't take no for an answer."

She finished off another box and pushed it toward him. "Does your granddaughter have friends like that?"

"I think so—I hope so. These two girls she's afraid are going to leave her behind have been friends of hers for a long time. In fact, she and Caylor grew up together. The one who married this weekend moved in with them in college a few years back."

Maureen's painted eyebrows rose. "Caylor. . .not Caylor Evans?"

"Yes, Caylor Evans." He knew the tall redhead almost as well as he knew his own granddaughters; she'd been around for so many of Flannery's childhood events.

The volume of Maureen's laugh drew the gazes of several nearby volunteers. "Caylor Evans is the granddaughter of my dear friend Sassy—Celeste Evans. You met Sassy in Sunday school—and at the game night Saturday. That would mean that your granddaughter is Flannery—of course! She was with you last Sunday on your first visit." She touched her fingertips to her temples. "How easily I forget details these days! I don't think your Flannery has anything to worry about. There will be a transition, certainly, as Caylor and Zarah figure out the new balance in their lives, but those two girls are spitting images of their grandmothers—at least as far as their personalities go. There is no way they'll allow Flannery to slip away from them. And I'll put a bug in Trina's and Sassy's ears, just to make sure."

"Thank you." Kirby set up several more empty boxes for both of them. "Flannery did say that she's agreed to allow her friends to set her up on some dates."

"That's good. No one will know her tastes as well as they do." Maureen fell silent a moment, chewing on her bottom lip.

"Now *you* seem pensive." He pulled down another flat of canned green beans and opened it.

"Oh—I was just thinking. . . . You know, there's nothing that says a grandfather can't also help his granddaughter find the love of her life."

Kirby chuckled. "I would have no idea of where to find eligible young men—and that's on top of the fact that I know nothing of her preferences when it comes to that."

A whistle blew, drawing their attention. Kirby turned and stepped aside so Maureen could see past him. A young woman wearing a shirt with the food bank's logo on it stood on a chair. "Thank y'all so much for coming out and helping us pack boxes this morning. We've more than filled our quota for this two-hour time slot, and we'd love to have you come back out anytime."

Maureen looked at her watch. "Goodness—I can't believe we've been at this for two hours already." She looked up at Kirby. "Are you still planning to come over to the shelter to help with the barbecue luncheon?"

"I am." Kirby wiped his forehead and the back of his neck with the red bandanna he kept in his back pocket.

"Good. Because someone's going to be there whom I want you to meet."

Jamie jumped, stretching his hands up as if to catch the red rubber ball but letting it just slip through his fingers. The young girl who'd kicked it squealed a giggle and then ran toward first base.

"Good job!" Jamie clapped his hands and turned to watch as she ran to second base. The kids defending the bases jumped up and down, yelling for the outfielders to get the ball in to them so they could try to get her out.

Yes, a game of kickball had been just the thing to keep the kids out of the way while Cookie and the other senior adults worked to get the food ready. And just the thing he needed to blow off the steam that had been building since last night—when he'd lain in bed, trying to sleep and been bombarded with questions. After the shock of seeing how much he'd have to pay for COBRA, he needed to find a less expensive health-insurance alternative until he found another job. But what if he couldn't qualify for individual health insurance? And what if he couldn't find another marketing job? Should he consider changing careers? What about going back to school to do something else? What else could he do? What else did he want to do?

Finally around three o'clock, he'd picked up his netbook from the bedside table and reread the most recent post from his favorite writer on the website. Then he'd gone into total fanboy mode and written an e-mail to the writer. At least sending it through the website protected his identity. All the writer would see would be his username, something that no one in real life would ever connect with him.

The ball came back to him, but not before the red team—wearing flapping red smocks over their T-shirts and shorts—scored two runs and the girl who'd just kicked landed on third base.

A little boy—probably no more than four years old—came up to home base. Jamie hunkered down and pitched a slow roller toward him—and then had to dive out of the way to keep from being smashed in the face when the kid kicked the ball harder than his little body should have been able to.

Jamie rolled onto his side and sat up, laughing and cheering along with the moms lining the side of the blacktop—a slab of asphalt just large enough for a half basketball court or the infield for a game of kickball.

Having dozed only fitfully after reading, he'd woken up with a headache and considered begging off helping with the cookout today. Now he was happy he hadn't.

A few dark clouds had rolled across the sky earlier today, but other than that, they couldn't have ordered up a more perfect Memorial Day. Bright sun, warm but not hot, slight breeze. Laughing kids. Cheering moms. And a bunch of senior adults bringing more food than everyone here could possibly eat in four or five sittings.

Perfect. Just what he needed to get his mind off himself and his own issues.

A dinner bell clanged.

"Okay, kids, that's the end of the game." He stood and tucked the ball under his arm.

The kids chorused their regret and begged to be allowed to continue the game after lunch, gathering around him and keeping him from escaping until he agreed. "Fine. After lunch, after you've had at least half an hour to digest your food—because I'm not cleaning up behind anyone who gets out here too early and pukes—we'll keep playing if that's what you want to do."

The amoeba around him cheered and, like a tidal wave, pushed him toward the food tables. His mouth watered at the charred aroma of grilled hamburgers and hot dogs. He helped a few of the smallest ones—who could barely see over the edge of the tables bearing all the food—fix their plates and then sent them over to the low plastic picnic tables under the trees beside the blacktop.

"You looked like you were having fun." Cookie handed him an empty plate.

He leaned over and kissed her cheek. "I was. They're great kids."

"Jamie, I'd like to introduce you to someone who's been visiting my Sunday school class." Cookie stepped aside, and a tall, broad-shouldered man stepped forward. "This is Kirby McNeill."

Jamie shifted the plate to his left hand and shook the older gentleman's hand. McNeill? Surely he wasn't. . . But McNeill was a fairly common last name, wasn't it? "It's nice to meet you, Mr. McNeill."

Cookie picked up a bottle of water and tried to wrap her gnarled fingers around the cap.

Jamie tucked his still-empty plate under his arm. "Here, let me do that for you."

With a grateful smile, his grandmother handed him the bottle, which he easily opened for her and handed back.

Before fixing his own plate, Jamie stood back and observed the food line, stepping in several times—to help one lady pour her iced tea, since her hands shook so badly she threatened to baptize the entire drink table with it; to help one of the most wizened men with a pair of tongs that had an industrial-strength spring in them and were hard to use; to lend an extra hand to someone else trying to get to a table across the grass with her food plate, cup, and dessert plate intact.

Once everyone but the ladies who were serving and the two men still at the grill turning out the last hamburger patties and hot dogs had gotten their plates and sat down to start eating, Jamie finally turned to get his lunch. Several of the dishes he'd wanted to try now stood empty, but that was okay—plenty of food still remained.

He piled his plate high then joined the little kids at one of the low plastic picnic tables—sitting in the grass at the end of it instead of risking overbalancing it with his weight.

He'd barely finished his lettuce-wrapped hamburger and started on his bunless hot dog when the kids began pestering him to play kickball again.

"How long did I tell you we needed to wait?" He looked around at the small crowd of kids.

"Half an hour," one of the older ones answered. "But what are we supposed to do until then?"

"You could help clean up," Jamie suggested.

Groans echoed all around him, just as expected.

"Why don't you play hide-and-seek or even just go lie down in the grass and close your eyes for a few minutes?"

The idea that he might want them to take a nap dispersed them quicker than cockroaches when the lights came on. He finished eating and then rose to help with the cleanup—starting with the mess the kids left behind.

Several of the senior ladies bustled around, pulling the butcher paper up around the plates, napkins, and cups left on the tables. He watched them carefully from the corner of his eye, just to make sure no one was becoming overexerted.

And then it happened. A lady who looked like she might be the oldest one there put her hand to her forehead and swooned, crumpling to the grass.

Jamie dropped the wad of trash he had in his arms and ran to her, dropping to his knees beside her. He wanted to help the woman but wasn't certain how. He looked around for a shock of familiar red hair. "Cookie! Cookie!"

His grandmother appeared at his side. "What happened?" She touched the woman's cheeks and forehead. "Burning up." She touched her fingertips to the lady's throat. "Pulse is rapid. Breathing is shallow and rapid. Heat stroke. Jamie, do you think you can carry her inside?"

He lifted the tiny woman in his arms and followed Cookie inside the shelter's common room.

"Put her there." Cookie indicated a sofa, and Jamie eased the lady down onto it.

"What can I do to help?" Mr. McNeill hovered behind Cookie.

She turned to look over her shoulder at him. "I need cool, wet cloths—damp, not soaked."

Mr. McNeill gave a terse nod and went off in search of someone to direct him to the supplies he needed.

"Jamie, call 911."

He'd already pulled his phone out in preparation to do just that. Once the ambulance had been dispatched, Jamie stayed on the line with the operator and relayed the woman's vitals as Cookie called them out. Pulse, respirations, temperature—the facility director had brought a thermometer with her—and that the victim was reporting dizziness and exhibiting slight confusion.

The paramedics arrived and got the lady onto a gurney with an oxygen mask and an IV before taking her out to the ambulance. Another member of the senior adult group had called the woman's daughter to meet her at the hospital.

"Praise the Lord you were here, Maureen. You may have saved her life." Kirby McNeill laid a large hand on Cookie's shoulder.

Cookie blushed and shrugged. "Anyone else could have done the same." Though she tried to sound casual and nonchalant, Jamie could hear the tremor in her voice.

He pulled her into a hug. "No, Cookie, not anyone else could have done the same. I wouldn't have known what to do." He didn't let go of her until her trembling stopped.

"Your grandson is right." Kirby nodded his head emphatically. "All I could think to do was pray. And while I know that's always the right thing to do, it's not always the most helpful thing to do. You knew exactly what she needed."

Cookie stepped back from Jamie and patted her hair to make sure it hadn't been mussed from his hug. He hid his smile. "I may have retired almost twenty years ago, but forty years of nursing isn't easily forgotten." She reached up and patted Jamie's cheek then smiled at Mr. McNeill. "And I had some wonderful assistants. Thank you. I couldn't have done it without the two of you."

The excitement over, everyone finished cleaning up and headed home. Jamie had to promise Cookie he'd stop by for dinner one night this week before she'd let him leave.

On the drive home, he kept running the scenario through his mind. What if Cookie hadn't been there? He wouldn't have known what to do—and he hadn't even thought to pray, as Kirby McNeill said he had.

But the satisfaction of seeing the old woman sit up and start to talk to them after he'd been sure she was dying, of knowing that he'd had some hand in helping her recover—was this what had drawn Danny to nursing? That sense of fulfillment, of accomplishment in knowing he'd had a direct impact on helping someone else?

Maybe he should give the idea some more thought. Perhaps, maybe, just a little bit, even pray about it?

# Chapter 8

$A$ small foam basketball bounced off Jamie's left cheek.

"Sorry, Boss." Ainslee scurried over from her desk to pick up the projectile. "Just a little game of horse before the day gets started."

Darrell and the two graphic designers stood beside Ainslee's desk. All of them early for work the day after a holiday—and the first day after learning they were losing their jobs?

Jamie set his black canvas briefcase down inside the door to his office, turned, and crossed his arms. "What's going on?"

Wade swished his head to flip his blond hair out of his eyes and took the ball from Ainslee. "What do you mean, Boss?"

"I mean you're all here early. And you're all wearing jeans." He uncrossed his arms and pushed his blazer back to rest his hands on his hips.

"We're just here because we have to be." Wade came up on his toes when he shot the ball across the large common room toward the hoop on his office door. It bounced off the rim and rolled back to him.

"Besides"—Ainslee picked up a small plastic football with an advertiser's logo on the side—"what's Armando going to do—fire us for wearing jeans our last week of work?" She lobbed the football at Jamie.

It hit the center of his chest and fell to the floor. He looked down at it, scowling. Why hadn't he thought to wear jeans today?

Oh yeah, because he might actually have a potential client to meet with. "Just don't forget that there's work to do this week."

"Yeah, like trying to find another job."

He heard Ainslee's muttered words just before he latched his office door closed. But he couldn't worry about the team—*his* team, whether he'd been promoted to director or not—right now. He picked up his bag and carried it to his desk. From the outside pocket he pulled out a business card, took a deep breath, and dialed the cell phone number on it.

"Cole Samuels."

"Good morning, Cole. Jamie O'Connor here." He flipped his planner open. "Calling to see if you know your availability this week so we can set up that meeting we talked about."

"Oh, yeah, yeah. Hang on just a sec. Amy Joy wrote everything down for me." The sound of rustling paper came through the phone. "Here it is. Let's see. . . . Thursday at ten in the morning."

Jamie waited a moment, but Cole didn't give any other time options. "Okay. Um. . .I'll have to call Flannery and let her know. I'm not sure about her schedule, but I imagine she can work around this."

"Great. How do I get to your office?"

*His* office? Jamie hadn't thought about that. This was his idea, something he'd come up with on his own, not for the Gregg Agency— or whatever the new name of it was now. But if he had Cole come here, Armando would get wind of it because no one in this office could keep a confidence. "I think we'll be meeting at the Lindsley House offices. And since I've never been there myself, I'll have to get directions from Flannery and e-mail them to you."

"That would be fantastic. I'll see you at ten Thursday morning then."

After Jamie hung up, he rested his face on his desk blotter. Why hadn't he called Flannery first and found out her schedule and made sure it would be okay to meet at her place?

The damage now done, he needed to face the consequences. He

sat up and picked up the phone to call Flannery. . .but didn't have her phone number. All right, then. He'd send her an e-mail.

No, he didn't have her e-mail address, either. He considered another face-plant on the desk, but he had work to do. Shedding his jacket, which he draped across the back of his ugly but ergonomic chair, he emerged from his office—into a heated basketball game between Ainslee, Darrell, and Wade.

Wade and Ainslee actually seemed to be playing more of a game of keep-away from the much shorter Darrell.

Well, that just wasn't fair. Jamie jumped into the fracas and stole the ball as Ainslee threw it toward Wade. He passed it low to Darrell, who floated an over-the-head hook shot into the basket. The two graphic designers, sitting with their backs turned to their oversized computer screens, cheered for each of the two teams—though not so loudly that their voices would carry down the hall to disturb others.

Like the previous department director, Jamie believed in the efficacy of physical activity to stimulate creativity. Or as a way to procrastinate from doing paperwork or other tedious tasks they wanted to avoid for as long as possible.

With a jumping fade-away shot, Jamie tied the score—and called an end to the game.

"Aw. . .come on, Boss. You can't really expect us to work this week." Ainslee tried to snatch the ball from him.

He hid it behind his back and dodged to keep her from it. "Yes, actually, I do. Remember, there's always the possibility that Armando will look to hire locally again. Do you really want to leave a bad impression behind?" Ugh. Why did he have to be the mature, responsible one? He desired nothing more than to goof off and ignore all of the paperwork and reports sitting on his desk to do this week.

Ainslee relented and flopped down in her desk chair. "I guess you're right."

"Good. Now while I make coffee, since apparently none of you has done it yet because Friday's leftovers are still sitting in it"—Jamie gave Ainslee a pointed look—"I need a favor from you. I need the contact information for Flannery McNeill at the Lindsley House publishing company here in town."

"Flannery McNeill? Seriously? Sounds more like the name of an Irish pub or something."

Her name was a little over-the-top on the Irish heritage. "Yes, seriously."

Ainslee jotted down the name. "M-a-c-n-e-a-l?"

"Um. . ." Come to think of it, he'd never seen it written down. "I'm not sure. But there can't be too many Flannery McNeills working at that publishing company, can there?"

"Phone number, e-mail address, or what?" Ainslee shook her mouse back and forth to wake up her computer.

"Whatever you can find." Jamie pulled the coffee carafe out and wrinkled his nose at the scummy residue ring left on the inside of the pot as the several-days-old coffee sloshed around.

Darrell perched on the corner of Ainslee's desk. "Boss, please tell me that this Flannery McNeill is some hot chick you met this weekend and you're trying to track her down to ask her out. I know. I heard your whole thing about wanting to leave a good impression behind." Darrell made a derisive raspberry sound. "But you can't seriously be starting a project you're just going to have to turn over so the Memphis office can take the credit for all your hard work."

Jamie couldn't lie to his teammates—but this thing with Cole Samuels. . .he could parlay it into at least part-time freelance marketing work, if not something even bigger. He couldn't let anyone here get wind of it.

So he'd tell Darrell what Darrell wanted to hear. "She's about five nine, long blond hair, hazel eyes. And when I saw her Saturday night, she was wearing a black dress that would have rendered even you speechless, D." And speechless would have been much better than yammering like a dork.

"I *knew* it." Darrell held out his fist, and Jamie bumped it with his as he went past, carrying the coffeepot and filter basket to wash in the break room at the end of the hall.

In the break room, two women rinsing out their coffee cups gave him furtive glances when he bade them good morning, and then they scurried away, not making eye contact with him. Good grief. It wasn't like getting laid off was contagious.

He'd have to come clean with Cole and Flannery Thursday morning—tell them that as of Friday afternoon, he no longer worked for the Gregg Agency and that he wouldn't have the kind of resources that he had here. He needed to come up with a full proposal of how he could do this freelance for them to look at and decide if they wanted to work with him or not.

He just hoped he hadn't sealed his fate with Flannery with the whole Dracula thing. If only life had a DELETE button.

∞

"I'm still not talking to you, Mr. Colby." Flannery flickered a glance toward the door.

Jack leaned against the jamb, his tie loose, his sleeves rolled up to the elbows. And it wasn't even ten o'clock yet. He held two white paper coffee cups in his hands. "I brought you something."

She leaned back in her chair and tapped the end of her pen against her chin. Why couldn't she have romantic feelings for Jack. . . which were reciprocated? She and Jack would be perfect together, the whole no-romantic-feelings thing notwithstanding. Maybe if the two of them could come to an understanding—a relationship based on their friendship and mutual respect for one another—she could stop worrying about relationships and love and marriage changing people.

She sighed. "Fine. Come in."

He set one of the large cups on the desk blotter and then settled into one of the chairs across from her desk—the one not stacked to teetering height with manuscripts and bound-book samples from different printing companies.

"What's all this?" He leaned forward and flipped through a stack of paper on her desk.

"Cover design options for my spring titles for the catalog meeting this afternoon. I was working on finalizing my frontlist release dates when you interrupted."

"I brought you coffee. Consider it a peace offering." Jack leaned back in the chair, slouching down a little, and lifted his cup to his lips. He sipped, frowned, and then pulled a ballpoint pen out of the Lindsley House–logoed cup on her desk and used it to make the vent hole in the plastic lid a little larger.

Flannery sighed again, uncrossed her arms, and picked up the coffee to taste it. She wrinkled her nose and opened her top desk drawer. Three packs of sugar should do it; though if Jack weren't here, she'd probably have added five.

Jack made a gagging sound as she sweetened the already semisweetened, french-vanilla flavored latte. She shot him a dirty look through narrowed eyes.

"Sorry." Though he didn't sound it. "You know I just have your best interests at heart, right?"

She snapped the lid back on her cup and tasted the latte. Yep, could have used two more packets. She'd wait until he left. "About adding what you think is too much sugar to my coffee or about something else?"

"How long have we worked together?" Jack looked totally unfazed by her snarky tone. One thing that annoyed—and pleased—her about Jack was the way he didn't give in to her moods.

She did a quick mental calculation. "Twelve years, if you don't count the two summer internships I did before I graduated from college." Jack had been the senior editor of one of Lindsley House's imprints back then and had hired Flannery as his editorial assistant. She owed him her career, as he'd mentored her and taught her everything he knew about the publishing industry, leading to her promotion to an assistant editor position eleven months later. "Why do you ask?"

"Flan, you know that I'm not close with my family—that it's all my brothers and I can do to be in the same room together without the police or paramedics being called after ten minutes."

She nodded and absently sipped the not-quite-sweet-enough coffee.

"You're the closest thing I've ever had to a sister, and I don't think I've ever told you how much I appreciate you and care for you." Though he didn't quite smile, his dimples appeared. "That's the only reason I give you such a hard time. Because I want to see you happy. And ever since Zarah and Caylor got engaged, I can see that you're not happy."

"Jack—"

"I know, I know, it isn't appropriate for us to talk about these kinds of personal issues at the office. But I felt really bad the whole rest of the weekend for giving you a hard time at the reception and teasing you about Jamie O'Connor. Forgive me?" Jack ducked his chin and stuck out his bottom lip like a five-year-old.

Flannery tried to stop herself from laughing but couldn't. "'You know I love you more than my luggage,'" she quoted from *Steel Magnolias*, trying to further diffuse the emotional tension in the room.

"And considering how much you travel"—he winked at her—"I know *just* how much that means." Reaching across the desk, he picked up her hand and leaned forward to kiss the back of it. He settled back in the chair again. "Now, let's discuss next year's spring frontlist."

Flannery went over the list of new titles already in the works for next spring, letting Jack make a few marketing and prerelease advertising suggestions just so he felt like he was once again in the editorial trenches instead of an administrator who got to focus only on the business end of things now.

Her desk phone rang a couple of times, but she let the calls roll over into voice mail when she didn't recognize the incoming numbers. She and Jack had just about wrapped up when Brittany Wilmette knocked on the almost-closed door.

"Come in, Britt. We were just finishing up." Flannery restacked her fact sheets for each of the spring titles and stuck them back in the folder to take to the meeting. "Oh, Jack, don't forget, I'm working from home Thursday morning because I'm flying out to Chicago that afternoon."

"Why are you going to Chicago?" Jack paused just inside the now-open door.

"Well, firstly because you asked me to do a few onsite visits with the printers up there. I also scheduled some meetings with a few of my authors in the area. And then I'll be taking appointments at that writers' conference next week."

Jack scowled. "So how long are you going to be gone?"

"I'm here today and tomorrow, and then I'll be out until a week from Monday."

Jack pulled out his smartphone and started tapping on the miniature keyboard. "I'm sure Mae already has it in my calendar, but I'll make a note of it. Just keep your phone turned on at all times."

Flannery almost snorted. "When do I not?"

He inclined his head to Flannery's assistant. "Brittany."

"Mr. Colby." Brittany stepped back from the doorway to let Jack get past her. He whistled as he walked away, still playing with his phone.

Flannery waved her assistant into the office. "You know you don't have to call him that."

"I know." Only a few weeks past her college graduation, the twenty-two-year-old still let her nerves get the better of her sometimes, even though she'd interned here the last two summers—just like Flannery had done.

"What's up?" Flannery reached in her drawer for the two packs of sugar her coffee still needed.

Britt handed over a slip of paper. "Some guy named Jamie called. He said he'd left you a voice mail about twenty minutes ago but wanted to make sure you got the message as soon as possible, so he zeroed out and got me."

Flannery wanted to crumple the note but refrained and finished doctoring her coffee. "Thanks, Britt." She handed the folder of fact sheets to the girl. "Will you please make ten sets of these for the meeting this afternoon?"

"Sure." Brittany took the folder back out to her desk.

Flannery stood and pushed the door almost closed again. Back at her desk, she picked up the receiver and dialed the number written on

Brittany's note. It rang three times.

"You've reached the office of Jamie O'Connor, senior sports marketing account executive with the Gregg Agency. I'm either on the other line or away from my desk at the moment, so please leave me a detailed message, including your name and phone number, and I'll get back to you as soon as possible. If you need immediate attention, please press zero and ask for Ainslee Urbanik."

He could read a script pretty well. Before the beep, Flannery hit zero. The line clicked a couple of times and then rang once.

"Sports Marketing, this is Ainslee."

"Hi, Ainslee. This is Flannery McNeill from Lindsley House Publishing. I'm returning Jamie O'Connor's phone call, and he made it sound urgent."

"Oh, hold on a sec. . . . Yeah, he's on the other line right now. Do you mind holding? I'm sure it won't be long."

"Sure, I'll hold."

"May I tell him what the call is regarding?"

If it would make him get off the phone any faster so they could get this over and done with sooner? Sure. "I believe it's about a meeting he's setting up for us with Cole Samuels to discuss a marketing plan for Mr. Samuels's books."

"Oh."

Flannery couldn't be certain, not seeing the woman's face, but her voice sounded as if this surprised her.

"Okay, let me put you on hold, and I'll go stick a note under his nose to expedite things."

"Thanks." Flannery pulled the receiver away from her ear when the on-hold recording came on in the middle of a spiel for how successful the Gregg Agency's clients were because of what the agency had done for them.

"Flannery?" Jamie's voice interrupted the stream of ads.

"Yes. Were you able to get a meeting set with Cole?" She pulled up the calendar on her computer. Of course, every block of time today and tomorrow was accounted for already—between meetings, phone calls, and time scheduled to work on stuff in her office.

"Thursday morning at ten o'clock."

Of course. "That's not the best for me. What about two o'clock tomorrow afternoon?" She could get out of the strategic planning meeting that way.

"Sorry, but Thursday morning is the only time he could meet."

"Great."

"What?"

"Nothing—I just have to catch a plane to Chicago at one o'clock that afternoon." And she was supposed to be working from home that morning—which meant in shorts and a tank top on the balcony in the sunshine. So much for that idea.

"Oh. That won't give us a lot of time, will it?"

"No, it won't." She sighed. "Look, why don't I come over at nine o'clock so that you and I can go ahead and hash some ideas out before Cole gets there."

"I can do the nine o'clock thing, but I told Cole we'd be meeting at your office. I figured it would be. . .calmer at your place than trying to bring him in here. Plus, you'd both have to pay to park in one of the garages down here, and there's no guarantee you'd find a spot."

Flannery curled her free hand into a fist and glanced around her office. No way she'd bring someone like Cole into this paper-hoarder's paradise. "I'll try to reserve one of the conference rooms so we can spread out." And if she couldn't get one of those, Jack's office would work just fine—especially since this had been Jack's idea to begin with.

"That'll work. Can you e-mail Cole directions to your office and CC me on it?" He read the e-mail address to her.

"I'll send that out before lunch." Of course this was turning into a huge pain in the neck. With Jamie O'Connor involved, why had she expected anything less?

"Oh, and let me give you my cell phone number. It'll be better—easier for you to get me that way."

She typed his number into the text box at the bottom of the meeting reminder before saving it to her calendar—which promptly warned her that the meeting conflicted with another appointment. She canceled the warning and deleted the block of time labeled WORKING AT HOME from the calendar.

"I guess I'll see you at nine on Thursday morning, then."

"I guess you will." Flannery flinched at the acidity in her own voice. "Thanks for setting this up."

"No problem." He paused.

She leaned forward, waiting for him to say something else—almost afraid of what it might be.

"Okay. Well, then. 'Bye."

" 'Bye." She frowned at the phone after hanging up. That guy was so weird. She just hoped he'd leave behind his awkwardness and stupid jokes and not embarrass her in front of Cole Samuels. She'd worked too long and too hard to land this contract for Jamie to ruin it for her.

# Chapter 9

$\mathcal{M}$aureen stared at the blinking cursor in the box for the e-mail's subject. She started and then erased several options. How could writing one simple e-mail make her feel like a socially inept teenager? And if she couldn't come up with a subject, how was she going to write the e-mail itself?

It wasn't as if this were her first time e-mailing him. Best just dive in.

**From:** Maureen O'Connor
**To:** Kirby McNeill
**Subject:** Weekend Plans

*Dear Kirby,*

She knew it looked old-fashioned—her grandson probably never addressed any of his e-mails as "Dear So-and-so," not even the business e-mails she knew he sent dozens of each day. But she couldn't help it. Surely Kirby would understand her formality. Hopefully, he'd appreciate it. He seemed like that kind of man.

*It was wonderful to have you join us at the food bank and women's and children's shelter on Memorial Day. We certainly*

*appreciated the extra help, and I hope you enjoyed yourself and got
to know some of the members of the Keenagers class.*

There. That was a pretty good start. What next? *I would like to
spend more time with you, so I hope you'll decide to join the church and the
class so I can see you more often.*

Her face burned from just thinking it. So, no.

She tapped her fingertips lightly against the keys. As one of the
volunteers in charge of outreach for the senior adult group, she usually
whipped out several e-mails a week to visitors and members alike.
She'd never had this kind of trouble figuring out what to say.

*We have some wonderful activities planned*

Wonderful activities? No, scratch that.

*Our summer schedule is full of activities, and I hope you'll
have time to join us for some of them. This coming weekend we
will be hosting a fish fry at the Hillsboro Village Assisted Living
Center—two blocks up Acklen Avenue from the church—on
Friday evening beginning at four o'clock for setup. Saturday,
a group is going to the Country Music Hall of Fame to see the
special Southern Gospel exhibit. And Sunday, there is a church-
wide dinner on the grounds to help the youth raise money for their
missions trip later this summer.*

She looked at the activities calendar and typed in a list of other
major activities coming up over the next couple of months. After
typing in only about half of the planned events, she read back through
them and cringed. They had far too many things on the schedule.

*I know this list may seem overwhelming—especially to
someone so recently retired. But I just wanted to give you a
sampling of all of the choices that the Keenagers group offers*

*seniors to stay active and busy, while also understanding that most
people aren't going to be able to participate in everything.*

If figuring out the subject line of the message had been hard,
coming up with an innocuous closing for the e-mail proved even
harder.

> *I hope*

What did she hope? She hoped he'd ask her out on a date—that
was what she really hoped.

"Maureen O'Connor, what is wrong with you?" She shook her head
at the silly schoolgirl thoughts. "You can't be thinking about dating at
eighty-four years old."

> *I hope you're having a good week, and we look forward to
> seeing you again soon.*
>
> > *Sincerely,*
> > *Maureen O'Connor*

And as she usually did, she included her phone number under her
name. Before she could second-guess herself, she clicked SEND, and off
the message went.

She moved on to uploading photos from the food bank and shelter
events to the group's Facebook page. After only a few minutes, the
computer chimed to let her know she had a new e-mail message.

She switched over to the e-mail program—and her heart gave a
little flutter when she saw the name of the sender on the only new
message in her box. She had to make her hand stop trembling to
double click on the message.

**From:** Kirby McNeill
**To:** Maureen O'Connor
**Subject:** RE: Weekend Plans

*Dear Maureen,*

She knew he'd be someone who would appreciate the formality of pretending like this was a real letter.

> *I had a wonderful time Monday participating with the group at the food bank and the shelter. Thank you for inviting me to come. I have printed your e-mail and will look at my calendar to see which of the future events I might be able to participate in.*
>
> *I will try to make it to the events this weekend, as my granddaughter will be out of town, so I will be on my own and in need of something to do. The weekend after, however, I will be in Alabama, visiting my son and his wife, so I will be unable to attend any events.*
>
> *I am thinking about looking for a small apartment or house to rent or purchase in Nashville so I don't have to stay in a hotel each weekend. Can you recommend the best areas to start my search? Unlike my granddaughter, I have no desire to live downtown, especially since I will only be there for the weekends. Nashville has changed so much since I was in seminary there that I do not know where to tell a real estate agent I would like to begin looking. Your thoughts?*
>
> *I look forward to seeing you again and to becoming a more active member of the Keenagers group.*
>
> *Until next time,*
> *Kirby*

Maureen bit her bottom lip. "*I look forward to seeing you*"—singular or plural? *You* as in the group, or *you* as in Maureen herself?

Gracious—she couldn't, shouldn't, do this to herself.

The computer chimed again with the notification of another new e-mail. She closed Kirby's e-mail and opened the new one—an automated message from Facebook.

*Kirby McNeill wants to be friends with you.*

Now she was certain she would go into a teenage meltdown. How did these young girls stand it—getting signals like this without knowing for sure if the man in question was romantically interested or truly just wanted to be friends?

She considered asking Jamie next time she saw her grandson. But given how much he liked to tease her about how addicted she was to social media already, she decided just to wait and see what happened with Kirby over the next few weeks before even mentioning him to Jamie. They'd met. That was enough for now.

And just to keep from seeming overeager, she closed the e-mail and went into the kitchen to start a batch of lemon cookies. She would answer Kirby's e-mail and accept his friend request later. She'd learned many, many years ago that it was sometimes better to make a man wait rather than to show one's eagerness.

But she would be accepting Kirby's friend request. And possibly any other requests he might put to her. And she wouldn't be dishonest in recommending he start looking for a place to live right here in Crieve Hall.

Sixty-five years ago she'd discovered the effectiveness of forcing patience onto an eager suitor when she'd made James wait a day or two for her responses to his letters and when she'd turned him down for dates requested hours before he wanted to go out.

But as a twenty-year-old nursing student, she'd had her whole life in front of her—unfortunately, James had fewer than twenty years remaining. But at least she got to spend that time with him before his heart failed.

She returned to the living room and sat back down at the computer. Neither she nor Kirby had twenty years left. And patience was overrated anyway.

# Chapter 10

❧

"Oh, come on. Don't act like this." Every time Flannery got one of Liam's claws detached from her T-shirt, he dug in with the other three.

"He knows you're getting ready to leave." Lola reached over to try to help, while Lala, Liam's mother, tried climbing up Flannery's knit leggings to get to her baby boy. Once Lola got Liam detached, Flannery reached down and pulled Lala off.

"Thanks so much for taking care of him for me. My friend who usually takes him is on her honeymoon, and I just can't stand to put him in the kennel. The only time I did, he lost a third of his body weight and half his hair because he went on a hunger strike in protest."

Lola held Liam up to her cheek and nuzzled him. "I can't believe you'd even think of taking this sweet thing to a kennel. No, he needs some Mama and Lola time. That's what he needs." The woman who'd practically insisted two years ago that Flannery take Liam began crooning to the cat in unintelligible baby talk.

Flannery leaned over and put the mother cat down inside Lola's door then backed away. "Here's the bag with his bed and toys and food, which should be enough to last for the eight days I'll be gone."

"When do you come back?" Lola didn't seem to mind at all when her cat started climbing up the silky fabric of her pajama bottoms.

104

"Early next Sunday morning. I managed to get the first flight out." It meant having to be at O'Hare by five o'clock in the morning, but it also meant she'd be back in Nashville before 8:30 a.m.—giving her all day to unpack, do laundry, get caught up on e-mails, and maybe take a nap before coffee with Caylor and Zarah. Because she definitely wasn't going to miss getting together with the girls on Zarah's first Sunday back from her honeymoon.

"Well, you just come by whenever you'd like to pick up the little dear"—the little dear who weighed twenty pounds and was currently growling in protest to the way he was being held—"or just leave him here and come by on Monday if you don't feel up to taking him back on Sunday."

"Thanks, Lola." Flannery backed away toward the door to the stairwell. "Again, I really appreciate this."

She jogged down the three flights of stairs and across the building to her own condo, where she showered at supersonic speed. Since she now had no time to dry her hair—a task that typically took at least half an hour—she french braided it, leaving a few tendrils loose around her face and ears. Makeup and then clothes—and instead of getting to be comfortable and wear jeans on the plane, she'd now be stuck in a business suit. She might as well make it her favorite—a tweed 1940s style with a cute kick-pleated skirt and a jacket with three-quarter sleeves and a peplum that flared out from a slightly raised waist, giving her the illusion of more curves than she owned. She pulled out a coral, wrap-front, sleeveless shell to wear under it and stepped into her comfortable burgundy-brown, round-toe pumps with the slight platform at the toe.

On second thought...

She grabbed a small overnight bag and threw a pair of jeans and a short-sleeved navy cardigan into it, along with socks and a pair of blue-and-coral plaid canvas sneakers. She'd change clothes before heading to the airport and just leave the suit hanging on the back of her office door until she came back. No point in making today any more miserable than it absolutely had to be.

She made it down to her car with her suitcase, the bag with her change of clothes, her laptop carry-on bag, and her purse right at eight thirty. Up until three months ago, leaving at eight thirty meant she'd walk into the office at eight thirty-five—if she drove the half mile from her condo building to their old offices on Lindsley Avenue, an additional ten minutes if she walked. But now that they'd outgrown that space and moved into new digs down in the Maryland Farm business park in Brentwood, the shortest her commute had ever been was twenty minutes.

On a regular day in the office, she'd have left here no later than seven thirty. But this was no regular office day. And since Jamie was supposed to be meeting her at nine o'clock, it would behoove her to be there before he got there.

She used the hands-free system in the car to call the office as soon as she pulled out of the garage.

"Hi, Flannery," Brittany answered after half a ring.

"I'm on my way in." She ran through a list of things she needed for the meeting with Jamie and Cole, which she'd figured on having time to pull together this morning. "If you can get that done for me, I'd really appreciate it. Oh, and another huge, huge favor—"

"I just started a fresh pot of coffee brewing, and someone brought in Krispy Kreme doughnuts this morning, so I set a couple aside for you."

She loved it—after just a few weeks as her full-time assistant, Brittany could already read her mind. "You are an absolute doll, Britt. I owe you big time."

She could almost hear the assistant beaming through the phone. "It's no problem."

"I'll be there in about fifteen minutes." She let Brittany go to get those copies made and files pulled and returned her full focus to the road. After praying that she'd make it to the office before Jamie got there, she relaxed a bit into prayer mode and spent the rest of the drive mulling over some things with God. Like safety for her trip, inspiration for a way to show her appreciation to Brittany, clarity on a few projects, and help to figure out her new relationships with Zarah and Caylor.

By the time she exited the elevator on the fourth floor of the building and pulled open the etched-glass doors of Lindsley House Publishing's offices, she felt pretty good about today.

Except for the whole Jamie O'Connor thing. And she knew better than to pray for patience with him—because God didn't *give* patience. God *taught* patience by putting her, repeatedly, through the situation she wanted the patience for.

"The coffee just finished brewing, I put the copies and files on your desk, and the doughnuts are"—the microwave beeped in the small kitchenette behind Brittany's work area outside Flannery's office—"warm and ready for you."

"Thank you, darling, darling girl." Flannery set her clothes bag and her laptop case on the empty guest chair in her office and then followed Brittany to the kitchenette while they discussed the information Brittany had gathered for her.

Flannery finished off her bottle of vanilla-caramel flavored liquid creamer—just enough left for this large mug of coffee—and she pulled a couple of paper towels out of the dispenser and dampened them with water from the sink before taking the small plate of doughnuts from Brittany, who'd taken it out of the microwave for her.

Brittany followed her back to her office and hovered in the doorway while Flannery settled down at her desk. She had ten minutes to eat and check e-mail before Jamie arrived.

"When the front desk calls, do you mind going up to the front to get Jamie? That'll give me a little extra time."

"No problem." Brittany gave her a jaunty salute.

"Thanks." Flannery set the mug on the coffee warming plate and turned on her desktop computer. She'd checked e-mail at home this morning while on the treadmill but had flagged a few to respond to once she was actually sitting at a keyboard instead of just scrolling through them on the laptop while jogging.

And as expected, a bunch more had come in since then. From the subject line of a message from one of her debut authors, she could tell it was one that needed to be dealt with quickly. Apparently after rave reviews in a couple of magazines and a bunch of online book-review blogs, in addition to a glut of four- and five-star reviews on the major online bookseller sites, the author had just read a scathing one-star review that had sent her into what Flannery liked to call Debut Devastation—that first experience with realizing that not everyone was going to like her book. In fact, there would be people who hated it.

She fortified herself with one of the warm glazed doughnuts, wiped the stickiness off her hands with the damp paper towels, and then set fingers to keyboard to both mollify the author's tender feelings and coach her in how to handle negative reviews. Many editors she knew told their authors just to ignore all reviews, never read them at all. Flannery believed an author could learn from just about anything, even the most negative reviews—sometimes the simple lesson of humility.

She read through her response a couple of times before sending the e-mail. Then she checked the time, thinking she might still have a minute or two.

Yikes! How had it gotten so late?

She stood and stepped out to Brittany's cubicle. "Where's Jamie O'Connor? He was supposed to be here fifteen minutes ago."

Brittany shrugged. "The front desk hasn't called to say he's here."

Oh, that man. Flannery spun and returned to her office, closing the door behind her. Brittany's tender ears didn't need to hear the blistering Flannery intended to give the inconsiderate lout.

She scrolled through the contact list in her phone and mashed the CALL button as soon as she got to his name. It dialed his cell phone number, which she'd put in as his default per his request.

Four rings and then voice mail. She disconnected and scrolled to his office number. Again, no answer. She didn't even let the message get beyond "You've reached—" before she hit zero. Two clicks and a ring.

"Sports. . .um. . .Hampton, Dixon. . .uh. . .Holcomb, and Gregg Marketing Solutions, this is Ainslee." The assistant sighed loudly.

"Hi, Ainslee. This is Flannery McNeill from Lindsley House Publishing. I'm trying to get in touch with Jamie O'Connor. We had a nine o'clock appointment this morning." She paced the short width of her office. Just wait until he got on the phone. She'd really let him have it.

"Um. . .yeah. He was getting ready to leave the office for your meeting when he was called in to Mr. Gregg's office. I haven't seen him since." Ainslee sounded a little worried about that.

Flannery stopped and leaned forward against the back of her desk chair. "I tried calling his cell phone, but he didn't answer."

"Well. . .his briefcase is in his office, so I think he's probably still in with Mr. Gregg. I'll have him call you as soon as he comes out and let you know his ETA."

"Thank you, Ainslee. I appreciate that." Flannery tucked the phone back into the holster clipped to the waistband of her skirt. She paced a little more and then returned to the desk, where she devoured the second doughnut to quiet her growling stomach and returned to answering e-mails. Nothing she could do until he got here.

Almost half an hour later the desk phone rang—and the ID window showed it was the front-desk receptionist calling. Brittany answered it before Flannery could reach the receiver.

What happened to calling her before he left the office? Maybe Ainslee had been away from her desk when he returned to the office for his briefcase and he hadn't gotten the message.

Flannery wiped her hands on the almost-dry towels and threw them and the empty plate in the trash can under her desk. She got a breath mint from the canister in the top drawer and then checked the front of her shirt for crumbs and brushed a few flakes of dry glaze away before buttoning her blazer.

She opened her door just as Brittany rounded the corner headed back from the front lobby. Behind her. . .

Flannery frowned and then schooled her expression.

Brittany led the unfamiliar man straight to Flannery and then returned to her desk. He extended his hand toward her.

"Hi, I'm Dustin Aaronson, senior sports marketing account executive with HDHG Marketing Solutions."

Flannery shook hands with the tall, stocky towhead—wondering how someone who looked about the same age as Brittany had enough experience to be a *senior* anything other than a student. "Flannery McNeill."

"I wasn't sure the first time I heard it, but is that *Flannery* as in—?"

"Yes, as in the author Flannery O'Connor." She sighed.

Dustin smiled at her. "May we step into your office a moment?"

Flannery backed through the door and motioned Dustin to enter. "I'm sorry I don't have anywhere for you to sit—I have a conference room reserved for. . .us."

Dustin closed the door and then turned his too-white smile back toward Flannery, taking a few steps over to stand across the desk from her. "I believe you were expecting to meet with Jamie O'Connor."

"Yes. He'd already shared some ideas with my associate publisher, which is why we'd set up the meeting with Cole Samuels while he's in town." Flannery started to cross her arms but didn't want to convey her discomfort through her body language. She rested her hands on the back of her chair. "May I ask why Mr. O'Connor didn't come to today's meeting?"

Dustin's thick pale brows raised. "He didn't tell you? He's been laid off. As of today he no longer works for HDHG Marketing Solutions. We didn't see any point in his taking this meeting when I was already in town working on the department transition." He lifted a plastic expanding folder from his soft-side leather briefcase. "Jamie gave me all of his notes and ideas, so I think we can make pretty quick work of this."

Flannery chewed the inside of her bottom lip as she turned to pick up her own file of ideas from her desk. "Let's go to the conference room then."

Halfway down the hall, her cell phone buzzed and then began ringing. She lifted it to look at the ID screen.

CALL FROM JAMIE O'CONNOR.

She almost answered it—but didn't want to do so in front of Dustin.

Jack stepped out of his office when he saw Flannery headed down the hall. His smile faded when he looked over her shoulder.

Flannery stepped out of the way. "Jack Colby, associate publisher for fiction, this is Dustin Aaronson from the advertising agency."

Jack recovered more quickly than she had, his smile extra wide as he shook hands with Jamie's replacement.

"Dustin, why don't you go ahead and have a seat in the conference room, and Flannery and I will be right in." Jack motioned to the open door just a few steps down from his office. He watched until Dustin disappeared in the room. "What's going on?"

Flannery glanced toward the conference room and then back to Jack and shrugged. "I'm not sure. The agency has a new name, and this guy told me that Jamie was laid off and *as of today* no longer works there."

Jack jerked slightly. "Really?"

"That's what he told me." Flannery chewed the nail on her right pinky finger.

Jack reached over and pulled her hand away from her mouth, a little twinkle in his blue eyes. "Don't tell me you're worried about Jamie O'Connor. I thought you didn't like the guy."

"I don't—I mean, he irritates me. But. . .to lose his job." She shook her head. "No one deserves that."

"Flan, my dear, I think there's hope for you yet."

"Don't count on it." She took a deep breath and then released it slowly. "And what's this about you coming to this meeting?"

"Hey—I have a few ideas I'd like to float out there, too."

"And you're a little starstruck with the idea that we're going to be publishing novels written by a big football great like Cole Samuels." Flannery rubbed her lips together. "Oh—you go in and entertain this Dustin kid. I'll be right back." She jogged back to her office, dug around in her purse, and pulled out her lipstick and compact.

Touched up, she stepped out of the office. Brittany hung up

her phone and came out of her cubicle directly across the hall from Flannery's door. "Mr. Samuels is here. Do you want me to go get him?"

"No, I'll go." Flannery straightened her jacket and ran her tongue over her front teeth, just in case the lipstick had transferred after she put the mirror away. She bared her teeth at Brittany, who nodded and gave a thumbs-up.

Starting down the hallway, Flannery lifted her cell phone and dialed into her voice mail. She had one new message. She ducked into the supply room.

"Flannery. . .it's Jamie. Look, I'm sure by now you've met the new rep. I—I'm sorry I didn't tell y'all Saturday night about the layoff thing but. . .well, I take full responsibility. I know that Dustin will be great for you to work with, and I. . .I wish you all the best."

Flannery accidently hit SAVE instead of DELETE. Oh well, she'd delete it later. She turned the sound off and reholstered the phone.

Cole stood in front of a display case of recent releases, making the small front office look even smaller. The *clack* of her shoes against the travertine tiles caught his attention, and he gave her a big grin.

"Cole, it's good to see you again." They exchanged the expected handshake. "Come on back."

"I've been looking forward to this. It's real exciting to do something new—different from sports. I've been writing since I was a kid, dreaming of being a published author someday." He stopped and touched her shoulder.

She turned to look up at him. Even with her in three-inch heels, he towered over her.

"I want you to know, I want you to be just as hard on me as you are on all of your other authors when it comes to edits. I know I'm going to take a lot of flack about being just another celebrity who thinks he can write a book. I don't want that to be what people say. I want them to be surprised because it's actually well written. And I may have a degree in English, but you're the pro here, and I want to learn from you."

Heat tweaked Flannery's cheeks. "It's a deal. I think you and I are going to work quite well together."

"And besides, football won't last forever. Maybe one of these days I can be angling for your job." He winked at her.

"Yeah, we'll just see about that." Flannery's good humor lasted until they entered the small conference room. Jack and Dustin stood and greeted Cole, who looked as confused as Flannery had been over the unexpected player substitution.

Instead of being able to come up with a few really good ideas and brainstorm how to put them in action, Flannery and Jack spent most of the meeting telling Dustin that everything he was suggesting were things that their marketing department already did. The plastic folder which he'd indicated contained all of Jamie's notes sat beside his tablet computer, unopened.

Flannery kept an eye on the clock, and at ten forty-five, she closed her folder—all of the copies of marketing campaign ideas they'd done in the past still in it.

"I hate to cut this meeting short, but I have a flight to catch." She stood and extended her hand across the round table toward Dustin. "Thank you for coming in, Dustin. I'll—"

"I'll get my assistant to show you out." Jack motioned Dustin toward the door, turned, glanced at Cole's back, and then gave Flannery a significant look.

Cole stood, his brows drawn close together. "That was weird. Who was that guy?"

"Well, apparently Jamie O'Connor got laid off this week, and this is his replacement." She caught the corner of her bottom lip between her teeth.

"I don't want to work with this Dustin guy. He didn't listen to a thing you said and doesn't know anything about books or marketing them. Jamie at least seemed to have an idea of how sports marketing and book marketing could work together."

From what Jack had told her they'd discussed Saturday night at the reception, Flannery grudgingly agreed. Jamie had apparently expressed some innovative ideas. None of which Dustin seemed familiar with.

She ushered Cole down the hall toward the front office. "Well, this was just an informational meeting. There's nothing that says we have to work with the advertising agency. Next week Jack and I will work on putting together our own marketing plan. Then when we meet with this guy—with Dustin again later in the month, we'll see if he has anything significant to add to it."

"Well, if I have any say about it, I don't want to work with that agency. I know Jamie O'Connor's been laid off and all, but I'd rather we figure out some way we can work with him." Cole turned and shook her hand when they reached the front office. "I'd rather work with Jamie O'Connor, if at all possible."

"We'll see what happens." Flannery stood in the reception area for a moment until Cole disappeared through the door.

Rushing back to her office, she tried to repress the response she'd really wanted to make, but it trumpeted through her head.

She'd rather work with Jamie O'Connor, too.

# Chapter 11

*❧*

"You don't have a window or aisle seat anywhere?" Jamie tapped his driver's license on the high countertop.

"No, sir. Center seats only. Three left. Rows eight, twelve, and sixteen." The airline rep looked up at him, brows raised in question.

If he had to squeeze in between two other people, he might as well be near the front. "Row eight."

"You will have a two-and-a-half-hour layover. Is that okay?"

After what transpired this morning? "Yes, as long as I can get a flight out today."

A few minutes later the rep strapped the barcode strip onto the handle of Jamie's small suitcase and then stapled the claim tags inside his ticket folder. "Departing at 2:04 p.m. Salt Lake City is your final destination. Arrival at 8:40 p.m. local time." She closed the folder and handed it to him. "Your flight will be departing from gate C-3. Enjoy your trip."

"Thanks." Jamie tucked his sheathed netbook in the crook of his arm and headed for the security gate. Thankfully, not too many people seemed to be flying anywhere at lunchtime on the first Thursday in June, so he didn't feel rushed in taking his netbook out of the case or removing his shoes—why had he worn athletic shoes instead of something easy to slip out of?

He made it to the other side with no problems and strode a few paces away to put his shoes back on. Before leaving the area, he hailed one of the TSA agents not currently doing anything.

"Is there a Starbucks somewhere near the C concourse?"

"There's a kiosk right here"—the guy motioned toward a large cart in the corner of the retail lobby the security gate opened out to—"but they're limited in what they can fix. There's a full-service store down near C-10 if that's what you'd prefer."

"Thank you." Jamie tucked his ticket folder into the outside pocket of the computer cover and slid his driver's license into his wallet and returned it to his back pocket.

While the line at security might not have been long, apparently the coffee shop hadn't gotten the message. But he had almost two hours to kill before the boarding time printed on his ticket, so he didn't mind standing in line. He let his mind wander—but not too far. He didn't want to turn into a frustrated, angry traveling man today by getting wound up about this morning.

Finally. Only two people in front of him. He swerved yet again to avoid the ginormous carry-on bag flailing precariously off the shoulder of the woman directly ahead of him. He graciously stepped out of her way after she finished her transaction. After he ordered and joined her at the other end of the counter to wait for his large, extra-shot, double-caramel latte—fat-free, sugar-free, extra-hot, no foam, please—he made sure to give her plenty of room.

The baristas here were fast, so a few moments later, Jamie snagged the last open table in the small café. He pulled out the computer and started it up.

E-mail first, as usual. Messages from Ainslee, Darrell, and Wade. He couldn't read those right now. He'd already turned his phone ringer off. Ainslee meant well; he just wasn't ready to talk about it yet. He'd barely been able to tell Cookie that he wouldn't be going back to the office after today and had decided there was no time like the present to go out to Utah to visit his mother.

He could tell from Cookie's voice that he'd worried her, but she didn't try to talk him out of it. He'd call her on his layover and try to explain things. If he could.

He clicked the second button on his "Favorites" toolbar, hoping to read something new from his favorite contributor.

"May I join you?"

Heart thundering, Jamie closed the lid of the small computer and looked up. No, his ears hadn't deceived him. "Flannery? What are you doing here?" He stood and motioned toward the other chair at the small table. "Please, join me."

"Thanks." She popped the lid off her large cup and added five packs of sugar to it.

*Like some coffee with your sugar there, Flannery?* Not that he had room to speak—with his double shot of the sweetened caramel flavoring in his own drink. But at least his was sugar-free.

"Oh—your flight—I forgot. . .you said you'd have to cut the meeting short to catch a flight. . . ." Even as the words tumbled out of his mouth, he cringed at his own discombobulation.

"Yes. So I should be the one asking what are *you* doing here." She stirred her latte, sipped it, nodded, and snapped the lid back on.

"I'm flying out to Utah to visit my mother."

"I assume this wasn't a planned trip." Flannery's short-sleeved, dark-blue sweater over a pinkish top with jeans gave her a comfortable, casual air that reminded Jamie of the first time he'd ever met her, at a cookout Cookie had dragged him to at the home of some of her friends last fall. The cookout at which Jamie had made his first great impression on Flannery by calling her Fanny. And then he'd done it again a week ago at the wedding rehearsal. Would he never stop messing up in front of her?

"No. It was sort of a. . .I–last minute decision." He might not be ready to talk to anyone else about it, but Flannery deserved an explanation. "Look, about this m–morning. . ."

Flannery set her cup down and looked at him with questions in her hazel eyes. She pushed her long, thick, blond braid over her shoulder. "I got your message. But Dustin had just arrived, so I couldn't answer your call."

Jamie thought a few very un-nice things about Dustin Aaronson—but regretted them when he looked across the table at the beautiful woman seated with him. Maybe not beautiful. Her pert nose and rounded chin kept her from being a true beauty. But not from bringing about a relapse of his stammer.

She would never think mean thoughts about someone.

"I should have told you. . . . Saturday night, I should have c—come clean and told you I'd been l—laid off. But I was kind of hoping to do this—maybe on my own. But I shouldn't have made you or Jack or Cole think I was still representing the Gregg Agency. Because I know that's why y'all agreed to m—meet with me."

Flannery sat there, looking regal and sipping her coffee for a long moment. "Yes, you probably should have told us that. I'm sorry you lost your job. I hope this didn't create any problems for you."

"Other than being called into Armando's office and made to sign a noncompete statement barring me from doing any work with Cole Samuels for at least six months or face being sued? Not really. I ended up not having to work the rest of today or tomorrow. But actually"—he tried to shift into cocky-grin mode—"that's not a bad thing. Because I'd been putting off all my month-end reports to do after the meeting with Cole. So it got me out of some tedious paperwork."

Flannery set her cup down on the table and toyed with the cardboard sleeve. "I can't help but think this is partially my fault."

She looked so forlorn, he wanted to reach across the table—not a long distance—and take her hand and offer her comfort. "No—why would you think that?"

"Because I'm the one who told the girl who answered the phone about our meeting with Cole the first time I called your office."

She'd told. . .but Ainslee wouldn't have. . .would she? Now he really wanted to check his e-mail. He tapped his fingertips against the cover of the netbook. "I don't think that had anything to do with it." *Liar.* "Even if that did play into it, it really didn't do anything other than show me that sports marketing probably isn't where I'm supposed to stay."

"What will you do now?"

He shrugged. "Go out to Utah and spend a few days with my mom and her family."

"Her family?"

"My stepdad and their kids."

"Wouldn't that make them your siblings?"

"Half. But they're both so much younger than me, and we've never lived together, so it's hard to think of them as related to me."

Flannery cocked her head. "You and your mom aren't close?"

He shrugged—less comfortable talking about his mom than what'd happened this morning. "After my dad died, she moved me into my grandmother's house and then left and traveled out West to 'find herself,' or something like that. She met Don, they got married, and she's lived out there with her new family ever since."

Flannery's eyes widened a bit more at each revelation of his past. "But you still saw her—at least for holidays, right?"

"Christmas, usually. But I think that was more Don feeling bad that Mom and I didn't get along very well." He pressed his lips together, thinking about the months before she'd left and the few times she'd come back before meeting and marrying Don. "We had a couple of really nasty fights, and when I was fifteen—right before she and Don got married—I told her I never wanted to talk to her again."

Jamie almost lost himself in the warmth of Flannery's gray-brown-green eyes. Only Cookie and Danny knew this much about him. Why was he telling this woman who, before today, had made it abundantly clear she didn't want anything to do with him?

"But you've reconciled since then?"

"Yeah. Don and Cookie—my grandmother—interceded and made us get together when I was in college. Ryan was a baby, and Mom had just found out she was pregnant with Chelsea. She flew back here, and Cookie invited me over without telling me Mom was at the house. Cookie swiped my car keys when I wasn't looking and took off, leaving me there with Mom. It was bad at first. We had a lot of stuff to work through. And we didn't get it all resolved right then. But it started us down a better path." He dragged his mind back from the past. "Mom's the one who made me start going to church again. I figured if she'd rediscovered her faith, anyone could, so I gave it a shot."

"And did it take?"

He shrugged again. "Sort of. I ended up at Christ Church because that's where all the people with money go, so it was good for my career. But I can't say I'm truly happy there."

"You should come visit Acklen Avenue someti—" Flannery's voice choked off, and she cleared her throat. "I'm sure if you visit around, you'll find a place you'll fit in."

Okay. . .he wasn't quite sure how to take that. "I'm sure I will."

She downed the last of her drink. "I think I interrupted you when I walked up. What were you working on?" She looked at the computer.

"Oh, not working. . .just. . ."

"Mr. O'Connor, I do believe you're blushing." The lilting giggle in Flannery's tone made his face burn even hotter.

He'd been honest with her about everything else so far, so why not with this? "You'll think I'm an absolute dork if I tell you."

She snorted a laugh—and turned bright red herself. "After the Dracula thing Saturday night, I don't *think* you're a dork, I already *know* you're a dork. So tell me."

"I was reading fan fiction."

Her smile faded. "Fan fiction?"

"Yeah, people who are fans of the King Arthur legends started up a website with community forums where people can chat about all the legends and books and movies. And it also has an area where people post stories they've written based on characters from the world."

Flannery's face had gone quite stiff. "Really? You read that kind of stuff?"

"Yeah. My favorite is the legend of Sir Gawain and Dame Ragnelle. There's someone on here who's doing a really good job re-imagining Ragnelle's story. . . ." Okay—he could tell from her freaked-out expression that he'd talked way too much already. "It's a hobby. It's not like I spend all my free time doing it. But there are some pretty good writers on there."

Flannery jumped and cocked her head to the side. "That's my flight they're calling." She stood and slung the straps of her purse and her carry-on bag over her shoulder. "I'm glad we had a chance to chat, Jamie." She picked up her empty cup and napkins.

He rose. "Me, too. Hope you have a good trip."

She nodded and backed away toward the exit. "You, too." She stuffed the cup and napkins into the trash, turned, and walked away, braid swinging down her back.

Jamie sank into his chair. He never should have told her. She'd looked at him like he'd turned into a troll right in front of her eyes. Which was exactly why, except for when a big blockbuster movie had come out and he and Danny had dressed up as their favorite knights to attend the 12:01 a.m. showing on opening day, he hadn't mentioned his affinity for the legend to a girl since middle school. For those few months around the time the movie came out, it had been cool to be a King Arthur fan. But that had faded quickly back to the realm of fanatics and weirdoes.

And frankly, if the anonymity of a made-up username hadn't protected his identity, he probably wouldn't have been participating in the online community.

That was something he needed this trip for—especially the hours of traveling today—to figure out which Jamie O'Connor he was: the guy with the expensive suits and the townhouse in the right part of town who attended church to be seen and network, or the guy who had a best friend with a shared interest in a fictional fantasy world who knew the real Jamie wasn't the suave, pulled-together guy he pretended to be.

He knew Flannery McNeill didn't like the first guy. And with her reaction to learning his hobby, he had a feeling she might not like the second. Would she like him if he became someone else completely different? Would he like himself better than he did now?

# Chapter 12

❧

"How do you do it?"

"Do what?" Jamie glanced at his brother and then followed Ryan's gaze to the woman in tight black leather pants who caught Jamie's eye and gave him a slow wink.

Ryan turned toward him, abject admiration on his face. "*That.* Make women flirt with you without even trying."

Jamie ran his hand over the seat of the low-slung, tricked-out motorcycle. If the bike didn't cost more than the first new car he'd bought back in college, he might do more than just drool over it. But with only three months' income guaranteed—his severance pay—and still no clue what kind of job he wanted, this impulse trip to Utah would be the last unbudgeted money he could spend.

He took another peek at the biker chick from the corner of his eye. Even though she seemed to be with a guy twice Jamie's size—in width, anyway—and dressed as if he spent a lot of time in a motorcycle showroom, she'd positioned herself so that she could watch Jamie. He raised his head, gave her a tight smile, and then turned his back toward her, not wanting any trouble.

"It's the not-trying part that's the secret." He settled his hand on Ryan's shoulder and led him toward the other end of the showroom. "You see, genetically, we've been blessed. Women are going to notice us." Could he sound like any more of an arrogant pig? "What I mean is that once we figure out how to look our best—which you've already got a handle on—women are going to look. And one thing I've learned they don't like is men who *know* they look good."

Ryan nodded, though his dark brows remained pinched together.

"And another thing I learned is that beautiful women aren't used to being ignored. They know they're beautiful, and they want men to admire them—so they can put us in our place by ignoring us. When we pay no attention to them, it makes them try harder."

"So I should ignore beautiful women, and they'll flirt with me?"

"*Ignore* may be too strong. Acknowledge, but leave it at that. It's the plain girls, the ones who never get attention—those are the ones you want to flirt with. Not only do they tend to be more the type you want to spend time with, but they're also less likely to cheat on you."

The words spewed out of Jamie's mouth like they came from someone else. Was that really what he did? Who he was? How he treated women? And would he be happy letting his little brother follow that advice?

If Flannery McNeill heard him say something like that. . .

"You know what? Forget what I just said. If you see a woman you like, talk to her. And when you do, just be yourself. Don't try to act like you're someone you're not. She may not like you in return, but at least you tried, right?" *And don't say anything about Dracula or King Arthur fan fiction. It freaks them out.* "Someday you'll run across one who likes you for who you are. I mean, look at Mom and Don."

Ryan seemed even more confused now than when Jamie had been spouting his sales pitch for flirting. But he nodded.

"Speaking of Mom. . ." Jamie pulled out his phone to check the time. "She's probably over at the restaurant waiting for me. Thanks for taking me hiking and hanging out with me this week, Bro."

"I wish you weren't going back to Tennessee tomorrow."

"We still have Chelsea's birthday dinner tonight." He cuffed his hand around Ryan's neck. "And I promise I'm going to try to get out here more often. After all, the skiing's nowhere near as good on the east side of the country as it is out here."

"You got that right." Ryan ducked out of his grasp and then gave Jamie a quick, one-armed hug. "Mom is going to drive you home, right?"

"Yeah. So go hang with your friends, and don't worry about me." Jamie squinted against the sun when they exited the store.

"Tell Mom I'll be home around four." Ryan slid mirrored aviator sunglasses down to cover his eyes—the same unusual dark-gray color as Jamie's and their mom's.

"I will." Jamie waited for the traffic on South State Street to clear before jogging across the thoroughfare to the Village Inn Restaurant.

Mom waved to him from a booth to his right. He gave a smile and a little wave to the hostess—who looked disappointed she didn't get to talk to him or seat him—and walked to the booth. He leaned over and kissed his mother on the cheek in greeting.

"Did you and Ryan have fun looking at motorcycles you'll never buy?" She clasped her hands atop her open menu and leaned forward as he slid into his seat.

"Motorcycles? I don't know what you're talking about. Ryan and I hiked Bell Canyon to the waterfall this morning." Jamie flipped open his menu, trying to keep a straight face.

Mom inclined her head to her left. Jamie looked out the bank of windows—which had a clear view of the motorcycle place across the street.

Busted. "We got done a little earlier than expected and just went in there to kill some time. He's a great kid. I'm sorry that I've missed out on so much of his life."

Mom pressed her lips together into a motherly smile. "I know that feeling." She reached over and squeezed his hand.

Their server arrived with drinks. A diet soda for Mom and...

"You remembered." Jamie took the glass of red juice from the server and tasted it. "Cranberry."

"I'm the one who got you hooked on the stuff as a kid. How could I forget?" Mom pushed her dark hair over her shoulder. Not the jet black he remembered from his childhood, but a softer dark brown that made her look a good ten to fifteen years younger than her real fifty-five.

Jamie studied the menu, debating between a couple of items. When the server returned, he made up his mind. "I'll have a cup of tomato-basil soup and a turkey sandwich, hold the mayo and cheese, with coleslaw instead of fries as my side."

Mom ordered a salad. They handed over their menus, and the server went away to put in their order. Jamie's stomach growled. Even though he'd filled up on a huge, protein-packed breakfast at the Black Bear Diner in Sandy before heading up into the canyon, the four-mile hike from the trailhead to the waterfall and back did a good job of burning it all off.

Mom reached over and took his hand again. "I'm really happy you decided to come out and spend the week. I'm sorry for the circumstances that made it possible, but I'm glad you're here."

"I'm glad I came, too. I don't know if it's losing my job, but everything seems different this time."

His mother's expression softened. "I think that's because you've changed. You're so much more relaxed this time. You're more. . .you." She gave his hand a squeeze and then released it. "I don't mean that in a bad way, just. . ."

"No, I know what you mean. It's like getting laid off has held a mirror in front of me and shown me that working in that place for so long changed me into someone I didn't recognize anymore." He'd told her and Don the basics of getting laid off, but she deserved to hear the whole story. And frankly, he needed to talk about it.

Their food arrived while he told her everything that'd happened, from finding out he was getting laid off to being asked to leave the building a week ago—including someone from Human Resources standing over him while he packed the few remaining items in his office to take home.

"It was humiliating," he said around a bite of sandwich, "but strangely satisfying."

Mom dipped her fork into the ramekin of salad dressing before spearing a cherry tomato and some lettuce. "I know you said your first night here that you aren't sure what you want to do. But now that you've had a week of rest and relaxation—and hiking and sightseeing—have you given it any more thought?"

Jamie wiped his mouth and took a swig of cranberry juice. "I'm not sure. I think I want to get out of the sales and marketing racket, though." He'd been wanting to ask her something all week, but the right opportunity had never presented itself. No time like the present. "Mom, I've kind of been"—he looked around and lowered his voice—"praying about it, and it feels like I'm getting an answer, but I'm just not sure."

Mom reached across the table and patted his cheek. "There's no shame in admitting that you've asked God's guidance, sweetheart. In fact, if I hadn't been sure you'd laugh at me, I'd have asked you if you'd prayed about it. I'm proud of you for doing so."

The heat in his cheeks from his admission of weakness—in not being able to make this decision on his own—receded. "Thanks."

"So what's this answer you think you're getting?" She took a dainty bite of greenery.

"Well, I'm not sure, because it's something. . .something I think D–dad would have told me wasn't the kind of c–career for a man." His whole body tensed just thinking about how his father would have reacted.

With a clatter of fork against plate, Mom also stiffened. She pressed her hands flat against the table on either side of her bowl. "Jamie, you know I loved your father. And I know you feel like you have to live up to his expectations for you. But, Son, you can honor your father better by doing what will make you happy, not what you think would fulfill some ideal you formed of what he wanted you to be when you were twelve years old."

Jamie set down the last corner of sandwich and reached for his glass, but regret and resentment clogged his throat.

"Your father was a good man. But you don't remember what it

was like to live with him as well as I do. He was a hard man to please, and he was almost never pleased with you. Do you realize that you start stammering again whenever you talk about him?" Mom's frown eased a bit. "Your grandmother warned me when I married your father that he had developed some strange notions of a man's place and a woman's place. Maureen said he hadn't been like that before he went to Vietnam, and that's not how he was raised. But Jamie, your father was wrong. He was wrong to pressure you to change; he was wrong not to accept who you were and let you do the things that interested you instead of what interested him."

She pressed her lips together for a moment, and her eyes turned glassy with unshed tears. "I bought you the knights- and castle-modeling kit you wanted for your birthday. Your father refused to let me give it to you, and he returned it to the store and came home with the workout set."

Jamie breathed slowly through his nose and tightened the muscles in his face, swallowing hard and blinking against the tears burning his eyes. "Why d–didn't you ever t–tell me?"

"Because the last thing I ever said to your father was that I wanted a divorce." Mom's chin quivered, and she wiped her nose with her napkin. "While you were in the living room with Danny and your other friends playing, I was in the kitchen telling my husband that I thought he was a horrible father and I wanted out—and I wanted to take you with me. And fifteen minutes later, he was dead."

Turning toward the window, Jamie held his breath against the remorse trying to erupt. "I always thought it was my fault. Because I never lived up to his expectations. Because he saw in my face how disappointed I was with that last gift." He sniffled, let out his breath, and turned to face his mother. "And I knew you blamed me for killing him, and that's why you left."

They really shouldn't be doing this in public. Mom's face twisted up in her effort to keep from crying. "No, Jamie. No. I never blamed you. I blamed myself. And every time I saw you, it was a reminder of what I'd done, what I'd said. I took your father away from you. And the way you acted toward me, as if you couldn't stand to look at me, I thought you knew. I thought you blamed me for your father's death. And I couldn't ruin a boy's memory of his father like that. So I left. It was the hardest thing I've ever done."

Jaw jutted forward and teeth clenched, Jamie reached across the table and took his mom's hands in his. He blinked, and two tears escaped and tracked down his cheeks. "We should have had this conversation a long time ago."

Mom chuckled through her sniffles. "We should have. I'm sorry. For everything."

"I'm sorry, too." He lifted her left hand and kissed the back of it, then sat back and wiped his eyes by rubbing them against the short sleeve of his T-shirt.

Mom pulled a compact out of her purse and dabbed at her eyes with the corner of her napkin. "So. . ." She gave her head a little shake and dialed up her megawatt smile. "As I was saying, what do you think you're going to do now?"

"I'm thinking about. . .you know how much I've always enjoyed going to the senior center with Cookie and helping out with the old folks?" He picked up his spoon and hovered it over the soup cup.

"Yes—you were always very good with both older people and little kids."

"I'm thinking I might want to do something with that. I'm thinking. . .about maybe going back to school for a nursing degree." Stirring the soup, he watched his mother's face for a reaction.

Her response was to smile even more broadly. "I think that would be wonderful. I've always seen you as someone in a more helping-oriented job."

Relieved, he put the spoon down and dipped the sandwich into the soup. "You don't think it's not manly enough?" He waggled his eyebrows to cover his self-consciousness.

"Sweetheart, following where God leads is the manliest thing you can ever do. Is this what you've been praying about? Nursing school?"

Shrugging, he took a bite and dunked the last remaining crust of bread in the little puddle in the bottom of the soup cup. "I guess so. Not specifically. I've just been sort of praying for God to show me what to do, and I keep thinking about nursing. Did you know Danny went back to school two years after we graduated from college and is a nurse now?"

"I know. He and Chae send us a Christmas card every year, and I occasionally exchange e-mails with him. But I didn't think you two had talked in a while." Mom picked up the receipt from the table. "Ready to go?"

He downed the last of his juice and slid out of the booth seat. "Ready." He followed her to the cashier stand and waited while she paid. After so many years on his own, it felt weird to let his mother pick up his lunch tab. But after a few meals out since arriving, he'd learned better than to argue.

"I guess you've talked about all this with Danny?"

Jamie held the door open for her, pulling his sunglasses down from the top of his head against the white-hot glare of the afternoon sun. "Some of it."

"You have the perfect opportunity to talk to someone who's made that choice. See if you can set up a time to shadow Danny at work. See if he'll introduce you to some of his teachers so you can talk to them."

Since she used the remote to unlock the doors of her luxury SUV, Jamie opened her door for her. "I'll do that."

Once she was in, he went around and climbed up into the passenger's seat.

"You know, there's something we haven't talked about at all since you've been here. And you're leaving tomorrow, so I'm not going to get another opportunity to ask." The vehicle beeped and lurched when Mom stomped the brake to keep from backing up into the car parked behind her.

Jamie released the overhead safety handle and finished fastening his seat belt as she put the SUV in DRIVE and headed out onto South State Street. "What's that?"

"Are you seeing anyone? Girlfriend? Possible girlfriend?" Tongue stuck between her teeth, she grinned at him. "A mother needs to know, dear."

An image of Flannery—not in the stunning black dress at the reception but in the sweater and jeans at the airport—popped into his mind.

"You're taking way too long to answer. There is someone, isn't there?"

"I. . .don't know. There's a woman I like—but every time I see her, I act like the biggest idiot in the world. I can't think straight when I'm around her. That hasn't happened to me since high school." Propping his elbow on the windowsill, he stared at the mountains in the distance.

"But you like her? You think she might be girlfriend material?"

He groaned. "I don't know. She's beautiful and smart. Tall. Blond. . ."

"What does she do?"

"She's an editor for a book publisher in Nashville. She's the one I was supposed to be with at the meeting on Thursday morning that got me kicked out of my job early." He leaned his head against the window. "I saw her at the airport that afternoon. It was kind of strange."

"Strange how?" Mom looked at him as she pulled to a stop at a light.

"She approached me. Asked to join me at the coffee shop. Always before, she's tried to avoid me—and I don't blame her. I can't seem to control what comes out of my mouth whenever she's in front of me. But we had a real conversation. And I didn't say anything stupid. . . until she asked what I'd been doing on the computer and I told her the truth."

Mom whipped her head around so fast her hair slapped against the seat's headrest. "What *were* you doing on the computer?"

He laughed at her aghast expression. "Nothing bad. I'd been about to log on to one of my King Arthur websites and read some fan fiction. That's what I told her. I had to explain what it was, and I think it freaked her out a little bit."

"Oh. . .well." She turned her attention back to the road. "What did she say to that?"

"Nothing—they called her flight for boarding, and she left. But I couldn't misread the expression on her face. I might as well have had *dork* tattooed across my forehead."

Mom reached across and tweaked his ear. "But you're such a cute dork. Maybe she's seeing the potential there."

He playfully swatted her hand away. "Right."

For the next few minutes, he let her concentrate on merging the giant vehicle into the quick-moving and heavy traffic on the interstate as she took them back toward the fabulous house in the foothills they'd recently finished building. Though he was slightly envious of its expansive luxury, his joy at seeing his mother so well taken care of far outweighed any jealousy he could feel.

"Jamie?"

"Yeah?"

"You know I'll support you in anything you want to do, right?"

Turning slightly in the seat, he studied her profile. Still a beautiful woman after all these years and everything she'd been through. "I know, Mom."

"And Don will, too. In fact"—she took a deep breath, glanced at him, and then returned her gaze to the road—"he asked me to tell you that if you want to move out here, he will make a job opening for you, and you can stay with us until you're ready to move on."

That catch in his throat came back. How had he never realized how fantastic his mom and stepdad—no, his *parents*—were?

"Work for a chain of high-end hair salons or go to nursing school? Hmm. . ." He tapped his index finger against his chin. But he couldn't joke away her offer. "Thanks, Mom. And I'll talk to Don when he gets home this evening. I'm glad to know I have a safety net if I need it."

But now figuring out if nursing school was the right direction or if he should pursue something else became even more important. Because with as much as he'd come to appreciate his immediate family over the past week, he couldn't imagine leaving Nashville.

Beauty parlors or nursing school. He could almost hear his father turning over in his grave.

# Chapter 13

❧

That's the plaza in Old Mesilla. At Christmastime they line all the buildings and sidewalks and the gazebo there in the middle with luminarias. That was one of the first dates Bobby and I had—we met at La Posta for dinner and then walked through the plaza after they'd lit all the candles. Obviously it looks a lot different in broad daylight in summer, but. . ." Zarah flipped to the next picture on the tablet computer she'd bought for Bobby as a wedding gift.

Flannery had a feeling that if Bobby ever wanted to use the device, he was going to have to buy Zarah one of her own. If she hadn't known she'd have a ton of work to do while in Chicago, she would have left her laptop at home and taken only her tablet with her. As it turned out, having both devices with her came in handy, as the tablet was a lot easier to carry around the warehouses and printing press areas of the vendors she'd visited—as well as being an unobtrusive way to take notes during the fifteen-minute appointments she'd had with wannabe authors for each of the three days she'd been at the conference. A few of the writers' pitches had intrigued her. She needed to remember to let Brittany know that there might be some manuscripts coming in that they'd need one of their readers to take.

She pulled out her phone—under the table—and sent a quick message to her assistant to get on that tomorrow. Then, stifling a yawn, she holstered the phone and leaned in toward Caylor to look at the pictures of the resort where Zarah and Bobby had spent the last part of their honeymoon.

"I know—this is more interesting to me than to you." Anyone else would have said it in a sarcastic tone. Not Zarah. She actually meant it.

Guilt plagued Flannery. "I'm so sorry. I love the pictures—it's making me rethink my decision not to go to teach at the writers' conference at Glorieta this fall. I'm not bored—I just didn't have a chance to get the nap I'd hoped for this morning, especially after never going to bed last night."

"Big party at the conference?" Caylor's blue-green eyes glimmered with the knowledge of having attended many writers' conferences herself.

"No, just hanging out with a few of my authors and some other editors and agents. You know how it is. . .once we get to talking, it's hard to stop. Especially when we all think we'll be able to catch up on sleep the next day." She yawned again, clapping both hands over her mouth. "Sorry—I'm going to get another Monkey Mocha. Don't look at any of the rest of the pictures without me."

She wended through the closely spaced tables—each packed with the twenty- and thirtysomethings who called the 12 South area of Nashville home and treated the Frothy Monkey coffeehouse like their living room—and approached the counter. The hippy-looking guy staring at the menu board didn't seem to be making up his mind anytime soon, so Flannery ducked in front of him.

A few minutes later, stifling another yawn, she sipped the cocoa-and-banana-flavored, espresso-heavy drink and made her way back to the table.

It didn't take long for Zarah to get through the rest of the pictures—of Albuquerque and Santa Fe and the mountains where they'd gone hiking. And Bobby seemed to have had no qualms about asking others to take pictures of them, as at least half of the photos featured both of them.

"Flan, did you bring any pictures to show?" Zarah turned off the tablet and returned it to her large purse.

"Y'all wouldn't be interested—mostly I took pictures for work of the warehouses and printing presses. And I'm sure you'll see all of the tagged photos of me online as people get home and upload everything from the conference. Oh, but I did get my bridesmaid dress back from the tailor in time to take it with me, and I wore it at the banquet the last night." She pulled out her phone and found the picture she'd had a colleague snap of her in the now just-above-the-knee black dress.

"Oh, wow—it looks even better as a cocktail-length dress than floor length." Zarah handed the phone back to her. "I'm glad we were able to find something that y'all could use elsewhere."

"Speaking of finding dresses. . ." Caylor's face went as red as her hair.

"What?" Flannery grabbed Caylor's wrist.

"Don't tell me, you've set a date?" Zarah clapped her hands together and then held them up in front of her mouth.

"Actually. . .yes. Sunday, after your wedding, Zare, Dylan came over to swim, and we decided that if we didn't want to wait until next year, we should go ahead and plan something small for this summer before school starts. And since my parents will be coming in from Geneva for Sassy's birthday at the end of July, we've decided to get married the last weekend in July." Caylor reached out and took Zarah's and Flannery's hands in hers. "He's already asked his brothers to stand up with him. Will the two of you stand up with me? Sage has already agreed, but I can't do this without the two of you, also."

Flannery's heart thudded a slow dirge. "I agree on one condition."

Caylor's forehead creased with her frown. "What's that?"

"That your sister is your maid of honor and that I'm just a bridesmaid." Both of Flannery's sisters had chosen a friend as their maid of honor over their own sisters, and Flannery didn't want to do that to Sage.

"I agree." Zarah nodded. "Sage should be your maid of honor. I know you two haven't always been close, but it would probably go a long way in healing your relationship to pick her over us."

Caylor looked between the two of them and then shrugged. "Okay. But I'm going to be counting on the two of you to help Dylan plan everything, because I know Sage will flake out."

"Help Dylan plan?" Flannery looked at Zarah, and then they both gaped at Caylor.

"Oh yeah, I didn't tell you that part. Dylan decided that since he can't contribute financially to the wedding, and because I have a book due in August, he's going to plan the whole thing. I agreed with the condition that if he gets stuck or needs help with anything, he's to call the two of you." She cocked her head and looked toward the ceiling. "And I just pray that his mother doesn't decide to try to take over."

At the thought of Dylan's mother—who'd made quite a spectacle of herself and her family in her bid for a state senate seat a few months ago—taking over the wedding, Flannery shuddered. "Don't worry. Zarah and I will make ourselves available to help with anything Dylan needs."

"So, tell us what you're planning."

At Zarah's request, Caylor launched into a detailed description of what she and Dylan had already decided for their midmorning outdoor wedding at the home of Dylan's grandparents. Flannery tried to pay attention; but exhaustion short-circuited her focus, and her mind wandered.

The conference. Work. Personal projects. More work. Printers' proposals. An unacceptable manuscript from one of her longtime authors. Traveling. Jamie O'Connor.

She shook her head. Where had that come from? She'd been trying not to think about the conversation they'd had at the airport. Mostly because it had been one of the most confusing encounters she'd ever had.

After a few meetings, she'd thought she had him pegged. Arrogant. Condescending. Creepy. But sitting there listening to him talk about his job and his family. . .she'd seen a whole different side to him. One that made her even more sympathetic toward him. One that scared her a little bit—because *that* Jamie O'Connor was someone she might actually like.

But she'd already made up her mind about him. He was one of those guys who was too good looking for her peace of mind. She needed to keep disliking him. Otherwise, she was in for a world of hurt—because she could very easily fall for him.

Of course, then there was the whole Sir Gawain and Dame Ragnelle thing.

"Flannery, do you think you will?"

She blinked a couple of times to bring her attention back into focus. "Will what?"

"See, I told you she wasn't paying attention." Zarah's brows raised, and she ducked her chin and gave Flannery a pitying smile.

Caylor sighed, but she looked more amused than put out. "I asked if you think you'll bring a date to the wedding. Right now, you and Zarah and Bobby are the only people outside of our families we'll be inviting."

Attend the wedding alone? Absolutely not—they'd spend the whole day trying to match her up with one of Dylan's younger brothers. "I might bring a date. If I can't find anyone else, Jack will always do in a pinch."

The ultracute blush that crept across Jamie's cheeks when she'd asked him what he'd been reading on the computer came back into clear view in her mind's eye. She'd always sworn she wouldn't fall for a good-looking guy but one who was more on the geeky side.

Did both possibly exist in the same man?

❧

Jamie patted the soil around the base of the last tomato plant and sat back on his haunches to survey the garden. Not a bad day's work, if he did say so himself. He enjoyed the benefits of Cookie's garden—tomatoes, carrots, squash, cucumbers, and roasted pumpkin seeds later on in the fall, pretty much the only vegetables he ever ate besides mushrooms, sweet potatoes, and white potatoes—so the least he could do was help her with the hardest part after she got each plant started.

"Are you finished?" Cookie called from a couple of rows over.

"Finished. You?" He rose and made his way to the squash row, dumping the remaining half bag of topsoil into the wheelbarrow beside her.

She spaded a bit more soil onto the base of the sixth and final squash plant. "Finished." She reached her hand toward him, and Jamie helped her to her feet. "Hopefully waiting this long to transfer everything to the ground won't adversely affect the yield. We just had such a stormy, cool spring that I didn't want to risk losing any of them by planting too early."

Jamie pushed the wheelbarrow back to the potting shed and laid a piece of plastic over it. After the first good, hard rain—forecast for later this week—they'd probably need to add the rest of this to replace what would be washed away.

"What are your plans for tonight?" Cookie removed her gardening gloves and set them on the high, heavy wooden table alongside stacks of empty plastic planters.

"Don't really have any. Figured I'd go home, take a shower, and eat some leftovers and watch one of the DVDs I got in the mail this week." The movie-rental subscription was just one item on a long list of things he would have to give up at the end of June if he still hadn't figured out what he wanted to do—and if he decided to go back to school, he'd definitely be giving up a lot of the things he now enjoyed, including the expansive (and expensive) digital cable service and the tendency to order delivery or pick-up takeout whenever he felt like it.

"Since you're thinking about changing churches, I thought you might like to try Acklen Avenue's Bible study for the young professionals' group tonight. It's my understanding that it's the group that includes the younger singles in the church, so those would be the ones you'd want to meet anyway."

"Younger? How young?" His experience with the "young adult" group at his church made him feel like an out-of-place old man—given that everyone in the group was college or graduate-school age. When he'd started getting strange looks from the older married couples who taught and volunteered with the group for being a good ten years older than anyone else in the class—especially the females—he'd stopped attending.

"Oh, I think you'd fit right in. Some of my friends have grand-children around your age who are involved in the singles' ministry, so I'm certain you'll fit right in."

Some of her friends. . .like Kirby McNeill? Jamie couldn't pass up an opportunity of having another good encounter with Flannery. "What time does it start?"

"Six." She looked at her watch. "So you'd better get a move on if you want to go home and shower and change clothes. Which you should." She wrinkled her nose at him.

He tossed his work gloves onto the table beside hers, kissed her on the cheek, and started across the yard to the gate. "See you later this week, Cookie."

"Have fun!"

Once home and in the shower, Jamie had second thoughts about attending the Bible study. But he'd promised Mom and Don he'd find a church where he could "plug in," as they put it. And Flannery had sort of invited him. . .before she thought better of it.

He'd go. And if Flannery gave him a hard time—or made it obvious she wanted to avoid him—that would be his sign as to whether or not to visit on a Sunday morning.

The drive to Acklen Avenue Fellowship took fifteen minutes—three times as long as his drive to Christ Church. He parked behind the imposing red-brick building and sat in the car for a few minutes. Several people who looked young adultish entered not the brick building but the modern glass-and-concrete building across a small courtyard from it.

He grabbed the slim, gray leather Bible from the passenger seat, checked his appearance in the rearview mirror—ugh, he needed a haircut—and followed two guys into the newer building. He waited behind them at the table set up at the end of the hallway that led into a large community center.

Once they walked away, he stepped up to the table. The young woman—emphasis on *young*—greeted him with a toothpaste-commercial smile. "Hey. I'm Cindi." He could tell by the way she said it she spelled it with an *i* on the end. "Is there something I can help you find?"

"I...uh..." He glanced into the large room beyond her, uncertainty eating at him. "I'm looking for the singles' Bible study."

"The *singles'* Bible study? I didn't know they had one."

Jamie inclined his head toward the people milling about in the community center. "What's this, then?"

"This is the young professionals' Bible study."

More confused now, Jamie shook his head. "What's the difference between singles and young professionals?"

"The young professionals' group is for unmarrieds, almost-marrieds, and newly marrieds between the ages of eighteen and thirty. The *singles'* group"—her nose wrinkled up at the word—"is for the older people who still aren't married yet—and maybe some who are divorced, but there's a divorce-care class, too."

Of course. Jamie sighed. "So you don't know if the singles' group has a Bible study or not?"

"They have a Sunday school class between the early service and the regular service. But I don't know if they do anything else." She cocked her head and her tone clearly indicated that anyone *that old* should probably be home eating rice pudding and having someone change their adult diapers for them.

"Okay. Well...thanks." So much for that idea. He returned to the car, never having felt as old or unwanted as he did at the moment.

And then he did exactly what he told Cookie he'd planned on doing: he went home, reheated some chicken curry—an experiment of Cookie's from a heart-health cookbook that turned out quite good—and put in a movie.

Before going to bed, he stood staring at himself in the mirror for a long time. When had those hairs in his sideburns and at his temples started turning gray? He forced a smile. Yep, he knew for certain those wrinkles hadn't been there last time he'd looked at himself. And he had some serious dark circles under his eyes.

No wonder Cindi had instantly pegged him for someone who didn't fit the description *young professional*. Not only did he no longer have a profession, but he definitely didn't look young.

He reached over and turned off the bathroom light, throwing himself into silhouette, with the bedside lamp casting a glow on the door behind him.

Needing something to settle his mind so that he might get some sleep, he propped a couple of pillows up against the headboard and sat in the bed with the netbook. Maybe his favorite fan-fiction author had posted something new.

Of course, every time he pulled up the site—or even thought about it—Flannery's look of distaste made him regret telling her about it. But even that wasn't enough to keep him from going to it.

Nope—no new post from his favorite writer. He thought about sending a note but decided instead to go back and read everything this writer had posted. She—he assumed it was a she, since her username, LadyNelle, was female—was posting a continuing story in installments. Ragnelle's backstory was that she was the hag who tricked King Arthur into making Sir Gawain marry her. Then in true Arthurian style, Gawain, through honor and integrity, managed to break the spell on Ragnelle and return her to the beautiful woman she was by giving her what she wanted—independence and the right to make her own choices. Jamie loved LadyNelle's take on the character— making her a strong, independent woman who seemed to be someone from a medieval culture and not just a modern woman written into the pseudo-historical setting. He also loved that the richness of the writer's description and history of the land of the misty other-times of England—not truly historical but not truly fantasy—added to the lore of his favorite legend instead of trying to change it to fit her own preferences. He also liked the fact that she added a spirituality to her version of the characters that wasn't in many of the stories.

The way this Ragnelle was written—unlike every other fan-fiction version of her he'd ever read—made Jamie truly believe her worthy of marrying his favorite character.

By the time he reached the most recent installment, his eyes drooped and he kept reading the same paragraph over and over. Giving up, he turned the computer off and set it on the nightstand.

He reached up to turn off the lamp and came to a sudden decision. Starting tomorrow, he was going to stop shaving until he got a job or enrolled in school, whichever came first. His last conscious thought before falling asleep was to pray that if God wanted him to go to nursing school, He'd show Jamie by sending him a job he could do part time or that he could work around his school schedule—because if he did go back to school, he wanted to get through it as quickly as possible.

Mom said to pray specifically, and he couldn't get much more specific than that.

# Chapter 14

$B$eing chased through the halls of the Gregg Agency wasn't the best way to start a Monday morning.

Jamie rolled over onto his back, heart pounding from the very realistic dream. He hadn't known what was chasing him, but he was pretty sure he didn't want to encounter it again.

He stared at the tray ceiling above his bed. Today was the first day of his laid-off life.

He could stay in bed all day if he wanted to.

He could get started on that long list of things he needed to do around the house.

He could have an all-day marathon of watching the extended editions of every single movie he owned that had anything to do with the legend of King Arthur.

He could start rewatching some of the TV shows he owned on DVD.

He could get his lazy carcass out of bed, take his computer, go someplace where he'd be around people, and start scouring the Internet for a job—and for information about nursing programs in the area.

Yep—he couldn't let himself fall into bad habits. He climbed out of bed—and turned around and straightened up the covers for the first time in ages, because he wasn't in a rush to get anywhere—and dressed in a T-shirt, shorts, and running shoes.

The mugginess of the morning air made him stop running after six miles. Ugh. First week of June and already shaping up to be a miserable summer.

Twenty minutes later, showered and dressed, he ran his knuckles over his jaw, happy with his decision not to shave for the time being. He'd never grown a beard—he had done the goatee thing about ten years ago but never a full-on beard. Maybe he'd like it. The goatee had taken way too much maintenance, and he'd shaved it off after a few weeks.

He'd just taken the Armory Drive Exit off I-65 when his phone rang. He didn't recognize the local number that showed up. Rather than answer it while trying to navigate the exit, he let it roll to voice mail. As soon as he parked in the Panera parking lot, he dialed in to listen to the message.

"Hello, Jamie. Shandi Patel from Lindsley House Publishing." The mellow-voiced woman had a slight accent—British, maybe? "I'm the marketing director, and your name was given to me as someone who might be interested in doing some freelance publicity work for us. We have some upcoming sports-related nonfiction titles that we'd like to talk to you about. We need to start moving on these pretty soon, so I'd love it if we can meet today or tomorrow—or sometime this week." She left her number—Jamie played back the message three times before he found a scrap of paper and a pen to write it down.

He punched the number in, but before he hit the button to put the call through, he took a deep breath and looked up—his gaze only going so far as the car's black fabric liner, but his spirit rising much further than that. Was this God's way of answering his prayer for a job he could fit in around a class schedule?

The phone rang twice and then, "Marketing, Shandi speaking."

"Shandi, hi, this is Jamie O'Connor. I understand you'd like to talk to me about some publicity work and that you'd like to do it soon. Does this afternoon still work for you?"

"Thank you for calling me back so promptly. I can see you...at two, if that works with your schedule."

Jamie looked at his watch. Almost ten o'clock now. "I should be able to make it at two."

"You know where we're located?"

"I do. Should I ask for you at the front?"

"Yes. Also, could you bring your résumé with you? And I'll need to have you fill out paperwork so that we can pay you, so you'll need your social security number. I know most people have it memorized, but I've learned over the years not to expect that."

"Certainly. I understand."

"Good. I'll see you at two, then."

After getting off the phone, Jamie went in to the restaurant, ordered a ham-egg-and-cheese sandwich on whole-grain bread and a large coffee for breakfast, then sat down to work on updating his résumé, something he hadn't done in ten years. There'd been no point since he hadn't dreamed of leaving his job.

It took two refills of the large cup of coffee to get his résumé updated to the point where he felt it adequately reflected everything he'd accomplished at the Gregg Agency but didn't take up more than two pages.

Getting a steak salad to go, Jamie headed home to get ready for his. . .what was it? Not really a job interview because it wasn't a job and he wasn't being interviewed—or at least Shandi made it sound like the freelance work was his if he wanted it.

After eating lunch, he dressed in a nice pair of gray trousers and a button-down blue shirt and then scrutinized himself in the mirror.

He *really* needed a haircut. But no time for that now. He rasped his fingers along his cheek. His whiskers halfway between stubble and scruff, he considered shaving for a moment. But no, he'd made the decision to grow the beard until he knew for certain what he'd be doing. If Shandi didn't give him the work because she didn't like the fact he wasn't clean shaven, then this wasn't meant to be.

He e-mailed his updated résumé to himself on the netbook and turned on his desktop computer, where he pulled up the e-mail and downloaded the attachment so he could print it. The big computer hadn't been used since before his trip to Utah, so he left it turned on and downloading updates while he drove a few miles east to the Maryland Farms business park. One thing was sure—if they wanted him to work out of their offices, he'd have a short commute.

All of the visitor spots near the building were taken, so he had to park in the far end of the lot, which wouldn't have been too bad except for the sweltering heat that seemed to have followed him home from Utah.

When he exited the elevator on the fourth floor, he paused. Across the hall directly in front of him were two glass doors, into which was etched LINDSLEY HOUSE PUBLISHING. He reached up to straighten his tie—and remembered he wasn't wearing one when he touched the open top button of his shirt.

He tucked his leather padfolio into the crook of his arm and pulled the right-hand door open.

A young man sat at the front desk, wearing a headset hooked into a large phone console. He held up one finger and smiled at Jamie.

"Just a moment, sir. I'll connect you." He punched a button, dialed four numbers, punched another button, and then pushed the microphone away from his mouth and looked up at Jamie. "Welcome to Lindsley House Publishing. How may I help you?"

"I'm here to see Shandi Patel. I'm Jamie O'Connor."

"Let me call her for you." He pulled the microphone down and dialed a four-digit extension. "Ms. Patel, Mr. O'Connor is here to see you." He punched another button and looked at Jamie again. "Ms. Patel will be with you momentarily. Please, have a seat or feel free to look around at the displays."

The open-front cases with glass shelves had caught Jamie's attention, so he gladly stepped away from the reception desk to survey the products—mostly books, but a few games and children's toys—on display.

He picked up *Courage and Comfort for the High School Athlete* and flipped through the gift book, packed with inspirational quotes from sports stars and coaches throughout the ages. He flipped open his pad and wrote down the title, wanting a copy for himself.

"Jamie?"

He set the book back on the shelf and turned. A Middle Eastern or maybe Indian woman stepped toward him, right hand extended. He shook it. "Jamie O'Connor."

"Shandi Patel." With a broad gesture, she waved him toward the archway. "This way."

For some reason he was surprised to enter a large room filled with cubicles. Why had he assumed everyone who worked at a publishing house would have a private office?

He followed Shandi out of the main room and into a hallway made up of tall cubicle walls on one side and the offices he'd expected on the other. The cubicles here opened up directly across from each office. They turned a corner at the end of the hall and—

"Jamie." Jack Colby stopped and shifted the box he carried under his left arm.

Jamie shook hands with the associate publisher. "Jack. Good to see you. I guess I have you to thank for this."

Frowning, Jack shifted the box back in front of him. "For what?"

Jamie inclined his head toward Shandi. "For offering my services to Shandi for freelance marketing work."

"Really? I mean, if I'd have thought of it, I would have done that for you. But. . ." Jack's expression went from consternated to amused in a heartbeat. "I think the person you should be thanking is Flannery, not me."

Seriously? "Oh. Well, I'll be sure to try to find her after we're finished. Thanks, Jack."

"I'll send her your way if I see her." Jack continued on around the corner, and Shandi led Jamie to her office.

It wasn't huge but at least as big and well appointed as his at Gregg had been. He sat in a tapestry-covered guest chair and set his pad on the desk while Shandi settled into her chair.

"Here's my résumé, as you asked."

"And here's the W-9 form for you to fill out. Just the fields I've highlighted."

Jamie pulled his pad onto his lap, opened it, and set to work filling out the Request for Taxpayer Identification Number and Certification while Shandi perused his résumé. Since the form only required his name, address, social security number, and signature, it didn't take him long.

Shandi put the W-9 form and the résumé into a folder. "I'm really glad to see you have both experience working with the media as well as in coordinating onsite events." She showed him the existing marketing materials for the four books she wanted his help with—what looked like standard forms and catalogs that went out to booksellers, a press release for each title, as well as some marketing and advertising text that had already been written.

Jamie offered some suggestions. Shandi added some comments. Two hours later, they'd come up with full-blown publicity plans for two of the four titles. Jamie would gladly have kept going, but Shandi's phone rang.

She looked at the phone. "That's a conference call I've been waiting for." Hand hovering over the receiver, she gave him an apologetic look. "Call me first thing in the morning, and we'll talk about everything else—including how you're going to get paid for this. Can you find your way out?"

He nodded. "Talk to you tomorrow."

She answered the phone, and he let himself out of her office, pulling the door closed softly behind him. If he turned left and followed the hallway, he'd be back at the front office. But he hadn't seen Flannery's name etched into any of the windows beside the doors of the offices he'd passed on his way here. So if he turned right, he should find her office.

He couldn't leave without thanking her. To be honest, he couldn't be this close to her without attempting to see her—to see if their somewhat-normal conversation at the airport had been a fluke or if it could happen again.

He followed the hallway, reading the names on each window. The office at the end of this hallway was Jack's—but he wasn't in. Jamie turned left and continued reading names until he came to the last office before the big open room again. And—yes, success! Flannery McNeill's office.

Raising his hand, prepared to knock on the open door, he looked in. She wasn't at her desk.

"Can I help you with something?" A very young woman with bright-blond streaks in her brown hair stepped out of the cubicle directly across from Flannery's office.

"I'm looking for Flannery McNeill." He nodded his head toward her office. "Do you know where she is?"

"She's in a Publishing Committee meeting for the rest of the afternoon. I'm Brittany Wilmette, Flannery's editorial assistant. Is there something I can help you with?" The way her eyes bored into him told him she *really* wanted to help him. . .with *anything*.

"It's personal. Can I leave her a note?"

"Oh, sure. There should be some paper or sticky notes on her desk, if you want to do that." She waved her hand toward the office.

He walked in—and was suddenly overwhelmed by a side of Flannery he'd never guessed at, though he probably should have. Framed photos and posters of Irish landmarks hung on the two walls that weren't dominated by dark-wood bookshelves. Displayed on those shelves in and amongst the books were Irish-themed trinkets and souvenirs. Leprechauns and four-leaf clovers. Small, cut-crystal bowls and cups filled with what looked like green-and-gold Mardi Gras beads.

A photo of Flannery, Caylor, and Zarah—all looking much younger—pretending to kiss the Blarney Stone hung over the return wing of Flannery's desk. The closer he looked, the more he noticed Flannery and/or Caylor and Zarah in most of the photos.

So, Ireland wasn't just a dream for her. She'd actually been—though it appeared it had been quite some time ago.

He sat at her desk and picked up a sticky-note pad. He thought for a moment before writing. What could he say that would truly express his gratefulness?

Seeing a felt-tipped pen in the cup bearing the publishing house's logo, he pulled it out and wrote the note, which he pulled off and stuck to her computer screen, just to make sure she'd see it when she got back to her office.

He stood to go—and then stopped, one of the hangings on the wall opposite her desk catching his attention.

It looked like something from medieval Ireland—a colorized print of an old woodcut image of a knight kneeling before an old hag under a tree. It blended in quite well with all of the other Irish-themed items with the greens and golds predominant in the coloring. But Jamie recognized it for what it was. And it made him question everything he'd ever thought about Flannery McNeill.

❧

Flannery rubbed her neck and almost lost her balance, catching herself on the doorjamb to keep from stumbling. She dumped the large stack of proposals into her in-basket and dropped into her chair. These meetings should be required to end by five o'clock. She'd only had four new items to pitch to the board today—and they'd wanted to nit-pick the minutia out of every single one. All she wanted to do was go home and sleep. After not sleeping Saturday night, she'd made the mistake of checking her work e-mail account at home last night when she got home from Vespers and All That Jazz at the Scarritt-Bennett Center. It had been after two before she'd finally given up and gone to bed—only to be back up at six to get ready so she could be at work early this morning to try to handle what she hadn't gotten to last night.

Speaking of e-mail. . .

She turned toward the computer. Oh, a note. Must be from Britt—but no, that wasn't Britt's handwriting. She rubbed her eyes from underneath, careful not to smudge her mascara. She pulled the note off the computer screen:

> *Thank you.*
> *Jamie*

Smiling for the first time in hours, Flannery bent to put the note in the trash. . .then changed her mind. She stuck it to the top right corner of her blotter.

Looking up at the wall across from her desk, she froze. Had Jamie been in her office?

Did it matter? She tried to tell herself it didn't. She once again turned toward the computer to check to see if anything needed to be addressed tonight or if it could all wait until tomorrow.

No—it couldn't wait. It did matter. She pulled out her cell phone and found Brittany's home number. She hated bugging the girl at home, but she had to know.

"Hey, Flannery—what's up? How was the Pub. Co. meeting?"

"Long. I hate to bother you at home, Britt, but I need to ask you something. Did you see a guy come by my office this afternoon while I was in that meeting?"

"Yeah—he was kind of wandering the hall, so I asked him if I could help him. He said he wanted to see you, but I told him you were in a meeting. So he asked if he could write you a note."

"So. . .did he write it and give it to you and you're the one who stuck it on my computer screen?" *Please let that be what happened.*

"No." Worry crept into Brittany's voice. "I told him he could go in your office to write the note. Was that wrong?"

She should never have called Brittany just to worry her about nothing. "No, Britt, it's perfectly okay. I just wondered. . .never mind. I'll see you tomorrow."

"I have a dentist appointment first thing, so it'll be nine thirty or ten before I get there."

Flannery wrote herself a note to that effect and then let the assistant go, guilty over having distressed the girl in her off hours.

She stared at the wall across from her desk, letting her gaze rove over all of the items hanging there. Photos and posters and tourist brochures from the trip she and Zarah had taken to Ireland when Caylor was in graduate school there. That trip had been when Flannery first accepted her overly Irish name and decided to embrace it by displaying the collectibles and souvenirs she'd brought back with her, first in her cubicle and then in the offices she'd had in the ensuing years.

One item, even though it seemed to fit in, was definitely not like the others. Her gaze came to rest on the framed, colorized woodcut print. Ten inches square, it wasn't easy to miss. But maybe he hadn't noticed it. Or if he had, maybe he hadn't realized what it was—that it wasn't something she'd brought back from Ireland or something someone had given her because it looked Irish.

She'd cling to that hope, but it was a fragile thread. Because if Jamie was enough of a fan of the legend of Sir Gawain and Dame Ragnelle to read the fan fiction, he'd probably seen the few pieces of classic art inspired by the story. And if so, he'd probably recognized the print and its subject matter.

Folding her arms on her desk, she buried her face. After all these years of keeping it secret, was her love of Sir Gawain and Dame Ragnelle about to become fodder for public ridicule once again?

# Chapter 15

◦∞◦

 "Who are you looking for, Cookie?"

"Who?—I—no one in particular." Maureen stopped craning her neck to watch the doors at the back of the sanctuary. No sense rousing her grandson's curiosity further. After all, she'd met Kirby McNeill only four weeks ago. But his absence last week, even though she'd been prepared for it, had made her long to see him even more. How would she explain that to Jamie when she hardly understood how she felt? She was too old to have an infatuation—a crush—on anyone. "Tell me more about this contract work you're doing for the publishing house."

Jamie obliged, and Maureen tried to pay attention. But with her lack of knowledge of marketing or publishing and her desire to see Kirby McNeill as soon as he walked in, she only listened with half an ear.

The organist started the prelude. One thing the older members of the church had insisted upon when the plans for the new sanctuary had been drawn up twelve years ago was that the pipe organ from the old sanctuary would be kept and integrated into this modern space with its screens and stage lights and theater-style seats.

She did have to admit that she appreciated the well-cushioned seats over the wooden pews and their thin seat pads that slipped around whenever one sat or stood. But she came to the early service so that she didn't have to listen to the raucous music they used in the eleven o'clock service, which many of her friends—and most of the young people—attended. But Jamie wouldn't hear of visiting her church and not attending with her.

She looked around toward the back of the sanctuary again.

"Okay, now I know you're looking for someone." Jamie crossed his arms.

"Don't do that; you'll crease your suit coat." She'd tried to tell him that none of the young men wore suits to church. But his argument that if he went to nursing school he might not ever have the opportunity to wear his expensive suits again made sense. Besides, he looked even more handsome than usual in charcoal gray—the same color as his eyes.

Jamie cocked an eyebrow at her but uncrossed his arms. "Who're you looking for, Cookie?"

"I just want to make sure I don't miss seeing anyone I should talk to after service, that's all." She patted his knee.

She was fairly sure she'd mentioned to Kirby that she attended the early service. But come to think of it, his granddaughter almost certainly attended the late service with the rest of the young people—the young professionals or the singles or whatever they were called. Jamie hadn't really been able to make sense of it for her after his failed attempt to attend the Bible study last Sunday evening.

Settling into her seat, she turned her attention toward preparing for worship by listening to the classically styled rendition of "Sweet Hour of Prayer" the organist played. If Kirby came to this service, fine. If not, fine. She'd see him in Sunday school in between and would content herself with that.

The choir entered the loft, and the medium-sized crowd quieted. They had just started the call to worship when something brushed against Maureen's left elbow. She glanced in that direction.

Kirby pushed the seat bottom down and sat. "I hope you don't mind if I join you," he whispered.

"Not at all." Maureen pursed her lips to keep the smile that wanted

153

to escape from exploding on her face.

Jamie leaned forward just a bit and looked around her. With a questioning look at her, he straightened and looked down at his order of service, but not before she caught a hint of a smile.

Let her nosy grandson think what he would.

When the music director turned and enjoined the congregation to stand for the first hymn, Kirby glanced around. "No hymnals?"

Maureen waved toward the front and the large projection screens on either side of the stage area. The organ began the introduction, and the music appeared on the screen—not just the words, as they did in the later service, but the actual staffs with notes on them above and below the words. "It's something we old-timers insisted on when they told us these seats wouldn't have anywhere to hold the hymnals."

"I've never seen that before."

"It took awhile for the music minister to figure it out, but it works wonderfully now. I don't even have to put my reading glasses on for the singing portion of the service anymore." Just standing beside Kirby McNeill gave her a thrill. He was so tall and so. . .sturdy looking. Not heavy, but large, thick. Like the old hickory tree in her backyard. Old Hickory. The epithet seemed to suit Kirby McNeill much better than it did President Andrew Jackson, for whom the Old Hickory suburb of Nashville and many streets in the area were named.

And when he sang. . .an assured, confident bass. She added her tremulous alto, and he smiled down at her, encouraging her to inject more energy to her singing. To her right, Jamie sang along with the melody, his voice clear and strong.

Joy clogged her throat and made it hard to breathe. She blinked back excess moisture. *Dear Father, if I could have this—standing between these two men, worshipping You—for what few years I have remaining, I will die a very happy woman.*

The sermon, about Esther and the Jewish feast of Purim, was interesting but not moving—especially for someone whose focus flitted between the sermon and everything the men on either side of her did.

Kirby took notes—not writing down everything the pastor said, just a few things here and there. Jamie braced his elbows on the armrests of his seat and leaned forward just a bit, frowning in concentration as if trying to memorize the preacher's every word.

Even after the invitation and closing hymn, Jamie's frown remained. But he released it when he turned to greet Kirby.

"Mr. McNeill, it's nice to see you again."

"And you, Jamie."

"Sir, do you have a granddaughter named Flannery?"

Kirby's gray-green eyes twinkled—making Maureen's insides quiver, which hadn't happened since she and James were courting more than sixty-five years ago.

"I can very proudly claim Flannery as my granddaughter. Do you know her?"

An odd expression came over Jamie's face. "I do—but not as well as I used to think."

"Will you be okay trying to find your Sunday school class on your own?" Maureen asked, ready to have Kirby to herself, even if just for the few moments it took them to get to the senior adult Sunday school room.

"I'll be fine, Cookie." He kissed her on the cheek. "You be good, now," he whispered in her ear before gracing her with a shameless grin and scooting out of the row.

"May I have the honor of escorting you, ma'am?" Kirby offered his arm.

Even sixty-five years ago, James had never been so chivalrous. She stepped out into the aisle and slid her hand into the crook of his elbow. "You may, sir."

"I trust you've been keeping well since last time I saw you." He nodded in greeting to people they passed, just as if they were on promenade.

"I have. Did you enjoy your visit with your son in Alabama?" Maureen listened with interest as Kirby talked about his son, a football coach at a small college in Birmingham, and daughter-in-law, the chief surgeon at one of the major hospitals down there. And she let the gaping and astonished expressions of her friends and acquaintances pass without acknowledgment. But she treasured them up in her heart.

∽

"Um. . .you do realize that you can't come to this class." Flannery blocked the door, barring Zarah and Bobby from entering. "It's for *single* people. And you no longer qualify."

Zarah looked up at her husband. "I told you she'd be this way."

"Some outreach director you are." Bobby moved forward, and rather than get run over by the former soldier who still had his high school football physique, Flannery moved out of the way and let them enter.

"Okay, but this week only. Then it's on to the appropriate class full of married people for you two." She returned to the greeter's table to make sure everyone was either picking up their existing nametags or making one to wear—the job Zarah used to do. One more reason for her to lament Zarah's marriage.

About half of the two dozen or so people in the room gathered around the newlyweds, and sure enough, the tablet came out of Zarah's purse so she could show the pictures everyone clamored for.

"Hey, Flannery, I think we have a visitor."

She looked up from the roll sheet she was trying to figure out at her helper's nudge.

No, no, no. He couldn't be here. Not now. Not if he knew.

"Hadn't you better go greet him?" the younger woman asked, though her eyes stayed glued to Jamie.

"I. . .yeah." She put the attendance record down, pushed her hair over her shoulders, straightened her blouse with a tug on the hem, and prayed all the way over to him that neither of them would say anything they'd regret.

Jamie scanned the room. Flannery stopped a few paces away and waited. A few seconds later, his gaze came to rest on her. Every plane of his face seemed to move infinitesimally as his expression shifted from concentration to pleasure.

"What are you doing here?" Okay, so that wasn't really the proper way to greet a visitor.

He had the audacity to grin at her. But with the short beard and mustache he now sported, she couldn't see the dimples in his cheeks or chin. She deplored facial hair. "You invited me, remember? At the airport."

"I didn't—" But she had said he should visit Acklen Ave. before she thought better of it. "Okay, so I did. Come with me, and we'll get your visitor information stuff filled out."

She watched—but tried to feign disinterest whenever he looked up—as he filled out the form with his personal information. She recognized the home address he listed—she'd considered looking at townhouses there to be closer to work.

"Do you like that neighborhood?" She took the form from him and stuck it in the folder with the rest of the attendance information.

"Yeah. I love it. I bought my townhouse about six years ago. It took me less than ten minutes to get to your office building the other day."

Flannery cringed. *Let's not talk about your being in* my *office. . .ever!* "I understand Shandi was able to put you to work immediately."

"Yes. Thank you for giving her my name and number. This work is going to help me out a lot when it comes to figuring out what I want to do next." He chewed the corner of his bottom lip.

"I have to ask. . .what's with the beard?" She couldn't help noticing the curious and admiring gazes of all of the women in the room, directed at Jamie. She took a measure of primal female pleasure in being seen tête-à-tête with arguably the best-looking man in the room, even if he was just the same height as she was in her thin-soled sandals.

He rubbed his hand along the dark growth. "I figured since I never had one, now that I'm unemployed would be the best time to experiment and see if I like it. What do you think?"

Flannery cocked her head as if studying and weighing the merits. She couldn't very well say she didn't like it because it hid his dimples. That would just go straight to his head. She leaned forward and pointed right where the facial fur hid the cleft in his chin. "Is that a gray hair?"

Pressing his lips together in a sardonic smile, he nodded his head. "Don't know what I did to deserve that, but that was a good one."

The couple who taught the class called it to order for announcements and the opening prayer. Flannery shooed her helper and Jamie off toward the chairs set in rows, filling three-quarters of the room.

Jamie took a few steps and then turned and came back over to the welcome table. "Aren't you coming?"

"I've got to finish taking the roll and get this put out in the hall before the hall monitor comes by to pick it up." She lifted the black folder.

"Oh." He looked over his shoulder at the chairs. "Want me to save you a seat?"

Flannery looked that direction, too, and caught Zarah looking at her, her eyes squinted in speculation. "No, that's okay. I'm going to sit with Zarah and Bobby. You go on over. I've got work to do."

A tinge of something—regret?—caught in her chest, but she dislodged it with the reminder that he had a tendency to say things that irritated her and that he possibly knew her biggest, deepest, darkest secret. Well, not the *deepest, darkest* secret, but still one that she didn't want anyone to know. Though Caylor and Zarah knew of her interest in the Arthurian legends, even they didn't know how far that interest was rooted. And if she couldn't tell them, how could she let someone like Jamie in on the secret?

❧

He'd done it. He'd had another normal conversation with Flannery. Well. . .normal by their standards.

Jamie wanted to copy his grandmother's actions from before the worship service had started earlier. He wanted to look over his shoulder to see if Flannery was still at the back of the room. Bobby had insisted on moving over and inviting Jamie to sit with them—so he knew he'd see Flannery when she joined them on the other side of Zarah. But what was taking so long?

Was she back to trying to avoid him? At least he hadn't lost his cool and babbled inanely at her this morning. What's more, if that gray hair comment hadn't been directed at him, he would have found it uproariously funny. She was right, even though she hadn't said it in so many words. He'd noticed gray hairs growing in the predominantly dark beard, and he feared it would make him look even older. Maybe he needed some of that men's hair color that worked on both head hair and facial hair. Or was there a separate product for each? He needed to pay more attention to the commercials.

Everyone bowed their heads—no, he needed to pay more attention to Sunday school. He bowed and listened to the prayer for people he didn't know, requests they'd just spent the last ten minutes listening to.

He prayed his own prayer once again about direction and figuring out what to do next as far as making a decision between working and school. Or between finding a job here, going to school here, or moving to Utah and working for his stepfather while he tried to figure out the rest.

Flannery finally came around and sat on the other side of Zarah. Just two people away, yet it seemed a chasm separated them. And he really wanted to figure out how to bridge the gap. Because the more he saw of her—and the more he stayed in his non-freaked-out-dork state around her—the more he saw glimpses of the Flannery who wasn't all prickles and attitude. That was the Flannery he wanted to get to know better. The Flannery who gave a funny toast at her best friend's wedding. The Flannery who had seen his need and done what she could to help him—and taken no credit for it.

After Sunday school, Bobby invited Jamie to sit with them in the church service.

"I went to the early service with my grandmother, and now we're going out for brunch. Maybe next time." He met a few other people but wanted to catch Flannery before she left.

Foiled, he promised himself that next week he'd plan to stay for the late service and not let her out of his sight.

He met his grandmother down at his car and opened the door for her.

Before getting in, she laid her hand on top of his on the top of the door. "I hope you don't mind, but I invited Kirby McNeill to join us for brunch."

Mind? With the way her eyes sparkled and her smile broadened whenever she mentioned the man's name? "I don't mind at all. I'll enjoy getting to know him better."

Watching his grandmother and Flannery's grandfather interact over their pancakes and french toast at Cracker Barrel, Jamie caught a glimpse of what his grandmother had been like as a young woman. Her conversation occasionally slipped into flirtation, and if Jamie had to choose a description for how Kirby acted toward her, it would have to be *courtly*.

For all that they noticed he was with them, he could have stayed at church and gone out to lunch with the singles' group, as invited. And since he'd picked Cookie up and driven her to church, she would then have needed to ask Kirby for a ride home.

Jamie had been aware for quite some time of his grandmother's subtle attempts to help him meet eligible young women. From the invitation to her friends' cookout last year—at which he'd met Zarah, Caylor, and Flannery (and called Flannery Fanny, but he wasn't going to think about that right now)—to the push for him to get more involved in his church, to this most recent suggestion of visiting the Bible study last Sunday and the singles' Sunday school this week.

He couldn't really blame her, he supposed. He was her only remaining blood relative. And she wasn't getting any younger. She deserved to see her great-grandchildren born while she could still enjoy them.

If he called her out on her attempts to find him a woman, she'd tell him she just wanted to see him happy. Well, she deserved some happiness, too. And since it seemed like she might find it with Kirby McNeill, Jamie would do what he could to throw the two of them together as often as possible—especially if it meant getting Flannery's help.

After all, when it came to matchmaking, turnabout was fair play.

# Chapter 16

**From:** TennesseeGawain
**To:** LadyNelle
**Subject:** Hope You're Okay

Jamie stared at the computer screen for a long time. *"Hope you're okay."* He didn't even know this person. And being honest with himself, he was sending this message for mostly selfish reasons. The user named LadyNelle hadn't posted anything new in over two weeks, and he was anxious to read more of her story.

Clicking into the message box in the website's contact form, he ran words through his head to see which would sound the least stalkerish:

> *You probably feel as strange receiving this message as I feel sending it. But I noticed you haven't posted anything in a few weeks, and I just wanted to let you know that I hope everything is okay and*

And what? *And please post something soon? And I don't care if you've been in the hospital having a kidney transplant—I want more of the story?*

He leaned back in his desk chair and rubbed the back of his neck. Why was he even sending this message other than to prompt this writer to post more of her story? Did he really care if this person was okay or not?

Yeah, actually, he did. Even though he didn't know who she was, he sort of felt like he knew something about her from the characteristics and personality she built into her characters. He genuinely hoped she hadn't experienced some kind of illness or tragedy. That's what he could say.

> *I hope that there has been no illness or family emergency. Even though I don't know you, I'm sending up a prayer for your health and well-being.*

Really? A prayer?

Sure, why not. After all, one of the aspects of her writing that he enjoyed was her inclusion of God in this fantasy world.

> *May blessings follow your steps.*

There. He closed with the phrase LadyNelle had created as the standard farewell for her characters.

Before he could second-guess himself, he clicked SUBMIT.

Though he hoped for an error screen that would tell him that not only had his message not gone through but the website had eaten it and it no longer existed, he saw a splash screen with a confirmation that his message would be delivered to LadyNelle.

Why couldn't he meet someone like her in real life? Not the user, of course—she was probably one of those strange, fairy-wannabe types who lived and breathed this kind of fantasy stuff—but the character she'd created out of nothing more than a brief appearance in one single story out of the entire legend.

Before he could log off the site, a box popped up in the corner notifying him that he had a new direct message from another user.

Surely she hadn't answered that quickly. He clicked over to his messages. Nope, not from her but...

**From:** Galahad37138
**To:** TennesseeGawain
**Subject:** Is that you?

*If this isn't the person I think it is, I apologize in advance.
But from your posts in the community forums, as well as the fan
fiction you've flagged as favorites, I'm taking a wild guess that
TennesseeGawain is someone I grew up with in Murfreesboro,
Tennessee.*

*Did you ever call that girl who gave you her number at the
King Arthur movie premiere?*

Jamie laughed and switched over to his regular e-mail program.
Before the big-budget film version of the Arthurian legend opened,
he'd spent months collecting and creating pieces and parts for his Sir
Gawain costume to wear to the midnight showing—right down to
growing out his hair. Of course, explaining the reason for growing
out his hair to people at work hadn't been easy—and had shown him
why keeping some things to himself was a good idea in the marketing
business.

**From:** Jamie O'Connor
**To:** Danny Seung
**Subject:** Yeah, It's Me

*You caught me. Yes, I'm TennesseeGawain on the King Arthur
fan site. And if I'd ever run across your username, I'd have figured
it was you, Galahad with a Murfreesboro zip code!*

*No, I never called that girl. In the light of day, and out of
costume, it just seemed a little strange to me.*

*How's the new job going? Is there a time soon when you can
get together for coffee or lunch or dinner or something? You see,
I've been thinking about nursing school and would like a pro's
advice.*

163

*Hope to catch up with you next week.*

—j

*BTW—Mom says hi.*

Out of habit, Jamie proofread the e-mail before sending it—even knowing he had the spelling checker turned on. That had been a lesson learned early in his career.

Danny didn't respond immediately, so he must have stepped away from the computer.

Jamie turned, facing out into the third bedroom of the townhouse, which served as his home office. If he was truly going to start working from home, and not just using this room for playing games on the desktop computer instead of the netbook, he should probably reorganize it, make sure he had appropriate office supplies so that he wasn't running to the store every couple of days, and get that six-foot folding table out of the garage and set up in here for some extra work space.

He should. . .but he'd wait a couple of days. Organizing an office belonged to Monday morning, not Friday night.

So, now what? Six fifteen on a Friday and he had nothing to do. Back in the day, back when he'd been gainfully employed, he'd be with a dozen or more people hanging out somewhere like the Flying Saucer or Rippy's or the Dan McGuinness Pub. For Jamie, it had been more about being around people and not having to face spending the evening alone at home. For everyone else, it had been about drinking away the workweek and starting the weekend with a hangover.

Well, whatever he did, he couldn't stay here, not with the walls closing in on him like this. Not after a week of seeing only the others who chose to work at Starbucks or Panera—but who were all so focused on their own laptops that no one had time to chat. He'd gone over to Cookie's house three days just to engage in face-to-face conversation with another human being—and because he knew he could indulge in the treats for which he'd named her as a child. She almost always had a batch of freshly baked cookies just waiting for someone to stop by and enjoy.

He turned back to face the computer. He supposed if he couldn't find anything else to do, he could start studying for the entrance exam the nursing program at Aquinas College—the program he'd been looking at—required for admission. He'd been out of college for thirteen years; he'd probably forgotten more in those years than he learned in the four years as a student at MTSU. And with a business administration major, he'd taken only the required general science classes. So he'd have some basic subjects to catch up on before he could start taking any nursing courses.

He'd just transferred the study guide to the netbook and turned off the desktop when his phone rang. Grabbing it just before it vibrated itself off the desk, he accidentally hit the answer button without a chance to look to see who was calling.

"Hello?"

"Jamie, it's your grandmother." She never failed to identify herself if he didn't address her by name when he answered.

"Hey, Cookie. What's up?"

"I know you're probably on your way out to have fun with your friends, but on the off chance you don't have plans, I thought I'd call and see if you'd like to go out for dinner tonight."

With the extra money coming in from the publishing house, he didn't see any point in denying himself some funds for entertainment. "I don't have any plans, and I'd love to go. Where did you have in mind?"

"I was thinking that we hadn't been for sushi at Hanabi in quite some time."

Jamie's mouth began watering. "You're right—we haven't. That sounds perfect."

"Good. I made a seven o'clock reservation for us."

God bless his grandmother for assuming he'd want to go. "I'll meet you at the restaurant at seven, then."

Which gave him plenty of time to change into something other than cargo pants and a T-shirt. Even though the Japanese restaurant boasted a casual dining experience, he couldn't disrespect Cookie by showing up in clothes he might wear to work in the yard or go hiking—or hang out at a coffeehouse or deli while working, as he'd done all day today.

Since he couldn't be sure that Flannery McNeill would ever give him the time of day, maybe tonight he'd give Cookie the go-ahead to start introducing him to all of the unmarried granddaughters of her church friends she kept talking about.

⚬❈⚬

"It looks awfully crowded. Are you sure we can get in?" Flannery hit the button on the remote to lock the car. "How did you even know this place exists? I work near here, and I've never heard of it."

"A friend recommended it. I'm sure we can get a table." Big Daddy opened the door for her and ushered her inside.

The crowd around the front door didn't look promising. Flannery excused herself to get to the person who looked like she worked here. Beyond the hostess, she could see a couple of empty tables. Good. That meant they should be able to seat the people already waiting, cutting down their time. "Table for two, please."

"Name, please."

"McNeill."

"About thirty minutes. Okay?"

"Thirty?"

"Okay?"

"Um...yeah, put us on the list for now. I'll go talk to my grandfather." Flannery made her way back to Big Daddy.

"Flan, look who I found." Big Daddy grinned down at a redheaded woman. "You remember Maureen O'Connor."

Flannery smiled—but then froze when Maureen's grandson entered behind her. "It's nice to see you again, Mrs. O'Connor. Jamie."

He smiled. She twitched in annoyance when her pulse fluttered at the way his laugh lines crinkled around his eyes. She turned toward her grandfather. "They said it's going to be thirty minutes for a table. There's another Japanese restaurant not far from here. We could go see if we can get in there faster."

"Oh—why don't you join us? We have a reservation, so we shouldn't have to wait at all." Maureen looked up at Big Daddy.

Flannery's pulse stopped fluttering. In fact, she was pretty sure her heart stopped altogether, not just from the flirtation in Maureen O'Connor's gaze, but also from the look of satisfaction that passed between her and Big Daddy. "We can't intrude—"

Big Daddy quelled Flannery with a glance and then smiled down at Maureen. "We'd love to join you."

The two seniors moved past Flannery, who watched them walk toward the hostess, confounded by the suspicions flooding her mind.

"Are you thinking what I'm thinking?" Jamie's shoulder brushed against hers.

"That this is a setup?" Flannery kept her eyes turned away from him so that she wouldn't have to admit how good he looked in his dark-blue, button-down shirt and khaki linen pants, despite the beard.

"But a setup for who?"

Both Flannery and Jamie ducked through the two or three parties waiting for tables when Maureen and Big Daddy motioned them forward. And though she wouldn't do it to anyone else, she just couldn't let Jamie's grammatical error slip by. If he was going to annoy her, she'd annoy him right back. "It's *whom* not *who*. And what do you mean, for whom?"

"I mean, did they do this just so they could see each other, or were they hoping to set the two of us up?" Jamie's hand lightly touched her back as he escorted her through the restaurant behind their grandparents.

A shudder shimmied up Flannery's spine from the feather-light contact. She tried to pretend it was revulsion at the thought of being set up with Jamie—but somehow, after that conversation at the airport a couple of weeks ago, instead of her hackles rising in annoyance whenever she saw him, she experienced a little wave of anticipation, of pleasure in seeing him.

Or maybe her fear of being left alone, left behind by Caylor and Zarah, blinded her to everything about him she'd found irritating in the past. Yes, that must be it.

Big Daddy and Maureen had already ensconced themselves on one side of the four-person table. Jamie held Flannery's chair for her and waited until she was situated before he sat down beside her.

See, that's what she meant. A couple of months ago, had he done that, she would have found it arrogant and condescending. But tonight. . .it was kind of sweet and endearing.

"Looks like we're one menu short," Maureen said.

"I'll share with Flannery, since it looks like y'all have different length requirements for your arms." Jamie raised his brows, ducked his chin, and winked at his grandmother—who did, indeed, hold the menu farther away while Big Daddy pulled his in close.

Jamie put the third menu—the one with the descriptions of the different sushi rolls—down on the table between them. Flannery's arm burst into flames when his shoulder pressed against hers as they bent toward it to read. Hmm. . .now she was starting to believe in spontaneous human combustion. Great. She knew being around Jamie wasn't a good idea.

"Ooh—I know what I'm getting." Jamie's low voice almost vanished into the din around them.

"What are you getting?" Three things on the menu looked great to her, but she could never decide until she knew what everyone else was having.

"A spicy crab roll and the spicy tuna roll. I probably won't be able to eat all of it, though. What are you getting—maybe we could share?" His shoulder pressed against hers just a little harder.

A faint aroma of citrus tickled Flannery's nose—something she'd noticed around him before. Citrus and maybe a little spice. Whatever it was, she liked it. Too much.

She couldn't fall for this guy. Not when their first three meetings had turned into scenes from a bad 1980s high school movie—embarrassing and better forgotten. But maybe, just for tonight, she could pretend. . . . After all, she didn't know anyone else who shared her preference for spicy sushi—he'd just named two of the three rolls she'd been considering.

"I'll get the spicy yellowtail roll, then."

"Niiice." He drew out the word, slowly nodding his head. They filled out their order sheets and handed them over when the waiter returned with four glasses of water and a pot of hot tea.

When Maureen offered to pour some for her, Flannery held up her hand. "None for me, thanks. Not really a hot tea drinker."

Maureen didn't even offer any to Jamie. She and Big Daddy got started talking about some of the restaurants they remembered in Nashville from when they were much, *much* younger.

Jamie turned partway toward Flannery, his gaze roving her face— and apparently liking what he saw. Yes, she could very much pretend tonight that she didn't dislike him and truly enjoyed his company.

"You know, I've been thinking."

"Have you written a press release about that yet?" She pressed her lips together, but she couldn't keep her amusement from traveling up to her eyes.

He quirked a lopsided grin at her and nudged her with his elbow. "Good one." He motioned toward their grandparents with a slight jerk of his head. "You know, I think they're kinda sweet on each other."

Flannery slew her gaze across the table without turning her head and bringing attention to herself. "What makes you think that, Captain Obvious?"

Jamie's expression slipped from smiling to stern. "Be nice, or I'm not sharing the crab roll with you."

She stared into his slate-colored eyes, noting the halo of lighter gray around the pupils, daring him to blink or smile first.

He had the longest, darkest lashes she'd ever seen on a man in her life. She almost reached out to touch them but stopped herself and rested her hand on the edge of the table.

Was that. . .a gray hair in his left eyebrow?

She cracked first, unable to hide her humor any longer. "Okay,

I promise. I'll be nice."

"Good. Because I'm going to need your help. We're going to have to work together if my plan is going to work." He leaned a little closer to her.

She leaned toward him. Another couple of inches and their foreheads and noses would be touching. And she wasn't sure that would be a bad thing. "What's your plan?"

But before he could launch into it, their food arrived. They both straightened. Cold, desolate, lonely air filled the gap between Flannery's shoulder and Jamie's.

Mercy, she could take this pretending thing a little over the top, couldn't she?

Jamie immediately put a couple of pieces of each of his sushi rolls on her tray. Flannery moved almost a third of her roll onto his.

He reached his chopsticks toward her condiment tray. "Are you going to use that wasabi?"

As if wielding a sword, she blocked his chopsticks with hers. "Yes, I'm going to use all of it, so don't you touch it. You can have the pickled ginger if you want that, though."

"Yeah, um, no thanks."

"Flannery, Jamie tells me you're an editor with a book publishing company." Maureen dipped a piece of salmon sashimi into her wasabi-and-soy-sauce mixture.

"Yes, ma'am. I'm the senior editor for Christian fiction at Lindsley House Publishing." She described a small portion of what she did—from acquiring new titles to scheduling release dates to working with authors and agents.

"So you won't be working with Jamie on any of the marketing projects he'll be doing?" Maureen's painted-on eyebrows raised almost to her fire-engine-red hair. On anyone else it would have looked garish. On Maureen, with her distinct, broad, bold features, it only added to her charm.

"No, ma'am. My understanding is that Jamie will be working with our nonfiction team right now." She swatted Jamie's chopsticks away as he reached toward her glob of wasabi again.

"I know he's already thanked you, but I just wanted to thank you, too."

Nooo—Flannery did *not* need the reminder that Jamie had been in her office and seen. . .possibly seen. . .the print. "No thanks are necessary, really."

Maureen engaged Big Daddy to tell her about what his other grandchildren did. Jamie leaned against Flannery's shoulder again.

"I don't believe I've ever seen you turn quite that shade of red before, Ms. McNeill." He straightened and swished a piece of the spicy crab roll through his wasabi-soy mix. "You really shouldn't be so self-deprecating when it comes to people expressing gratitude to you when you've done such a great service."

She turned and gazed at him through squinted eyes. He thought she'd blushed because of his grandmother's expression of gratitude? Then he hadn't noticed, hadn't recognized—

"Of course"—he finished chewing and swallowed—"I wouldn't tell anyone that you're trying to pass off a print of Sir Gawain and Dame Ragnelle as a piece of Irish artwork, if that's why you turned beet red when my grandmother mentioned my thank-you note. Nope." He licked the ends of his chopsticks. "Wouldn't tell a soul."

Ooh—he irritated her so much!

# Chapter 17

❦

**From:** Kirby McNeill
**To:** Maureen O'Connor
**Subject:** RE: Idea

*Dear Maureen,*
*You were correct. Though I believe Flannery would have protested the idea of having dinner with Jamie, once we were there, she did seem to get along with him quite well.*
*The food was good, and the company was excellent. I look forward to "running into" you and your grandson again.*
*Until next weekend,*
*Kirby*

**From:** Jamie O'Connor
**To:** Flannery McNeill
**Subject:** That plan I mentioned

*I never got to tell you the other night about my plan. It probably wouldn't have been a good idea to discuss it in front of them, anyway.*
*So, here's the thing—my grandmother likes your grandfather, and it's obviously reciprocal. But I have a sneaky suspicion that*

172

*unless you and I find ways to push them together, they're not going to admit that they want to spend time together.*

*My plan is this. . . .*

*Big Daddy mentioned that he's looking for a place to rent or buy in Nashville so he doesn't have to stay at a hotel every weekend. (Until he sells his house in Pulaski, right?)*

*I have a three-bedroom townhouse. He can stay in my guest bedroom on the weekends until he finds something more permanent. Then you and I can figure out some activities we can all do together—the four of us—so that he gets to see my grandmother but also gets to spend time with you.*

*What do you think?*

*—j*

*BTW—Have I mentioned recently that I promise I would never say anything about the Sir Gawain print to anyone else? I am curious about it, though.*

**From:** LadyNelle
**To:** TennesseeGawain
**Subject:** RE: Hope You're Okay

*Yes, it was a little strange to receive a message like yours from a complete stranger, but thank you for the sentiments. There has been no illness or family emergency, just life intruding, the way it can sometimes do. I'm humbled by the fact someone who doesn't even know me would pray for me.*

*Thank you.*

*PS—I posted a new chapter tonight. I hope you enjoy it.*

**From:** Maureen O'Connor
**To:** Kirby McNeill
**Subject:** RE: RE: Idea

*Dear Kirby,*

*There did seem to be some flirting going on across the table from us, didn't there? Until seeing them together, I had forgotten how the sparks flew between the two of them at a cookout Jamie and I attended last autumn. It is rare that I see a young person with as much poise and humbleness of spirit as your granddaughter. I would feel blessed indeed to welcome Flannery into my family, should things develop to that stage.*

*I understand my grandson has written to invite you to stay with him on the weekends until you have more permanent arrangements. This would work greatly to our advantage in planning activities that bring Jamie and Flannery together, as I believe she would find it logical and reasonable if you began to include Jamie, and possibly me, in your plans.*

*Do not feel I am pressuring you to accept his offer. You must do what you feel is right, of course.*

*Cordially,*
*Maureen*

**From:** Danny Seung
**To:** Jamie O'Connor
**Subject:** RE: Yeah, It's Me

*I knew it! You're so obvious.*

*The guys and I are gaming this coming Saturday if you'd like to come join us and see what it's all about.*

*I only have thirty minutes for lunches this week, so meeting for lunch is out of the question. And since we haven't found a house up there to buy yet—mostly because we're waiting on the M'boro house to get some offers first—I've pretty much got to head straight home after work so that I don't get stuck in the worst of rush-hour traffic.*

*Why don't we meet at the IHOP right there at the corner of Harding and Nolensville (in front of the Walmart) for breakfast some morning? That's closest to the hospital, so I'll have a little more time if we meet there. My shift starts at 7:30 a.m., and they open at 6:00 a.m. I know you've never been an early morning person, but if you're really serious about going to nursing school, you're going to have to get used to it sooner or later, because the newest nurses get the worst shifts.*

*Just let me know if you want to meet one morning, and I'll plan for it.*

*Danny*

**From:** TennesseeGawain
**To:** LadyNelle
**Subject:** New Chapter

*Seriously? You're going to leave me hanging like that? What a horrible (and absolutely awesome) way to end a chapter!*

**From:** Jamie O'Connor
**To:** Danny Seung
**Subject:** RE: RE: Yeah, It's Me

*Ugh—6 in the morning??? Maybe I'll just stay up instead of trying to get up that early.*

*How does Wednesday sound?*

*I've got a houseguest this weekend (and every weekend for the foreseeable future). I probably won't be able to swing the gaming session this month, but I am really interested, so keep letting me know when you're meeting.*

*—j*

*BTW—The townhouse two doors down from mine just went on the market this week. Three bed/two bath. Renovated kitchen. I think it's a foreclosure, so you might be able to get a good deal on it.*

**From:** Kirby McNeill
**To:** Maureen O'Connor
**Subject:** RE: RE: RE: Idea

*Dear Maureen,*

*I just sent an e-mail to your grandson, accepting his offer. I plan to drive up early on Friday and hope that you might be available for lunch so that we can discuss your ideas face-to-face, without Jamie or Flannery being there. I've told Jamie not to expect me before three o'clock.*

*I hope you know that it is not only discussing the grandchildren that leads me to asking you to lunch. While I desire nothing more than seeing my youngest granddaughter find the happiness that my sons and other grandchildren have found, I cannot claim to be completely selfless in this endeavor.*

*I enjoy spending time with you and hope that we will make opportunities to see each other regularly.*

*With affection,*
*Kirby*

**From:** Jamie O'Connor
**To:** Chae Seung
**Subject:** RE: Dinner

*Thank you so much for the invitation to dinner with your family. Yes, I will bring a guest. I'm not certain who it will be at this point, but I will bring someone.*

*It's been a long time since I've had Korean food, and I look forward to it, especially since it sounds like your mother and grandmother will be doing most of the cooking. ;-)*

*—j*

*BTW—How long did you know Danny before he told you about his Sir Galahad obsession? What did you think when you first found out?*

**From:** Maureen O'Connor
**To:** Kirby McNeill
**Subject:** Lunch on Friday

*Dear Kirby,*

    *I, too, enjoy spending time with you, and I would be delighted to meet you for lunch Friday. Since you will be driving up from the south side of town, why don't we meet at Chef Paul's on Mallory Lane in Cool Springs, just off the new McEwen Drive exit. Is eleven o'clock too early for you?*

*Until Friday,*
*Maureen*

**From:** Flannery McNeill
**To:** Jamie O'Connor
**Subject:** RE: That plan I mentioned

    *My grandfather (and no, you may not call him Big Daddy, so don't do it again; it's Mr. McNeill to you) just called me to tell me he's going to be staying with you on the weekends.*

    *While I like the idea of coming up with ways to give my grandfather and your grandmother time to spend together, since it's your plan, it probably needs some work. I can't believe I'm about to suggest this—I'm taking a half day off on Friday. We should probably meet for lunch and talk before my grandfather arrives in town. Let's meet at the Panera in the Target shopping center on Old Hickory Blvd. at one o'clock Friday afternoon.*

*Flannery*

*BTW—Have I mentioned recently that you're a dork? It's a sneaking suspicion, not a sneaky suspicion.*

# Chapter 18

❧

Kirby left the motor running a moment after pulling in to the parking space in front of Chef Paul's and prayed for energy. Not since the month before his open-heart surgery and the installation of his defibrillator seven years ago had he experienced this level of exhaustion.

A small blue car pulled up beside him, and he recognized Maureen's red hair. He climbed out of his pickup and met her on the sidewalk, opening the restaurant door for her. He assisted her with getting seated and then took the chair opposite so that he could see her beautiful grayish eyes as they talked.

After they ordered, Maureen folded her hands in her lap. "I hope you don't mind my asking, but I would love to know more about your wife."

The first few years after she'd died, Kirby couldn't talk about her. But now, he appreciated it when people asked him about her—it kept her memory fresh and alive. But he never assumed they wanted to hear too much. "Her name was Beatrice. We married young. Had three boys—though we lost one in Vietnam.

Maureen stirred a pack of artificial sweetener into her iced tea. "How did you meet?"

"We both grew up on adjoining hog farms outside Pulaski. The drive up to her parents' place was half a mile down the road from ours,

178

and I had to pass it on my way to school. Bea was a few years younger, so I didn't pay her much mind for a while on those walks to and from that one-room schoolhouse. And there were some years there when she downright got on my nerves." Warm tenderness filled him at the memory of the little girl with the golden braids. "But a few years later, I asked if I could carry her books for her. And then a few years after that, we would stand at her gate talking until her ma rang the dinner bell looking for her. Though she loved learning and reading, Bea hated school. She loved farm living and knew she wanted to be a farmer's wife."

"So of course you went off to college and majored in agriculture." Maureen's eyes danced. "To be that space-age farmer who was going to revolutionize the agricultural industry."

He smiled and nodded. "After doing my patriotic duty—I still have the piece of shrapnel in my hip that ended my military career after just nine months. Bea was still just a sophomore in high school when I came back. We would have married the summer she graduated from high school, but there was too long of a waiting list for married-student housing. So we waited a year until I graduated from college. As a graduate student, it was easier to get housing for the both of us. So she joined me."

"And I would imagine she hated living in Knoxville, on campus, being a farm girl at heart." No condescension or censure came through Maureen's voice, only sympathy.

"But she put up with it for the five years it took me to complete my master's and doctoral work. Because she believed as soon as I was finished, we'd be moving back out to the country and starting our own little hog farm on the piece of property between our folks' farms that they gave to us as a wedding present. And she didn't have it easy. All three of our boys arrived in those five years, and things would have been lean *without* three extra mouths to feed."

Kirby's reminiscence was interrupted by the arrival of their food.

"I assume, then, that Bea did not take it well when you told her you felt God calling you into the ministry." Maureen liberally salted her red beans and rice.

Kirby squeezed three of the lemon wedges they'd given him over his grilled salmon and double portion of steamed broccoli. "That's not exactly what happened. After I finished, we moved back to Pulaski as I'd promised and started the farm. Our fathers had built us a small house while we were in Knoxville and gave us our start with a few prize hogs from their own herds. And I spent that first year wrestling with God. It wasn't so much that I didn't want to follow His calling; it was that I couldn't break my word to Bea."

Maureen closed her eyes and shook her head. "I cannot imagine being in such a difficult position—between the woman you loved and the God you wanted to serve."

"Eighteen months after we'd been on the farm, I came in for dinner one night to find Bea packing suitcases for herself and the boys."

Maureen gasped. "No."

"Yes." After a couple of bites of salmon and broccoli, he continued. "When I asked her where she was going, she said, 'To Nashville.' And then she pointed at an envelope on the bed. I picked it up and looked at it. It was a letter of acceptance, addressed to me, from the divinity school at Vanderbilt. Knowing that I would not break my promise to her, but that I was also not obeying God, Bea took the decision out of my hands and submitted the admission application for me. She said she couldn't live with a man who would willingly disobey God. So either she was taking the boys and moving to Nashville without me, or we were all going together so I could do what I knew I was supposed to do, which was become a preacher."

"And she didn't worry that you would be called to preach at a church in a large city?"

Chuckling, Kirby set down his fork, not really full, but simply tired of eating. "That was her sole condition. She agreed to live in Nashville with me while I was in seminary if I agreed to apply for positions only at rural churches, preferably within easy distance of the farm we already had. Apparently God decided to reward her faithfulness, because almost as soon as I finished seminary, I got a church not fifteen miles from the farm. And for the rest of her life, I was never called to a church more than twenty miles from the farm, and I was never without a church. So she got her dream of being a farm wife—though my brother and hers, who eventually took over our parents' places, ran the hogs—and I fulfilled the call to ministry God had for me."

"And when did God call her home?"

"Eighteen years ago, a few weeks after our forty-sixth anniversary. It was her third recurrence of cancer, and it metastasized and spread to her liver, kidneys, and stomach. All of the children and grandchildren were able to be there with her at the very end to say good-bye. She had a beautiful, peaceful passing. And her last words were to thank me for giving her the life she'd dreamed of."

A tear trickled down Maureen's cheek. She blotted it with her napkin. "I think I would have liked her very much."

Kirby nodded. "Everyone did."

"You're blessed that you had all the extra years of your childhood together. James and I met in high school, and I made him wait for three years after I graduated before I'd agree to marry him. He'd trained to be a pilot in preparation to join the Army Air Corps as soon as he turned eighteen, but the war ended a month before his eighteenth birthday. I was determined to go to college here, at James Robertson, but there weren't many opportunities for a young, green pilot in Nashville. So he went off to Atlanta to fly for Eastern Air Lines while I stayed here and became a nurse. After a couple of years, Eastern allowed him to transfer to Nashville, and after almost a year of making him wait and ask several times, I said yes, and we married. James wanted a large family—we'd both been the only child in our families—but that wasn't to be. Our son, Jimmy, came a year after we were married. We had fifteen more years with James before his heart failed and he died driving home from the airport late one night. Three years later, Jimmy enlisted in the Marine Corps, but unlike his father, he turned eighteen during the height of the Vietnam War. He served three tours of duty but was then discharged for health reasons—a weak heart, they said— and he came home and enrolled in the police academy."

"You said before that your son was angry at God over his father's death. Did joining the military or the police force help him with that?" Kirby had seen it so many times—young men distraught over the loss of a parent finding their way to healing through the discipline and order military service provided.

"No. He came home a changed man. Still angry, but it presented in a different manner. He developed notions about men's and women's roles, both inside the home and publicly. And he became very controlling. I believe that's why he married a woman so much younger than he—Jackie was only nineteen when they married; Jimmy was twenty-six. Jamie was born a year later."

Kirby's back began to ache—these chairs were not designed to encourage long conversations. "And where do your son and daughter-in-law live now?"

Maureen looked down at her plate, pushed it back, and then looked back up at him. "Like his father, Jimmy's heart was weak—and he refused to acknowledge it or see a doctor. Medical intervention earlier in his life could possibly have prolonged it. But he died of heart failure on Jamie's thirteenth birthday. Jackie was still quite a young woman—only thirty-three—and she needed to deal with the grief in her own way."

Maureen pressed her lips together. "And she had not only the loss of her husband to grieve, but she needed to grieve the fact her marriage had not been happy. Jimmy was a hard man, making unreasonable demands of both his wife and his son. Frankly, I was surprised Jackie hadn't left years before. I loved my son." Maureen's gaze pierced Kirby's, and he knew she needed him to believe her. "But Jackie deserved better. She went out to Utah to live with a friend. She ended up meeting someone else and remarried two years later."

Kirby did understand and believe Maureen's complicated feelings for her only child. "And when did Jamie move back to Nashville?"

"He never left. Like Jimmy and me, Jamie and his mother had problems after his father's death. I offered to let Jackie leave Jamie with me—I needed Jamie as much as he needed me."

Given his own health crises and issues, fear niggled the back of Kirby's mind. "And does he share his father's and grandfather's health problems?"

Maureen glowed with pride. "He was raised by a nurse and received regular medical checkups. As science progressed, they were finally able to discover a congenital defect—a small hole between the two upper chambers of the heart—that would eventually make his heart fail. He had corrective open-heart surgery when he was eighteen. And though I'm not certain he's as cautious as he should be with what he eats, he gets plenty of exercise and monitors himself and sees his doctor regularly."

Kirby didn't know quite what to say. He'd been in his late seventies when he'd gone through open-heart surgery, already a widower. For Jamie to have needed it so young. . .

"I know what you're thinking, Kirby." Maureen reached across the table and wrapped her knobby fingers around his. "I don't want Flannery to end up a young widow, either. But if they are meant to be together, nothing we can do will stop them. And would you give up the years you had with the love of your life if you had known how soon she would be taken from you?"

He did not know that forty-six years of marriage was "soon," but he understood her meaning. "No one is guaranteed tomorrow, but everyone deserves a chance at finding true love."

⚓

Flannery pressed her fingertips to the ache just above her left eye. "Tell the production designer to stop work. If the single quotation marks were replaced with double quotes all the way through, the entire thing will have to be proofread again and fixed manually. Find a free-lancer who doesn't mind working over a holiday weekend, and tell them we'll add five dollars an hour to the regular rate. We'll need it back before start of business Tuesday if we're going to keep our production schedule."

Pacing the sidewalk in front of Panera, Flannery talked with the assistant editor—who managed their stable of freelance copy, content, and continuity editors—for a few more minutes about the issue the production designer had discovered in the manuscript that the proofreader had missed—and shouldn't have. She'd have to deal with the in-house editors who also missed the error on Tuesday.

"If you can't find a freelancer who can take it this weekend"—she sighed—"e-mail it to me along with the series continuity guide and the style sheet, and I'll do it myself."

"Flannery, no, you can't. I'll do it."

She shook her head, as if the editor could see her through the phone. "You have your family reunion this weekend. I don't really have any other plans." She forced a smile to try to instill confidence and enthusiasm into her voice. "Besides, I have faith that one of the freelancers will come through for us."

The assistant editor ended the call to go find that mythical saint, and Flannery clipped the phone to the waistband of her jeans and entered the bakery and sandwich shop. The call had made her a few minutes late, and Jamie hadn't walked in past her, so either he was running even later, or he was already here.

He wasn't in line to order. She walked around the different areas of the restaurant, searching for tables with only one person. There—at the round-table booth in the corner. Dark hair and beard, wearing a dark-blue T-shirt and olive cargo pants, head bent over something.

She approached the table and set her tablet computer on it—and finally looked to see what Jamie was doing.

He held the library book at such an angle that she couldn't help but see the cover and spine: *A Good Man Is Hard to Find and Other Stories* by Flannery O'Connor.

Without lifting his head, he looked at her over the top edge of the book and winked.

Flannery picked up her tablet and headed for the door. Ooh—he irritated her so much. She would never forgive him for this.

A hand grabbed her elbow. "Flan, I'm sorry." But the amusement in his voice belied his words. "Please, come back to the table."

"I should have expected this after the whole *Fanny* thing. If anyone was going to tease me and make a big deal of my name, it was going to be you." She allowed him to lead her back to the table, where the book now sat closed, face down—but she would say *dragged* just to make it sound more dramatic when she told the girls Sunday at coffee.

"This Flannery O'Connor was a good writer." He rested his hand on the book. "I don't know why you don't want to be associated with her."

"It's not so much that I don't want to be associated with her—it's that I'm tired of *only* being associated with her. I'm my own person. But to most people I'm the one with the same name as that author they were forced to read in sophomore lit. I get it almost every time I meet someone new. '*Flannery*—oh, as in the author Flannery O'Connor?' At least my sisters' names are somewhat normal and not necessarily automatically linked to the authors they're named after." She slid into the seat and dug in her purse to pull out her wallet.

"Emily and Sylvia?"

Frowning, she glanced at him as she stood again, ready to go to the front and order her lunch. "How'd you know their names?"

"I was standing there when you went through that whole explanation with Amy Joy Samuels. And I have to say, you should be glad you got the name Flannery. It's unusual and distinctive. Emily and Sylvia—they could be just anyone. But Flannery—it's not every day you meet someone who not only has that name but also is unusual and distinctive enough to carry it off. People will remember meeting a Flannery but probably not an Emily or a Sylvia." He grinned at her.

Forgiveness and pleasure warmed the cockles of her heart (whatever heart cockles were), and she followed Jamie to the counter to place her order. He let her go in front of him.

Her stomach gurgled with the demand to be fed. She knew what she wanted without looking at the board. "I'll have the Pick Two—Mediterranean veggie sandwich and bowl of broccoli cheddar soup, with a baguette and a regular fountain drink, and go ahead and add on a toffee-chip cookie."

She handed over her frequent-diner card, which the clerk ran through

185

the scanner on the side of his monitor. "Welcome back. . .Flannery—oh, hey, I did my literary criticism thesis on Flannery O'Connor this semester. Cool." He handed the card back to her.

Flannery looked over her shoulder at Jamie, who smirked at her. He leaned forward. "See, now he'll go home tonight and tell his girlfriend or whoever that he met someone named Flannery today, just like Flannery O'Connor." His breath tickled her ear and cheek, and she took and released a jagged breath. Wow—she shouldn't be having this reaction to him.

By the time they'd fixed their drinks—Flannery needing the extra boost of caffeine and sugar in Dr Pepper, Jamie opting for iced tea—their food was ready, so they carried everything back to the table.

"What have you been up to today—besides figuring out new and not-so-unique ways of torturing me?" She cast a pointed glare at the book, now on the half-circle booth seat between them.

"After I put fresh sheets on the guest bed and vacuumed and dusted in there and cleaned the bathroom, I spent a little while studying for the entrance exam that's required for the. . .school program I'm thinking about. And then I spent some time on some online job websites, seeing what's available. And then I talked to my stepdad for a while."

Though Flannery hadn't known him well—and hadn't wanted to—when she made the fateful decision to join him in the coffee shop at the airport, the difference in his tone of voice when he mentioned his stepfather spoke volumes about what his trip out to visit his mom "and her family" had done for his relationship with all of them.

"What did you talk to your stepdad about?"

He shrugged. "Jobs. Things. What I like to do. What I might want to do. The possibility that if I can't figure it out within the next couple of months, he wants me to go out there to work for him."

Flannery pulled most of the sliced red onion off her veggie sandwich before taking a bite. This should fill her vegetable quota for the weekend. "Sounds like you and your mom's family are getting along better now."

"They're *my* family, too." He looked at her as if she'd just insulted not just them but his grandmother, too. She refrained from reminding him those words had been his own description of them a month ago. "My parents, my brother, and my sister." Even the beard couldn't hide the softness, the nostalgia that stole over his features.

"So your stepdad is helping you figure out what you want to do careerwise?"

"Yeah. There's. . .there's a lot of stuff in my past, issues from before my father died, that I'm still trying to work through about who I am and what my life is about. Don has really been there for me with that in a way that Mom would never be able to do." Wonderment filled his voice. Then he shrugged one shoulder. "Of course, I don't have long to get it all figured out before I need to know what job I'm supposed to be looking for or going back to school for."

"I'm sorry the whole thing with Cole Samuels didn't work out. I know you'd have done a great job on that marketing campaign." She leaned over her plate to take another bite of her sandwich, not wanting to see him preen over such a compliment.

"How's Dustin working out for you?" His voice sounded flat—but in an *I'm-trying-not-to-sound-jealous* kind of way, not a disinterested way.

She hid her smile. "We ended up keeping it in house. Dustin couldn't come up with anything for us that we weren't already prepared to do. And. . .Jack had a few ideas that someone had shared with him at a wedding reception of all places." She ventured a glance at him.

Yep—he looked quite pleased with himself. "I'm glad I was able to pass those ideas along before it became illegal for me to do so." He sighed. "Now if I can just figure out what it isn't illegal for me to do. . . ."

"What can you imagine yourself doing?" Flannery stirred the thick, cheesy soup, but instead of lifting the spoon to her lips, she broke off a piece of the small, crusty sourdough baguette and scooped the soup up with that.

Jamie held his fork in front of him, a large piece of lettuce dangling from the end of it. "What do you mean?"

She couldn't believe she was about to tell him this. Caylor and Zarah didn't even know about it. "When I started college, I had no idea what I wanted to do. I wasn't like Caylor with her love of literature and writing or Zarah with her passion for history. My dad's a football coach, and my mom's a chief surgeon at a hospital. My sisters went into banking and computer programming. By the end of my sophomore year, I had to declare a major. So since Caylor was majoring in English, and since I liked reading and writing, I decided to major in English. But I still had no idea what I wanted to do."

"But you figured it out by imagining yourself doing something?"

"I'm getting there—hold on." She grinned at him to soften the rebuke of his fractious tone. "I was involved in a small-group Bible study, and when I mentioned to the leader that I didn't know what I wanted to do, she told me I shouldn't just pray, but I should meditate."

Scorn joined the irritation in Jamie's expression and body language.

"Yeah, that's what I thought, too. I had no idea what meditation was—other than just thinking really hard about one thing, and sitting on the floor Indian style, you know, with your hands like this. . . ." She set her hands on the table, palms up, and touched the tips of her thumbs to the tips of her middle fingers. "And doing the whole *ooohhhhmmmm* thing."

"And that helped?" He took a huge bite of his salad. At least chewing kept him from making faces at her.

"Not because of the sitting position, and I didn't do the *ohm* thing, either. And at first I wasn't sure. I'd go into my room and close the door and the blinds and turn off the light and sit in the middle of the floor like that. And I'd pray. I'd ask God to show me what He wanted me to do with my life. I'd concentrate on the things I enjoyed and was good at. Reading. Writing. Helping other people improve their writing—I worked part time in the writing lab as a tutor. And after doing this a few days, instead of remembering myself doing those things in classes or the lab, I suddenly visualized myself working in an office where I was doing those things. I was reading stuff. And I was helping to fix it and make it better. I wasn't sure what this meant. But I tried it again the next day. And in that. . .vision, for lack of a better word, someone handed me a manuscript and said, 'I need you to edit this.'

Day after day, I spent time doing this—starting with prayer first, just to make sure I was focused on God and not myself; and day after day, this became not just something fun to do, but it became a passion—I wanted to be an editor."

A somewhat-bemused expression replaced his incredulity. "That's how you figured out what you wanted to do with your life?"

Flannery shrugged. "I call it praymagining. And it's worked for me in a lot of situations." Of course, she hadn't been using it in *this* situation. Could she imagine herself *with* Jamie O'Connor? Ugh—if she was with Jamie, as in, if they ended up getting to the point where marriage was a possibility, that would mean changing her name. . .to Flannery *O'Connor*.

No way! That was *so* not going to happen. If it were any last name other than that, she would change hers—maybe hyphenate, so she could still display her Irish heritage and her pride in whose daughter and granddaughter she was. Just not O'Connor.

But even with her utter abhorrence of having the name she'd learned to dread hearing, she could suddenly see herself walking up the church aisle toward Jamie—who was wearing a tux just like he'd worn at Zarah's wedding. He held out his hand toward her, and she placed hers in his. He kissed her hand, then bent forward and—

"Flannery? You okay?"

"I—yeah. I'm fine." She swallowed hard, blinking rapidly to clear the image of Jamie leaning toward her to kiss her.

Because now that she'd visualized it—or praymagined it or whatever she wanted to call it—she wanted it to happen even more than she'd wanted to become an editor.

# Chapter 19

❧

Jamie paused on the landing at the top of the stairs and waited for Kirby McNeill to catch up with him. He hadn't noticed in their previous encounters that the elderly man had problems with stamina, but he supposed that was to be expected in someone his age. It took Cookie almost twice as long to get up to the second floor of his townhouse as it was taking Flannery's grandfather.

"This will be your room." Jamie ushered Kirby into the slightly larger of the two extra bedrooms, the one he actually had set up for guests. He set Kirby's duffel on the low chest of drawers that also served as a nightstand for the bed.

"Thank you." Kirby sounded winded, as if having trouble catching his breath.

Jamie tried not to let his concern show. "The bathroom is the door directly across." He stepped across the narrow hall and flipped the light switch on. "I put some extra towels out, and there are some extra toiletries in the cabinet under the sink if you need anything."

He stepped aside so Kirby could enter the bathroom to put his shaving kit on the vanity. "This is a nice place you've got here. So much larger than Flannery's apartment."

"Where does she live?"

190

"High-rise in downtown. The entire back wall of the apartment is windows that give her a view of all the big buildings. It's pretty at night—until you're ready to go to bed and all the blinds have to be messed with just to make it dark enough to be able to sleep."

"She lives downtown and works in Brentwood?" Talk about backward.

Kirby nodded. "Don't know where that girl got the notion that she's a city gal, since she grew up in Green Hills before it was all developed the way it is now, but she seems to love it."

Loved it enough that she had asked Jamie about this neighborhood. "Well, you won't have to worry about city lights bothering you here. Cookie made sure when she helped me decorate that I installed blackout blinds under the curtains in each of the bedrooms."

Coming out of the bathroom, Kirby looked into the room right beside the guest bedroom.

"This is my office. I have wireless Internet in the house, but if you'd like to bring your laptop in here and sit at the table"—he entered the room and pulled the box still holding the few items he'd been forced to pack up under guard the morning he left the agency from the second office chair—"please feel free."

"I should send Flannery a message to let her know I arrived safely." Kirby stepped from the doorway of this room into his adjacent room and returned a scant moment later with his laptop case.

Jamie sat on the old, wobbly office chair—having rolled his newer, more comfortable, sturdier chair over to the table for Kirby to use— and turned to his desk. He jiggled the mouse to wake the machine up to check his own e-mail.

A new message from Ainslee. Probably another apology for having gotten him in trouble by mentioning to Armando's executive assistant that Jamie was spending his last week trying to land new business. He'd deal with responding to her later.

Behind him, Kirby's fingers began tapping on his keyboard. He still sounded winded, but some color began returning to his cheeks the longer he sat.

Jamie turned around at the cessation of typing. Kirby turned toward him.

"Mr. McNeill, I was hoping to—"Jamie's cell phone began to trill. He turned to pick the phone up off the desk, looking at the screen as he did so.

"Hey, Cookie. What's up?"

"Is Kirby there with you?"

He turned back to look at Flannery's grandfather. "Yes, ma'am. He's right here."

"Good. So I guess that means he found your place without any problems."

"It would appear so."

"Why don't you both come over here for dinner tonight? I put a corned beef brisket in the slow cooker this morning."

Mouth instantly watering at the thought of his grandmother's corned beef and cabbage, Jamie couldn't pass up that offer. "With parmesan smashed red potatoes?"

"I picked up the potatoes while I was out running errands earlier."

"I—let me check with Mr. McNeill and make sure he doesn't have plans for tonight already." Jamie lowered the phone and extended Cookie's invitation to him.

"I don't have any claim on Flannery's time this weekend, so I have no other plans and gladly accept."

Jamie relayed Kirby's acceptance to Cookie.

"And why don't you call Flannery to see if she'd like to join us, if she doesn't have any other plans."

Jamie stole a glance across the room at Kirby. Would Flannery be more likely to come if her grandfather invited her? No telling. But their time at lunch hadn't been long enough, and he could do with talking to her again, even if just for a brief time. "I'll do that."

He hung up with his grandmother and pulled the phone down to look at the contacts list as he scrolled through it. "Cookie wants me to invite Flannery, too."

Pressing the phone to his ear, he heard just one ring before she picked up. "What now, Jamie?"

He sure hoped that was *feigned* exasperation in her tone. "My grandmother just called and invited me and Big Daddy"—he grinned at purposely using her nickname for her grandfather when she'd teasingly told him not to in that e-mail—"to dinner at her house. She'd like it if you could come, too."

Flannery groaned. "I'd love to—because I'd love to experience some of what you've seen between the two of them. But I can't."

"Big date?" His voice held enough humor that she hopefully wouldn't notice the catch of vulnerability.

"Don't I wish. No—a project blew up at work today, and now I'm going to have to spend my whole weekend re-proofreading a book. I can't let the schedule get off, so it has to be finished before we all get back to work on Tuesday. Which probably means all-nighters tonight and tomorrow night just to get it done. So much for my holiday weekend, huh?"

When she'd said she was passionate about being an editor, she meant it. "I'm sorry to hear that. Have you gotten a break at all since Memorial Day?"

"A few hours here and there on the occasional Sunday afternoon. But. . .this is the life I chose, so I just have to suck it up and pick up the slack when necessary. Is Big Daddy there?"

"He got here about thirty minutes ago. He just sent you an e-mail to let you know he arrived safely." Across from him, Kirby nodded.

"Oh—well, I turned off my modem so I wouldn't be tempted to get online while I'm working. Tell him I'll call him tomorrow to let him know what the rest of the weekend looks like." She yawned. " 'Bye."

" 'Bye." Jamie passed Flannery's message on to her grandfather, who'd risen and moved over to look at the items displayed on the shelves over Jamie's desk.

Kirby picked up one of the still-boxed Arthurian action figures, looked at it from several angles, and then returned it to the shelf. He turned and looked around the room. Jamie did, too.

More action figures—all still in collectible condition in unopened packaging—framed posters from several different movies, and the costume he'd made for the movie premiere, which he'd mounted on the wall.

"I see you're a King Arthur fan." Kirby sat down again, continuing to look at all of the collectibles in the room.

"Yes, sir. Those are some of the first stories I remember reading as a kid." Looking at his office decor, he considered that to someone like Kirby, a retired pastor, it probably looked quite juvenile.

"Those were Flannery's favorite stories growing up as well."

Jamie went quite still, not wanting to do or say anything that might keep Kirby from continuing.

"It always annoyed her sisters that when they were told to play together, she never wanted to play school or house or with baby dolls. She wanted to act out the stories from Arthurian legend. When she was quite young, she would pretend she was Guinevere—after all, that was the female character who had the most stories about her. But then as she grew older and she read more than just the children's versions of the stories, she changed who she pretended to be. She wanted to be Reggie or Raggie or something like that. And when I asked her why, she told me she didn't like the fact that Guinevere cheated on King Arthur. And then she told me she liked Sir Gawain better anyway. So she wanted to be this other character, because this other character was the girl Sir Gawain ended up marrying."

"Ragnelle." Jamie could barely breathe.

"Yes—that's it. I should have guessed you'd know it. She made up all kinds of stories about this Reg. . ."

"Ragnelle."

"Ragnelle. Yes. She made up stories about Ragnelle because, she said, there wasn't really much about her in the legends. Once she hit her teens, when she still indulged in this playacting, her older sisters teased her unmercifully about it. For a while, I believed she gave it up. But then she told me when she was fifteen or sixteen, when I saw her highlighting something in one of the books, that she was studying it for the story she was writing. But she made me promise not to tell her sisters, because she didn't want to be teased about her continued interest in the stories."

It couldn't be—could it? No. There must be thousands of fans out there who wrote Ragnelle-centric stories. He'd thought, maybe, that the e-mails he and the writer had been exchanging sounded a little like Flannery—but that had just been wishful thinking. Hadn't it? He'd read too much into them in his desire that she wouldn't be so freaked out by that part of his life.

There was absolutely, positively no way Flannery was LadyNelle, his favorite fan-fiction author. Was there?

⚬⚬

Flannery grabbed Liam and set him down on the floor for the umpteenth time. "No, you can't lie on the keyboard." For all that Ragdolls were supposedly "floor cats," Liam liked to be up—on the bed, on the coffee table, on the sofa, on the treadmill, and especially on the desk if Flannery had docked her laptop to be able to use a real keyboard, mouse, and monitor for working. Fortunately, the kitchen counters were too high for him to heft his considerable bulk up onto—which was a good thing. The idea of a cat walking around on the surfaces where she might set food down grossed her out.

Liam started his crying *meow*, winding around and between Flannery's ankles. She glanced at the lower corner of the screen.

How had it gotten to be seven thirty already?

"Sorry, buddy. Didn't realize how late it was." She pushed the wooden-slat chair back and stretched, feeling her back pop in several places. The movement dislodged the pencil she'd used to hold her hair in a bun. She grabbed it before it could fall completely out, shook her hair out, massaged her scalp for a moment, and then finger combed her hair back and twisted it around into a tighter knot before sticking the pencil back through it.

She fed and watered Liam, then stood with the fridge door open for several minutes—long enough that she started to feel chilled. Closing the door, she turned and opened the top left drawer in the island.

Chinese. Thai. Chinese. Pizza. Pizza. Chinese. Chicken wings.

Blech. Why were these the only options for delivery? She could call in an order to Past Perfect and run up the block to go pick it up. . .but that would steal time from her work—and necessitate energy she just didn't have.

The doorbell rang. Had she ordered delivery and lost all memory of it? She skirted around Liam, who took up considerable space at his food dish at the end of the island, and answered it.

Jamie grinned at her from the hall. He hefted two canvas grocery bags. "Cookie sent me with leftovers." He stepped into the doorway and breathed in deeply through his nose. "Hey, do I smell coffee?"

He entered and left her standing there, holding the door open. He set the two bulging bags on the island then crouched down. Liam lifted his head from his bowl and meowed at Jamie. Jamie scratched the cat behind his ear and along his jaw.

Flannery could hear Liam purring from where she stood—with the door still open. She closed it and drifted over to the bar.

"How did you get in here? There's security. The concierge—"

Standing, Jamie held up a building security card. "Your grandfather loaned me this."

He washed his hands and dug into the first bag, setting disposable plastic containers on the island's granite countertop beside the sink. "Let's see. . .we've got corned beef and cabbage—packaged so that you'll have a good four meals from that. Roasted red potatoes"—he pulled out a lumpy, foil-wrapped package—"which need to be eaten tonight. We'll warm those up in the oven in a minute. Irish stew she made earlier this week—again, four meals' worth."

He stacked the four containers of stew next to the four containers of corned beef and cabbage and then pulled out a large glass casserole with its own plastic lid. "And a leftover shepherd's pie that didn't get eaten last night." He grinned at her across the island. "You can't call yourself Irish and not love my grandmother's shepherd's pie." He moved on to the second bag and continued pulling more plastic containers out.

Flannery hoisted herself up onto one of the tall bar chairs and rested her chin on her fist. Having grown up with a father who did most of the cooking—because of her mother's long hours first as a medical student and then as an intern and surgical resident—contentment and coziness embraced her at the sight of a man working in the kitchen, relaxing the muscles in her shoulders and neck.

"Where are Big Daddy and your grandmother? I thought you were all having dinner over at her house."

"There's some big-band, swing dance thing that she'd heard about that one of the churches in town holds every month for their senior adult group. So Cookie asked Big Daddy to take her dancing."

Her grandfather...dancing? Flannery wished she were there to see it. But then, she would have missed watching Jamie working in her kitchen.

Jamie stepped to the other side of the walk-through kitchen and studied the back of the stove for a moment before pressing some of the buttons on the black panel between the knobs for the five burners.

The appliance started beeping at him, and he looked over his shoulder at Flannery. "How do you get this thing to preheat?"

She shrugged. "I think the manual's still down in it."

He opened the oven and pulled out a deep metal pan that had a plastic sleeve filled with stuff taped to it. Straightening, he turned to face her. "Flannery, did you just get this range?"

"No. It's been here since I moved in."

He set the pan on the counter on the other side of the sink from all the food. "And how long have you lived here?"

"Just a little over three years—I was one of the first people to move in when the building was finished." Flannery slid off the bar chair and crossed to her desk—only a few feet away—to retrieve the cup of coffee she hadn't finished yet.

When she came back, Jamie stood with both arms locked, his hands braced against the edge of the counter. "You're telling me that in the three years you've lived here, you've never *once* used the oven?"

She paused, halfway back up onto the chair. "What? You're telling

197

me that you bake all the time?" Settling onto her seat, she pointed to a small appliance on the strip of counter between the stove and fridge. "I have a toaster oven. It's big enough for pizzas and a six-cup muffin pan. What would I need to use the big one for? It's just a waste of electricity. The toaster oven doesn't take as long to heat up, and it doesn't put as much heat out into the room." At least that's what the materials that came with the device had said.

Jamie's head dropped, and he shook it vigorously. But he smiled when he raised it again. "Point taken. But just in case you do decide to use the oven someday, I'm going to put the broiler pan in the storage drawer down here and let you file the owner's manual and instructions wherever you have those for the rest of your appliances."

Flannery took the paperwork and watched curiously as Jamie pulled open a small drawer under the oven. "That's a storage drawer? I thought it was another oven."

"It amazes me that you've survived living by yourself for this long." Jamie straightened and leaned over to turn the toaster oven on. He pulled the top of the foil package open, set it on the rack, and closed the door.

She stuck her tongue out at his back and then smiled as she carried the booklets over to her desk. Opening the file drawer, she found the file labeled APPLIANCES and stuck everything down in it. She stayed kneeling by the drawer for a moment when it finally caught up with her that Jamie O'Connor was *here*, in her condo, fixing a meal for her on a night when she'd started thinking that just skipping dinner would be the easiest thing to do.

Jamie O'Connor was *here*. She glanced around, making sure that everything looked okay. A sweater lay draped across the arm of the sofa. Her tablet computer and a stack of papers took up one side of the small dining table. She hadn't made the bed this morning; but even though it didn't have a door to close it off from the rest of the apartment, she didn't think she'd be showing Jamie her bedroom.

Knees beginning to ache against the wood floor, she stood and walked the few paces back to the kitchen. Jamie had started whistling as he moved the food containers from the counter to the fridge.

"This is just sad, you know." He jerked his head toward the fridge's interior. "A few takeout boxes, a bunch of sodas, a lot of condiments, and not a vegetable in sight." He clicked his tongue. "We're going to have to do something about that."

His *we* sent a tremor of anticipation rushing across her skin. "Big Daddy said that as soon as his vegetables start coming in, he's going to bring me some when he comes up for the weekends."

"Have you ever been to the farmers' market over at the Bicentennial Mall?"

"A couple of times. There's a really good Jamaican restaurant there."

Jamie sighed loudly. "I know you can't go tomorrow because of this editing project, but next Saturday, I'm picking you up early, and we're going to the farmers' market."

"I don't like vegetables."

"I watched you eat a vegetable sandwich yesterday along with broccoli soup." He popped the corner of one of the single-serve containers of corned beef and put it in the microwave, which hung over the stove.

He had her there. "Well, okay, yes. But that's pretty much my quota of vegetables for the week."

Jamie came over and leaned his crossed arms on the counter directly across from where she sat. "I'll let you in on a little secret. I don't like most vegetables, either. But there are a few I do like, and those are the ones I concentrate on. The rest. . .Cookie does a pretty good job of hiding them in dishes like stew and shepherd's pie—which she tops with creamed cauliflower instead of mashed potatoes."

She could almost see Maureen standing over Jamie, forcing him to eat veggies. "Does she cook for you a lot?"

Gray eyes soft, the corners of his lips raised in a tender smile. "Sort of. She cooks a lot. She always makes more than she needs to for the different Bible studies and ladies' luncheons she goes to every week. And I know she's concerned that I'm not taking good enough care of my health, so I think she always makes a little extra, especially of the healthier stuff, just to make sure that I'm not eating hamburgers or pizza for every meal."

He turned and went to the left side of the stove, to the coffeemaker. "Do you mind if I help myself?"

"Cups are in the cabinet right above it. So's the sugar. There's half-and-half in the fridge." She finished off the last bit of her coffee and, careful not to tip the chair over, stood on the bottom rung, leaned over, and put her cup on the counter beside the sink.

The microwave beeped, and the toaster oven dinged. Jamie pulled out the potatoes first and then the corned beef. "Plates are. . . ?" He made a slow turn in the middle of the small kitchen.

"Upper cabinet between the microwave and fridge."

"Ah. Logical placement. I'm impressed." He shot her a wink over his shoulder.

A month ago his teasing would have annoyed her—*did* annoy her. Now. . .well, she didn't want to think about how much her reaction toward him had changed in just a few weeks. "I can be that way sometimes."

"Logical or impressive?" He scooped the meat and cabbage out onto the plate and poured a little of the liquid left in the container over it. He then set the potatoes—still in their foil nest—onto the plate, which she appreciated, because they weren't down in the meat juice that way.

"Both. Aren't you fixing a plate for yourself?" Eating in front of him—knowing he'd be watching her—was not really her idea of comfortable.

"I ate over at Cookie's house before I came." He set the plate in front of her and then faced the other side of the kitchen again. "Now, if I were silverware, I'd be. . ." He opened the drawer between the stove and fridge. "Yep, you're right. Logical and impressive again."

He handed her a fork and table knife. "The meat has already pretty much fallen apart, but there are still a few chunks you might need to cut up. Do you want more coffee, or do you want one of the cans of soda from the fridge?"

"Lemon-lime soda, please." The first bite of corned beef melted like ambrosia in Flannery's mouth, tender and juicy, with spices that coated her tongue and filled her nose with their pungent aroma. She closed her eyes and chewed.

"Told you it was good."

She didn't open her eyes, even at the *clink* of the aluminum can against the granite bar. "Don't watch me eat, please."

When he grunted, she finally opened her eyes. "You're a heavy guy, aren't you?" He straightened, holding Liam. He picked up his large, bright-green ceramic mug of coffee. "We're going to go sit in the living room and get better acquainted. That way, I can't watch you but we can still talk if you're so inclined."

"Be careful. Liam likes coffee." The first bite had triggered Flannery's hunger, and she ate quickly but still enjoyed the wonderful flavors and textures of the soft meat and cabbage and the crisp edges of the parmesan-sprinkled, smashed, roasted, baby red potatoes. He was right, she should eat like this more often. And she would if someone else cooked for her.

Liam's tags jingled in the living room. "Liam. That's interesting. Where'd his name come from? Is that a nickname for a longer name?" Jamie sat with his back to her in the chair-and-a-half that faced the wall of windows.

Flannery almost choked on a mouthful of cabbage. She finished chewing and swallowing. "His name is Liam. Just Liam. It's Irish."

"But why Liam?" Jamie persisted. He took a drink of his coffee and then set the cup on the end table to his right. "Of course, one could make the leap that you named your cat after Liam Neeson, who played Sir Gawain in *Excalibur.*"

The last bite of potato stuck in Flannery's throat. She coughed and wheezed, eyes watering, trying to dislodge it. When that didn't work, she took a swig of soda to wash it down. Finally, it cleared, and she caught her breath just as Jamie made it to her side and started pounding her between the shoulders.

She waved him off. "I'm okay. Just inhaled when I should have swallowed." She cleared her throat, trying to get rid of the croakiness. No one could have ever made that connection. She'd picked the actor's first name because *she* knew it connected back to her favorite character, but for everyone else it seemed like just another way in which she embraced her Irish heritage.

Jamie pulled out the bar chair beside her and turned it then sat facing her. He took the fork from her and set it on the now-empty plate and took both of her hands in his, making her turn slightly in her seat to face him.

"Flan, there's something I need to ask you."

*Oh, dear Lord—no. He can't. We haven't been. . . .* She knew she'd been flirting with him a little bit, but surely he didn't think they were *there* yet! She started running rejections through her head—not wanting to hurt him, but not ready to make any kind of commitment yet.

"You don't, by any chance, write Sir Gawain fan fiction under the username LadyNelle, do you?"

She would have preferred the premature proposal.

# Chapter 20

❧

$\mathcal{H}$e wasn't sure what she thought he was going to ask her—because she'd looked terrified—but she certainly hadn't been prepared for that question.

"I. . .uh. . .I. . .What do you mean?" Flannery yanked her hands out of his, turned, and practically jumped off the opposite side of the tall chair. "What are you talking about?"

The urge to cover his ears at the high pitch of her voice almost outweighed his determination not to offend her by teasing her about what might be her biggest secret. "I mean, I know that you're. . ." He really needed to choose his words carefully. "Seeing that print in your office, knowing it's from the legend of Sir Gawain and Dame Ragnelle, and your nonverbal admission your cat is named after an actor who once played Sir Gawain, the pieces kind of fall together."

Only to someone with extremely twisted logic—or knowledge he would never tell her he had. If she found out what her grandfather had told him, she'd never forgive Kirby.

"If you are LadyNelle, there's something you should know. I'm the one you've been e-mailing with through the website. I'm the user who goes by the name TennesseeGawain."

Flannery leaned over the small dining table, hands braced on the corners. Maybe he shouldn't have sprung this on her right after she ate.

But if he was going to become a nurse, cleaning up after someone got sick would be part of his job. He would have to start getting used to it some time or another.

"I should have guessed." She straightened and stalked down the length of the open-concept, kitchen-dining-living room.

He turned, resting his elbow on the back of the bar chair. "Should have guessed what?"

"I told myself those e-mails seemed familiar because we've been going back and forth so often. I should have picked up on the cadence and the *seriously*s and the *by the way*s at the end—though you don't use *BTW* with those on the fan site e-mails the way you do on your regular e-mails." Standing in front of the floor-to-ceiling windows, she crossed her arms. The knot of hair at the back of her head hung lopsidedly, as if about to fall completely loose.

"I only posted my writing there because I thought it would be completely anonymous. Because I was confident that no one I knew would ever go onto a website like that."

Jamie slid off the barstool and moved a little closer—perching on the high, padded arm of the oversized chair. "Hey, I thought it was anonymous, too, but I got an e-mail through it this week from a friend—my best friend—who'd figured out it was me because of some of the discussions I posted on and some of the things I had marked as favorites—like your story. You're one of the best writers I've ever read. Why aren't you published?"

Shoulders sagging, Flannery turned and sank onto the end of the sofa. She leaned her head back against the high cushions and covered her eyes with her left hand. "Because Arthurian fan fiction is all I've ever written. I've tried writing other stuff before, but it just comes across as a cheap imitation of someone else's work."

She lifted her hand and looked at him without raising her head. "You *have* to promise me that you won't say anything about this to anyone. No one can ever know I still do this."

He moved from the arm of the chair down onto its seat, dislodging Liam—who jumped right back up into his lap. "You mean your best friends don't even know? Caylor? Zarah?"

Flannery shook her head. "Not really. They know that I occasionally still dabble with writing fan fiction. But they have no idea that I've been posting any of it publicly. I knew that would come back to bite me. I should have just kept it to myself. But I went out to see what others were doing, and I was so disappointed in their characters and writing ability that I felt compelled to post mine, just to give fans an alternative to a lot of the. . .really bad stuff I found. But if you figured it out, who else will? It'll be public humiliation all over again."

"Public humiliation?"

She covered her eyes with her hand again. "When I was seventeen, my sister Sylvia and I got into a huge fight. I don't even remember how it got started, but she accused me of reading her diary. I hadn't, but with Emily egging her on—because I had read Emily's diary when I was all of about eight years old—Sylvia believed her. When I was out at my riding lesson that day, Sylvia went into my room. She found my notebooks, filled with stories I'd been writing for years based on the Sir Gawain legends. When my boyfriend came to pick me up for prom that weekend, Sylvia started telling him all about how I was in love with a fictional character from a book and how I wanted him to change his name to Sir Gawain and wasn't it childish that I spent all of my free time pretending that I was part of a fantasy world. It was horrible."

Having seen how girls reacted to finding out he was something of a fanatic himself, he completely sympathized with her. "Tell me he didn't leave you standing there and didn't take you to the prom."

"Oh, no! That would have been better. He took me. And made a complete fool of me when he laughed about it with all his football team buddies. I ended up calling my mom to come pick me up—I was so humiliated. Thank goodness there was only a week of school left after that before graduation. Of course, by the time we all got there for the start of exam week Monday morning, everyone in school knew. I was never one of the most popular girls, but I'd had a large circle of friends. That last week, you'd have thought I had exploding boils all over, the way people avoided me. Which is why I now avoid just about everyone I went to high school with. Because that's always the first thing that comes up."

She sat up and hugged a pillow to her chest, drawing her feet up under her. "Of course, I would imagine they all went to see the movie *King Arthur* when it came out several years back, because then it was cool to be a fan of Arthurian legend. But about six months after that movie came out, I ran into a girl whom I'd considered a friend since fourth or fifth grade. And not two minutes into the conversation, she starts in on, 'Hey, how's that fantasy boyfriend of yours. . .now, which one was he in the movie?' I mean, come on! It's been sixteen years, and people still can't let it go."

"You know, being an Arthurian-legend junkie when I was a kid didn't win me a lot of friends, either." Under his hand, Liam rolled onto his back, clasped Jamie's hand between his paws, and started licking his fingertips. Jamie shuddered and pulled his fingers away from the rough tongue.

"It's different for you." She shook her head, her tone dismissive.

"Why is it different for me?" Setting Liam on the floor, Jamie pushed himself out of the chair and crossed to sit near her, in the middle of the sofa.

"Because you're a guy. You can do geeky stuff like that as a kid, but then if you grow up to be good looking and successful, people forget all about it."

Contentment vibrated through him like one of Liam's full-body purrs. She thought he was good looking and successful. "No, believe me—that kind of stuff stays with you no matter how successful you are. And let's not forget I'm not only the dork who was into all that kind of stuff as a kid—and who couldn't talk to pretty girls to save my life. I'm the guy who was that dork who's now *still* a dork who has trouble talking to pretty girls sometimes *and* is unemployed."

"Ha! With the way women start drooling the moment you walk in a room? I'm not buying it." She popped him with the pillow.

Grabbing onto the corner of it, he leaned forward. "Um, hello—

remember Fanny and the Dracula comment?"

"I remember." She stilled; the smile slipped slightly from her pouty lips. Lips he really wanted to kiss.

He pointed at himself. "Dork." He pointed at her. "Pretty girl."

Rolling her eyes, she yanked on the pillow again, and he let it go. "Whatever."

"It's true. Those first few times I was around you, I couldn't think straight. And when I can't think straight, words get past that filter in my brain—you know the one that says, 'That's stupid; don't say it'?—and they spill out of my mouth, and I can't control them." He wrapped a few silky threads of the pillow's thick tassel around his finger, imagining doing the same with her hair.

"You seem to have been doing a pretty good job of it lately." She shifted so that her back pressed against the arm of the sofa and she faced him.

Turning, he bent his left knee up onto the sofa, almost touching hers. "It wasn't easy. But I knew I needed to work at making you see I wasn't just some weirdo with no social skills."

She raised her eyes toward the ceiling, puckered her lips, and cocked her head. "Weirdo with no social skills. Hmm. . . Actually, I was thinking arrogant and condescending jerk, but six of one, half a dozen of the other."

"Seriously? You're going to go there?" He put on his best arrogant, condescending, tough-guy bluster. "Because I'll go there, Fanny, I will."

Finally she laughed. Not just a giggle or a chuckle, but a head-tossing, full-throated laugh.

Something fell out of her hair and hit the floor, and the blond mass tumbled around her shoulders. Jamie's hands itched to feel those loose curls wrapping around his fingers, to brush back the piece that came to rest on her cheek.

Flannery tucked it behind her ear and pushed the rest over her shoulders.

Words started boiling up in Jamie's brain, words that wanted to come loose. But even more than that, the compunction to lean forward and kiss her came so forcefully that it scared him. He'd kissed lots of women before—too many, probably. But the desire to kiss Flannery, to hold her in his arms, to cradle her head in his hands, to run his fingers through her hair. . .this was completely new.

He shot to his feet and backed away from her.

She set the pillow aside and stood, too, frowning. "What's wrong?"

"I'm about to say one of those dorky, socially inept things." Better to let the words spew out than to offend or embarrass her by giving in to the need to kiss her. "I really want to kiss you right now."

She lowered her head a little and arched her brows as if expecting more.

"I—that's it. That's what I needed to say." He turned and headed toward the kitchen. "I'll go now."

"Jamie, stop." The forcefulness in her voice stopped him as much as her words.

He didn't—couldn't—turn around.

"Please look at me."

Flinching at the nearness of her voice, he did as bade.

She stood just out of arm's reach. "I want you to kiss me, too."

His knees gave out, and he grabbed the back of the nearest bar chair.

"But—"

He should have known there'd be a *but*. There was always a *but* when it came to him and women.

She moved closer, and he straightened, meeting her eye-to-eye. When she reached up her hand and ran her fingers along his bearded cheek, the bar chair's feet started rattling against the floor. "Tell me the truth behind why you're growing a beard."

As soon as her hand dropped back to her side, a little bit of oxygen returned to his brain. He had a beard? What? Oh—right. "After praying and not really receiving a clear answer, I decided I wouldn't shave until I'd made a firm decision of what I want to do."

"And what do you want to do?" Her hand joined his on the back of the bar chair—not touching, but near enough that the slightest shift would bring them into contact.

He'd forced her to share her big, embarrassing secret. It only seemed fair to allow her to do the same to him. "I'm thinking about going to nursing school."

She didn't balk, didn't laugh, didn't run screaming in the opposite direction. "That's a big change from marketing."

"I know. I had breakfast with Danny—my best friend—Wednesday morning to talk about it." He told her a little about Danny's leaving the ad agency and going to nursing school. "Even though he didn't have some of the hang-ups about it that I do, he had other pressures—cultural and family—that made it difficult."

"Hang-ups?"

Just how much about himself did he want to share with her? "My dad—my real dad, not Don—was kind of. . .demanding and difficult. He'd been a marine and fought in Vietnam, and, according to Cookie, he came back with some weird notions about women and how they should behave and what they should do. When I was growing up, he was a cop. And it really bothered him when his department started hiring a lot more women. My mom was only nineteen when she married him, and I was born eleven months later. She'd had a year of college before they got married, and she wanted to go back, but he wouldn't let her."

"What did she want to do?" Flannery shifted her weight, and her pinky finger pressed lightly against his thumb. She didn't move it.

"She w–wanted"—he drew a deep breath and tried to quell the chaos going on inside his head from Flannery's nearness and the swirl of memories—"wanted to get her degree in business—in marketing, actually. He told her that was a man's world—business and marketing—and if she wanted to go to school, he'd pay for her to go to beauty school or nursing school, because those were appropriate jobs for women."

"So did she?"

"Yeah—she went to cosmetology school. And as soon as I started first grade, she got a job at a hair salon in our neighborhood so that

I could walk there after school, sit, and do my homework while she finished up with clients, and then we could walk home together."

"Is that why you ended up going into marketing? Because your dad said that was a man's world?"

Could she cut to the chase or what? With a sigh, Jamie pulled out the middle bar chair and sat. He motioned for Flannery to do the same. This could take awhile. He told her about the way his father had yelled at him for failing PE, for getting kicked off the peewee-football team, for being more interested in reading than in sports or hunting. And the arguments his parents got into because of it. Then he told her about his thirteenth birthday, including what Mom had just told him.

"So the last words my dad ever said to me was that he didn't want to be disappointed in me anymore. That I was thirteen years old, and as the Bible said, it was time to put away childish things and be a man. Less than half an hour later, he was dead."

Flannery reached over and took his hands in hers. "Oh, Jamie."

"I hated him. But I loved him—he was my dad." Jamie looked down at their entwined hands. "And ever since then, I've been trying not to disappoint him. But as both Mom and Don have pointed out to me recently, I've done that to the exclusion of making sure that I'm not disappointing myself. Oh, and that the 'putting childish things away' doesn't appear in the Bible quite the way Dad paraphrased it."

"How did your mom and Don meet?"

He told her about Mom's leaving six months after his father died. "She had a friend from high school who'd moved out to Salt Lake for college and then stayed, and she invited Mom to go out and live with her. Mom needed a job, so she went around to all of the salons in the area to apply. Several of them were salons that Don owned, so he brought her in for an interview. They got married two years later."

"Wait—your stepfather owns hair salons?" A little chuckle of disbelief preceded a smile.

He liked it when she smiled. "Yep—started out as a hairdresser, put himself through college, got his MBA, and started buying up salons all over the area—especially in the ski resort towns—and turning them into high-end 'experience' salons and spas. Mom went to college, got her business degree, and is now the vice president of marketing for the company."

Flannery stared down at their joined hands for a long moment. He didn't interrupt. This was a lot for anyone to take in.

"I can see why you're struggling to figure out what you want to do. Your real dad, the one whose blood you share, made you believe that if you didn't have a profession he deemed masculine enough, you'd always be a disappointment to him. Your stepfather, who sounds like he'd love nothing more than to have a genuine father-son relationship with you, is the antithesis of everything your real dad stood for and believed." She looked up at him. "You're having to choose between them. Like, if you choose to go to nursing school, you're picking Don over your dad."

Jamie swallowed hard. Without even knowing all the facts and details, she'd managed to pinpoint his exact problem and put it into succinct words. Don's advice of seeking out objective feedback had been right.

"I told you that I want you to kiss me, too. But I don't think now is the right time. I don't want to distract you while you're trying to make this decision. I also don't want our first kiss to be with you in a beard." The corners of her eyes crinkled up. "You need to figure out what you want to do with your life, what God is calling you to do. You told me that one of your options is going out to Utah to work for your stepfather. If that's where God wants you to go, I don't want to stand in your way. I want you to know, though, I will support you in whatever you decide, so long as you're following God's will and not your own—or someone else's."

She leaned forward and planted a soft, lingering kiss on his forehead. "I'll be praying for you," she whispered. She untangled her left hand from his and touched the shaggy hair at his temple. "Did you also decide not to get this cut until you figure everything out?"

"No, that's just me being lazy."

"I guess you deserve a few weeks of laziness after working for so many years." She slipped down from the bar chair and went around the island into the kitchen and started washing the plastic container the corned beef was in.

In other words, he'd had a month, and now it was time to get on the ball. Message received. "What are you doing for the Fourth of July?"

Shaking the excess water off the container, she looked across at him. She pulled four paper towels off the roll beside the sink—far more than she needed—and rubbed the container vigorously, making sure to get into all the nooks and crevices. "I usually go with Caylor and Zarah to a family cookout in the afternoon. But that's assuming I can get this editing done."

"Cookie invited your grandfather and me over to her friend Perty Bradley's house for their cookout Monday afternoon. So I guess I'll see you there, if you can make it."

Flannery passed the folded grocery bags and the washed container to him. "I guess I should try to get the project done by Sunday night so that I can."

He backed toward the door. "Good idea. What are you doing that morning?"

"Why?"

"Do you have any plans for that morning?"

"No. Why?" She stalked toward him.

He reached behind him to make sure he didn't hit the door. "Because if you're willing, there's somewhere I'd like to take you that morning. Somewhere. . .I think we can get to know each other a little better." He wrapped his fingers around the lever-style door handle.

"You're being awfully secretive about this." Suspicion oozed out of her.

"It seems to be a night for secrets. So will you go with me?"

"Do I get to know where?"

He could tell her—and have her decide she wouldn't be able to get that editing project finished after all. "No. I'll come pick you up at nine o'clock sharp. Wear comfortable clothes—we'll be inside, but you might work up a sweat." He pushed the handle down and stepped forward as he pulled the door open.

"Nine o'clock Monday morning?"

He backed into the doorway. "Nine o'clock Monday morning."

"All right. This had better be good. I'll be waiting for you in the lobby, so you can just pull up on the street. Wait—what kind of car do you drive?" She reached for the edge of the door and held it open as he backpedaled into the hallway.

"Big, black, four-door Dodge Charger with tinted windows."

"Jamie—"

The breathlessness in her voice almost drew him back to her side. "Flannery?"

"Be careful!"

He looked over his shoulder—and swerved to keep from running over one of Flannery's neighbors. The young woman shot him a dirty look and let her apartment door slam.

Jamie flourished his arms in a bow. "Sir Dork will now be leaving the building." With that, he turned and escaped to the elevators before he did anything else to embarrass himself tonight.

He took a few deep breaths as the elevator sped toward the ground floor. Inviting Flannery go to with him Monday morning was quite a risk. But she needed to see that side of him, to know what was important to him, before they went any deeper and one or both of them ended up getting hurt.

# Chapter 21

**From:** Chae Seung
**To:** Jamie O'Connor
**Subject:** RE: RE: Dinner

*Thank you for letting me know you'll be coming to dinner and bringing a guest. Danny's parents often ask him about you, so I know they'll be happy to see you. Please let me know once you have the name of the guest you will be bringing. My mother likes the formality of place cards, even though this is a casual, family dinner.*

*I've gone back and forth with this, but I've decided I must be perfectly honest with you. I wasn't thrilled when Danny suggested inviting you to come. I know he's always thought of you like a brother, but I think it's pretty rotten that just when you start getting successful with your career, you drop him from your life. Then when things look like they're about to get tough, all of a sudden you want to be buddy–buddy again. Danny believes that you're truly sorry for having done that. And because I love my husband, I want to believe it, too. I could make all kinds of threats, but I know I could never do anything to you that would rival you hurting my husband again. So all I can do is trust this is a genuine act of friendship, that you do want to participate in his life, and pray that his faith in you is well placed.*

*Now, as to your question about Sir Galahad. After we
were married, Danny admitted to me that the matchmaker his
grandmother hired told him in no uncertain terms that he was
not to mention to me anything about the King Arthur stuff, or
paintballing, or anything else the two of you used to do together.
Ever. Not even after we got married. But because Danny is who
he is, he can't keep anything to himself if he is interested in it. He
told me on our first date. I admit, I was a little concerned about
his level of interest in a fictional world—and that was before
he'd started the weekly (now monthly) King Arthur gaming
with his nurse friends. But I came to realize that having a rich
imagination is part of what makes Danny who he is, and it's a
big part of why I fell in love with him. It helps that he does have
other interests and doesn't talk about it nonstop—the way one
of his friends does. Now that guy, he's obsessed with that stuff so
much that it's a little scary to be around him.*

*I assume you asked because you like someone and you don't
know how to tell her about this. My advice is just tell her. If she
freaks out and doesn't want to see you again, she's probably not
the right person for you. And you never know, she may turn out to
share that interest and be the perfect person for you. If you never
tell her, how will you ever find out?*

---

"Wow—you look absolutely wiped out." Zarah draped her beach towel
over the wooden deck chair to Flannery's right.

Caylor handed Zarah and Flannery each a can of soda and returned
to her position on the chaise on Flannery's left. Hanging out at the
pool in Caylor's backyard had been a much better idea than going to
the crowded, noisy coffeehouse.

"Could be because she hasn't slept in forty-eight hours." Caylor
pinned her with an accusatory glare.

Flannery yawned. "I took a couple of naps here and there. But I
got the project finished so that I can enjoy what remains of my holiday
weekend."

"By sleeping it away?" Zarah sat and started rubbing sunscreen onto her arms and legs.

"I don't want to hear it from either of you. I know quite well that both of you have had to pull all-nighters to get a project finished just within the last couple of months."

Neither could argue, so they stopped ragging on her. She waited until Zarah was settled on her lounge chair to drop her news on them.

"I've been meaning to tell y'all—I'm not going to go out with Pax Bradley."

As expected, Caylor's head popped up, and she frowned at her. "You promised."

"I know. But. . .I also know whom I'm going to invite as my date to Caylor's wedding."

Both Caylor and Zarah sat up from their reclining positions.

"What?"

"Who?"

"It's probably just Jack, and she's teasing us." Caylor swung her long legs around to sit sideways on the chair, facing Flannery.

"It's not Jack." Flannery took a deep breath, maintaining her relaxed pose and a straight face. "It's Jamie O'Connor."

That drew even more drastic reactions from her two best friends.

"You've hated him ever since that first time you met him and he called you Fanny."

"And I distinctly remember you complaining on several occasions about his inclusion in my wedding party." Zarah turned onto her side so she could see Flannery.

"Which is exactly why I've been debating whether or not to tell y'all. Because I knew you'd never let me live down that initial impression of him. But I'm telling you, he's changed in the last few weeks. And most of it comes from his whole life being shaken up when he got laid off a month ago."

"That's terrible—a month ago? But the wedding was a month ago. How come I didn't hear about this?" The guilt for having been wrapped up in her wedding when someone else was going through a hard time would eat at Zarah for some time to come, if past experience had taught Flannery anything.

"He didn't tell a lot of people in the beginning. But then he went out to Utah to visit his family"—she grinned over his new attitude toward them—"and he came back almost a completely new person. And I like that new person."

Adjusting her sunglasses, she stole glances at her friends from the corners of her eyes. "We had lunch Friday, and then he came over and brought me dinner that evening."

The girls demanded details. Flannery gave them what specifics she could—he came over with the leftovers from Cookie, fixed her dinner, played with the cat, they talked, he shared some of his background, he left.

It sounded rather dull and dry the way she told it.

"So you just talked—at lunch and at dinner. Just. . .talked?" Caylor leaned forward and scratched her foot.

"He's got a lot of stuff going on in his life right now, and he needed someone to talk to, someone without a vested interest in what's going on." Except she did—because she definitely didn't want him moving to Utah. Not now.

Were there any major fiction publishers in Utah? Or maybe Jack would let her work remotely. No—that would never work. She'd have to figure out how to make a go of it as a freelance editor. If that's what she must do, she had the industry contacts to be able to make it work.

"Not vested *yet*." Zarah—ever the romantic. Or at least for the last nine months or so, since the love of her life, her first love, had come back. "It sounds to me like you're starting on a good foundation of friendship. You should have that trust in each other—knowing that you can tell the other person anything and they'll never judge you or think less of you, even if it's something you can't tell anyone else."

Flannery turned her head and studied the usually taciturn historian. The idea Zarah would have any secrets in her life that she felt she couldn't share with her and Caylor. . .Flannery couldn't imagine it. "But that's why I don't want to go out with Pax. I want to see what this thing with Jamie is before I go out with someone else."

Pushing her sunglasses up to the top of her head, Flannery straightened into a more upright position. "Speaking of secrets, there's something else I need to tell you two. Something I've been keeping from you for a while now."

"Sounds serious." Caylor touched her arm. "You know you can tell us anything."

"I know." Now that Jamie had called her out and made her admit the truth, it seemed silly that she'd kept it from her two closest friends. "You both know that I sometimes spend my free time writing Arthurian-legend fan fiction."

Both nodded.

"You've done it your whole life. You used to torture me by reading it to me." A wink followed Caylor's tease.

"But, Caylor, you remember what happened at prom—what ruined it for me."

"I don't," Zarah said.

Caylor launched into an explanation, relieving Flannery of the emotional expense of having to tell the story again this weekend.

"Those people are just lucky that I didn't go to your high school." Caylor rubbed her hands together.

"It wouldn't have mattered even if you did—you were finishing up your first year at Vanderbilt."

"True."

"Anyway"—Flannery turned more toward Zarah, who didn't know as much of this backstory as the woman she'd grown up with—"after that, I made sure that no one knew that I wrote fan fiction. I even invested in a locking file box in which to keep my notebooks. Once I had my own computer, I password-protected the files and gave them coded names that only I would understand."

She took a sip of soda, her throat dry from the long talking sessions and the lack of sleep she'd had the last two days. "But the thing about writing fan fiction is that we have a tendency to want to share it with other fans of the original story. After that movie came out several years ago—the one with Clive Owen in it—a bunch of Arthurian-legend fan sites, as well as a multitude of places to share and read fan fiction, cropped up. For the longest time, I read—the stories and the discussion forms—but didn't participate, and definitely didn't post anything. But I finally got so tired of the poor quality of stuff I'd read—not to mention how raunchy and sometimes downright depraved some of it is—I needed to provide an alternative, especially with the story of the characters who are my favorite. So about six months ago, I created a profile on one of the sites and started uploading my completely revised and updated story about Dame Ragnelle's life."

"Publicly? On the website, for anyone to see? After everything you've been through?" As a published author, Caylor should have understood the need to share what she'd written.

"It's published under my username, which has no connection to me or any way for people to find out who I am. So I thought I was safe from discovery, that I would remain anonymous."

"If this turns out to be another tragic story about someone finding out you do this. . ." Zarah fanned herself with her broad-brimmed straw hat—something she'd bought in New Mexico out of necessity.

"Well. . .sort of. Not the tragic part, though. You see, the story installments caught someone's attention and. . .we'd been e-mailing back and forth through the site. Usernames only—no personal information whatsoever. And the e-mails turned a little flirty."

"So there's another guy in addition to Jamie?"

"No—I'm getting there." She told them about Jamie's visit to the office and seeing the print of the Gawain-Ragnelle woodcut. About Jamie figuring out Liam's full name. "He asked me if I was that user—and told me he was the person I'd been e-mailing with."

Zarah laughed. "It's just like the movie *You've Got Mail.* You disliked him in real life, but under the protection of an assumed identity, you fell for him."

"Yeah—except I'd already started falling for him in real life before things got flirty on e-mail. So not only does he know that I'm a closet geek, but he actually appreciates that about me, being a former dork himself." A giggle bubbled up at the memory of his flourished bow and departure Friday night.

"What is it, Caylor?" At Zarah's question, Flannery turned to look at their friend, too.

"I've known Flan since before I can remember. I've been with you through every relationship you've ever had—from the initial euphoria of the crush to the ice cream and Dr Pepper of the breakups. But I have never—*never*—seen you like this before."

"Like what?" both Zarah and Flannery asked.

"In love."

"Ha!" Jamie whipped the card down onto the table. "One thousand miles."

Cookie and Kirby groaned. Yet it had been their idea to play *Mille Bornes*, a card game Jamie hadn't seen since elementary school. Apparently, they must have been practicing with it—because up until this sixth hand, they'd been trouncing him. But not this time.

Kirby's phone rang. He squinted at the screen and then smiled, slid his finger across, pressed a button, and held it to his ear. "Hello, Flan."

Jamie tensed, hoping to be able to hear her, but no such luck. An unreasonable surge of jealousy took him by surprise. Seriously? He was going to get jealous over Flannery calling her grandfather instead of him?

"I'm sorry to hear that, but I'm glad you'll be able to make it tomorrow. Sleep well. And don't worry about me, I'm well entertained." He said his good-byes and returned the phone to his shirt pocket. "I won't need to leave in an hour after all. Flannery finished her work project, but she said she didn't get much sleep. She's going to turn in early tonight so that she can enjoy all the activities tomorrow."

"How disappointing for you. I know you've said how much you enjoy the music program at the arts center." Cookie carefully stacked the cards and put them back in the box. "Would you. . . I know I am no replacement for your granddaughter, but if you still want to go, I would like to go with you."

Jamie left the dinette table and moved into the kitchen, where he promptly opened the refrigerator door and crouched down behind it so the two older folks could pretend like they were alone.

"That would suit me right dandy." Like his granddaughter, Kirby was usually very well spoken. But occasionally, he'd pop off with one of these countryisms, reminding them of his rural, farm-boy roots. Jamie imagined it was something he learned to do as a preacher, not only to relate to his congregants but also to keep them on their toes.

"Jamie?"

He stood, closing the fridge door and coming away empty handed at his grandmother's call. "Ma'am?"

"Will you be all right on your own without us tonight?"

Trying to keep from jumping up and down, Jamie leaned on the peninsula that separated the kitchen from the eat-in part of the kitchen. "I think I can manage on my own."

"That settles it, then. We'll take my car, and then I can drop you off at Jamie's house afterward."

Jamie didn't miss the fact that his grandmother laid her hand on top of Kirby's, nor that Kirby turned his hand over and clasped hers with it.

Too sweet—his grandmother was holding hands with her boyfriend. The childlike excitement that came from getting just what he asked for as a gift made him giddy. He wanted to call Flannery and tell her.

Even though lunch on Friday had been meant to discuss their plan for figuring out ways to put their grandparents together—though, on his part, it had really just been to see Flannery—Cookie and Big Daddy seemed to be doing just fine without them.

Measuring his pace so that it didn't turn into a happy dance, Jamie went around and kissed his grandmother's cheek. "I guess I'll see you tomorrow, then."

"We won't be out too late." Kirby looked from Jamie back down at Maureen. "Maybe grab some grub afterward?"

Cookie nodded.

"You kids be good now." Whistling, Jamie pulled his keys out of his pocket and headed out to the car.

Almost as soon as he hit the interstate, his phone rang. He hit the button to answer his phone through the car's hands-free system. "Hello?"

"Hey, it's Flan."

He clutched the steering wheel tighter—because raising both arms in victory wouldn't be prudent while flying down the highway. He did pound the fabric-lined ceiling a couple of times with one fist, though. "What's up?"

"I'm working on my story, and I've gotten to a point at which, in the past, I've written it a few different ways. I was thinking maybe I could run them past you and get your opinion on which one you like best."

Seat dancing—mostly just moving his shoulders and head—was something he could do in the car. "I'd love to help out with that. Hey, by the way, your grandfather and my grandmother are going out again tonight."

"How did you arrange that?"

"I didn't—you did, by calling and canceling on your grandfather. Cookie offered to go in your place. They invited me go with them, but I declined, of course."

"Of course. So where are you now?"

"I'm on I-440 about to get onto 65 and head home."

"Want to come over?"

Jamie changed lanes quickly to take the north exit instead of the south exit. "I'm on my way. Want me to pick up something for dinner?"

"There's a new Thai place that delivers. Why don't we do that?"

Thai, Chinese, pizza, cardboard. Would it really matter? "I'll be there in a few minutes."

"Do you still have the security card to get in?"

"Did you really think I was going to give that up once it was in my possession?"

"I guess not. So what are you going to want to eat?" She read the menu to him.

By the time he'd told her what he wanted and she repeated it to him, he'd pulled into a parking space on the street. "Don't order yet. I'm on my way up."

Moments later, he knocked on her door, heart hammering. Flannery didn't want him to kiss her until he'd figured out what he wanted to do with his life. But really, the only thing he wanted to do with his life was spend time with her. He doubted she'd take that as an answer, though.

The person who answered the door was definitely not the Flannery he was used to seeing. With her hair pulled back in a partially up/partially down ponytail, no makeup, and wearing sweatpants and an oversized T-shirt, and from the dark circles under her eyes—and the fact she couldn't seem to get them open all the way—Jamie could understand why she had canceled on her grandfather, claiming fatigue. Definitely not a ploy on her part to make Kirby and Cookie spend more time together.

She handed him the menu—with a sticky-note on it containing her order—and left him in the kitchen while she padded in her socked feet over to the armchair. Not quite the width of a loveseat, it just about swallowed her whole, leaving only the top of her head and the screwy ponytail showing.

Something brushed against Jamie's leg. As soon as he looked down, Liam started meowing—though it sounded more like a little kid crying.

"As soon as you order, would you mind getting a can of food out of the pantry and feeding Liam?"

It hadn't been a poor connection on the phone—her voice really was low and gravelly tonight. Jamie quickly scanned the menu, though he'd been certain of what he wanted. Flannery's sleep-deprived brain just hadn't been able to process it.

He placed the order—which was promised in thirty minutes—then turned his attention to Liam. The pantry would be one of those two doors. He opened the one closest to the end of the kitchen. Yep—well, a utility closet with the water heater taking up most of it. But judiciously placed shelves maximized the small space. A couple dozen cans of cat food occupied a high shelf. Never having dealt with feeding a cat before, he grabbed a can without reading the label.

Liam's crying intensified.

"Oh, cat, shut up." The moaning complaint from Flannery could barely be heard over the cat's begging cries.

Jamie bent to pick up the empty bowl from Liam's mat, happy the can had a pop top, since he didn't see a can opener on the counter anywhere, and he didn't feel like digging through her drawers to find a handheld one.

He pulled the lid off the can—and strangled out a gagging cough. "Is it supposed to smell this bad?"

"Yeah." Flannery lethargically waved a hand over her head. "It usually smells pretty bad. Please rinse the can out before you put it in the recycle bin so it doesn't stink up the whole place."

Jamie used the bent can top to scrape the foul-smelling brown stuff into the bowl. He thought Liam might keel over of an apoplexy with the way the cat stiffened as Jamie put the bowl back on the mat, but instead the cat hunkered and chowed down.

After making sure every morsel of the foul-smelling stuff was gone, he found the recycle bin and tossed the can and lid into it.

Finally, he made his way to the living room, dropping onto the end of the sofa closest to her. "What've you got for me?"

Sitting cross-legged in the big chair, Flannery had her laptop balanced on her right leg, one spiral notebook on her left knee, and two more notebooks on the coffee table, which she'd pulled over in front of the chair.

They spent the next hour reviewing the scenes she'd written five, twelve, and twenty years ago. The Thai food was great, in that it was delivered on time and hot, but mediocre in its quality. However, Jamie would gladly sacrifice quality food for quality company.

Around eight o'clock, as they discussed the pros and cons of different events from each of the scenes, Jamie got up to put the leftover food away and rinse the plates and utensils to put in the dishwasher.

An idea for a totally new scenario hit him. Shutting off the water so she'd be sure to hear him, he told her exactly what he could see happening in the scene.

Silence met him when he finished.

"Flannery?" He dried his hands and walked over to the chair. In the semidarkness—with no lights turned on in the living room, only the glow of the city beyond the windows—he could easily see he'd lost her. Rescuing the laptop before it slid off onto the floor, he set it and the notebooks on the coffee table, which he pushed back to its original position in front of the sofa.

He considered trying to carry her to her bed, but though she was slender, she was the same height as he. And a runner, if the 10K charity run T-shirt she wore was any indication, meaning muscle tone would make her heavier than she appeared. Plus, she looked so comfortable and peaceful—he didn't want to disturb her. Instead, he pulled the soft throw from the back of the sofa and covered her with it, tucking it around her shoulders.

Almost jumping out of his skin with the urge to kiss her, Jamie pushed a loose strand of hair back from her cheek, leaned over, and kissed her temple. That was all Flannery would do the other night, so that was all he would allow himself.

Opening the laptop to jot down his idea for her, he discovered he couldn't when it came up to a screen asking for a password.

Well, he had access to paper and pen. Turning one of the notebooks to a blank page, he started writing. Somehow, in getting the high points of it down in black and white, it seemed a bit cliché, maybe even silly. But he'd let her be the judge. She was the writer, not him.

The blinds provided him with a challenge—figuring out that they were electronically, not manually, controlled and then actually getting all of them to close. He left the light over the stove on, just so she wouldn't wake up in the dark and hurt herself.

But before he could leave, he had to do one more thing.

He picked up the notebook and took it into the kitchen where he could see. On the last blank page in it, he drew a heart that went from

225

edge to edge, top to bottom, running the gel-ink pen over it several times to thicken the line. Then inside, he wrote a note that he hoped Flannery would understand.

As quietly as he could, he tore the page out. Pulling two magnets off the side of the refrigerator, he hung the note on the front, right over the water dispenser, where she wouldn't miss it.

At the front door, he paused and turned to look back. He could barely see the bump her head made on the arm of the chair. "Good night, LadyNelle."

His gaze fell on the note on the fridge.

*Gawain + Ragnelle*

The names of their two favorite characters contained in a heart.

*Jamie + Flannery*

That was the note contained in his heart. He prayed it was in hers, too.

# Chapter 22

Flannery pulled her pinky finger away from her mouth when she realized she was chewing the nail. Ever since Jack had brought the habit to her attention, she'd cut down on the physical display of her nerves. But sometimes...

A large, aggressive-looking black car pulled up to the curb. Black with tinted windows. That's what he'd told her.

Taking a deep breath, she slipped her sunglasses on and stepped out into the hot morning sun, reflected as it was off the glass building behind her and the concrete and asphalt of the city sidewalk and streets. One thing about summer—city dwelling seemed to make her only too aware of just how hot it got in Nashville.

The driver's door of the car swung open, and Jamie—dressed in tan cargo shorts and a light-blue T-shirt with ankle socks and athletic shoes that showed off his toned, tanned lower legs—jogged around to the passenger side and opened the door for her. The *back* door.

"Good morning." His shameless grin made her only that much more nervous.

Until she peeked into the car. Big Daddy turned and looked over his shoulder. "Morning, darlin'."

She straightened and pinned Jamie with the glare that usually made editors and graphic designers squirm and agree to her deadlines no matter how tight. "Where exactly are we going?"

"Just get in the car."

With one more glare, she climbed in, her twill khaki shorts sliding easily on the smooth leather seat. Jamie closed the door behind her. The cool, dim interior of the car made her shiver from the contrast to the heat outside. She pulled her glasses off again.

"Big Daddy, where are we—"

"I promised I wouldn't tell." Her grandfather exchanged a conspiratorial grin with Jamie. She didn't really like either of them right now.

Granted, she wasn't necessarily a morning person. And even after getting up around ten last night and moving from the chair to the bed, her neck still hurt. Caylor'd been telling her about the absolutely fabulous massage therapist she'd found—she treated herself to a massage at the end of each semester as well as each time she finished and turned in a novel to her publisher. Flannery pulled out her phone and made a note to be sure to get the name and number from Caylor and set an appointment. She deserved it, after all the extra time she'd been putting in at work so far this summer.

In the front, Jamie and Big Daddy talked about some cutthroat game of cards they'd played—though it didn't sound like any card game she'd ever heard of. Familiar landmarks rolled by as Jamie drove down Broadway, angling toward Vanderbilt and then slowing as the road narrowed in Hillsboro Village.

When he put on his turn signal to turn onto Acklen Avenue— right in front of the church—Flannery leaned forward, as far as the seat belt would allow. "Where are we going?"

"Ten seconds and you'll see." Jamie smiled at her through the rearview mirror.

Two blocks up, he turned left into a tree-shaded parking lot.

"Hillsboro Village Assisted Living." She hadn't been here since her early twenties, when the college group from the church took on the senior center as their volunteer project.

Big Daddy opened her door for her and offered her his hand.

Though she didn't need it, she took it and continued to hold it as they followed Jamie into the building.

Red, white, and blue bunting, streamers, and balloons hung from every corner of every wall and desk and countertop in the place.

Maureen met them near the reception counter and introduced Flannery and Big Daddy to several of the staff and the center's director. Flannery filed each name away, grateful for their name tags on a day when she would be meeting dozens of new people.

A large contingent from the church's senior adult group gathered in the front lobby, and after a few minutes—with Big Daddy and Maureen introducing Flannery and Jamie to everyone they hadn't yet met—the director led them back to the community room.

"We need help setting up chairs in rows to face the stage, and tables along the back for food. And for those who can't do that kind of heavy lifting, we could use your help with arts and crafts in the dining hall."

Jamie and Flannery joined the nursing staff and a few other younger volunteers in setting out chairs, while Maureen and Big Daddy joined the group going to the dining hall.

"I suggested to Cookie that your grandfather probably shouldn't be doing much vigorous activity today." Jamie pushed a cart stacked high with heavy wood-framed upholstered chairs to the end of a half row already set out.

Flannery spun, watching her grandfather as he disappeared into the other room. "Why? What's wrong?" She started toward the dining hall.

Jamie grabbed her arm and pulled her back toward the stack of chairs. "He says it's allergies—that it always happens around this time of year. He's just having a little trouble with catching his breath and his stamina."

As a fellow seasonal allergy sufferer—probably inherited from him—Flannery could sympathize. But worry chewed at her enough that she spent the first few minutes of helping Jamie set out chairs praying for her grandfather.

"You. . .um. . .so are you surprised that this is where I wanted to bring you?"

Startled, she almost tripped over the chair she'd been pushing to the end of the row. Jamie stood there, hands in his pockets, rocking from heel to toe, deep lines between his brows, bottom lip pulled completely into his mouth. Wow, he was even cute when anxious.

"Yeah—a little. But it's a good surprise. I used to volunteer here when I was in high school and college—and I've been meaning to get back. But you know what they say about good intentions."

A slow smile softened his features—what she could see of them around the mustache and beard. He'd trimmed it, but she'd really much rather see his dimples. She gulped a couple of deep breaths. Beard or no, the temptation to kiss him grew greater each moment she was with him.

Especially after seeing the note this morning.

*Gawain + Ragnelle.*

She'd taken it off the refrigerator and had been about to file it—to protect it, she told herself—in the lockbox with all the notebooks from yesteryear. But as she knelt there by the box in her closet, she thought about what the note represented.

Past pain.

Secrets.

Humiliation.

Embarrassment.

Personal joy.

Relaxation.

Contentment.

Fun.

Acceptance.

Love.

She'd put the note right back on the fridge. If she had time this week, she'd get over to the craft store and find a frame for it, because it did need to be protected.

*Jamie + Flannery* needed to be protected. Not *Flannery*. That's how she'd entered—and ended—every relationship she'd had since high school. No matter what, protect herself from getting hurt.

Her knees gave out a little when she gave in to the urge to take a break and stand back and watch Jamie work. For all that he'd been an office-job guy, he must have spent a lot of time at the gym. His arms bulged with muscles as he lifted three and four chairs at a time from the stacks. Even with his T-shirt untucked, she could see enough of his shape to know that he had a trim waist.

How could a guy who looked like that—like some of the worst world-class jerks she'd ever had the misfortune of meeting—be the kind, caring, funny, self-deprecating dork (to use his own word) she'd always told herself she'd someday fall for?

Jamie finished setting out the chairs in his stack then turned and looked around the room. The creases between his brows vanished, and the corners of his mouth drew up into a smile—no, not just *a* smile, *her* smile, the one he gave just to her—when their eyes met.

A wave of euphoric dizziness almost pulled her into its undertow, and she grabbed the edge of the table behind her.

She loved him. She barely knew him. But she loved him. Enough that she'd do anything he asked of her, especially change her last name to O'Connor.

❧

Jamie enjoyed getting to see Flannery in action. And the girl could move. Her lithe figure belied her strength, as she held her own against the burly orderlies in the physical labor of getting the community room set up.

Once the director deemed they'd put out enough chairs, she asked for help in decorating the space—hanging bunting, draping streamers, and blowing up balloons.

"I'll do the balloons." Flannery eyed the ladder a maintenance man carried into the high-ceilinged room, chewing on the nail of her pinky finger. Not fan of heights, huh? He'd file that away for future reference.

"Oh, I wouldn't ask volunteers to go up on the ladder—staff only.

Cuts down on liability. But do as many balloons as you can. What we don't use for decorations in here, we'll tie to the residents' wheelchairs and walkers or give to the kids who come out to visit this afternoon.

Jamie offered to be a spotter, holding the base of the ladder steady while the guy at the top jiggled it around as he worked. He handed up tools and supplies as needed and helped move everything around the room.

They'd just reached the last corner when high-pitched laughter caught Jamie's attention. It sounded like Flannery. . .but not. He exchanged a curious glance with the maintenance guy—two rungs up with heavy bunting hanging across the entryway to the dining hall.

Jamie turned. Three orderlies stood in a semicircle around Flannery, who—at that very moment—put a balloon up to her mouth and inhaled. She said something in a cartoonishly high voice, and all four of them laughed.

He didn't know whether to join in the laughter or go pull her away. Couldn't she see the three men were smitten with her?

"You're a lucky man." The maintenance guy tapped Jamie's shoulder.

"I'm—what?" Tearing his gaze away from Flannery, he looked up.

"I've seen the way that gal looks at you. It's not very often that a fella finds a woman who'll look at him as her one and only, and that's the way she looks at you. It's easy to tell y'all have been together a long time, too. Not many would feel comfortable letting other men try to get their woman's attention. But when you're confident she loves you, and you alone, there's nothing to worry about, is there?" He pointed to Jamie's left side. "Now, hand me that hammer."

With a man's safety depending on him, Jamie had no choice but to steady the ladder, turning his back on Flannery. The laughter died down, replaced once again by the steady rhythm of balloons being filled and tied off.

That was just it, wasn't it? He'd fallen, and fallen hard, for Flannery. But he really didn't know her all that well. He knew her deepest, darkest secret—or at least, he hoped she didn't have any others—but he didn't even know her birthday or exactly how old she was, though he assumed within a year or two of his own thirty-five.

His new weekend roommate could be a fantastic source of all that kind of information—Jamie just needed to figure out how to get it without interrogating her grandfather.

They'd been e-mailing back and forth almost daily through the fansite—but not sharing anything personal. Through regular e-mail, several days lapsed between messages and responses—though she'd e-mailed him a couple of times a day since lunch Friday.

Cookie had told him that she'd fallen in love with his grandfather through the letters they wrote back and forth while James lived in Atlanta and Cookie was in college and nursing school. Could he and Flannery be doing the same thing—only with a compressed timeline due to the speediness of electronic mail?

Before he could join Flannery at the helium tank, she finished tying a long string to the last balloon, which she let float up to the ceiling. The orderlies had disappeared, and the maintenance guy collapsed the ladder and carried it out.

Jamie sauntered over to her, hands in his pockets, whistling to hide any trace of the doubts and questions plaguing him. "Having fun?"

She pulled her hands out from behind her back. Pinched between her fingers and thumbs were the necks of two balloons. She put one up to her lips and held the other one out toward him. "I couldn't leave you out," she said in her little-girl-cartoon voice.

Jamie inhaled a little bit of the helium. "Thanks for thinking of me."

Flannery giggled, her voice returning to normal. They stood there for ten minutes, talking like little cartoon kids when they weren't laughing too hard to form words.

With the last little bit of helium, Jamie said, "I'm really glad you came with me today."

Flannery flung her arm around his neck and took in the last bit of her helium. "I'm really glad you asked me."

Jamie put his arm around her and rested his hand in the small of her back. Their bodies weren't touching anywhere else, but with only a little pressure, he could have her in his arms in a nanosecond.

"Where's the party?"

They both turned in the direction of the loud voice, dropping their arms as if they'd been doing something wrong. An elderly man with a walker ca-chunked into the community room.

Jamie stepped forward, ready to assist if needed. "We were waiting for you. We can't have a party without you, Fred."

Fred's entrance began the wave of people moving from the dining hall into the community room, ready for the day's program to begin. Jamie offered his assistance to one of his favorite little old ladies, and Flannery was about to offer hers to another when the director pulled her to the back corner of the room. He couldn't tell what they talked about, but the director seemed worried. Then Flannery reached out and touched the woman's crossed arms, smiling and nodding as she responded. The director smiled and hugged her, pinning Flannery's arms to her side briefly.

Whatever it was about, Flannery seemed to have made the woman's day.

It took awhile for all of the residents, their family members who'd already arrived to spend the day, and the senior group from the church to shuffle into the room and take their seats.

The little kids, whose voices they'd occasionally heard from the dining hall during arts-and-crafts time, trooped up onto the stage. One of the two ladies with them sat down at the baby grand piano. The other one stepped out to the front of the stage.

"Please stand as you're able for the Pledge of Allegiance and the singing of the national anthem."

Jamie hurried to join Flannery at the back of the room as about three-quarters of the people in the room struggled back to their feet.

He got there just in time to "assume the position"—the stiff little soldier-man stance his father had drilled into him as a small boy—for the Pledge and anthem.

After the anthem, Big Daddy waved them over to the back row on the other side of the room. Flannery slipped her hand around Jamie's elbow.

His feet didn't touch the floor until they got over to where their grandparents had saved them seats and Flannery released his arm. He went in first—which meant Flannery sat beside Cookie, who put her arm around her shoulders and gave her a squeeze. Flannery leaned close and pressed her cheek to Cookie's, and they both gave a silent air kiss.

Jamie collapsed into his chair. Cookie hadn't liked any girl he'd ever introduced her to as a date, much less a girlfriend. Did Flannery meet her approval simply because Cookie had a crush on Flannery's grandfather?

No. Because if Flannery and Cookie ever had a chance to sit down and talk privately, they would probably walk away from it best friends. Or close friends, anyway.

Flannery mouthed the words along with the children's choir— "America, the Beautiful"; "My Country 'Tis of Thee"; and the big finale of "This Land Is Your Land."

Toward the end of the last song, the music leader turned around and waved her hands at the audience. "Everyone join hands and sing along."

Flannery didn't just put her hand in his—she twined her fingers through his in a very nonplatonic gesture. Her shoulder pressed against his, and he swayed with her to the rhythm of the music as they both sang as loudly as they pleased—no one could hear them over the cacophony of voices filling the large room.

He was holding hands with Flannery McNeill. *God, this is what I want. My career doesn't matter. I'll do whatever You want. I'll take a job as a garbage man or a street sweeper if that's what You want. But my part of the bargain is that no matter what career it is, I get to keep Flannery.*

Either God heard and answered or Flannery made the decision for Him, because when the song ended and everyone else in the room released each other's hands, Flannery didn't budge hers.

The center director took the stage as the children stomped down the steps and were then led out of the room. "And now we have some special guests with us who are going to do some readings."

Flannery released Jamie's hand. Maybe she'd just forgotten—

But then she stood up and left him—scooting past Cookie's knees. Big Daddy stood so she could get out of the row, and she walked toward the front of the room.

"Some of you may remember her from years ago when she would come in and read to you for hours and hours each week. Flannery McNeill is going to read the poem 'Paul Revere's Ride' by Henry Wadsworth Longfellow." She stepped aside from the podium.

Flannery adjusted the microphone, moved something around on the stand, and then looked out at the audience, making eye contact and smiling. " 'Listen, my children, and you shall hear of the midnight ride of Paul Revere. . . .'"

Read? Ha! Try *recite*. In all the years Jamie had spent the Fourth of July here, the program hadn't changed, just the people participating in it. And no one had ever given such life to Longfellow's poem. Jamie leaned forward, elbows on knees, and closed his eyes, nodding his head to the melody and rhythm of Flannery's voice. When she finished, loud applause and cheers went up for her. And over even that, he heard a woman's voice crackle out, "That's her, I'm telling you!"

Obviously someone remembered her from her volunteer days.

She smiled and waved as she walked to the back row. Jamie wanted to kiss her. Instead he settled for putting his arm around her atop the back of her chair and resting his hand on her far shoulder.

Her ponytail tickled his arm when she leaned toward him. "Did I sound okay?"

He squeezed her. "You sounded great."

The pastor from Acklen Avenue got up and read the Declaration of Independence—to a light smattering of applause, and then Kirby McNeill was invited to the stage to recite the Gettysburg Address.

Kirby braced his hands on the pulpit—and Jamie tried to envision him preaching a fire-and-brimstone sermon, then laughed at the absurdity of that idea.

"Whew. That's a long walk up here from the back." Light laughter met his banter. After a couple of deep breaths—Flannery and Cookie looked at each other, and Jamie could see the concern in Cookie's eyes—Kirby started. " 'Four score and seven years ago. . .'"

Once started, he did just fine, and he received more applause and cheers than the pastor, but not quite as much as Flannery.

The program continued with a little more music and closed with a recognition of the veterans. Kirby stood when the U.S. Army song was played—and that didn't surprise Jamie at all. According to Cookie, Kirby was a few years older than James, so he'd have been the right age to serve in World War II. Most of the men in the room around Kirby's age stood as well, during one or the other of the military theme songs.

Flannery slipped her hand into his again, and when he looked at her, tears glistened in her eyes. She smiled and wiped away an escapee. "This part always gets me. I should remember to carry tissues in my pocket on Independence Day."

Jamie made a show of patting the multiple pockets of his shorts, then slid his fingers under the sleeve of his T-shirt and stretched it out toward her. "This is what I use."

Laughing through her sniffles, Flannery gave him a little shove with her shoulder. When the music ended, she was the first to jump to her feet, cheering and clapping. Jamie joined her, as did the rest of the younger people in the room. She leaned over Cookie, who sat to applaud, and hugged her grandfather.

"Lunch will be served in the dining hall in fifteen minutes, so please make your way into the other room."

Instead of getting in the way, they stayed seated while the room buzzed with activity around them.

Cookie put her arm around Flannery and pulled her close. "You did such a lovely job reading the poem. It's obviously one you know well."

"I had to memorize it in eighth grade, and it's stuck with me ever since. It's always been one of my favorites."

"Excuse me, Ms. McNeill?"

Flannery turned at a voice behind them. A middle-aged woman stood with her husband and children and a very frail older woman in a wheelchair.

"I told you she came," the older lady said.

Jamie stood and moved his chair so that Flannery could stand and move around to talk to them.

The woman introduced herself to Flannery and started to introduce the old woman, but Flannery crouched down beside the wheelchair. "You're Addie Parker. I used to read to you." She took the woman's ivory, veined hand in hers.

Addie beamed up at the family towering over her. "I told you. Flannery O'Connor used to come and read to me every week."

Flannery looked stricken—but only for a moment before she laughed. "Mrs. Parker—I used to come and *read* Flannery O'Connor *to* you. My last name is McNeill." She stood but kept hold of the lady's hand.

"You can't believe how worried we've been about her mind over the last ten or so years. Every time she'd start in on why Flannery O'Connor never came to read anymore, we just thought she was going senile. Flannery O'Connor was always her favorite author, so we thought she was just confused."

Flannery patted the back of Addie's hand. "Because of people always connecting my first name with Flannery O'Connor, I avoided reading her as long as I could. But Addie didn't want anyone else but O'Connor, so we read her. I think that's the first time I ever had an appreciation for the writer my mother admired so much as to name me for her."

Proud of her for not going off on her rant about how much she hated that comparison, Jamie couldn't help but be grateful she hadn't been the daughter named after Sylvia Plath.

Addie's family wheeled her away—after Flannery promised to come read to her again sometime soon.

Most of the crowd had made it into the dining hall. Jamie held out his hand toward Flannery.

"Y'all go on ahead. I'll be along in a minute." She headed out the opposite door.

Jamie followed Cookie and Big Daddy into the room, and they

found four seats at a big round table in the corner. Food was served family style, with large platters of baked chicken and corn on the cob, and bowls heaped with potato salad and coleslaw. Jamie served plates for both himself and Flannery, but he waited to start eating until she came.

But when she still hadn't come when everyone else at the table was halfway through with their food, he knew something was wrong. Excusing himself, he stood and went back through the community room to the hallway into which she'd disappeared.

Flannery leaned against the wall, hand covering her eyes, her breathing ragged.

"What's wrong?" Jamie pulled her into his arms.

"I'm such a horrible person."

He almost laughed—until he realized she was serious. "No you're not. What are you talking about?"

"Addie," she sobbed out. "She's been asking about me for ten years. But did I ever make the time to come back here? She wanted me— needed me—and as soon as I finished school and got out into the real world, I completely forgot about everyone here. I'm so s–s–selfish and self-centered."

He thought about teasing her that *selfish* and *self-centered* were pretty redundant with each other—the way she teased him about his inadvertent, and sometimes purposeful, grammatical errors in his e-mails. But grief rattled through every breath she took—now wasn't the time for teasing.

"You can't change the past. But you can change. You can start coming up here with me every week."

She pulled back from him, and her teary eyes darted back and forth looking into his. "Every week? What do you do up here every week?"

"I'm the caller for Thursday night bingo. I have been since I was thirteen years old, when Cookie would bring me up here because she couldn't leave me at home alone." He reached up and pushed the damp ends of her bangs out of her eyes. "So while I'm calling bingo, you can

239

come up and read to those who want it. How does that sound?"

Flannery ran her fingertips down his jaw, tickling his beard. If he had a purr box, he could definitely out-purr Liam right now.

He couldn't stand it any longer. Hooking his hand behind her neck, he pulled her forward and kissed her. The pillow softness of her lips was even better than he'd dreamed. Her hand flattened against his cheek, and she kissed him back.

Heart racing, he pulled back and then gave her another light kiss. He blinked a few times before he could see her clearly. "I'm s–sorry. I know you d–didn't want the b–beard—"

Flannery pressed two fingers against his lips. "It's not so much the beard as what it represents." She frowned. "Well, actually, it is the beard, too."

He captured her hand in his and kissed the fingertips touching his lips. "The beard will be gone before the cookout this afternoon—if you don't mind being a little late so that we can stop by my house on the way so I can shave. Either that, or you can ride with Cookie and Kirby over there, and I'll just meet you."

"I'll go with you." She watched her own fingers as she ran the backs of them down the facial hair. "So you've made up your mind?"

He took a deep, shuddering breath. "I have. I'm—"

His cell phone rang—the new ringtone he'd assigned to Cookie. He released Flannery to pull the phone out of the cargo pocket on the side of his shorts' leg. "Hey, Cookie, what's—"

"Is Flannery with you?" Her voice sounded frantic.

"Y–yeah. What's wrong?" He flashed a concerned look at Flannery, grabbed her hand, and started toward the dining hall.

"It's Kirby. I think he's having a heart attack."

# Chapter 23

$\mathscr{H}$e can't be having a heart attack. He has an automatic defibrillator—an ICD." Flannery's voice preceded her, and Maureen looked up from Kirby's pallid face as his granddaughter flew into the room.

She shifted so Flannery could kneel beside her but kept her fingertips pressed to the inside of Kirby's wrist, the deep groaning prayer in her soul never stopping. "It's probably tachycardia or fibrillation. His pulse is weak and rapid, and just before he passed out, he complained of dizziness. And he's been having trouble catching his breath all weekend."

Kirby groaned. Flannery stroked his cheek. "Big Daddy, are you okay? Can you hear me?"

"He has been responsive but sluggish." Maureen chewed her bottom lip. She'd been a pediatric nurse, so her knowledge of providing support for a cardiac event had been limited twenty years ago when she was still practicing. And so much had changed since then.

She looked up at Jamie, who knelt with one hand on Flannery's shoulder—the other rubbed the center of his own chest.

*Oh, dear Lord. I can't have found Kirby only to lose him the same way I lost James and Jimmy. Please, please, don't take him from me.*

Finally, someone in a nurse's uniform leaned over Kirby with a stethoscope. Flannery moved out of the way so another nurse could wrap a blood pressure cuff around his upper arm.

"His pulse is 120." That was the only thing Maureen had been able to do. Sit here and count his heartbeats, wondering if the next would be his last.

Jamie stood over her, his hand extended. "Come on, Cookie, I know you want to help, but let's let them take over for now." He wrapped his arm around her and pressed her head to his chest—where she could hear the steady, strong beat of his heart. Jamie held out his other arm, and Flannery accepted his one-armed embrace.

"At least it happened somewhere with medical personnel on site." Flannery held her left hand up to her mouth and tapped the nail of her pinky finger against her bottom teeth while she watched the nurses monitor her grandfather's vitals.

The crowd around them stirred and parted. Relief touched Maureen's panic to see the paramedics arriving. Jamie pulled her and Flannery back to make room for the gurney.

With a little help, Kirby got to his feet and onto the gurney under his own power. As the emergency responders unbuttoned his shirt to place the heart monitor leads on his chest, he reached his hand out in their direction.

Maureen was about to step forward and take it when Flannery broke away from Jamie and went to her grandfather's side. Of course he wanted his family, not someone he'd only known for a little more than a month.

"I'm sorry, darlin'. Sorry this happened."

"Oh, Big Daddy, it's not your fault." Flannery swiped her cheeks with the back of her free hand. "They're going to get you to the hospital and get you sorted out. And then we're going to get you well and home again."

"Do me a favor—don't call your dad or the rest of the family until we know what's going on."

"Big Daddy, are you sure? They should know. They'll want to be here."

He gave his granddaughter a wan smile. "That's what I'm afraid of. Let's find out if it's serious or not before we go ruining everyone else's holiday."

Flannery's ponytail bobbed when she nodded her head. "Okay."

"Where's. . . ?" He lifted his head a little, but one of the EMTs gently pushed it back down onto the thin pillow. "Where's Maureen?"

Jamie propelled her forward. Flannery gave her a teary smile and passed Kirby's hand to her. Maureen clasped the big paw in both of hers. "You gave me a little scare there."

"Sorry. Not the best way to impress a pretty girl, is it?"

"You don't have to try to impress me, Kirby McNeill. You just have to get better." She kissed the back of that strong, solid hand.

"Ma'am." The paramedic who'd been setting up the heart monitor now stood at the head of the gurney, ready to push.

Maureen kissed Kirby's hand again and released it. "What hospital are you taking him to?"

"Vanderbilt," Kirby groaned out. "That's—that's where my cardiologist is."

The crowd parted again to let them through. Maureen followed, with Jamie and Flannery behind her.

"Come on, Cookie. We'll all go in my car." Jamie held the front door for her and Flannery—who pulled out her phone, pressed a button or two, and held it to her ear. Maureen almost reminded her of the promise she'd made to Kirby, but it wasn't her business.

"Hey," Flannery greeted whoever answered. "We're not going to be able to make it to the cookout. . . . Um, Big Daddy, Jamie, Maureen, and me. . . We're on our way to the hospital. Big Daddy got dizzy and passed out at lunch at the senior center—he's talking and seems to be getting better already—but we're going to go find out what's going on."

Impressed with Flannery's calm voice and her ability to understate the problem to keep from worrying anyone else, Maureen allowed Jamie to help her into the front passenger seat of his car. He closed her door, and in the mirror, she watched as her grandson drew the pretty blond into his arms, said something to her, and then kissed her tenderly.

More tears flooded Maureen's eyes—tears of joy for her grandson and tears of fear for herself. She couldn't lose Kirby. She just couldn't.

∽

For all that Flannery kept calm and cool on the outside, inside. . . garbled, short-circuited thoughts tumbled through her head. Her heart went from racing to a slow pounding. And it was all she could do not to call her mom and dad.

Once again, she thanked God Jamie and Maureen were with her so she didn't have to do this alone. She glanced up and caught Jamie looking at her through the rearview mirror.

She looked away. She didn't need pity right now; she needed strength. She needed him to hug her and reassure her and kiss her. Again.

Pressing her forehead against the window, she almost gave in to the threatening tears. She didn't *want* to need Jamie's presence. She didn't want to need his strength, his confidence, his assurance that Big Daddy would be okay. She wanted to find that within herself. She'd lived this long without needing someone else. After just five weeks of being around him, of flirting back and forth—sometimes without even realizing it was him—she'd gone and done what she'd vowed to herself she wouldn't.

She'd changed. She'd given up her independence. And all because some cute, dorky guy made her lower her defenses and let him see her vulnerabilities.

As soon as Jamie pulled into a parking space in the garage, Flannery jumped out of the car and headed for the elevators. She was still jamming her finger on the call button when Jamie and Maureen caught up with her.

Jamie and Maureen murmured behind her, but Flannery couldn't bring herself to focus on their words. She needed to think, to concentrate. To pray.

Only, she couldn't seem to get past, *Dear God. . .dear God. . .*, but she made it her mantra all the way from the car to the information desk in the emergency room.

"My grandfather was brought in by ambulance. Kirby McNeill." She spelled both the first and last names without being asked.

The woman at the computer typed it in. "Your name?"

"Flannery McNeill."

"Please have a seat. We'll call you when you can go back." She didn't even look up from the computer.

"But, I'm—he shouldn't be alone."

The woman barely spared Flannery a glance. "Ma'am, they're still getting him situated and running tests and getting all of his information, so you'd just be in the way. And we have to clear visitors with the patient, due to privacy concerns, so please have a seat, and we'll call you when you can go back."

"Flan, come on."

She considered resisting Jamie's tug on her elbow, but from the expression of sheer unconcern on the hospital employee's face, she figured she wouldn't accomplish anything more than making a scene and getting more people upset.

Jamie led her to the bank of seats where Maureen sat staring at her hands resting in her lap. No, not her hands, but something she held. A handkerchief.

Big Daddy's handkerchief. He'd handed it to Maureen when she'd gotten choked up during the finale of the program. Flannery found a glimmer of humor. Big Daddy had offered Maureen a pristine, delicate, white handkerchief on which to wipe her tears. Jamie had offered Flannery his shirtsleeve. Both offered unconditionally, neither worrying about makeup stains or, in Big Daddy's case, if he'd get it back. If that wasn't love. . .

Maureen looked up at Flannery and Jamie's approach, and she reached her hand out toward Flannery.

Flannery didn't want to need anyone. But honestly, she did. If Jamie and Maureen hadn't been with her, she would have called Caylor and Zarah to be with her. If she couldn't have them, she would have called Jack or other coworkers or friends from church.

If it wouldn't take Mom and Dad three hours to drive up here, she'd have called them.

For years, she'd put on a big show about being independent and taking care of herself and not wanting to put her trust in anyone lest she end up getting hurt; but as a human being, she must depend on others. That's how the world worked. That's how God intended it. And because Maureen and Jamie had been with her when this happened, God wanted her to depend on them.

Leaning down, she gave Maureen a hug and then sat beside her. Flannery, in turn, extended her hand toward Jamie, who took it and eased down into the seat beside her.

"Sorry I freaked out there a little bit. It was rude."

Maureen patted her leg. "It's forgiven and completely understandable."

"He's my last living grandparent." Flannery finally gave voice to her greatest fear.

"How old were you when. . . ?" Jamie left the end of the question unasked.

"Sixteen when Mimi—Big Daddy's wife—died. She'd been fighting cancer for three years, so we had time to prepare, but still, even though her passing was expected and peaceful and we were all there with her, it was hard to say good-bye. I was in college when my mom's parents died. We weren't really close with them. They lived in Oregon and didn't travel at all—meaning that to see them, we had to go all the way out there. And with Dad's school schedule and all the years Mom had no say in her work schedule, trips out to Oregon had been few and far between. We got to see Big Daddy and Mimi all the time— they could come to all of our school programs and recitals and church musicals and graduations and all that kind of stuff." Flannery leaned hard against Jamie's strong shoulder. She couldn't lose Big Daddy now. She wasn't ready.

Jamie pulled his hand out of hers and put his arm around her instead. "You're lucky. I never knew either of my grandfathers. One died before I was born, and the other, when I was just a baby."

246

Flannery wondered which had been Cookie's husband but didn't feel right asking.

"I guess that's why I've liked volunteering at the nursing home and helping out with the senior adult group at church. And why I've liked having Kirby around so much recently."

"Big Daddy," Flannery corrected.

Jamie kissed her temple. "Big Daddy. I like having him around because it's like he's my long-lost grandpa."

Flannery stole a quick glance at Maureen, who was back to staring at the handkerchief, but the corner of her mouth did quirk up a little at Jamie's statement.

They all jumped when Maureen's cell phone rang. She looked at the screen before answering and then stood and went out through the automatic sliding doors to talk outside.

Jamie frowned. "Wonder what that's all about."

"I imagine Caylor told her grandmother, who called Dylan's grandmother, who called Zarah's grandmother, who called Bobby's grandmother, to see who knows what's going on, and now it's one of them calling your grandmother to try to find out."

"Yeah...that wouldn't surprise me." Jamie let out a hybrid chuckle-snort—a snuckle? "Actually—it kind of would surprise me that they're just calling and haven't already descended upon the waiting room. We couldn't seem to get rid of them when I was eighteen and had—"

"Family of Kirby McNeill?"

Flannery shot out of the chair and dragged Jamie by the hand toward the woman standing in the double doors to the main part of the ER. "Yes—family of Kirby McNeill."

Maureen joined them.

"You're all family?"

"Of course." No way was she going to leave her only support system out here while she went in to see Big Daddy.

"Come on back, then. Oh, and you will need to turn your cell phones off." The nurse looked pointedly at Maureen, who hadn't put hers away yet.

Flannery handed hers to Jamie to deal with as they followed the nurse through the labyrinthine emergency room.

Big Daddy had been put in a room rather than one of the curtained-off areas. Leads and wires connected him to several machines, not to mention the IV in his hand and the oxygen tube under his nose.

And suddenly Flannery understood why Mimi hadn't wanted her grandchildren visiting her in the hospital until they'd unhooked her from everything.

But he was sitting up, and he smiled at them. "Doc says the old ticker has finally gone back into rhythm." He thumped his chest between the heart-monitor leads. "That's all it was, the ol' heart being stubborn and wanting to make its own rhythm."

"Don't joke about it, Big Daddy. Why is your heart going out of rhythm? Isn't that what your ICD is supposed to keep from happening?" Flannery looked at the monitor recording his blood pressure (110/60), pulse (82), and $O_2$ (98).

Big Daddy gave a laughing groan. "Believe me, it was trying its hardest to shock my heart back into the right rhythm. Felt like that time Ol' Bert, the mule, took a disliking to me and showed me just how much by applying his back feet to my chest."

Maureen's arm brushed hers. "Pressure's still a little low, but not bad. The rest of your vitals look good. Your pulse rate has come down quite a bit."

"It was even lower than that just a minute ago, but then you walked into the room." Big Daddy waggled his bushy eyebrows at Maureen, who turned almost as red as her hair.

Flannery dropped her left hand from her mouth and tapped Big Daddy playfully on the shoulder with her fist. "Easy there, big fella." But even though he still looked somewhat gray and weak, the fact that he could not only joke but also flirt helped her believe he would be okay.

The doctor came in, introducing himself as the on-call cardiologist.

"Mr. McNeill had a ventricular tachycardia episode—meaning the heart started beating too fast and irregularly. We downloaded the information from his ICD, which shows it was working correctly, but it just took awhile for the heart to respond. We're going to admit Mr. McNeill for observation for at least twenty-four hours to make sure he doesn't have another event, as well as run more tests and find out if we need to adjust his medications."

"What kinds of tests?" Her mother would ask, so Flannery needed to know.

"We'll need to test for damage and to see if any adjustments need to be made to the ICD—or even if it needs to be replaced. His regular cardiologist will determine exactly what tests are needed."

"His regular. . ." Flannery crossed her arms. "So you're saying that he's not going to have these tests today?"

"A few—especially to check for damage. But most of the others can wait until tomorrow, when we're back up at full staff." He looked down at the pager on his belt. "Please excuse me."

"Thank you, Doctor," Jamie called after him.

"Flan, now you can go call your folks. But be sure to tell them I *don't* want them coming up here. I'll be out of the hospital in another day—there's no point in them taking time away from their jobs and responsibilities to come up for nothing more than this. Jamie—why don't you go with her?" Kirby inclined his head toward the door.

Before she could argue, Jamie clamped his hand around her elbow and led her out of the room, back to the waiting room, and out through the doors they'd entered.

"What was that all about?" She accepted her phone when he handed it to her.

"I think your grandfather wanted to have a word alone with my grandmother." He grinned at her.

She rolled her eyes. "Whatever." Turning her phone back on, she made the call to her parents. When she got no answer at their home number, she remembered that they usually went to their church's cookout.

Instead of face her mother's questions immediately, she called her dad's cell phone number. After all, he was Kirby's son, so he should be the first to know.

And he did know first—and then handed the phone to Mom so that Mom could grill her with medical questions the cardiologist probably wouldn't have been able to answer.

"No, Mom—I don't know. I've told you everything the cardiologist told us. Tests. For damage today and then they're going to look at everything else tomorrow. . . . Yes, he said at least twenty-four hours so they can keep him under observation." After ten minutes, she'd repeated herself at least four times. "Look, once Big Daddy is moved up to the medical floor, I'll make sure he calls you and explains. And if that isn't good enough, tomorrow we'll try to get his cardiologist to call you and explain."

"He won't have to. We'll be there in three hours."

"No—Mom, no. He doesn't want you to come."

"He may not want us, but he's going to get us."

Flannery grabbed hold of Jamie's wrist and squeezed—hard. "No, Mother. He doesn't want you coming."

Before she could stop him, Jamie snatched the phone out of her hand. "Mrs. McNeill. . .no, I'm not his doctor. I'm Flannery's boyfriend, Jamie."

Flannery slapped both hands over her face and then smoothed them back over her hair. She was in for it now.

"Oh, she didn't tell you she had a boyfriend? I can understand. It's a pretty recent development. Anyway, I wanted to tell you that my grandmother and I were with Flannery and Big Daddy when this happened, and we're here at the hospital. And my grandmother has four really good friends who are, even as I speak, heading this way to come and gather round and pray and make sure that your father-in-law recovers. Frankly, I think if you came now, you'd just be in the way."

Flannery turned toward the parking garage, and sure enough, four elderly ladies marched toward them.

"Yes, ma'am, I understand that you're concerned. And I know Big Daddy appreciates that. But he's going to have enough on his hands dealing with my grandmother and her friends."

Perty Bradley, Sassy Evans, Trina Breitinger, and Lindy Patterson formed a semicircle around them.

Jamie shot Flannery a big grin. "Yes, ma'am, Maureen O'Connor... Yes, ma'am. I would say it's pretty serious.... Well, she's very fond of him, too. And so am I.... How long have Flannery and I been dating?"

Flannery jerked the phone out of Jamie's hand. "Mom, we really need to go."

"How could you not tell me you have a boyfriend?"

She had to hold the phone away from her ear. And from the smiles exchanged amongst her friends' grandmothers, they heard every single word.

"Mom, really, we've got to go. I promise I'll call you...later." Maybe in a month or two, once Mom got over the shock of finding out this way that Flannery was seeing someone. She disconnected and then punched Jamie in the arm. Not softly or teasingly, either. "How dare you tell my mother you're my boyfriend!"

He grabbed her around the waist and pulled her close. "Because I *am* your boyfriend. And it got her thinking about something else."

"Just saying you're my boyfriend doesn't make it true—"

His lips crushed against hers. She smiled and pressed her hand to his hairy cheek as she kissed him back.

And the meddling, matchmaking grannies cheered.

# Chapter 24

⌒∞⌒ (decorative knot)

$\mathcal{F}$lannery flipped back to the previous page and reread it. But after a second reading, she still didn't follow.

Maybe trying to read new book proposals while sitting in her grandfather's hospital room wasn't the greatest idea in the world. She closed out of the reader and switched over to solitaire. Playing round after round after round of it didn't help in keeping her work from piling up, but it did suit the chaos in her head. And even though she'd spent the morning at the office—until Jack ran her out—every minute she spent away from her desk, her workload increased exponentially.

But she couldn't leave Big Daddy here by himself, and Maureen and Jamie couldn't be expected to stay here with him all day.

His light snores paused, and she looked up. He blinked a couple of times, reached up to rub his eyes, and looked at the IV in the back of his hand as if he'd forgotten where he was.

She set her computer pad down on the extra chair and rose to stand beside the bed. "How're you feeling?"

"Good. Hungry."

She checked the clock. Only three thirty. "Want me to see if I can scrounge you up a snack—something that your doctor would approve?"

"No. I can hold on till supper. Where are Maureen and Jamie?"

"Maureen had a meeting over at church she couldn't get out of, and

Jamie had to run down to the office to take care of something on one of the projects he's doing for us."

"Good. I was hoping to get a chance to talk to you alone."

Flannery perched on the edge of the bed and took his hand in hers, being careful not to knock off the pulse/oxygen monitor clipped to his finger. "You look like the Cheshire cat."

"I feel sort of like that grinning critter." He squeezed her hand. "You like Jamie, don't you?"

"Of course I do." Her breath caught in her throat with the delayed impact of his question. "Why?"

"'Cause when I look at you with him, it's the happiest I've ever seen you. Maureen agrees—this is the happiest she's seen her grandson pretty much in his whole life."

"You two have been talking about us?"

Big Daddy had the decency to look chagrined. "I have to admit, we've talked a couple of times about ways we could plot to bring the two of you together."

"Like. . ." Flannery narrowed her eyes at him. "When we 'accidentally' ran in to them at the Japanese restaurant?" She shook her head and tried to keep her expression stern. "I should have known."

"Are you upset with me?"

She bent forward and kissed his cheek. "No, Big Daddy. I'm thankful for you."

"And I'm thankful for you, too. But I've been worrying about you."

"And you're blaming that for your heart problems?" She grinned at him but couldn't stop the guilt that nudged at her from the very real prospect that she'd caused him undue anxiety, which landed him here.

"No. No. Not that. I'm worried about what you told me a few weeks ago—about moving to New York because you felt like your friends had left you behind."

Flannery straightened and looked at the back of his hand, held in hers. "I was being stupid. I mean, I know I can't help feeling the way I felt, but I'd let myself forget that Caylor and Zarah and I are closer than I ever was with my sisters. And they've gone out of their way in the last few months to make sure we haven't stopped getting together or talking or being there for each other. And frankly, I know if I needed them, Bobby and Dylan would be there for me, too. I haven't lost my friends; they've just brought more people into the mix for me to be friends with. I almost feel like I'm closer to them than I was before, and I know that'll continue for the rest of our lives."

"So you're not considering moving to New York anymore?" He squeezed her hand.

She leaned forward and kissed his cheek again. "I can't go to New York and leave everyone I love behind."

He pressed his palm to her face and rubbed the apple of her cheek with his thumb. "I hope this incident hasn't scared you away from Jamie. He's a good man."

She sat up with a laugh. "He's been great through this incident. Why would you think it would scare me?"

Her grandfather's expression clouded. "Because of his heart problem."

"His—" Flannery slid off the edge of the bed and took a couple of steps back. "What are you talking about?"

Big Daddy tried to push himself up and then reached for the controls and raised the head of the bed. "He hasn't told you?"

"Told me *what?*" Panic chewed the edges of Flannery's mind.

"I guess that's a question you'd better ask Jamie."

"Ask me what?" Jamie strolled into the room.

Flannery turned on him, fists planted on her hips, her own chest pounding with the frantic denials in her heart. "You have a heart problem? After all this, how could you not tell me?"

Jamie came toward her and reached for her upper arms, but she lurched away from him, holding her hands up between them.

He sighed. "I *used* to have a heart problem." He unbuttoned the placket of his Henley-style T-shirt and pulled the neckline apart, revealing a thick scar down the middle of his chest. "I had what's called ASD—an atrial septal defect. I had a little hole between the two upper chambers of my heart. But I had surgery, and they fixed it." He buttoned three of the four buttons again—just high enough to hide the top of the scar.

"They fixed. . .is that what your father and grandfather died from?" She squeezed her fists tight to keep her hands from shaking. This couldn't be happening. It just couldn't.

"Most likely. It is a congenital problem. But theirs was undiagnosed and unmonitored. Mine was diagnosed when I was little; and once the doctors determined it had closed as much as it was going to on its own, they did the surgery." He reached for her again, and this time she let him settle his hands on her shoulders. "Flannery—I would have told you, but it didn't seem important. I had my appendix and tonsils out when I was a kid, too. I have as much risk of dying now from those surgeries as I have from the ASD."

"But. . .doesn't it mean you're going to be more prone to. . .heart attack and other problems?"

"Sure, maybe. They don't know. But I take care of myself—I exercise, I try to eat well, I see my doctor, I take my vitamins, I drink plenty of water, and I try to get enough rest. That's all any of us can do to try to stay healthy, isn't it? And frankly"—Jamie glanced at Big Daddy and then back to her—"looks like you have just as great a risk of heart problems as I do, if this runs in your family."

"Not to mention your grandmother's cancer," Big Daddy chimed in.

"You're not helping." Flannery raised her voice slightly but didn't look at her grandfather.

Jamie dropped his hands and jammed them into the pockets of his jeans. "This is probably a lot for you to take in right now. I promise you, if I thought it would be a problem, I would have told you straightaway." He rocked from heel to toe. "I'm going to head home and get some work done. Call me when you're ready to talk about this. . .or if you need me for any reason." He tapped the end of the bed. "Kirby, you hang in there."

Jamie almost bowled over his grandmother in his rush toward the door. They exchanged a few words, but Flannery's head buzzed so loudly she couldn't make out anything they said.

Maureen entered and placed a floral arrangement on the wide windowsill then leaned over the head of the bed and greeted Big Daddy with a kiss. They murmured to each other before Maureen stood and straightened his blanket and then looked at the machine monitoring his vitals.

"I. . .I've got to go." Flannery stuffed her tablet into her purse and escaped the room, barely able to catch her breath.

Jamie had the same heart problem his father and grandfather had died from. Probably. Most likely. And from what she'd heard, both men had died in their thirties or early forties. Jamie was already—how old? She didn't know. But from the few silver hairs here and there, he had to be midthirties at least. How long until he—

No! She swerved from the vehemence of her mental protest. She couldn't entertain thoughts like that. She couldn't. She wouldn't.

But then, wasn't she just in a state of denial if she didn't?

Needing to scream but lost in the corridors of the huge medical center, Flannery struggled to breathe.

Minutes later, she made it out to the parking garage. Instead of waiting for the elevator, she took the stairs up to the sixth level, needing the physical outlet for her anger and confusion.

She needed something to get this off her mind. Work. Yes. She'd go to the office and bury herself in the work she'd yet to catch up on from being away from the office the first week of June.

She headed south from the hospital. . .but didn't end up in Brentwood. She pulled the car up behind the white SUV in the carport at Caylor's house. Putting the car in PARK, she turned it off—but couldn't move.

Caylor stepped out onto the balcony above the carport from her upstairs bedroom-office loft space and waved. Moments later, the redhead came out from the kitchen. She opened Flannery's car door.

"What is it? What's wrong?"

Unable to control herself any longer, Flannery hugged the steering wheel and pressed her forehead against it. "Jamie. . .his heart. . .I can't. . ."

Somehow, Flannery ended up inside Caylor's house on the sofa in the family room area of the newly renovated, open-concept house.

Caylor slapped a cold, wet cloth on Flannery's forehead and dropped a tissue box in her lap. She didn't say anything, just kicked off her flip-flops and curled up on the other end of the sofa, facing Flannery.

Flannery covered her face with the damp washcloth, crying into it with all the energy she had. She hated being this way—she hated for anyone to see her being this way. But it was only Caylor. And Caylor had seen her *much* worse than this. And if she didn't get it all out at once, she'd explode.

And if that happened, Jack would do his I-told-you-so dance of victory.

"Are you crying or laughing?" Caylor asked.

Flannery scrubbed at her face, then wiped under her eyes to eliminate the smeared mascara she knew would be there.

"Missed a spot on your left cheek."

"Thanks." She made judicious use of the tissues to clear out her now-stopped-up nose.

"You ready to talk now?" Caylor handed her a soda.

"Yeah." Flannery popped the can open and took a few gulps, relishing the burn of the carbonation as it went down.

"Sometime today?" Caylor reached around behind her and pulled out a small wastebasket, which she swept the wadded tissues into from the coffee table. She set the basket down near Flannery's feet.

Flannery launched into the recounting of everything she'd been through in the last twenty-four hours—giving Caylor the look of death when Caylor exclaimed and clapped at hearing that Jamie'd kissed her.

Caylor's joy disappeared, though, with the details about Big Daddy's heart "event," and returned at the news that he was doing much better—enough to admit his part in the matchmaking scheme.

"And then Big Daddy asked me if this scared me when it came to me and Jamie."

"What did he mean?" Caylor ran her fingers along the braided piping at the top of the cushion she leaned against.

"That's what I asked. And then Jamie came into the room." She launched into what Jamie had told her about his heart problem and surgery.

"And you don't believe him?"

"I believe him. I'm just not sure if I trust him."

Caylor's head jerked in a confused gesture. "What do you mean? You don't trust that he's telling you the truth about his risk factors in the future?"

"No." Flannery flung her arms toward the ceiling in frustration. "I don't trust. . .I don't trust. . ."

"You don't trust him not to die and hurt you."

And there it was. Bald and out in the open. Flannery dropped sideways onto the center couch cushion and drew her legs up into the fetal position. "I don't trust him not to die and leave me alone and in pain."

"Flan?" Caylor poked the top of her head with her bare foot.

Flannery sat up, brushing at her hair with both hands as if she could wipe away Caylor's foot cooties. "What?"

"Do you still drive the interstate to work every day?"

"Four days a week. Five if I just can't work from home one day."

"Do you realize how much risk you're putting your life at by doing that?" Caylor reached sideways to set her soda can on the glass-top coffee table. "I've never heard of this condition Jamie said he has— had—whatever. But if what he tells you is true, you may have a greater chance of dying young in a terrible, burning, exploding car crash and leaving him alone and in pain than he does of dying from heart problems." Caylor tapped her chin. "Or you could just be maimed— scarred all over from the burns. Or lose a limb or two. Maybe go blind. Be paralyzed, and then he'd have to decide if he loves you enough to sacrifice his life to take care of you for the rest of yours. . . ."

Flannery grabbed a throw pillow, buried her face in it, and yelled as loudly as she could to drown out what sounded like Caylor brainstorming a new—and morbidly melodramatic—novel.

"What? You don't like my version of the way things could turn out?"

Flannery threw the pillow at her best friend. Caylor batted it back to her.

"Look, it's not like he's asked you to marry him. You've really only been getting to know him for, what, a little less than two months?"

"Not quite—barely over a month. But in the last couple of days, we've been e-mailing back and forth like crazy—four, five times a day sometimes; so it seems a lot longer than that. How could he not have found a way to tell me in one of those e-mails?"

"Give it some time. Give him some time. Do some research on his condition. If that doesn't help, get him to set up an appointment with his doctor and take you with him so you can grill his doctor about his condition. But just do me a favor."

Flannery crossed her arms over the pillow. "What?"

"Don't give up on him the way you've given up on every other guy you've dated. This is different—you're different."

"Different? You mean I've changed because of him?"

"We all change when we fall in love. We can't help it. The important question is have you changed for the better. And from where I'm standing, the answer is yes."

"You're not standing, you're sitting."

Caylor picked up another pillow and popped Flannery with it. "You know what I mean. So will you?"

"Will I what?" Exhaustion—physical and emotional—clouded Flannery's brain. She fell over onto her side again, putting the pillow under her head.

"Will you promise not to give up on Jamie?"

"I'll think about it."

❦

"She totally freaked out when I told her about the heart surgery."

"You should have expected that." Don's voice crackled on the other end of the connection.

Jamie adjusted his earpiece phone and then returned to weeding. "Expected her to freak out over nothing?"

"Jamie, even you know it's not nothing. If you didn't, you wouldn't take care of yourself the way you do."

He rocked back on his haunches, considering his stepfather's words. "But the food choices and the exercise and the regular doctor visits—that's how I was raised. It's just part of who I am."

"And she needs a chance to get used to that idea, to learn that about you, for it to become part of who you are together. Son, you've only been seeing this girl for. . .a minute, in the grand scheme of things. Don't be in such a rush."

Jamie attacked a weed with the trowel. "But what if. . . ?" He couldn't put it into words.

"What if. . .what? What if you wait and something happens to one of you? That's a chance you have to take. That's a chance we all take. Human life is frail. That's something we all have to accept."

Jamie pulled a few dried-up leaves off the nearest tomato vine. Another week or two and many of these would be ripe and ready to pick. "What if I promise her forever and can only give her a few years?"

"What if she gets pneumonia and dies? What if she's in a car accident that leaves her brain damaged? What if Jesus comes back next week?" Don sighed. "You can what-if yourself to death if you're not careful. How confident are you in your feelings toward her? Have you prayed about your relationship and its future?"

"Every day. I'm more sure that I'm supposed to be with her than I am about anything else, even nursing school, and I just sent my registration and initial tuition check in for that."

"Then you have to show her that confidence. That's the conclusion I reached when I couldn't get your mother to agree to marry me. She was picking up on my own self-doubts, my own issues of inadequacy, and my feeling that she deserved better than me. Because as long as I felt like she could do better than me, I was making her feel the same way."

Jamie sat down in the dirt between the tomatoes and squash plants in Cookie's backyard. Sweat dripped from every surface of his skin under the brutal July sun. But the dirt and sweat didn't matter. "How did you know you were in love with my mom?"

"I knew it from the first moment I laid eyes on her. Except, of course, as soon as I saw her, I reverted back to feeling like nothing more than a small-town hairdresser trying to convince everyone in Salt Lake that I could make something of myself and my grand business ideas, even though I already owned seven salons. I convinced myself she wouldn't want to have anything to do with me—I'm ten years older, I was a closet science-fiction geek, and I'd never had a real relationship with a woman in forty-three years of life. She was thirty-three and, even though grieving, a vibrant, outgoing, beautiful woman. I still think she deserves better than me."

"I don't. You're just who Mom needed. . .and me, too. I just wish I'd realized it a lot of years ago." Jamie wiped his face with his shirttail. His face itched so badly under his beard. . . .

His beard! He pushed himself up to his feet.

"I know. But now we've got the entire future."

"Yep. And I know just how to kick that future off to a better start." Brushing the dirt off his jeans, Jamie jogged around to his car in the front of the house. "I'll talk to you again soon, Dad. And hopefully, I'll have some good news."

# Chapter 25

❧

**From:** Jamie O'Connor
**To:** Chae Seung
**Subject:** Dinner Guest

*Chae, thank you for being so honest with me. I understand where you're coming from, and I respect that. I promise you (for whatever that's worth) that I will do my best to make sure I'm always there for Danny and that I never again will do anything to hurt him—or you. But I can only prove it to you by showing you. And I promise to do so.*

*The name of the guest I'm bringing to dinner is Flannery McNeill. Yes, Flannery as in Flannery O'Connor. So please don't say anything about her name when you meet her. She's a little touchy about it.*

*See you next week.*

**From:** Jamie O'Connor
**To:** Flannery McNeill
**Subject:** Dinner next week?

*Flan—*
*My friend Danny and his wife, Chae, have invited us*

to dinner next week. It'll be a traditional Korean meal, with Danny's and Chae's mothers and grandmothers helping cook it. It's next Tuesday night. I hope you'll go with me. Danny and Chae really want to meet you, and I want you to meet them.

About the whole heart surgery thing. I'm sorry I didn't tell you. But that's one of those awkward things to work into conversation. "Oh, by the way, I had open-heart surgery when I was eighteen years old to correct a hole in my heart that might have killed me if they hadn't fixed it." I guess I could have worked it in around talking about Gawain and Ragnelle or your dirtbag of a high school boyfriend. Or maybe in one of the e-mails about our favorite TV shows from childhood or bands from the '80s. But there's never seemed to be a spot in any of our conversations so far that invited talk about it. (And for the record, MacGyver was absolutely the best show.)

Seriously, my doctors give me a clean bill of health. And though right now I'm trying to figure out how I'm going to afford to pay for health insurance, I want to assure you that I will continue going for my annual checkups. You can go with me to my next one in August, if you really want to. Okay?

Please let me know about dinner next week as soon as you can.

—j

BTW—I won't be at church Sunday. I'm going up to Louisville this weekend to help man the Lindsley House booth at a book fair.

**From:** TennesseeGawain
**To:** LadyNelle
**Subject:** I'm sorry

Just in case I didn't make it clear in my other e-mail, I'm sorry. Hope to see you next week.

**From:** Chae Seung
**To:** Jamie O'Connor
**Subject:** RE: Dinner Guest

*Thanks for understanding, Jamie. And I'll hold you to those promises.*

*Also, thanks for letting me know about your dinner guest. But who's Flannery O'Connor? Is that a relative of yours?*

**From:** Danny Seung
**To:** Jamie O'Connor
**Subject:** RE: Pulled the Trigger

*Congrats on being accepted and getting registered for your first semester! The first semester or two are going to be hard, getting in all those science classes you didn't take the first go-round in college. Take as many placement tests as they offer so that you can get out of as many of the math and other basic classes as you can. That way you can get to the clinical classes sooner—and you'll need total focus for those. And don't forget, if you need help with anything or need a study partner. . .well, let's just say I'm glad all that is behind me. :-) (You know you can always count on me.)*

*Chae told me Flannery is coming to dinner with you next week. Way to go, dude! Who knew that you could go from insulting her with Dracula to bonding over her secrets (which I still want to know) in just a few weeks? You're even smoother than you were in college.*

**From:** Kirby McNeill
**To:** Maureen O'Connor
**Subject:** When you come tomorrow

*Dearest Maureen,*
*You've only been gone fifteen minutes, and I already miss you.*

*Being locked up inside this place is enough to make me loony, and your presence has helped make it a little less oppressive. Thankfully, Flannery showed me how to do e-mail on my phone when she was here earlier, so I can spend time this evening contacting friends and family to stop them from worrying about me.*

*If you have a chance tonight, can you get my Bible and journal from the bedside table at Jamie's house? If they're going to keep me another full day, as they're hinting, I would very much like to have those.*

*I miss you.*

*All my heart (which you may or may not want at this point),*

*Kirby*

**From:** Flannery McNeill
**To:** Jamie O'Connor
**Subject:** RE: Dinner next week?

*Jamie,*

*I'm sorry I freaked out on you at the hospital earlier today. I hope you'll forgive me.*

*Dinner with your friends next week sounds great. I've never had Korean food, but I've liked every other Asian cuisine I've ever tried, so I'm sure I'll love it—especially since it'll be homemade.*

*They're keeping Big Daddy in the hospital at least one more day. But your grandmother is going to be there with him, since I have to go back to work. I've already got a stockpile of work to do and can't afford to be away another day. Plus, Big Daddy pretty much ran me out of the room when I went back up there tonight. (He can be such a grouch when he doesn't get his way!) I may not make it to church this weekend either—I'll probably be at the office trying to get caught up on projects.*

*I think I told you in another e-mail that Caylor and Dylan are getting married the last week of the month. They'd like for us—you and me—to go out with them and Zarah and Bobby next* weekend (week from Saturday) so we can all spend some time together, since you're going to be my date for the wedding. I know you and Bobby know each other pretty well, but the girls would like to get to know you better. I'll probably know when and where by the time I see you on Tuesday.

—f

PS—Should I plan on meeting you at your house Tuesday after I get off work so we can go to your friends' house together?

PPS—Simon and Simon *was so much better than* MacGyver!

**From:** Jamie O'Connor
**To:** Flannery McNeill
**Subject:** RE: RE: Dinner next week?

*Who said I'll be your date to Caylor's wedding? You're assuming an awful lot there, girl.*

—j

**From:** LadyNelle
**To:** TennesseeGawain
**Subject:** RE: I'm sorry

*I'm sorry, too.*

**From:** Maureen O'Connor
**To:** Kirby McNeill
**Subject:** RE: When you come tomorrow

*My darling Kirby,*
*I have your Bible and journal. And Jamie and I had a good, long talk tonight. He and Flannery have already exchanged a couple of e-mails, and it seems everything there is on the mend.*

*I'll bring the paperwork I downloaded and printed when I come tomorrow, too.*

*I also talked to your nephew as you requested. He seems only too happy to take care of everything on the farm for you for as long you need him to. In fact, I think he may be calling you tomorrow to talk about what's going to happen to the farm going forward. I think your idea of selling it to him instead of to the developers is a grand one, even though you won't make nearly as much money. I imagine that's what Bea would have wanted—to keep the land in the family and make sure it stays a farm.*

*Love,*
*Maureen*

**From:** Flannery McNeill
**To:** Jamie O'Connor
**Subject:** Caylor's Wedding

*If you don't want to go to the wedding with me, I guess I can always call that guy I met during Zarah's bachelorette party and ask him to go. He was very tall and gorgeous. . .and gainfully employed.*

*—f*

**From:** Jamie O'Connor
**To:** Flannery McNeill
**Subject:** RE: Caylor's Wedding

*Ouch. Suddenly I'm feeling like I'm in a Shakespeare play.*

*—j*

**From:** Flannery McNeill
**To:** Jamie O'Connor
**Subject:** RE: RE: Caylor's Wedding

*Are you comparing me to Katherina Minola of Padua?*

*—f*

**From:** Jamie O'Connor
**To:** Flannery McNeill
**Subject:** RE: RE: RE: Caylor's Wedding

*If the shrew fits. . .*

—j

**From:** Flannery McNeill
**To:** Jamie O'Connor
**Subject:** RE: RE: RE: RE: Caylor's Wedding

*You're a dork.*

—f

**From:** Jamie O'Connor
**To:** Flannery McNeill
**Subject:** RE: RE: RE: RE: RE: Caylor's Wedding

*But I'm an irresistibly charming and handsome dork. However, if you really want to start calling names, we can go there, Fanny.*

—j

**From:** Flannery McNeill
**To:** Jamie O'Connor
**Subject:** Name Calling

*Okay, I give. (But you really need some new material— Fanny? Really? That's so last season—well, three seasons ago, since it started last fall.)*

**From:** Jamie O'Connor
**To:** Flannery McNeill
**Subject:** RE: Name Calling

*And, Princess Flannery, that's one of the things I love about you so much. . .the way you can just forget and move on.*

*And yes, I realize I used the word "love" in the sentence above. And I used it because I meant it.*

*Love, love, love, love, love, love.*

*Great, now that Nat King Cole song is stuck in my head. You know, the anachronism song.*

*—j*


*BTW—Jamie loves Flannery.*

**From:** Flannery McNeill
**To:** Jamie O'Connor
**Subject:** RE: RE: Name Calling

*You know, I've heard that speaking of oneself in the third person is a sign of extreme narcissism. And you're starting to ramble—given that it's after 2:00 a.m., I guess that's understandable.*

*And I will take this opportunity to reiterate that you're a dork—it's an acrostic not an anachronism.*

*Good night.*

*—f*


*PS—Flannery loves Jamie, too.*

# Chapter 26

&#10086;

$\mathcal{M}$aureen climbed out of the car into the oppressive mid-July heat and humidity for all that it was at ten o'clock in the morning. She could have wished for better weather but not a more perfect day.

"Are you certain you want to do this here, today, like this?" Lindy shut the front door of the big Cadillac.

Maureen turned to help Trina and Sassy out from the backseat. Perty got out on the other side.

"I'm certain. If we wait—no. There would be too many complications." With her four dearest friends in the world, Maureen crossed the courtyard and entered the red-brick church. Beyond the worship center and the new education wing, they entered the old portion of the building.

"Let me go in and make sure everything is ready." Perty pushed through the door at the end of a short corridor and disappeared.

Trina fluffed Maureen's hair, and Lindy turned Maureen's pearl necklace so the clasp was in the back again. Sassy stood back watching—but unable to see well enough to help with the fine details.

"They're ready." Perty was a bit breathless.

With Trina and Lindy to her right and Sassy and Perty to her left—in a slightly wedge-shaped formation—Maureen processed down the aisle toward the altar in the century-old chapel. Kirby stood at the front with Victor Breitinger and Greeley Patterson. Gerald Bradley stood in the center of the platform in his black judge's robes, holding a small white book.

"Too bad none of us plays the piano," Perty whispered.

"I could have sung," Trina offered.

"I probably could have figured out how to hook my MP3 player into the sound system."

They all looked at Sassy, who just grinned at them.

"No, this is fine. I don't need music." The song in Maureen's heart was enough.

Kirby reached his hand out for her and turned with her to face Gerald.

"Beloved friends, we are here in the sight of God and the presence of these witnesses to join in holy matrimony this man and this woman."

Maureen had eyes only for Kirby. He stood there, so tall, so proud—so much better than he'd looked yesterday morning when they'd released him from the hospital. She'd driven him down to the farm to get what he needed for a while, which they'd dropped off at her house. Then they'd gone downtown to get their marriage license and then out to dinner with the Breitingers, the Pattersons, the Bradleys, and Sassy to tell them the news and ask them to be here today.

As a former judge, and not a preacher, Gerald used the short-and-sweet, cut-and-dried version of the ceremony. And before Maureen realized what had happened, Kirby leaned down and kissed her.

"I now pronounce you husband and wife," Gerald said belatedly.

For good measure, Kirby kissed her again. Maureen liked it even better the second time around. He hugged her tightly. Tears slipped from her eyes. No one had cherished her like this in forty-six years. If only she and Kirby could have met a long, long time ago.

After a celebratory wedding brunch at Perty and Gerald's house, Maureen and Kirby left in a shower of flower petals—picked hastily, Maureen was certain, from Perty's extensive flower beds.

Kirby drove straight to Jamie's townhouse. Unfortunately, Jamie wasn't home. While Kirby went upstairs to pack up his toiletries and a few remaining belongings, Maureen called Jamie's cell phone number.

He answered on the third ring—and sounded quite out of breath. "Hey, Cookie. What's up?"

"Where are you?"

"Up at the gym playing basketball with a few of the people I used to work with. Why?"

"Do you think you'll be heading home anytime soon? There's something...something I need to tell you."

"What, that you and Kirby McNeill are sneaking off to get married?" Jamie laughed.

Maureen couldn't answer.

"I knew it! You two have been far too secretive the last two or three days—and I saw the marriage license application sitting on the end of the kitchen counter Tuesday afternoon when I came over to pick up my leftovers for the week."

"Well...we're not actually *sneaking* off to get married. We just *got* married. Gerald Bradley did the ceremony—he's a retired judge, you know."

"I'm really happy for you, Cookie. But if you just got married, I can't imagine you really want me around right now."

"Oh stop." But she laughed at the teasing tone in her grandson's voice.

"Does Flannery know yet?"

"That's our next stop."

"You're going to tell her at work? Cookie, I don't know if that's such a great idea."

"No, we're picking her up and taking her out to lunch. But we'll tell her either outside or in the car—somewhere private, not public." Maureen looked up at movement on the stairs.

"Good—because I've had a few too many emotional conversations in public recently, and I know Flannery has, too."

Maureen chewed her bottom lip. "Do you think she'll...?"

"I think once she gets past the initial shock, she'll be very happy for both of you."

"I hope so." She said good-bye and tucked the phone in her pocket.

Kirby set his duffel bag down on the coffee table and sat beside Maureen on the sofa. "Are you having second thoughts?"

She picked up his near hand and held it in both of her own. "No. I know this was the right thing to do. But I know you're worried about how your family will react—especially knowing there's no prenuptial agreement."

"Franklin will be more of a problem than Craig. Franklin's wife has convinced him that there's a fortune to be inherited, and they're going to make a fuss if they think they won't get their windfall when I die."

"Franklin is your older boy, the one who lives in Michigan, right?"

Kirby nodded. "Married to Jill, two boys, neither of whom have made much of themselves."

"And Craig is Flannery's father." Maureen dug through the dusty, dim recesses of her memory. "And his wife is. . .Nina, the doctor. Two other girls are—wait, don't tell me—Sylvia and Emma." She smiled in triumph.

"Emily." He leaned over and kissed her cheek. "Are you ready to go?"

"We did the right thing, didn't we?" Maureen clutched Kirby's hand when he moved to get off the sofa. The adrenaline rush of the planning and actual event of the wedding ebbed, leaving plenty of room for doubt to rush in.

"What did Jamie say on the phone?"

The amusement in her grandson's voice did make her smile a little. "He said he was happy for us."

"And you don't believe him?"

"No—I know he meant it. It's just. . ."

"Ah, I see. It's my family you're afraid of."

She shrugged. Over the past few weeks, he'd told her enough about his sons—especially the older son, Franklin—to know that not everyone in Kirby's family would be happy for them, which was why they'd done things the way they had.

"We can always undo it."

Maureen tore her eyes away from the framed Monet lithograph on the wall and looked at Kirby. No, not just Kirby. Her husband. "I don't want to undo it."

A smile spread and softened his craggy features. "I hoped you'd say that." He bent and kissed her, long and slow, full of passion and gentleness and the promise of forever.

∞

Flannery retwisted her hair and tucked two pencils through the bun this time to try to keep it up and out of her face as she leaned over the cover proofs in the art vault.

Her phone beeped, and she pulled it out. A new text message from Jamie.

CALL ME AFTER YOU GET FINISHED WITH LUNCH WITH COOKIE AND BIG DADDY.

She texted back a quick confirmation, put her phone away, and turned her attention back to the proof and what the designer was trying to tell her about the colors and the UV coating and the stock.

Why did Jamie want her to call him? And how did he know she was going out to lunch? She hadn't known until this morning when Big Daddy called to see if she'd be available—and now Maureen was coming along, too?

What did Jamie know that she didn't?

Her phone rang. "Yes, Brittany?"

"The front desk just called looking for you. Your grandparents are here to take you to lunch."

"Thanks, Britt." Her grand*parents*? Of course, whoever was working the reception desk could have assumed, if Big Daddy said he was her grandfather, that Maureen was her grandmother.

"Let's pick this up again after lunch. It doesn't have to go back out until tomorrow, so why don't you come up with the option you like best, and we can look at the cost." She left the designer in the bright, climate-controlled room, rushed back to her office to get her purse, and then headed up to the front office.

Sure enough, Maureen stood there with Big Daddy, both of them looking at the shelves of displayed products.

"Here I am. Are y'all ready to go?" Until she knew otherwise, she would just pretend like everything was normal.

*What did Jamie know?*

She willingly folded herself into the backseat of Maureen's small hybrid, turning sideways to keep her knees from pushing Maureen's seat forward.

Big Daddy turned to look at her over his shoulder. "Darlin', there's something we need to tell you."

Flannery swallowed hard. She had a suspicion. "What?"

"Maureen and I got married this morning." He held up his left hand to reveal a plain gold wedding band. "It was small, just Maureen's friends and us."

"M–married?" The air around Flannery got very thin, and she stiffened. "Married? I thought you were going to tell me you were engaged."

"Nope. We got hitched." He sobered. "Are you unhappy?"

"Un. . .no. Not unhappy, just surprised. Isn't this a bit sudden? I mean. . .you haven't known each other very long."

"Flannery, I'm eighty-six years old. And what happened this week drove home the message pretty clear: I don't have a lot of time left. So I'm not going to waste what I have on hemming and hawing and wringing my hands before making a decision. I love Maureen. She loves me. I asked; she said yes." He glanced at Maureen with a smile that made Flannery's heart melt.

"So, you didn't tell anyone? Dad? Uncle Frank?" Actually, she worried more about her mother's and sisters' reactions than her dad's.

"No, we haven't told any of the rest of our family yet. You're the first to know."

*The first to know?* "I don't think so. I think Jamie was the first to know. He texted me and told me to call him after lunch. The rat. He's just sitting there reveling that he knew before I did." She pulled out her phone and texted him.

He texted back a few seconds later.

She erased it. But grinned. He'd get an earful tonight.

Big Daddy and Maureen—Cookie, she insisted Flannery call her—told her all about the event when they arrived at the restaurant.

"You mean to tell me that when you sent me out of the ER—Jamie and me—that's when you proposed?" Flannery shook her head and buttered another soft, sweet yeast roll. "I should have known there was something going on and why you sent Jamie with me. Of course, when Big Daddy confessed to trying to set the two of us up, I thought that was all it had been about."

Cookie gaped at Big Daddy. "You told her about that?"

He shrugged. "I figured it was only fair, since I figured they'd been trying to do the same to us."

Flannery choked when she tried to inhale a bite of bread. "What are you talking about?"

"Don't try to deny it. You two aren't as sly as you think. Besides, Jamie admitted it to me last night when Maureen dropped me off at his place. We spent a long time talking, about a lot of things." His hazel eyes twinkled at her.

She didn't need or want to know what had passed between the two of them about her. She turned her attention back to Maureen—Cookie. "So who was there with you?"

It didn't surprise her that the others involved in this were Zarah's, Bobby's, Caylor's, and Dylan's grandparents. After all, the four grandmothers had been at the hospital with Maureen for hours when Big Daddy was in the emergency room.

"Well...so what are you going to do now? What's going to happen to the farm?" She'd spent so many happy days and weeks at the farm, she couldn't imagine never seeing it again.

"Drew—Mimi's brother's oldest boy—is going to buy it from me and add it back into his place. So it'll still be in the family."

But not in the immediate family. Of course, she hadn't been down there except to pick him up or drop him off on the way to and from Birmingham for the holidays in the past ten years since Mom and Dad moved down there. But just knowing it was there and she could visit if she wanted to was comforting.

"You're going to be living with Cookie now?"

"I didn't think Jamie would want me staying with him." Big Daddy waggled his brows.

She couldn't help but laugh. "Okay, sorry. Dumb question. When are you going to tell the rest of the family?"

"I'm going to call Craig and Franklin tonight," Big Daddy said. "They can call their children and let them know."

Flannery gave a mock gasp. "Are you telling me you're too chicken to call your grandsons and granddaughters to tell them the good news?"

"I wouldn't mind calling the boys. But. . ." He grimaced.

"But you know that Sylvia and Emily are going to go off their rockers about why they weren't informed ahead of time or invited. Which is why I completely understand why you didn't invite me but told me afterward. Are you going to tell Dad that I already know?"

"I am. But I'll be sure to specify that you weren't at the wedding and didn't know anything about it so he can assure your sisters of that when he tells them."

"Tells them? He'll send them an e-mail if I know him. He doesn't like breaking family news to them any more than any of the rest of us do." She'd seen the big lug of a former-football-player-turned-coach done in by those two girly-girls too often in her life.

They finished up lunch, and before Flannery left them at the front of the building, she hugged both Big Daddy and Cookie. "Congratulations. And welcome to the family, Cookie. Just bear with everyone the next couple of weeks. They'll come around once they get used to the idea."

"I'm just glad we have you on our side." Cookie squeezed her tightly.

She waved as they drove off and then entered the building and jogged up the four flights of stairs to the office. Waving off a few people who would have waylaid her, she made a beeline for her office.

"Flan—"

"Just give me a minute, Britt." She closed the office door and pulled out her phone.

Jamie answered on the first ring. "So?"

"You are the world's biggest brat. You had to rub it in, to somehow let me know they told you before they told me."

"Only 'cause I'm their favorite."

"You're Cookie's only grandchild. If you weren't her favorite, you'd be in serious trouble."

"They told you face-to-face—and at least you got taken out to lunch. Cookie told me over the phone while I was in the middle of a basketball game with Darrell, Wade, and Ainslee."

"Aren't you too short to play basketball?"

"Aa-*shrew*." Jamie faked a sneeze to call her a name.

"You owe me this one." She spun her office chair around slowly. She really should be diving right back in to work, but talking to Jamie had just improved her day tenfold.

"Okay. Yes, if I were to try to play professionally, I'd probably be cut for being too short. But Darrell's a good four or five inches shorter than me. So we put him on Ainslee's team because she needs the handicap."

"She's the one who played pro a season or two, right?"

"Yeah. They can't wait to meet you."

She twisted a lock of hair around her finger. "I'm looking forward to meeting all your friends." Someone knocked on the door. "I've got to go. Real life beckons."

"I wish we could get together before Tuesday."

"I know. Me, too. If only you weren't leaving for Louisville tomorrow afternoon."

"If only. I'll e-mail you later." A pause. Then, "Flan?"

"Yeah?"

"I love you."

She held her breath a moment. To see it written in an e-mail was one thing. But to hear it in his mellow voice made it all the more real. So why did she still feel like something was missing? "I love you, too."

# Chapter 27

*J*amie let the drapes fall back in place as soon as the little, dark-gray four-door pulled into his driveway. The last four days, though busy with travel and the book fair, had been the longest of his life—stretching for an eternity before he could see Flannery again. He dashed upstairs, not wanting Flannery to know he'd been standing in the front window for the past twenty minutes waiting for her to arrive.

But when the doorbell didn't ring after several long moments, he jogged back downstairs and peeked out the window again.

Flannery stood near the tail end of her car, looking up toward the back part of the complex, hand shading her eyes.

He opened the door and stepped out onto the stoop. "Something interesting?"

"I was just looking at the grade of the road." She turned and pointed toward the hill. "You run that every day?"

"Yeah—sometimes up to eighteen or twenty laps a day." He stuffed his hands into the pockets of his black pants and stepped down onto the narrow sidewalk that connected the stoop to the driveway. "You should come run with me sometime. Get you off that treadmill and let your feet pound the pavement. Then we'll see about you and your ten or twelve miles a day."

She rolled her eyes and met him on the sidewalk.

He stood still, trying to look relaxed but wanting to grab her and kiss her.

Her gaze stroked his face—and then her hands followed, her warm palms and fingers running along his cheeks and jaw. "You shaved. So I guess that means you've come to a decision."

He hadn't realized how sensitive the skin would be to even the lightest variations in temperature or physical contact after weeks covered with a beard. He shuddered and grabbed her wrists, unable to bear the intensity of her touch. He kissed her palms even as he drew her hands away. "I not only made a decision, but I've already taken some steps toward it."

Taking one of her hands in his, he led her up the steps into the house.

"Are you going to tell me?"

In the middle of the living room, he turned to face her. "I've decided to move to Utah and work for Don."

The expression on her face was priceless—and just what he'd hoped for. Dismay mixed with a slight tinge of devastation. "O–oh. That's not... I thought you were leaning in another direction."

He couldn't torture her any longer. "Kidding. I'm staying here. I was accepted to Aquinas College's nursing program. Last week I registered for my first semester and made my first tuition payment."

Flannery yanked her hand from his and started slapping—none too softly—at his arms. "That's not funny!"

"You should have seen the look on your face." He grabbed her in a hug—effectively trapping her arms—lifted her from the floor, and spun in a circle. "I'm going back to school."

Flannery finally joined him in his laughter. "You are such a pain."

He set her down on the floor and loosened his embrace. She maneuvered so that she could put her arms around his waist.

"You're just like a little boy on the playground who picks unmercifully on the little girl he secretly likes." She shook her head, and her thick curls bounced and swung, tickling his arms.

"Except it's no secret that I like you." Seizing the moment, he pulled her close and kissed her. But she didn't respond the way he expected. He backed up enough to focus on her expression.

She frowned.

Frowned? When he'd kissed her? "What's wrong?"

She grimaced. "I don't know. I've gotten so used to kissing you with the beard that it's weird kissing you without it. I don't know if I like it or not." She looked away and then looked back at him, concern filling her eyes. "This could be problematic."

"Why?"

Contorting in his arms so she could raise her hand between them, she lightly pressed her finger to the dimple in his chin. "Because I like being able to see your whole face like this. But when I'm kissing you, I have my eyes closed. It's such a dilemma. I don't know how I'll ever get used to kissing you like this."

Words of protest jumbled in the back of his throat—until she looked at him again with a twinkle in her hazel eyes. Oh, so that's how she wanted to play this?

Instead of giving in to her subtle goading to kiss her again, he released her and shrugged. "You're right. It is a dilemma. But since I'm never going to grow another beard, I guess if you ever want to kiss me again, you'll have to figure something out."

She gasped and planted her fists on her hips. He turned and headed back toward the kitchen so she wouldn't see his smile.

"Did you remember to pick up the basket for me?"

"After three text messages and four e-mails?" He returned to the living room with the gift basket she'd ordered from a small boutique in Brentwood.

"Thank you. I never even got a lunch break today, so there's no way I'd have been able to get it before they closed at five." Plucking her keys from her purse, she turned toward the door but then stopped and looked at him again. "Are we taking my car or yours?"

"I know where we're going, but I can guide you there just as well as drive. And you are parked behind me."

She flung the strap of the large, square, black leather bag over her shoulder. "I guess I'll drive, then."

He shrugged into his blazer and then followed her out to the car and around to her side to put the basket on the backseat, right where she wanted it.

With one hand on the car roof for balance, she bent over and pulled one of her pumps off, replacing it with a plain, flat, black shoe. The hem of her wide-leg, gray pinstripe pants pooled on the pavement.

"What are you doing?" He'd been around professional women long enough to know that there were very few things that would make them take off their high heels before going somewhere people would see them, especially people they didn't know.

"Changing shoes." She didn't look up at him as she exchanged the shoe on her other foot.

"Why?"

"Because. . ." She pushed her hair back over her shoulders.

"If it's for any reason other than your feet are killing you and you can't stand the idea of staying in those shoes for the rest of the night, we're not going." Closing the car's back door, he crossed his arms.

"My feet hurt." She still couldn't look at him.

"Liar. Those are your favorite shoes." Wild guess, but he'd seen her wear this pair of shiny black shoes, with a good three-inch heel and an extra-thick sole in the front, several times.

"Not my *favorites*, but. . ." She tossed her hands up in a frustrated gesture. "Ugh. You make me so mad. I'm changing shoes so that I won't be taller than you in front of your friends. Is that what you want to hear?" Finally, she made eye contact with him.

"If that's the truth, then yes, that's what I want to hear. Are you embarrassed to be seen with someone who's shorter than you?"

"You're not shorter than me—only when I wear heels."

"Are you embarrassed by that?"

"No!"

"Then why are you changing your shoes?"

"Because I don't want *you* to be embarrassed because I'm taller than you when I wear heels." She blushed so intensely, he wouldn't have been surprised if her hair had turned red, too.

Jamie reached out and settled his hands on her waist, looking her directly in the eye. "Put the heels back on, please. You like wearing them, and they look good on you. Besides, I kinda like the idea of being seen with a gorgeous, statuesque woman on my arm. Every man looks at me and has to wonder what I did to deserve you." He kissed the tip of her nose.

Wonder filled her eyes. "And what did you do to deserve me?"

The moment of wonder was nice while it lasted.

"Well. . ." He waited to go around to the passenger side of the car until she changed shoes again. "I called you Fanny, twice. I suggested Dracula would want to bite you. I freaked you out by telling you I read fantasy fan fiction. I forced you to tell me your biggest secret. . . ."

Flannery rolled her eyes and got into the car.

He climbed in beside her and leaned over the console. "And I'm so charming and handsome, you couldn't resist me."

Speculative scorn filled Flannery's expression. "It's because you're handsome and charming that I didn't want to have anything to do with you."

Stunned, he straightened. "Seriously?"

"Seriously." She put her seat belt on and started the engine.

He took his time buckling his own seat belt. "You treated me like I was pond scum for months because I'm handsome and charming?"

"Yep." Flannery slid on a pair of sunglasses and backed out of the driveway. "I learned a long time ago not to trust good-looking guys. Remember the dirtbag boyfriend from high school? Handsome and charming."

"So. . .what was it that did make you fall for me?"

The car rolled to a stop at the gate, and she turned to look at him, leaning on the console. "Because when I sat down to talk to you at the airport, you were hurting. You were vulnerable. You stuttered. And you were a complete dork. And I told God a long time ago that I didn't want to marry a good-looking guy; I wanted to marry a nerd, geek, or dork."

Jamie wouldn't need to lean far to be nose to nose with her. His heart pounded at her use of the *M*-word, not once but twice. Could she really be there mentally and emotionally? Ready to make a lifelong commitment to him? "And God did you one better and sent you a handsome dork."

They both jumped at the sound of a car horn behind them. Flannery straightened and pulled out onto the road.

"Of course you know what this means," he said after directing her to turn right onto Old Hickory Boulevard and head east.

"What?"

"That you think I'm handsome and charming."

The car jerked a little as she shifted from second to third. "Whatever."

"I've already told you tonight that you're gorgeous and statuesque. Would it help you admit my assets if I told you I also think you're talented and gifted?"

Pink crawled up into her cheeks in a very becoming way. He hated that the thick arm of her sunglasses kept him from seeing her eyes.

"It might. . .if I didn't worry that any compliment I give you would be the pin that explodes your already-overinflated ego."

With a laugh, he settled in for the forty-five-minute drive—or longer, depending on how bad traffic on the interstate would be this evening—and continued picking on the girl he not-so-secretly liked.

❦

By the time Flannery pulled up to the refurbished bungalow on Cherry Lane in Murfreesboro, she'd pushed her sunglasses up on top of her head due to the growing shadows—and she'd heard the entire story of Jamie's heart surgery.

"Mom came out to be with me, but I was so horrible to her she went home after only two days. That's why Don and Cookie devised their plan to intervene and force us to talk to each other a couple of years later, because I'd pretty much decided to cut off all contact." He bounced his head back against the headrest. "I was such an idiot."

Flannery ran her knuckles along his smooth jaw—and electricity coursed all the way up her arm. "You were just young and hurting. And you're trying to make up for lost time now, which is all you can do."

"I guess." He looked at the front of the gabled craftsman. "Ready to go in?"

She opened her door. "Ready."

The red, paned-glass front door provided the only pop of color in an exterior done all in shades of gray. She liked the effect.

The door opened before Jamie could ring the bell.

A young couple met them at the door. The man stepped out and gave Jamie a backslapping hug. "Good to see you, man."

"You, too." Jamie inclined his head to the delicately beautiful woman. "Chae."

"Jamie."

Flannery looked between the two of them, concerned by the frostiness in Chae's voice.

But Jamie's smile didn't falter. He put his arm around Flannery's waist. "Danny and Chae Seung, this is Flannery McNeill."

Having read up on Korean etiquette online last night, after seeing Danny's greeting of Jamie, she wasn't certain how to greet them—bow, handshake, nod of the head?

Danny solved it for her when he extended his hand toward her. She shifted the gift basket to her left hand and shook Danny's. Chae stepped out onto the porch and extended her hand to Flannery as well. For as fine and delicate and petite as she looked, she was almost the same height as Jamie—and Flannery herself when she didn't have her shoes on.

Oh—she should have changed shoes before she left the office! Then Jamie never would have known, and she wouldn't be standing here, towering over him and Chae.

Flannery extended the basket toward Chae and Danny with both hands—as she'd read was proper. "Thank you so much for inviting us to dinner. I've been very curious to meet Jamie's friends."

Chae took the basket, giving Flannery a warm smile. "Thank you."

Danny's eyes almost disappeared when he smiled like that. "And Jamie's friends have been very curious to meet you. Please, come in."

But instead of immediately following his friends inside, Jamie braced one hand against the wall and started kicking off his shoes.

Flannery looked down, dismayed to see several pairs of shoes lining the wall of the house near the door. No wonder Jamie hadn't cared if she'd worn heels or flats—she'd be barefoot anyway.

When she'd read online that, as in most Asian cultures, it was tradition to take one's shoes off before entering the house, she'd assumed that since Danny and Chae had been born and raised in America, this would be one of those old traditions they'd let fall by the wayside.

No such luck. And it had been more than a month since her last pedicure. She grabbed Jamie's shoulder for stability and glared at him as she stepped out of her shoes and pushed them into line beside his.

Jamie grinned at her. "Don't look so concerned. If you haven't noticed, your pants completely hide your feet."

And if she'd realized she'd be barefoot tonight—which, yes, was her fault for assuming Danny and Chae wouldn't follow this tradition—she would have worn something else, not pants cut to be worn with three-inch heels.

Danny closed the door behind them once they'd stepped onto the plush, oriental-style rug in the entryway. "Sorry about the shoe thing, but we have to revert back to the old ways when the grandparents are here."

Chae gave her an apologetic grin over her shoulder. "I hate going barefoot," she whispered. "But when Hamo and Habo are here, it's a mortal sin to wear shoes even in our own house."

Hamo and Habo turned out to be Chae's maternal grandparents. Though Flannery prided herself on immediate retention of names, keeping track of six grandparents and four parents with names unfamiliar to her brain and tongue proved difficult. She did get to practice her bow, much to the giggling of the grandmothers, who gave her an impromptu lesson on posture and angle and where her eyes should point.

They sat down to dinner almost immediately. Dish after dish of food appeared on the table, each person having multiple individual bowls and plates to eat from. Flannery wasn't sure what most of it was—even with Chae's and Danny's explanations, but she tasted everything, including the vegetables.

Just when she thought she wouldn't be able to eat anything else, two of the grandmothers came out of the kitchen with a sticky-rice dessert. Unusual and complex in its flavors, the dessert grew on Flannery enough so that she finished her whole serving. While she would have loved a good hazelnut coffee to go with it, she settled for hot tea to wash it down.

Flannery volunteered to help in the kitchen, but the mothers and grandmothers shooed her and Chae out. The fathers and grandfathers retired to the living room, but Danny suggested they go sit out on the deck where they could talk.

The scorching heat of day hadn't dissipated much. But the deck caught a nice cross breeze, and so long as Flannery sat still, she stayed pretty comfortable, since she'd been instructed to remove her blazer as soon as she entered, leaving her in a sleeveless blouse.

Jamie rolled the sleeves of his white dress shirt up to his elbows and sat on the rattan love seat with Danny. Chae led Flannery a little farther down the expansive deck to two armchairs with deep cushions.

"I thought maybe you and I could have some time to talk." Chae motioned for Flannery to sit before she did.

"I'd enjoy that."

"How did you and Jamie meet?" Chae crossed her legs and braced her elbow on the arm of the chair, leaning toward Flannery.

She told her the story of the cookout last fall, Zarah's wedding, the work project that didn't happen—at least for Jamie—and running into him at the airport.

"So, when you first knew him, you thought he was...conceited and disdainful of others' feelings?" Chae narrowed her eyes and glanced down the deck at her husband and Jamie.

Flannery followed her gaze. Jamie and Danny sat side by side talking, legs crossed the same direction—even their arms draped across their laps the same way. In their white shirts and dark trousers, they looked like the most bizarre pair of twins she'd ever seen.

"*Condescending* and *arrogant* were the words I used—*irritating*, too." She turned her attention back to Chae.

"But now you're dating him. What changed?"

"He did. . .and I did." She shook her head. "Even though I vowed to myself I wouldn't."

"Wouldn't. . .change?"

"At my friend's wedding. I've seen so many women become unrecognizable when they fall in love and get married. And I vowed I would never do that—I would never let falling in love change me. But I guess that's because I'd never actually been in love before."

Flannery leaned toward Chae, lowering her voice to ensure Jamie couldn't hear her, though it was probably an unnecessary precaution. "Over the last week or so, I've struggled with the idea that falling in love with Jamie has changed me, until I realized something very important."

"What's that?" Interest sparkled in Chae's dark eyes in the twilight.

"That the change is for the better. I'm not a different person than I was before. I know so many women who talk about how they weren't 'complete' before they fell in love. But for me, falling in love didn't 'complete' me—it's enabled me to be more completely myself than I've ever been in my life. And I think that's a pretty positive change." She looked back down the deck toward Jamie.

He caught her looking, ducked his chin, and gave her a secretive, smoldering grin.

Her toes curled against the deck—hidden by the long hems of her pants. Yes—she'd never felt so alive, so free to be herself, to say whatever came to mind without having to worry how Jamie would take it.

She vowed to herself she'd never make another vow like that again.

# Chapter 28

Jamie ran his finger under the tight collar. "Is the tie really necessary?"

"I thought you loved wearing suits and ties. At least that's what you said at church when I teased you for wearing that." Flannery reached up and straightened the knot at his throat.

"I don't know." He stepped into the bathroom to check his appearance in the mirror. "I know it's been less than two months since I got laid off, but I think I've gotten used to wearing T-shirts and shorts or cargo pants every day. This itches and strangles."

Flannery headed out the door, her "Whatever" trailing behind her. He grinned at his reflection. He loved getting under her skin—though he'd tread lightly tonight. After a spur-of-the-moment overnight trip to Birmingham to meet Flannery's parents yesterday, she'd been pretty grumpy on the way back to Nashville this afternoon. And she'd been even grumpier when she remembered that dinner with Zarah, Bobby, Caylor, and Dylan had been changed into an evening at an art gallery opening for a last-minute exhibit Dylan had landed, requiring business-formal attire.

When he arrived at the condo to pick her up, he'd found her still dressed in jeans, hair in rollers, makeup half on.

The speed in which she'd finished getting ready impressed him.

"Are you coming?"

Better not poke the sleeping dragon any further. He turned off the bathroom light—and the kitchen light as he passed through—and waited in the hall as Flannery locked the door behind them.

Sullen silence filled the elevator on the way down to the ground floor. Jamie tried to think of something to make her laugh, but everything that came to mind would probably annoy her instead. So he sighed and kept quiet.

She stalked out ahead of him when the doors opened. The knee-length, bright-blue satin dress looked even more spectacular on her than the black one she'd worn at Zarah's wedding. She'd pinned her hair up so that a cascade of fat curls tumbled down her back, only partially hiding what the crisscrossing straps of the dress revealed of her shoulders and upper back.

And he just now noticed she was wearing flats. Good thing he hadn't seen that upstairs; he might have made the mistake of commenting on it. He probably wouldn't have been able to convince her today that he really did like it when she wore heels—because *she* liked to wear them, and he liked what she liked.

He jogged across the marble-tiled lobby to catch up with her just in time to open the door for her. She gave him a tight, tired smile and exited. Thankfully, he'd gotten a great parking space on the street right in front of her building.

He opened the car door for her—but blocked her from getting in. "You don't have to go. You can call and tell Caylor you don't feel well—headache or whatever. I can go, make an appearance and spread apologies all around, then pick up something for dinner and bring it back here."

The tight lines in Flannery's forehead and around her eyes and mouth melted into fatigued gratitude. She reached up and caressed his cheek. "Thanks, but I need to go. Just give me a few more minutes to be in a bad mood, and then I promise I'll be pleasant for the rest of the night."

"Maybe this will help get things going in the right direction." He cupped her cheeks with both hands and kissed her, ever so gently.

She sighed a little and leaned in to the kiss, tangling her fingers in his hair.

After two more little pecks, he hugged her, cradling the back of her head with his hand. "I love you. Even when you're cranky."

"And I love that you still love me even when I'm cranky. And I'm sorry for being cranky. But if I'd known Sylvia and her family were going to choose this weekend to drive up from New Orleans to surprise Mom and Dad, I wouldn't have suggested we pop down and surprise them." She kissed his jaw right in front of his ear, and a shiver rattled his spine. She chuckled and stepped back. "Now, we'd better get going. I know this is one of those events at which showing up late is fashionable, but—"

"But you hate being late. I know." He stepped aside and waited until she was seated and situated before closing the door and going around to the driver's side.

Neither of them had been to this area of Franklin before, so Flannery used the GPS app on her phone. But that seemed to get them even more lost. Finally, when she was to the point of trembling with frustration, he took the phone from her, scrolled through her contacts, found the one he wanted, and called.

"Hey, Flan, where are you?"

"Hi, Caylor, it's Jamie—and we're lost." He told Flannery's friend where they were—and Caylor guided them the rest of the way in—on a street that didn't connect all the way through town but was interrupted by Franklin's old town square.

"We're here. Thanks, Caylor. We'll see you in a minute." He pulled the car around to the side of the building and parked.

Flannery pulled down the visor and checked her appearance in the mirror then pulled out lipstick and put some on. A rosy pink, just a few shades darker than her natural color.

"Do you know how much I want to kiss you right now?"

"Do you know how much I'll never get tired of hearing you say that?" She smiled at him—and just like someone had flipped a switch, the sparkle had returned not just to her eyes but to her smile and her demeanor. She kissed his cheek then wiped off the transferred lipstick with her thumb. "And do you realize that we just took our first road trip without getting into a single fight? That's better than we do at home sometimes."

"I don't know what you're talking about, because as far as I know, we've never had a fight." He got out and went around to open her door and offer her his hand in assistance. She popped out of the car as if she'd gotten a full night of sleep last night and a nap this afternoon—instead of only about four hours total.

"Um. . .let's see. The thing with the shoes Tuesday night before we went to Chae and Danny's."

Jamie puckered his lips and made a raspberry sound. He tucked Flannery's hand in the crook of his elbow and escorted her toward the front of the gallery building. "That wasn't a fight. That was a discussion. Princess, you'll know when we have a fight. But I don't see that happening."

"If you call me *princess* in public, it will." She squeezed his arm, but a smile accompanied the threat.

"Yes, my lady." He flourished his hand in front of him.

She laughed. And he relaxed and forgot about the itchy collar and tight tie and constricting suit coat.

Once they entered the gallery, Jamie immediately flashed back to social gatherings with clients and sponsors. He ran his finger under his collar, reminding himself he wasn't here to sell anything or try to impress anyone tonight—except for impressing Flannery's friends.

"Sorry the directions were confusing." Caylor came forward, a glass of what looked like fruit tea in each hand. Flannery took one, and Caylor handed the other to Jamie. Wearing a purple dress made out of some kind of sparkly fabric that set off her red hair and blue-green eyes to perfection, Caylor drew more attention than the artwork—at least from many of the men milling around the room. Jamie recognized several people, owners of large companies and corporations in the area. If Dylan drew this kind of clientele, he must be making pretty good money with his art.

Even though Jamie'd seen him in a tuxedo not that long ago, Dylan seemed quite out of his element dressed in an expensive, well-tailored suit as he hobnobbed with guests.

"He hates this part of getting a showing." Caylor sighed. "But he's so concerned about having gone without full-time income for so long that he's willing to do just about anything for the prospect of earning a little money. Even put on his suit."

"He's just not a suit-and-tie kind of guy." Flannery sipped her tea. "Besides, most artists—and I include writers in that—are introverts. If half of my authors could do as well as he's doing right now with walking around and talking to people at book signings, those events would be four times as successful."

Jamie left Flannery and Caylor to talk about one of their favorite subjects—the publishing and book world—and wandered around to look at Dylan's art. He'd been forced to take an art appreciation class in college for his fine arts credit, but he didn't really remember much. If all of it had looked like Dylan's art, he might have paid more attention. Each piece told a story, complete with characters and background and mood. Castles and medieval costumes seemed to be a theme in his paintings, though there were some with different imagery of interior spaces or more obviously American architecture—like three paintings featuring his requisite cast of characters in a tableau in front of Old South plantation houses.

"He's quite the talent, isn't he?"

The hairs on the back of Jamie's neck tingled at the husky female voice. And this was the other thing he hadn't missed in the two months since he'd gotten laid off. "Yes, he's quite good." He turned and acknowledged the woman—probably in her fifties, but well preserved, most likely through plastic surgery.

"Are you an art connoisseur, Mr. . . ?"

"O'Connor. And no, not really. I'm a f—friend of the artist." His unease increased when the woman moved close enough that her arm touched his. The cloying sweetness of her perfume ran circles in his sinuses and made him dizzy.

"I like friends of artists." She pulled a card out of her purse. "I'm Mandelisa. Call me sometime, and we can talk about what it's like to be friends of artists." She ran a taloned finger along his jaw and then turned and moved on.

He needed another shower.

"I see you met my wife."

Jamie almost dropped his glass at the familiar voice from behind him. He spun and found himself face-to-face with the last person in the world he'd ever wanted to see again. "Mr. Gregg."

"Oh, please, it's Armando. I never made you call me Mr. Gregg when you worked for me." He shook Jamie's hand vigorously.

Had Armando always come across as this fake? Jamie used to think him one of the most genuine people he'd ever met.

"How are things, Jamie? Where are you working these days?" Armando sipped what smelled like hard liquor.

"I'm working as a freelance publicist and marketing specialist for Lindsley House Publishing." Jamie flagged a server and divested himself of his glass before he dropped it. . .or worse.

Armando downed the rest of his drink and set his glass on the tray then waved the server away. "Freelance, huh? I'm surprised. Any marketing firm or ad agency in town would be lucky to have you."

"Except yours." The words popped out before Jamie could filter them.

Armando inclined his head. "Touché. But that's why I'm glad I ran into you tonight. You see, I've been meaning to call you this week." Armando ran his fingers through his salt-and-pepper hair. "Once we got everything settled and I was able to assess the skills of those who replaced everyone I had to lay off, I realized that some of them were nowhere near as talented as those I let go. The other partners have agreed we need at least two sports marketing reps here in Nashville. I offered one of the positions to Mitch, but he's already accepted a job at a firm in Milwaukee. One of the two positions is yours, and then you can bring on anyone from your former team you want to work with you."

Jamie's pulse throbbed against his tight collar. He could get the old team back together. Make sure everyone had jobs—and the numbers would work, since Ainslee had just accepted a coaching job in Chattanooga. "What about graphic designers?"

Armando shook his head. "Just two account executives. You'd have to share the administrative assistant and graphic designers from the Major Accounts Department."

"Then I know exactly who the two people you need to hire are. Darrell Keesey and Wade Vaughn. They're the best sports marketing guys you're going to find in Nashville." The graphic designers had probably already found other jobs, anyway.

Armando rested his hand on Jamie's shoulder. "No, you're the best sports marketing guy in Nashville. This offer is for you. I'll be setting up a nationwide recruitment plan if you turn it down."

"Jamie?"

He turned, dislodging Armando's hand from his shoulder. Flannery's brow knit with questions that reflected in her eyes. He slipped his arm around her waist and kissed her cheek. "Flannery, I'd like you to meet Armando Gregg. Armando, this is my girlfriend, Flannery."

Recognition of the name flickered in Flannery's face. She shook hands with the smarmy, insincere snake.

"Mr. Gregg just offered me my job back."

Flannery showed no external reaction other than a slight catch in her breath. "Oh, is that so?"

"Yes. And you arrived just in time to hear me give my answer." He looked at Armando again. "Thank you for the offer, Armando. But my answer is no. I'm going back to school in September to become a nurse, so I'll be completely leaving the world of marketing, book publishing or otherwise, in another few years."

Armando threw back his head and laughed. "A nurse? You? Come on."

Jamie kept his cool—but it had been a really good idea to get rid of that glass of tea. "Yes. A nurse. Just like my grandmother and my best friend."

Realizing Jamie wasn't joking, Armando's mirth ceased abruptly. "And to think that when I realized you were getting ready to try to steal business from us your last week on the job, I believed you were the kind of guy I could groom into being my junior executive when I take over the corporation." He snorted. "What a waste."

He started to walk away.

"Oh, Armando?" Jamie pulled away from Flannery and closed the gap between him and the man he wanted to be absolutely nothing like.

"What?"

He held a card out toward him. "You can give this back to your wife. Tell her I *won't* be calling her to talk about being friends with artists or any other kind of friends." Without waiting for a response, Jamie returned to Flannery, kissed her, and then took her by the hand and led her to the back of the gallery, where Bobby and Zarah stood with Dylan's grandparents and Caylor's grandmother.

He sent up a quick prayer of gratitude for God intervening and getting him out of that business before he did end up like Armando Gregg.

They spent the rest of the evening at the event—Jamie turning into a front man for Dylan once he learned enough about the paintings and Dylan to answer questions with confidence. Not that anyone asked him to do it. He just couldn't help it.

After the last client left, the gallery owner asked Jamie how much he would charge to come in and do that at all their show openings—he'd booked more sales in one night than he usually did in an entire showing.

Before he thought better of it, Jamie gave him a business card—one he'd had made with his personal contact information—and invited him to call so they could talk about it.

"Y'all hungry?" Dylan handed his coat and tie to Caylor, unbuttoned his shirt, and pulled it off, leaving only his white T-shirt. Under the sleeve, the bottom of an elaborate, full-shoulder tattoo showed, and another—three faces with some writing below them—decorated the inside of his other arm near the elbow. Jamie had thought of getting a tattoo before. Maybe he should have Dylan design one for him.

"Starving." Bobby worked his tie loose.

"It's late—there won't be much open." Caylor handed Dylan's clothes back to him, then used his shoulder for stability as she put her high-heeled, strappy sandals back on.

"I know I'm the new guy, but this is one of those discussions that could go on all night." Jamie's stomach growled loudly, and he joined in the laughter. "So let's just all meet over at the Waffle House on 96 near the interstate." Jamie raised his brows and pressed his lips together, hoping he hadn't just overstepped his bounds with this group.

"Perfect. I've been craving some greasy-spoon recently." Bobby wrapped his arms around Zarah from behind. "Because someone insists on making us eat healthy stuff most of the time."

"Hey. . .you're the one who was complaining about gaining weight with all the eating out we were doing before the wedding. I'm just trying to help you meet your goal." Zarah tilted her head to look up at her husband.

"Thanks, dear." He kissed her forehead and released her.

Jamie took Flannery's hand in his. "Shall we?"

She covered her yawn and nodded her head. "Yes. Take me to coffee."

In the privacy of the car, Flannery let out a jaw-popping yawn.

"Better?"

"Am now. What was that about—back with Armando Gregg?"

Jamie told her everything Armando—and his wife—said to him. "What an arrogant, condescending jerk."

"Gee. . .where have I heard those words before? Oh yeah, I said them about someone in this very car." She reached over and squeezed his arm.

"I was never *that* bad."

"Maybe not as bad as he was tonight. . .but, sweetie, you were headed that direction. If God hadn't intervened. . ."

He lifted her hand and kissed the back of it. "Believe me, I will say a prayer of gratitude every day that He got me out of a world that wasn't good for me, drew me closer to Him, and showed me what He really wanted me doing."

"Just like I'll thank Him every day that through that process you became the man you were always meant to be—humble and caring and considerate." She returned the favor and kissed the back of his hand.

"Careful, now, or you might start inflating that ego again."

"Oh, don't worry—I carry a concealed ego meter. I'll know when it's about to pop, and I'll deflate it back down to a manageable size."

They were the first to arrive at the restaurant and grabbed the big round table in the corner, sliding into the middle.

Zarah and Bobby arrived, then Caylor and Dylan—who'd managed to change into jeans and sneakers between the gallery and restaurant.

"Wouldn't you know he's the only one who thought of bringing a change of clothes?" Caylor rolled her eyes and slid into the booth next to Jamie. "At least Flan was smart and wore comfortable shoes."

"These are my go-to pair for conferences and trade shows—I know I can stand in them for hours on concrete floors and not end up throwing my back out of whack."

"Hey, guys, while you're both here—I want to invite you both over to my grandparents' house Friday night. I'm not going to have a real bachelor party, but my brothers and I are into some pretty cutthroat video-gaming, and I thought maybe you two might like to come over and join us for pizza and hang out with us for a while."

"You know I'm there." Bobby reached his fist across the table, and Dylan bumped it.

Jamie did the same. "I'm there, too. Just tell me when and where."

Three months ago, he'd wondered why Bobby Patterson had asked him, someone he barely knew except through casual acquaintance and because their grandmothers were close friends, to be an usher at his wedding. Now, with Flannery at his side and surrounded by these new friends, he still didn't know why—except to rejoice that God knew what He was doing all along.

# Chapter 29

❧

Tight searing pain blocked Flannery's throat. Tears stung her eyes. Bright-white dots danced in her peripheral vision. She needed to sit down.

Then she remembered to bend her knees, and the dizziness vanished. Mostly. Even though they'd picked ten o'clock in the morning for the ceremony time, the last Saturday in August was usually one of the hottest days of the year.

As a recorded version of some classical music Flannery'd never heard before played over the borrowed sound system, Caylor walked through the split in the small crowd gathered under the spreading hickory tree surrounded by flower gardens in the yard of Dylan's grandparents' home.

Carrying two white roses, Caylor came toward them dressed in a white sundress that fit her to perfection. They'd managed to get a few of the sprigs of baby's breath to stay stuck in her artfully messy, short red hair. Her bare feet sank into the thick grass, and she grinned at Dylan.

Flannery sniffled and exchanged a smile with Zarah, who was in pretty much the same condition. Unlike the last wedding she'd been in, this time, all of Flannery's tears were tears of joy—for Caylor and for herself (and for Zarah, since she'd missed out on getting tears of joy from her).

Caylor's father kissed her on the cheek and placed her hand in Dylan's and then stepped back.

"If you'll all gather round." Mr. Bradley raised his arms slightly, and the semicircle of the nine family members not involved in the wedding—plus one nonfamily member—closed and drew in tighter.

Jamie had chosen to stand on Dylan's side of the circle, even though he had more family here. But Flannery didn't really mind all that much. After all, she could look right at him without even having to turn her head. But she didn't do more than glance at him every so often, because he gave her such outrageously flirtatious winks and smiles that she was afraid she'd bust out laughing. And that wouldn't do at all. Not with Dylan's mother and maternal grandmother standing close enough to smack her around if she disrupted the ceremony.

Caylor took each of the single white roses Flannery, Zarah, and Sage held, and she and Dylan gave one to each of their mothers and grandmothers.

Why did only mothers get recognized with flowers during a wedding ceremony? Shouldn't something be given to the fathers as well? Flannery would have to think about that for her wedding.

She stole a glance at Jamie—and the knowing expression on his face sent a flash-fire of heat over her shoulders and up to her hairline, as if he knew what she was thinking. About her wedding. About *their* wedding.

Within just a few minutes, vows, rings, and kisses had been exchanged. For now, Caylor had told them Sunday at coffee, they were exchanging very simple, inexpensive gold bands. But later—maybe for their first anniversary, once Dylan had been working full time for a year—they would buy a real wedding set.

After hugs and kisses all around, everyone adjourned into the blissfully cool, air-conditioned house for the catered gourmet brunch provided by Dylan's parents.

"I have to hand it to Dylan." Flannery stacked mini-waffles on a small plate and then piled strawberries and whipped cream on top of them. "He knows how to throw a wedding."

Zarah, cutting into a wedge of quiche, nodded. "If I'd known he was this good at it, I'd have hired him to plan my wedding. Of course, he would have been at loggerheads with Beth most of the time." Zarah widened her eyes, and Flannery laughed. With Zarah's own mother gone since she was eight and her father and stepmother not interested enough in Zarah to even attend the wedding, Bobby's mother— with Bobby as her only child—had gone a wee bit mother-of-the-groomzilla on them.

Flannery scanned the open-plan parlors in the remodeled Victorian until she found Jamie—laughing and cutting up with Dylan's brothers on the sofa in the room across the entry hall. When—if—no, *when* they got married, she'd make sure his mother felt as involved as possible, though given the distance, with her in Utah, that might be hard. Of course, with her own mother a three-hour drive away, it wouldn't be all that easy to involve her in all the little details.

But that was okay. She had Caylor and Zarah to help her with that. And Cookie. Yes, Cookie would definitely need to be involved.

Caylor came over and hugged both of them again. "I still can't believe I'm actually married." She looked down at her left hand, and her smile gave no indication that she missed the presence of a diamond ring or fancy wedding band. She looked up and winked at Flannery. "I guess you're next, huh?" She turned and positioned herself between Flannery and Zarah and looked toward Jamie.

If she'd meant to tease Flannery, it didn't work. Flannery sighed and smiled. "I hope so."

~❦~

After Dylan and Caylor's wedding, what had been the best and most eventful summer of Jamie's life finally settled into a good routine. He went to the Lindsley House offices two days a week to work with the marketing team on his assigned projects and attend the nonfiction book team's weekly meeting. Even though he was only a contractor working on a project-by-project basis, he started to feel like part of the team, part of the community.

And he got to have lunch with Flannery on those days.

The other three days, he worked a few hours at home and then took his computer to a coffee shop or restaurant where he could work in the noise and chaos that best suited him.

His acceptance to school had been provisional, based on receipt of his test scores, which they did receive, and his status went from provisional to full acceptance the second week of August.

While Cookie and Big Daddy traveled to Alabama, New Orleans, Florida, and then Michigan to visit Kirby's family, Jamie took care of her garden. And he and Flannery reaped the bounty—especially when Flannery told him she'd enrolled in a healthy-cooking class offered at the community college.

Now when she came home the three nights she didn't go to class—coming to his place after work, since it was just down the street—she couldn't wait to get into the kitchen with him and try out new recipes and techniques.

"That's not how you're supposed to cut a tomato." She pushed him out of the way and showed him the very slow, cautious method she'd learned in class.

He let her do it, enjoying the sight of her in a kitchen—in *his* kitchen. "We're going to have to go over to Cookie's house tomorrow morning and pick all those tomatoes and take a bunch of them to Caylor and Dylan's with us."

"I hate to see those go to waste. We're supposed to be learning how to make marinara next Tuesday night. Maybe I could do that—make a whole bunch, buy some nice jars, and can it, and then we won't have to buy the expensive stuff anymore." She hunkered over the cutting board and started on another tomato.

The bacon would be completely cold by the time she finished slicing it, but they'd have the most beautifully cut tomatoes on their sandwiches anyone could ask for.

"What time do you want me to come over so we can go pick them tomorrow?"

As tempting as it was to offer to let her spend the night—in his guest bedroom, of course—he couldn't put her in a compromising position like that. So it was a good thing he planned to do something about that. . .and soon.

"What time are we supposed to be at Caylor and Dylan's?"

"Around three or four. They said something about starting to grill about six o'clock. Did you ever hear back from Danny and Chae?" She took the slices and fanned them out on a paper plate, just so.

"Yes, and they're looking forward to coming and to meeting everyone. Let's go over to Cookie's to work in the garden early— because it's supposed to be a scorcher tomorrow. Say nine?" At her nod, he slipped his arms around her waist from behind and kissed the side of her neck. "Thank you for cutting the tomatoes."

"You're welcome."

They took their dinner out onto the back deck and enjoyed the sounds of the neighborhood—people coming home from work, kids playing—and the aroma of grills that intensified as the evening progressed.

After they finished eating, Jamie reached across the table and took Flannery's hand. "What do you want to do tonight?"

"I thought. . .since we've never done it before. . ." She blushed and looked away.

Where was she going with this? "What?"

"I thought maybe we could watch some of the King Arthur movies together. Just one tonight, of course. Or maybe two."

Jamie stood, leaned across the table, and kissed her. "That's why you're my princess."

*Watching* meant, naturally, discussing as the movie progressed. At one point, Jamie had to pause the DVD, go upstairs, and get one of his books that contained comprehensive information on all of the legends so that he could try to prove something to her. And he learned a very important lesson.

"Repeat after me: 'I will not doubt Flannery when it comes to details about the legends of King Arthur and the knights of the round table.'"

He crossed his arms and sat on the floor in front of the sofa instead of beside her. "I'm not saying that. You were right *this* time. It doesn't mean you're going to be right *every* time."

She mussed his hair and stretched out on the sofa behind him. "Do you really want to find out? I wrote my senior literary criticism piece on these legends. I took both a medieval literature course *and* a seminar focused just on these legends as an undergrad."

"I've *got* to take you to one of Danny's gaming nights. You'd be able to save them so much time just by being a walking encyclopedia of the legends."

"Sounds like fun. Once or twice. I don't intend on becoming a geek about all this."

"No, because knowing all the stories backward and forward, including all the more recent stuff, doesn't make you a geek about it." He shot her a wry look over his shoulder.

She pushed his face away. "Until you came along, I managed to keep it very well hidden and under wraps. This still isn't going to become some big, public thing for me."

"If you insist."

They got caught up in the movie again—and when it was over, Flannery groaned and complained about the long drive back to her condo downtown.

"You know, there is something you could do to change that." Jamie carried the empty popcorn bowl and glasses back to the kitchen. He rinsed the empty cranberry-grape juice bottle out and tossed it in the recycle bin.

Flannery leaned on the breakfast bar, cheeks pink. "Oh yeah? What's that?"

"That townhouse two doors up is still on the market. I hear they just dropped the price." Oh, he was so bad.

She flung a dish towel at him and then flounced toward the door. "I'm going home."

He walked her out to her car and gave her a very unsatisfying good-night kiss. He knew all too well that until she became his wife, he wouldn't be satisfied with a kiss and a wave at the end of an evening together. But tonight, he could live with it. Because tomorrow, he would put his plan into action.

~∞~

"I am so not ready for classes to start next week." Caylor fanned herself with her straw hat.

"I am." Dylan did a cannonball into the pool, splashing them with water.

The cool droplets felt good on Flannery's legs, but the relief from the oppressive August heat didn't last long. "Don't get started with me about the whole 'Waa, I have to go back to work' thing. Some of us actually have to work all year long."

"Hey, I wrote a whole novel this summer. And edited it. And turned it in more than a month early."

"And I painted all summer."

"Oh, to have the freedom to spend all summer writing or painting." Flannery pressed the back of her hand to her forehead in a melodramatic pose. "I shall now be forlorn because I chose the wrong profession."

"All you have to do is finish your master's degree, and I know JRU would hire you in a heartbeat to teach composition and grammar."

"And have to grade all those essays for the composition classes? I don't think so!"

"You thinking about changing jobs?" Jamie held the bottle of water over Flannery so ice and water dripped on her.

"Hey!" She grabbed the bottle. Jamie put his down beside her lounge chair and then followed Dylan's lead and jumped into the pool, making as big a splash as he could.

Zarah and Bobby arrived, and it wasn't long before Bobby splashed them, too.

"We've decided we're going to go to Italy in May next year as soon as school lets out." Caylor took a sip of water and then dribbled some of it over her shoulders and arms.

Since money was limited—at least as far as Dylan was concerned, as he didn't want Caylor paying for everything—they'd spent a few days in a cabin on the lake at Fall Creek Falls State Park after their wedding. But their dream honeymoon was Venice.

"It should be gorgeous in May—not yet oppressively hot."

The sound of the doorbell echoed through the screen door, and Caylor went in to answer. Flannery followed.

Chae and Danny looked a little uncertain, but as soon as Caylor greeted them by name, their ready smiles appeared.

"I'd hug y'all, but I'm damp and covered in sunscreen."

"We brought a couple of side dishes, as suggested." Chae held forward a huge bowl of cut melons and another of berries.

Caylor took one, and Flannery took the other, leading Jamie's friends through to the kitchen. Caylor showed them where they could change clothes, but they'd come prepared, with their swimsuits on under shorts and T-shirts.

With everyone having arrived and the weather too hot to stay out of the water, Flannery, Caylor, Zarah, and Chae risked entering it and were splashed and chased around for their bravery. But eventually they got a heated game of volleyball going—with the guys on the deep-end side of the net, of course.

As Jamie and Flannery had hoped, Danny and Chae fit in with the group perfectly—as if they'd always been around. Chae wasn't afraid to speak her mind—a very important quality for someone in this group of big opinions and even bigger attitudes—even to the point of staring down Bobby and getting him to admit he'd touched the net when he spiked the ball. And since her conversation with Flannery after the dinner at the Seungs' home, Chae acted much warmer and friendlier toward Jamie, as if she, too, could see the changes in Jamie that Flannery had seen.

At six, the guys made a big production of getting out of the pool so that they could "cook dinner for the ladies."

"Of course, we're the ones who'll actually do all the work," Zarah muttered, scrubbing at her wet hair with her colorful beach towel.

"As if you've ever complained about that before." Caylor pushed Zarah's shoulder.

"Well. . ." But Zarah conceded the point with a shrug.

After getting dried off and changed, they took over the kitchen, checking the potatoes baking in the oven (which, to Flannery, had been a revelation—she'd never seen a baked potato cooked anywhere but in a microwave oven in her life), finishing off side dishes, and setting out all the food.

Flannery and Chae were sent out to set the long table on the deck with a set of cute melamine dinnerware that one of Caylor's fellow professors had given them as a wedding gift. The purple-and-turquoise wavy stripes on it recalled the colors from the wedding—Flannery was so glad her dress had been aqua, not lavender—and were perfect for poolside dining.

Everyone exclaimed over the tomatoes and squash from Cookie's garden.

"Please, take some home with you. We've got more than enough already, and more ripening every day." Jamie passed the platter around again.

Dinner lasted until well after dark, with no one wanting to leave the table even to go get the ice-cream-sundae bar set up.

Finally, Zarah started to get up. But Bobby stopped her with a hand on her shoulder. He dropped a kiss on the top of her head and stood. "Guys, I think we should clear the table and go get dessert ready."

Impressively, they managed to get everything in just two trips.

"Zarah, you're the only one who can see around the corner into the house. You'll have to tell us what they're doing." Caylor munched on a piece of ice from her glass.

Zarah tipped her chair back. "Looks like they're washing dishes."

"Amazing." Chae tucked a stray napkin under the citronella candle in the middle of the table to keep it from blowing out into the yard. "I should probably go in and take pictures. I've never seen Danny do the dishes before."

Talk turned to Chae and Danny—with Caylor and Zarah especially fascinated to learn that they'd met through a professional matchmaker. They exchanged smiles.

"We sort of had matchmakers, too, though not of the professional variety." Both told how their grandmothers—as well as Bobby's and Dylan's—had done what they could to push them together.

"And you, Flannery? Did you have a matchmaking grandmother?"

Flannery shook her head. "Grand*father*. Of course, it backfired on him."

Chae frowned, concern obvious in her expression. "Oh? How?"

"He ended up marrying Jamie's grandmother. When they were trying to plot how to get the two of us together, they ended up falling in love with each other. As Jamie put it, turnabout's fair play."

"How long is it going to take them to put out ice cream and toppings?" Zarah leaned back again to check their progress.

Caylor stood. "I'll go see." She disappeared around the corner into the house.

Moments later, the floodlights on the eaves of the back of the house blazed on. Flannery held her hand up and blinked against the blinding light.

A shuffling and clinking and rustling drew her attention to the main part of the deck up near the door.

"Um, y'all need to come see this," Caylor called.

Flannery, Zarah, and Chae stood and hurried around the corner of the house—and Flannery's knees almost gave out as soon as she cleared it.

Standing in the middle of the deck, in the spotlight created by the light on the corner of the house, stood. . .

She doubled over, trying to catch her breath. She'd seen the Sir Gawain costume in Jamie's office, but she'd never thought she'd see him in it.

And behind him—three more knights in varying degrees of early medieval armor stood in a row.

The way Caylor held her digital camera, she was probably video-recording the whole thing.

Jamie stepped forward; then, amid protesting costume pieces, he went down onto one knee in front of Flannery. "My lady. I humble myself before you, a poor, lowly knight, laying my honor at your feet, to beseech thee for a favor from your great magnanimity."

Flannery pressed her fist to her mouth to keep from laughing aloud at Jamie's nonsensical speech. She took a deep breath, steadied herself, and dropped her hands to her side. "What favor might this lowly knight ask of me?"

He grinned up at her for playing along. "My lady would do this lowly knight the greatest honor by granting him the boon of her hand in marriage."

Now that, she hadn't been expecting. Her voice died in her throat, along with her ability to breathe.

He shifted, his costume creaking and clicking. "Flan. . .will you marry me?" He lifted up his hand, and the small, dark object in his hand caught the light—which flickered and flared off the diamond ring inside it.

She cleared her throat. "Aye, Sir Knight. I will grant thee the boon of my hand in marriage." And before he could launch into any more ridiculous speeches, she bent over, grabbed him, and kissed him. "And it took you long enough to get around to asking," she whispered.

"What can I say? I'm not the smooth operator your grandfather is." He stood, and after using his teeth to remove one of his gloves, he put the ring on her finger. "So seriously, it's yes?"

"Seriously, it's yes." She threw her arms around his neck—and regretted it when the costume bit into her skin.

He kissed her again then turned. "Um. . .do y'all mind giving us a few minutes? There's something I need to talk to Flan about."

The guys, already pulling off the hot, heavy costumes, didn't protest, and the girls went in to put out the sundae fixings.

As soon as the sliding door closed behind Caylor, Jamie pulled off the top half of his costume, to reveal his T-shirt beneath. "Now, I know you aren't really keen on the idea of becoming Flannery O'Connor when we get married."

"Jamie, I don't mind it, really."

"Well, I do. I don't want you to have to go through the rest of your life with people commenting on your name—it's bad enough they do it with just the same first name."

"I've thought about that, too; but Jamie, as much as I'm attached to my family's name, I want people to know that we're a family, too, because we share the same name."

"I know. I feel the same way. But something you said awhile back has really made me think a lot about family and about what my family identity is." Jamie took her hand and led her to the deck chairs, where they sat, facing each other.

"What did I say?"

"About how I felt like I was having to choose between my birth father and my stepfather in making my career choice. And you were right. I was. I was having to choose between a father who was demanding and unforgiving and a father who's shown me nothing but acceptance and unconditional love. And I want to show that acceptance and unconditional love back toward Don. Flannery, when we get married, I want both of us to change our last name to Don's."

Flannery chewed her bottom lip. At least by changing her name to O'Connor, she still kept her Irish identity. "What's Don's last name?"

Jamie grinned. "Murphy."

"Murphy. . .but that's—"

"Irish, I know."

Flannery flung her arms around his neck again, so relieved she wouldn't have to be Flannery O'Connor *or* give up having an Irish last name. She sat back and wiped at the tears streaming down her cheeks. Could today get any more perfect?

"So, you see, it's like a reverse adoption—I refused to allow Don to adopt me when I was a teenager, so now I'm adopting him by officially taking his last name."

She ran the backs of her fingers along his jaw. "You're a good son."

"He's a good father."

Flannery leaned forward and kissed him. "I love you, my knight in shining armor."

"I love you, my princess."

# Epilogue

$\mathcal{M}$aureen blotted her cheeks with a handkerchief as she carried the white rose to the front of the chapel. Just over five months since her wedding, and now, here she was again.

She looked up and thanked the young man who'd escorted her up the aisle, then took her seat on the groom's side of the room. Kirby winked at her from his place on the platform. Soon Jackie and Don joined her, and Jackie took hold of her hand. Maureen handed her the handkerchief to dry her tears, too.

Their boy was getting married.

The chapel turned out to be the perfect size for the Christmastime wedding. Flannery looked stunning in her simple white gown, and Jamie, more handsome than ever in his suit. Their ceremony lasted a little longer than hers and Kirby's had—but they had a preacher, not a retired judge. And Kirby had a pretty good wind in the pulpit. Fortunately, Flannery had talked him out of "sermonizing" on the history of marriage. And by asking her grandfather to officiate the wedding, she'd solved the problem of which side to seat him and Maureen on—or whether to separate them and have one on each side.

Soon, Kirby pronounced them husband and wife, and Jamie kissed Flannery. And kept kissing her to the point where the crowd began to titter and giggle. And then he kissed her again, just for good measure, apparently. Everyone cheered and clapped when Jamie turned and pumped his arms up in the air in a victory gesture. Flannery took him by the hand and made him leave the chapel.

All the pictures had been taken beforehand, so everyone headed across the cold courtyard to the community center for the reception—a simple affair that seemed more like a Christmas party, especially with people taking turns on the stage at the far end singing all manner of holiday songs with accompaniment from musicians from Caylor's school.

Maureen had barely had time to congratulate her grandson and granddaughter-in-law—twice over—when she found herself surrounded by her four dearest friends in the world.

"It's hard to believe that it's only been sixteen months since we stood right here"—Trina Breitinger paused—"well, over there in the worship center, and bemoaned the fact that none of us had married grandchildren."

"And look at us now." Perty Bradley beamed up toward the stage, where Caylor had dragged Dylan, Zarah, and Bobby up to sing "White Christmas" with her.

"All of us with at least one grandchild married—and we got Maureen married off in the process, too." Lindy Patterson gave Maureen a one-armed squeeze.

"I would say, all in all, we make pretty successful matchmakers." Sassy Evans squinted toward the stage and smiled and waved at her granddaughter and grandson-in-law.

"I agree." Maureen raised her glass of cranberry-flavored punch. "To the matchmakers. May we make many more successful matches for our—well, *your*—grandchildren."

"Hear, hear!" cheered the others.

After taking a sip, Trina set her glass down and took Lindy's hand. Lindy did the same, taking Maureen's hand; and soon all five had joined hands in a circle. Trina bowed her head. "Lord, I know we probably didn't set about this with the best of intentions, but You blessed our meddling, matchmaking efforts anyway. Now, we ask that

You bless our grandchildren with happy, healthy lives and homes, and guide them in Your pathways. Amen."

"Amen," the other four murmured.

Sassy, however, didn't lift her head or let go of Perty's or Trina's hands. "And Lord, if it's Your will, bless us with lots of great-grandbabies soon. Amen."

They all laughed. "Amen!"

**Kaye Dacus** is a graduate of Seton Hill University's Master of Arts in Writing Popular Fiction program. She is an active member and former vice president of American Christian Fiction Writers (ACFW) and current president of Middle Tennessee Christian Writers. Her *Stand-In Groom* novel was a Christy Award finalist in 2010. Find out more at kayedacus.com.

OTHER BOOKS BY KAYE DACUS:


BRIDES OF BONNETERRE SERIES

*Stand-In Groom*
*Menu for Romance*
*A Case of Love*


THE MATCHMAKERS SERIES

*Love Remains*
*The Art of Romance*